Frogs and Toads Forever
The War at Sea

by

A. Anthony Oseguera

RoseDog Books
PITTSBURGH, PENNSYLVANIA 15222

ISBN: 978-1-4349-8295-7
eISBN: 978-1-4349-4540-2
Printed in the United States of America

First Printing

For more information or to order additional books, please contact:
RoseDog Books
701 Smithfield Street
Pittsburgh, Pennsylvania 15222
U.S.A.
1-800-834-1803
www.rosedogbookstore.com

To my wife Maggie, my family, my friends,
and classmates who once called Frogtown their home

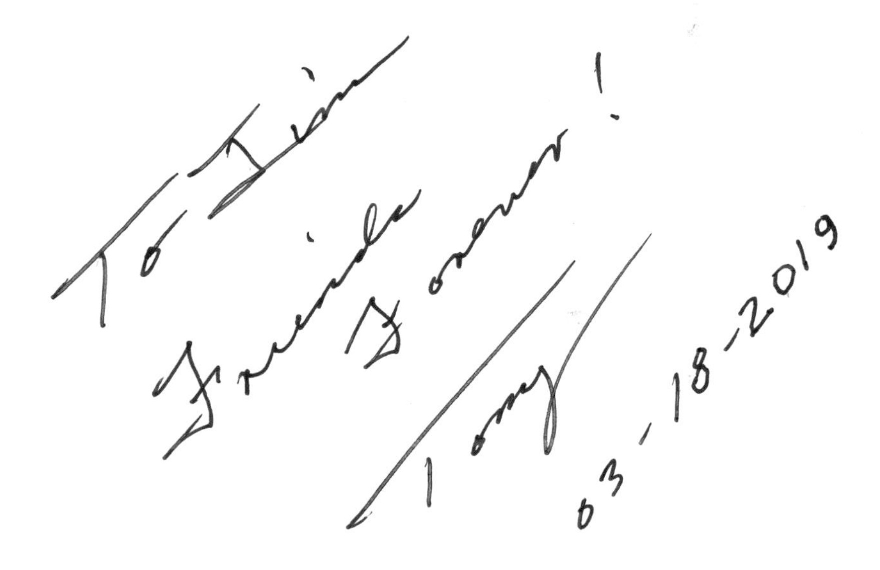

Table of Contents

Chapters

Chapter One

In the Beginning

Once upon a time, in a Kingdom nearby and not very long ago, there lived in the future-past, a great King who ruled over all the Frogs of Frogland. His name was King Josue II. Josue was also called Osee as a child, but the name Josue seemed to suit him best; maybe it's because that's the name his friends chose for him. Some say kings receive their names from heaven. Since children listen to the angels they see in the sun, the moon, and the stars, oftentimes too in the clouds and in the rainbows, they, the children, know best what heavenly name to call their best friends.

The Frogs of Frogland were a proud yet humble race, and they were very capable of winning wars over all their enemies. There was one enemy, however, they really feared: the monster Crickets! These Crickets came from way beneath the earth's surface. One of the Professor Frogs said that there had been a great explosion under the desert that caused the Crickets to get so gigantic. What was worse, the Crickets appeared to be excellent cliff climbers. They had captured the Frog Princess in the tower and made good their escape! The Frogs demanded of their leaders, "why" and "how" could the Crickets perform such a terrible deed and against our King, the most powerful King in the region: now, through knowledge obtained by excellent sources, they learned the Crickets were holding the princess for ransom. What were the Frogs to do?

Just across the magnificent Jordan River and toward the east, there reigned a powerful King in Toadland named Gideon III. He was very protective of his people and made certain his borders were well fortified against any hostile acts that some foolish army might undertake. Long ago there had been an informal understanding between the Toads and the Frogs. With just a mere handshake, they sealed their intent to respect each other's borders and to make the Jordan River a permanent boundary between their two nations; thus, they all lived in peace in that region. As a result, both the Frogs and the Toads prospered, while living on opposite sides of the Jordan River. Neither of the two countries had been in a major conflict for years. Now, however, it seems things have changed for the Frogs. They find themselves without their Frog Princess and with no plan in sight on how best to free her from the dreadful, ugly Crickets!

The Frogs had a superb army, but they had let their navy practically disintegrate: their vessels were hardly seaworthy anymore; whereas, their neighbors to the east, the Toads, had continually improved and increased the quality and quantity of their vessels: their larger ships made them the envy of nations from all around. The Crickets, in the meantime, had learned to swim in deep water and now were quite confident they could fight on the sea, as well as on land. They had pushed down from the North years earlier but were waiting for the opportune time to strike from their newly acquired lands, just north of Toadland.

The Crickets were ruled by two leaders, the Blue Vampire and the Red Vampire: Cornwalter and Reynaldo, respectively. They were called the Vampire Leaders because some said they drank the blood of their victims. They ruled over the Land of the Black Crater and maintained great discipline over their warrior nation. The master soldiers were trained from early age in all the arts of war. Most of the female Crickets ran the community, while some were in the military. Their youngsters trained at the Cricketstan Academy under the supervision of senior officers. To qualify for the rank of senior officer, the soldiers had to have graduated from the best of the Cricket Academies and to have fought in three major military campaigns that brought new lands to their ever-expanding Cricket territory.

The smaller nations, all around, were becoming very nervous and extremely concerned, because a major war in the region would engulf them as well. They would have to choose whether to support their neighbors, the Frogs and the Toads, or whether they, the smaller nations, would fare better by joining forces, now, with the Crickets. They reasoned: These Cricket mutants would be the probable winners, in the event a war broke out! The Crickets, their logic told them, had sheer size, that is, superior numbers; they could muster more than 200,000 Cricket soldiers, besides another 50,000 Cricket navy personnel, almost immediately!

As it turns out, the Kingdoms of Frogland and Toadland had never even signed the "Mutual Defense Initiative Treaty of the Middle East" (MDITME). The MDITME was an old document, a frog archeologist had discovered in an abandoned castle near the Jordan River, some thirty years ago. It stated simply that at one time in the history of the region, it had been necessary for adjacent nations to coalesce, in order to defend against an imminent attack. This offense was most probably perpetrated by outside marauding hordes, coming mostly from the north and others coming from the east. They thought about the looming situation on each side of the Jordan: What should they do if the Crickets launched an attack on their territories?

After much debate, the separate Congresses of the Frogs and Toads determined that the only chance they stood against the mighty Crickets was to resurrect the ancient document and sign the MDITME, alongside their regal dignitaries. Therefore, they would send their respective emissaries to each other's nations, going back and forth across the Jordan in record time, in the hopes of ratifying the MDITME, now referred to as the "Treaty." The two nations, absolutely, had no time to waste! But, who could possibly speak to bring them together at this crucial crossroads in their history? The answer would not long delay in coming.

The Kingdom of the Frogs had a splendid, no, a superb statesman who was also the most eloquent speaker in the Frog Senate; he was addressed by his Greek name, Plato. Plato's family had moved to Frogland many years ago, when his great-grandparents had escaped from Greece, in order to avoid a plague in that country. They traveled for days up and across the Mediterranean, until they finally felt it was safe to set foot on what was for them virgin territory. As it turns out, there was a small colony of Greek Frogs who met them at the port of disembarkation and made them feel right at home in Frogland.

Plato, thus, was born in Frogland—in this new "land of milk and honey"— after two generations had passed and his ancestral family had already grown to maturity. He was considered a Frogland native: a great distinction and privilege. Still, when Plato was young, his grandfather had taught him to be proud of his Greek heritage. He stated that one should remember how democracy had first come to the world through Greece; democracy had to be "won" and had to be "defended," even at the cost of one's life! Now, Plato saw that his nation was in peril, and that he had to do all in his power to persuade his fellow countrymen to stand for democracy!

Plato, speaking to his colleagues, was quick to point out the facts as he understood them. First, they, the Frogs, were vastly outnumbered by the enemy Crickets; secondly, their navy was hardly seaworthy; thirdly, their soldiers had not fought a war in generations; they didn't even know what it was to slay another being, since their Holy Book taught them that unjustified killing was against the Creator's Commandments. Still, he pressed on, "Extraordinary times call for extraordinary measures." Surely the Creator of the universe did not intend for them to be exterminated or to become vassals for merciless, dictatorial rulers! Peace seemed to be a far-off dream now. He told his fellow senators about a walk he had taken by himself the night before:

> As I walked by the Jordan at night, the smell of the river was sweet, and I recalled how sweet and privileged my life has been until now. I looked up to the heavens and prayed that the Great Force in the universe would hear my plea. "Send us faith and courage and intelligence to meet the challenges that will soon confront us: Make us warriors again that our race may vanquish the menace before us!"
>
> Suddenly, a quiet peace descended upon me, and an angel appeared to ease my spirit. The angel stated: "Behold honest and noble

> frog! He that sent me has heard your prayer and commands you to send an emissary to the Toad Nation. If you join forces with them, you will defeat the Crickets. The Frogs and Toads, however, must turn away from any disagreements they may have with each other, including their fellow countrymen, and embrace the Force of all nature, and that is 'Love'."

No sooner had Plato spoken these fine words than the entire assembly rose to their feet in a tremendous applause that spoke louder than words, saying, "We have found our emissary; we have found someone who can persuade the Toads to join us in our hour of need!" The Treaty would, after all, benefit them as well.

That night, after the King appointed Plato Prime Minister and the assembly approved him by acclamation, a post not needed for decades, he spent some time at a local cafe sipping coffee with close friends. After discussing family and friends, their talk turned, once again, to more serious matters: the best manner in which an alliance with the Toads might be forged. Plato's older white-haired friend, Seneca, shared his views with the intimate group. He began:

> For the better part of half a century, we have known peace with all of the nations, surrounding territories, and their communities; now, we are faced with a do-or-die situation. I never thought the day would come when, once again, we would have to enlist our young men and women to fight, in order to maintain our tranquil way of life. How foolish of me! We must do what we must! I urge you, Plato, to impart to our friends, the Toads, the need to band together, if we are both to survive. Their leadership must be made to understand the severity of the moment. With their powerful navy and our formidable army, we can make the enemy retreat. Our combined air force can provide us with the proper reconnaissance that will enable our land and sea forces to outmaneuver the Crickets. Logistics are paramount! Once we make them sue for peace, they will deliver our princess, Sophia.

Plato listened attentively as Seneca spoke with fervor and passion in his voice; mostly, however, it was the logic and immediacy of the moment that caught Plato's attention. Seneca had always been a trusted friend and now, when the world seemed to be coming to an end for them, they were standing together: standing tall! He addressed Seneca saying, "There is nothing left to do but forge ahead with all deliberate speed." Plato assured his friend that he would be leaving that very night to cross the Jordan for an emergency meeting with Gideon III, the Toad Judge (In those days, a Judge was another name for a champion of the people, a leader, and in Gideon III's case, a King as well). Much remained to be done! Plato was very fortunate to have a fantastic wife, Ruth. She would assist him with taking care of all the details and extras that a trip of this nature required.

When Plato had finished what needed to be accomplished with his wife's great assistance, he was sped away in an unassuming military vehicle, to a restricted airfield where King Josue II was already there to bid him *bon voyage*. The Frog King said to Plato, "Upon your shoulders rests the hope of our nation. As our emissary to the Toads, please convey my warmest regards and deepest respect for their friendship in this our hour of need. As the King of Frogland, I will continue to give direct orders to all our Cabinet ministers and our very able military generals and admirals, until you return. We will be ready with a resolve not seen in our land for a century, or more. May the heavens bless you as you move and speak before the Toad Congress! I know the Eternal Force is with us, and He will help give you the words necessary to sway their leaders to our cause." The two stood looking intently into each other's eyes; no more words were necessary; still, the King was moved to embrace his emissary in an expression of love and concern. They smiled politely, shook hands firmly, and Plato was on his way.

Within the hour, Plato found himself getting off the new *X9 Super Fighter Aircraft,* the latest edition of many new military aircraft the Frogs had at their disposal. The flight had been smooth and uneventful, just the way he had hoped. While the Frogs had not been to war, they continued to create and build the best aircraft technology in their sphere of the world, so much so, that other nations paid great sums of money to purchase Frog airplanes; nevertheless, the Frogs were careful not to sell their most prized aircraft, and the *X9 Super Fighter* was definitely in that class: designated "Top Secret."

The Toad emissary was at the airport to greet the Frog emissary with all the protocols of state. Since it was still nighttime, however, no band was required, just a high-level honor guard with additional representatives from the various branches of the Congress, that is, the Toad Congress elite. It was a kind of surreal experience for all present, because there had never been such a meeting in the lifetime of any of the participants present; moreover, the light was just beginning to gleam over the beautiful Jordan River, and the birds of every kind began their early morning songs.

Samson, the Toad emissary, had once been an Olympic champion in the decathlon. He was still very strong and quite personable. He maintained a build that is reserved for those who swing on the flying trapeze. His wife Esther had disappeared quite unexpectedly less than a year ago. The two had been very much in love; she was as beautiful as he was handsome. It seems as though her beauty was renowned throughout the Toad Kingdom and the entire Jordan Valley. Samson believed Esther was being held against her will. This person or these persons wished him and his associates ill will, to say the least. In spite of his personal situation, Samson knew that the meeting with his Frog counterpart just might hold the key to his wife's disappearance and, of course, the answer to the impending doom that their nations must confront and resolve.

After the formal salutations, the Toad entourage escorted Plato to the King's palace that was located on the summit of a high hill overlooking his kingdom. The palace looked more like a fortress built to withstand any enemy attack, rather than the ostentatious palaces of Europe. With the sunrise now complete over the Jordan, Plato saw himself being introduced to King Gideon III. The King was not at all what he had expected to find, based on all the stories that circulated about him: they suggested a man much older, perhaps with a wise brow and portly body; instead, he was also quite comely and athletic of appearance.

King Gideon addressed his Frog guest with all due respect, yet he conveyed an informal air that said: relax, you are in your home, or *"mi casa es tu casa"*! Without any fanfare, the King invited Plato to enjoy breakfast with him, together with Samson and a few close ministers. The Toad Congress would no doubt listen to Plato's address later that morning. Notwithstanding that appointment, now was the time to rekindle past friendships and to discuss the salient issue at hand: war! In an unusual change in the King's traditional protocol of welcoming guests, the King chose to acquire information regarding the many questions he had concerning the enemy. Besides, time constraints also needed to be considered, so Gideon dispensed with his usual no-business-at-the-breakfast-table ritual.

The King was fascinated with the culinary arts and breakfast was just as important as the other meals. A body needed strength that only came from a proper diet that by no means precluded a pleasant display. This presentation included fresh flowers at the table, with all the accouterments, including the finest china, silver implements, and the crisp linen napkins. Breakfast consisted of fruits, cereals, eggs, meats, milk, breads, and light pastries, and much, much more! Plato was overwhelmed for the moment. His diet generally consisted of a simple bagel or muffin with cream cheese, some choice nuts, milk or coffee, but rarely tea. Yes indeed, he knew not to embarrass the King, so he joined in the feast with an outward delight: Faking would not do! Had he been missing something, he mused?

After the two friends had discussed the long-running friendship of their respective nations, the King said to the Frog Prime Minister, "Now we can discuss the business we both find so pressing. I am sure it will go better if we each have a favorite to drink; what is your choice of beverage?' Plato replied, "Thank you for offering! I'll take some coffee, please." "Sugar and cream?" the Toad King asked politely." "No thanks, just nice and dark like my beautiful wife, the Frog emissary said with a smile." Plato's smile turned to a concerned and disturbed expression when he began to relay all that the Frog Central Intelligence Agency (FCIA) had conveyed to their Frog King. At first, Josue II had been startled by the news, but then the Frog King's resolve had quickly replaced fear with determination: Any doubts to the final outcome were summarily removed!

What Josue had learned, Plato continued, was that the Cricket army and navy were large and formidable. Intelligence indicated that they had defeated every military that was thrown against them. One of their greatest strengths seemed to be their incredible discipline. No army or navy that lacked the proper training could stand up against them! Their leadership was a no-nonsense type of administration. They removed any combatants who came up short, in this regard; duty, discipline, courage, and loyalty to officers, and officers' loyalty to superior officers, all made the Cricket army and navy victorious over their prey. If they had any deficiencies, it was difficult to discern. Perhaps it was what was so obvious to others but not to their enemies: more like one's nose on one's face. Wow! No one had ever mentioned an air force!

Why did the intelligence reports to the Frog King leave out that critical information? Surely, the Crickets, who seemed to possess everything else aggressors possess, also had an air force, or did they? Some of the Frog Central Intelligence Agency (FCIA) officers, however, had not returned from their most recent spy mission. Thus, Is it possible they possessed photographs or other recorded data that had, obviously, not yet made it back to FCIA Headquarters? In the immediate haste of preparing for war, a tangled labyrinth, it now appears the Frogs did not possess all the facts vis-à-vis their Cricket adversary's full potential to make war!

Gideon III had been listening very intently. After a heavy sigh, he exclaimed, "If you don't mind my saying so, we have known for a long time that you Frogs have the best aircraft money can buy. Moreover, we also know that you are smart enough not to sell your best airplanes. We, on the other hand, have an equally superb navy with some of the best, if not THE best aircraft carriers in this part of the world! What I have not shared with you Plato is that for some time now, we have also been spying on your Cricket friends." The King had a bit of sarcasm in his voice. "We, as you now suspect, have come to the conclusion that they do possess a hi-tech air force, too! Oddly enough, no one has any record of these in combat. It seems that their ground and sea forces are sufficiently superior to all other foes, that to date, they've not needed to use their air power.

"You must know that because of our nations' very warm relations across the Jordan, over the years, we would never think of abandoning you, in this desperate hour: No, not at a time when our fates are tied together. I do sincerely want you to address our joint members of Congress, so that you may share what you have discussed with me and express anything that is on your mind. As they say in Toadland, we're all ears, ha, ha!" The King, now with his coat on, continued speaking, as his attendant turned to assist the Frog Prime Minister with his trench coat, "Now the time has come to get going!" The King, then, moving with grace towards the huge, ornate door, beckoned Plato to join him. As the door automatically opened before them, Gideon lll, directing his voice to his newly found friend, began to sing, "When the going gets tough..." and Plato, in his baritone voice, finished the oft-said American phrase, "the tough get going!"

As Plato entered the well of the Toad Senate, the senators and representatives rose to give their visitor a warm welcome. They were in various degrees of readiness to hear the Frog, because it was still very early in the morning and some had gotten to bed quite late the night before, discussing business of state and military matters, too. On this very important occasion, Samson, the Toad Prime Minister, came to the podium to introduce Plato. He began by simply saying, "We are indeed privileged to have one of the most respected orators and statesmen of the Frog Kingdom with us this morning. He is a person, as many of you already know, of great integrity and sincerity. I, therefore, present to you, with no further words that will delay his most important message to us, the Prime Minister of the Frog Kingdom, Lord Plato!" Once again, the Congressional auditorium burst into a stirring applause. Plato got up from his comfortable chair with the confidence of a Shakespearean actor ready to play his part to the hilt, to the utmost; except that this was no play; it was, as they say, "the real McCoy": the real thing! Fortunes and destinies would be decided, won or lost, based on his speech. He mustn't hold back any of his talents of persuasion. Plato began:

> Friends and countrymen of Toadland—you, our most time-honored allies—I come to you today with a very heavy burden, but also with a very cheerful heart, because I know that I am in my home, when your King says to me "mi casa es tu casa"! And, I say to you, dear Toads of Toadland, "Mi casa will always be your casa!

He barely finished his phrase when the house broke into a spontaneous applause, and they all started to chant: "Plato, Plato, Plato, Plato, Plato," until Plato raised his hand in a salute and begged them to return to their seats. Plato continued:

> Life is a curious thing. Just when you think you've got it all figured out, a challenge appears that stops you right in your tracks. You ask yourself, "Why did this have to happen?" Or in our case, "how can we prevent this from happening, a war with a not-too-unambiguous enemy, such as the Monster Crickets?" What did we ever do to them that they should want to destroy us and take away what we hold most precious: our princess, our loved ones, our land, our way of worshiping, our way of living from dawn to dusk, our waking and our sleeping under starry skies, all our hopes and dreams, our children and our grandchildren, all that we hold dear: yes, our very lives? The spirit that is within each Frog and Toad will rise to the occasion! With your help, together, we Frogs and Toads can defeat any enemy, be they Crickets or Martians. Yes, they will be a formidable-opponent, but we are even more formidable!

After a few additional speeches by the host leaders, a Toad messenger rushed into the chamber of the Senate and announced "The Crickets have landed on both sides of the Jordan and have begun their assault on major defense installations." The Prime Minister of Toadland raised his hands to calm the assembly and began:

> Our military has anticipated such an attack and is as ready as can be to thwart the enemy's aggression. We mustn't panic. What is called for is for each citizen, of each of our respective countries, to do their

assigned duties. If you are a leader, lead, if you are a follower, follow, and if you are a baker, then bake! Each of us has a job to perform by leading, obeying our leaders, and providing all the services that are necessary for the good of the nation and our respective communities. Now, let's go to work and defend our way of life! May the Everlasting be with each and every one of us!

The Prime Ministers' speeches had been equally stirring. Thus, no further need remained compelling the King to address his subjects, except to say:

> Please kneel and bow your heads for the Eternal Force's blessing: As you follow the good advice of Prime Minister Samson, remember that we have survived throughout our long and illustrious history by following the traditions, customs, and laws of our ancestors; therefore, at this time of peril, Great and Gentle Force of the Universe be with us during our tribulation. We implore Thee! Thank You for all past blessings! We know, in our hearts of hearts, if You are with us, who can possibly defeat us! You are now and forever our King of Kings. Amen.

With that, the assembly calmly and quickly left the senate and representative chambers of the Congressional building. They would soon meet with their previously assigned groups to accomplish the King's and Prime Minister's directives. While Plato did not expect the attack that morning, he certainly was not taken by surprise. Now that the war was on, he somehow felt the better for it. After all, is this not why he had crossed the Jordan, he mused. Yes, we will win; the Everlasting is on the side of His angels and those who commit to do His will on Earth: We are such a people; he introspected. The motorcade, he and the King were riding in, went into the underground Pentagon, where the Toad Four-Star Generals were already at work, looking at their computer screens to verify Cricket positions.

Samson was very eager to introduce Toadland's only two Four-Star Generals to King Gideon III and to Prime Minister Plato. The generals, however, were extremely careful to alternate being presented to Gideon III and Plato, due to the need to secure defense positions on the front lines of the battlefield: Not even a second could be wasted! The Toads' Western Command had communicated to their Central Command Headquarters that it was quickly losing ground to the encroaching Cricket invaders! Prime Minister Samson, therefore, in an effort to minimize interruptions, promptly introduced General Schwartzwait. Schwartzwait had been positioned closest to the entourage. He pivoted from his position, where he had been studying the battle images reflected on the enormous 3-D computer screen. The General saluted the King and then quickly saluted the Prime Minister, as well. Or, was it the other way around? With the mirrors and computers all over, it was difficult for Plato to determine. Finally, General Schwartzwait, wearing a concerned smile, shook hands with the King's distinguished guest, The Frog Prime Minister Plato!

Schwartzwait called all the top officials' attention to what the large 12 X 20-foot 3-D screen was presenting. "You see, your Highness and honored guests, our best tanks are no match for the Crickets' new antitank weapons. Those weapons are certainly impressive, but I believe we've got a few surprises in store for them, don't we General Lopez?" Lopez swiveled around on his high seat and stood at attention, as he, too, saluted the Toad King, the Toad Prime Minister, and the Frog Prime Minister. "Yes we do Red!"

"Red" was what Lopez had called Schwartzwait, ever since they had first met at the Toadland Military Academy as freshmen, more than thirty years ago. At that time, Schwartzwait's hair was almost carrot-red. The nickname held; still, no one else was permitted to address him by that "handle!" Similarly, as Plato's family had emigrated to Frogland from Greece, many decades before, Lopez's grandparents had, instead, emigrated to Toadland from Iberia. The Jordan region seemed to welcome immigrants who displayed a hard-work ethic and a desire to improve their status in life. These new citizens contributed by making the most of the opportunities afforded to them, in that free and democratic society.

General Lopez also pointed to the right side of the screen, where large laser guns were moving into position to clear the antitank bazooka-type weapons. Up until now, these antitank weapons had wreaked havoc on the honor unit: The **Fighting 333 Scarlet Berets** Toad defense line. Within minutes, the Toads' huge laser weapons were in place and destroying the Cricket guns. The Toad **M-245 Shermann** tanks, with the enemy's might reduced, went swiftly back to work by pursuing and offending the enemy! "At the moment" Lopez shouted "we've got them on the run, in full retreat!"

Plato could not help but wonder what was occurring on the other side of the Jordan; how were his countrymen faring against such a formidable foe? The answer to his question was short in coming. The Crickets had sent their first and best army against the Frogs for a surprise and sudden victory, the strategy of the Crickets being that, "if we can defeat the Frogs by a sudden attack, then we can throw all our resources against the Toads." Aha, the strategy seemed to be working! What the Toads had viewed as a Cricket retreat was in fact a pullback of strength, in order to support the Western Front Offensive: a reinforcement of their elite **Panther Division,** attacking the outskirts of Frogland.

In theory and practice, the attack against the Toads was really a feint, a false attack to test enemy strength. The Crickets had gained much valuable information in that military encounter: They quickly learned that the Toads had advanced laser technology, worthy of any adversary's respect and probable humiliation, if the attacking armies were not well-coordinated. Thus, the Crickets, newly reinforced on the Western Front, moved swiftly with their "blitzkrieg!" The Frog Commander, on the other side of the telephone, was asking Plato to deliver a message of great urgency: Could they, the Toads, engage the enemy at sea with their latest nuclear carriers, airplanes, and experienced personnel, thereby thwarting any further reinforcements on the part of the Crickets?

Meanwhile, back at the ranch or, in this case, aboard *The Stingray*, flagship to the immense Cricket Flotilla, the Crickets were strategizing how best to take the Frogland Western Front. Cornwalter, the more raucous of the two Cricket leaders, pointing to the electronic map before them in the strategy room, began with much animation and declared, "We can defeat them after nightfall and before daybreak, if we move at 21:00 hours. Tonight, our ancestors are with us! They have provided us with ground and sea cover, since there will be no moon!" The Blue Vampire's glossy blue eyes glistened, and his brows began to seek each other. A wicked smile made its way to his mouth, "Ha, ha, you frogs will provide us with a delightful dish of 'frog legs' when this attack is completed or sooner, ha, ha!" "Enough," interrupted Reynaldo.

The Red Vampire Cricket had been listening very attentively to what Admiral Cornwalter had been saying and had been thinking along the same lines. "So far, things are going our way, but we mustn't underestimate their strength and their strategy. We've tested them and found them very able. Who would have suspected that they had such advanced technology with their lasers and all! No, I believe they will, in some capacity, be up to the task. Still, we do outnumber them, don't we?" But he would not yet smile; instead, his countenance displayed an expression of firm resolve to defeat and conquer, as he had done so many times before, by thinking things through, meticulously planning, and executing with exquisite diligence.

Plato had received a secret encoded e-mail from his sage friend Seneca! In the communiqué, it stated: "Spies behind enemy lines have learned that although the Princess Sophia has been well guarded, somehow or other she has, with the assistance of others, been able to escape!" In spite of the fact that the Crickets were very disciplined, apparently they were unfair. Some of the middle-grade officers had been passed over for promotion. These officers had spent many years fighting in various campaigns, but realized they would probably never be elevated to the senior-rank status because of political nepotism. Several of these middle-grade officers, therefore, sought to embarrass Admiral Cornwalter, the Blue Vampire Cricket, who along with Admiral Reynaldo, the Red Vampire Cricket, was co-Emperor of the mighty Cricket military! The rebellious Crickets had formed a cadre of five experienced and brave middle-grade officers. They, in turn, contrived a scheme to rescue the Frog Princess Sophia for a tidy ransom of ten million pounds, deliverable at a secret designated location, in gold and sterling silver bouillon, that is, five million of each!

In so doing, these officers were *risking* their lives; if they were caught, the punishment was certain death by unspeakable, horrible means. Still, more than being passed over for promotion, or even the money, if they could obtain it—a big if—it was the opportunity to advance justice! After so many years of fighting and so much real estate conquered, these special Crickets felt they no longer had the stomach for unjustified conquest. They already had more land by conquest than Rome would ever acquire in its long history. Perhaps the return of the Princess would cause the Cricket leadership to sputter in its effort to overtake the Frog and Toad kingdoms!

The Group of Five, known only to a very few select people, went by the name of *Goh. Goh*, it turns out, is the number five in Nipponese! The story is told that several decades ago a disillusioned, or a disenchanted Samurai soldier, had boarded a ship in Nippon that was bound for the Middle East. Long before the ship could arrive, it was hit by a tremendous typhoon: one so enormous that it destroyed the large ship and the vessel became toy-like in the vast ocean. It was thrown in every direction, up and down, until it was utterly in shambles! Miraculously, only a barrel containing a man inside was found on the high seas by a passing Portuguese man-of-war. The Samurai's name was Fumihiko, or just *Shihan* meaning *honored teacher*.

Fumihiko had been a *superior* knight in the Nipponese Emperor's personal guard. The Emperor had sent his most trusted servant-guard to teach the young men of the Hawaiian Islands the art of war. Some say that the Emperor's advisors had spread a rumor that Fumihiko was dissatisfied with his post, but this was only a ruse to mislead the Emperor's enemies. The Nipponese Emperor hoped to reinforce his army with Hawaiians whose parents had emigrated there many centuries earlier from Nippon. The Portuguese man o' war, unfortunately, was captured by Cricket submarines that came, it seems, from an undersea other world civilization.

Almost immediately, the Crickets recognized the value of having found such a treasure as Fumihiko the Samurai. They treated Fumi with the utmost respect accorded a *special teacher*, a *Shihan*, a Samurai. "We need your Oriental martial arts knowledge to help our students of the Cricket Military Academy. If you will also teach us your ways, we pledge to assist you in defending your Nipponese Emperor." Having no real choice but to oblige, the Samurai said he would offer his services for three years and then he would hold them duty- and honor-bound to support his Imperial leader! The two parties agreed! Soon, Fumi the Samurai became the most respected and famous of the Cricket Academy's martial arts teachers. Amazingly, at this very time, five new recruits—from the Cricket Academy—began their studies with this much-heralded teacher from the Orient.

The *Shihan* said to the Academy Administrators that he would prefer to begin with small classes, and then his best students could assist him with teaching the others: They agreed. The five new recruits soon became the Samurai's best students. In the evening, around the campfire, the *master* teacher taught them more than the "art of war"; he taught them "the art of living." He spoke to the young Cricket cadets about a code of honor, only after he felt secure in this new relationship: "Yes," he introspected, "together, we have formed a bond and these choice Crickets can be trusted!"

Fumi needed honest friends, so far from his homeland. Needless to say, these five Crickets blossomed into fierce warriors, who also embraced the *Samurai Code* of honor above self, respect for all living things, helping the meek, the poor, the disenfranchised, the widows, the orphans, and many others. "The power of the universe," Fumi proclaimed, "is manifested all around us. If we are to perform the Great Spirit's will, we must find our inner harmony. Follow the true light of the forest by day, just as the mariner-captain, who wishes to protect his ship and crew, finds the celestial star of the evening-light, to guide him throughout the night." Then quoting from his credo, he espoused, "On the high seas, true faith—real faith—calms even the mightiest squall."

Their *Shihan* had spent three years as a loyal military teacher of the young Cricket cadets; nevertheless, the new senior officers did not keep their part of the bargain: to return Fumihiko to his native Nippon and help his Emperor. The Samurai, brokenhearted, became depressed and fell ill. No longer of any use to the Cricket command, he was sent "out to pasture," as they say. In order not to cause a revolt among the junior officers, Fumi's life was spared. He was even given a small living quarters but barely enough of a stipend: to feed himself and to take care of his life's necessities.

The Group of Five, the *Goh*, when they learned of the shameful way their *Shihan* had been mistreated, vowed that someday they would find a way to return the Samurai to his native country. In one of their last *formal* meetings around a secret campfire, located some distance from the Cricket barracks, Fumihiko the Samurai, in spite of his present condition, found the energy and the will to perform a *special* ceremony. Here, each of the *Goh* members was transformed into Samurais! Each of the newly installed young Cricket Samurais, out of respect for their *Shihan*, took a new name, known only to the Samurai and to themselves. The names, as one might suspect, were Nippiness:

Hiroshi: generous
Michio: man with the strength of three thousand
Roka: white crest of the wave
Toru: from the sea
Toshiro: intelligent, talented

Twenty years had passed since that ceremony had taken place! Hiroshi recommended that the *Goh* ought to meet now, rather than on their customary monthly meeting time, when the moon was full!

"Well that's OK with me," replied Toshiro, "but the rest of our members won't be returning from the field-of-operations until tomorrow." He continued, "What's on your mind?"

Hiroshi answered, "Now that we have successfully been able to free the Frog Princess Sophia from the dungeon-like cell in the tower, we must escort her safely to a halfway house. Once there, she will join the *avant garde* comprised of Frog Seals." Hiroshi then paused as the others waited to hear more. He looked up at the starry sky, where all who were present began feeling the chill of the night air. For a moment there was a silence that seemed to meld with the heartbeat of eternity. His face, outlined by the campfire, betrayed the stress of one struggling with the consequence of delaying. He recalled from his military history that Napoleon had once stated, "Ask me for anything but time!" He suddenly seemed to return from the universe above. He broke his silence and started to speak, adding, "If we do not move her from her present place of hiding, then we risk the possibility of having our plans foiled!" Hiroshi's voice echoed around the canyon's walls, reminiscent of nature's own conviction when warning that winter is fast approaching.

Toshiro seemed stunned that Hiroshi would want to move so swiftly. He spoke with his own deep concern, "Did we or did we not agree to wait until the end of the month, only a week away?"

Hiroshi replied, "That may be so, but our Cricket Central Intelligence Agency (CCIA) is looking high and low for the Princess and those who helped with her escape!

Roka, seeking to break the impasse, offered, "Do you recall the lecture from another of our visiting French military strategists? He quoted the same French General, to whom you infer, 'Ask me for anything but Josephine!'" Instantly, everyone broke into hilarious laughter! With all of the tension they had been through, the laughter brought a release that was long overdue! Maybe now they could all relax and move confidently toward a successful rendezvous with the Frog Seals.

Hiroshi still laughing, in spite of himself, then calmly answered, "Yes, yes I do, Roka." Toshiro, with a change of heart, then quickly offered, "In that case we have no time to waste! I will do my utmost to reach the rest of our group by use of our specially encrypted code, that has to date been indecipherable over short-wave radio." Toshiro continued, "I usually talk to Toru right after nightfall; he can pass the encoded information on to you, after you join them. If you leave within the hour, Roka, we can all be together by midnight tomorrow."

The next afternoon the two *Goh* members, who would remain on shore, met. "Let's synchronize our audio-video watches," Hiroshi exclaimed! Continuing to speak, he indicated, "It is now 13:05 hours." "I believe you're right, from what I see on the park's Senior Administration Building," Toshiro affirmed. "I must be a few minutes slow; maybe I need a newer watch like yours," Toshiro quipped, with a smile. He knew, as one of the more intelligent officers in all of the Cricket Special Services, that oftentimes it is necessary to act normal when the stress of life tries to interfere with the quality of life. He acted out his motto as he moved through life; it seemed to be: "Smile in the face of adversity, and take courage; these two coupled with intelligence will win the day!"

The two best of friends had agreed to meet at the Middle Grade Cricket Officers' Dining Hall and, from there, proceed to the business at hand. Toshiro would contact Toru, as he had promised, and Hiroshi would pretend to be involved with his research project: "Oceanomics and Its Application to Seafood for the Cricket Navy" at the Academy's superb library.

The time was now 18:00 hours, exactly, and things were becoming very tense on both sides of the Jordan, as well as on the Jordan itself. The Cricket admiralty had already ordered that any leave to officers of middle-grade status—and up—be denied! By 21:00 hours the planned second Cricket major offensive, against Frog defenses on the Western slopes, would go into effect. It was precisely at 18:01 hours when Toshiro had encrypted a message to his *Goh* counterpart, Toru. Toru, expecting this nightly radio-transmission from Toshiro, knew he had to get away from his classified meeting very soon. Fortunately, the meeting was just breaking for coffee. Toru, therefore, used this window of opportunity to slip away to a quiet corner to listen to Toshiro's recorded radio transmission.

Toru was alarmed to learn that their plan was being changed: to move now rather than next week. He responded to the message by simply saying: "No can do! There is absolutely no way that I can leave the SSCA (Secret Service Cricket Admiralty) without permission from the commanding officer. Recommend you and Hiroshi move on your own; Roka and Michio are in the same fix; nevertheless, I will relay the info to them and the first opportunity we have, we will jump ship! Stay in touch for a meeting place. Is the halfway house still available? If so, we will find a way to meet you there. Need to stop here; being called back to our top-secret briefing! Toru. PS: Give my best to Hiroshi, and good luck!"

As the rest of the Cricket flotilla continued to move down the Jordan, under the cover of darkness, anxious family members and friends of the Frog Defense League were gathered together at the FDL headquarters, to learn the latest of what was happening on the Western Front. Seneca, Plato's wife Ruth, and several other prominent townspeople of Frogland were seated on the stage, near the front of the assembly that numbered some 4,000 citizens. Various individuals began jumping up and down trying to get recognized by the prestigious board. Seneca quickly jumped to his feet and began to speak on the public address system, saying:

"Please, please, one at a time, you'll all have a chance to speak! While I am taking questions from the floor, the rest of you can write down your questions on a slip of paper, and the assistants will collect them, so that our panel can review them and then pass them on to us. We will, of course, choose the questions we feel are most important to the security of all, those questions we feel best reflect the sentiment of the entire assembly."

An old farmer, who had had his hand up for some time, was recognized by Seneca and began to speak:

"Thank you for calling on me" he said in a hazy husky voice. "I am concerned with how we might bring our produce to market, since all of the highways are crowded with military vehicles and our trucks continue to be rerouted on detours that lead to nowhere: the whole thing is ridiculous! Tell me, how are our troops supposed to eat, if we can't get food to them?"

Without hesitation, most of the Frogs began to applaud while some even jeered and stamped their feet, to let out their frustration and to lend steadfast support to the agricultural community.

"Here, here," Seneca bellowed over the microphone, "We'll have none of that! Once again, let us be civil. Are we or are we not a respectable citizenry?" With that, other Frogs in the audience stood up and turned to their fellow citizens and asked them to comply with the FDL Chairperson's wishes. A hush fell over those present and many leaned forward to catch every word coming from the front table's speaker. Seneca continued in his elegant voice, "I know how difficult this episode in our lives has been for all of us. As I speak, the last of the military convoys have passed the busiest sectors of Frogland and are headed toward the Front. You should, it appears, now have little or no problems getting your food and supplies to market! As you know, the larger portion of the food must be sent to our soldiers-in-arms; still, there should be plenty available for the rest of us and our families."

Ruth, just finishing reading to herself one of the handwritten messages, began by quickly turning to Seneca, in order to hand the missives to him. He was beginning to show his age, and he politely asked Ruth to replace him on the podium for a spell. She smiled a yes at him and then rose to speak. A thunderous applause welcomed her! They all knew what a fantastic Frog she was and what a handsome, intelligent, and courageous husband she had in Plato. Furthermore, they knew that Plato, as Frogland's newest Prime Minister, had been very successful at winning over the Toad King, the Toads' Congress, and the hearts and minds of the Toad community. She continued smiling and beaming with a radiance that was so incredibly self-assuring.

"My fellow Frogs and friends of our beloved country let us be assured that our military with the able assistance of the Toad Nation will defeat the enemy!" More applause and shouting punctuated her delivery and they began to chant: "We love Ruth, we love Ruth, we love Ruth!" She raised her long arms to quiet them and with a smile, after blowing them a kiss, she continued: "My husband, the Prime Minister," more cheers interrupted her speech, "has relayed to our Board of Directors that our newest *Mushroom Jets*, that are able to ascend and descend vertically, are now landing on the *HTMS Supreme,* His Toad Majesty's personal aircraft carrier! This war effort is a joint military operation with dual commanders in charge of land and sea operations. Our navy defending our shores is at present under the command of Admiral Wisemann; conversely, our Toad friends' current commander is their most experienced and highest-ranking naval officer, Admiral Da Vinci." The Frogs were decidedly impressed with the leadership that would be directing the naval operations of their two nations. Others were still anxiously waiting and wondering whose question she would answer first.

"I see that some of you have been following the *Frog Military Times* and have learned that the Crickets prefer attacking their enemies by nightfall. This first question then reads, 'Will the Crickets attack tonight and, if so, are we prepared?' An excellent question, to be sure, and one I know you are all asking yourselves." With a determined smile she continued. "What I can tell you from Frog and Toad Military Command Headquarters (HQ) is that HQ has considered that precise possibility. Right at this very moment, our combined navies are moving swiftly to overtake the Crickets! Trust me! They'll never be able to disembark on our beaches with their main force's landing crafts! We will kick their ugly behinds back into the River Jordan!" Much laughter erupted!

"The next question reads, 'Are their any female Frogs or Toads involved in these operations?' Once again, a superb question!" Ruth remarked. "Our Admiral Wisemann has said that, thus far, most women aviators are confined to defending the home front, that is, defending our shores, our beaches, and our installations: arms factories, foundries, electronic bases, all sorts of important plants, and the like. Since we first began to allow women in our military academies, we have been very pleased with the results.

"If our female pilots prove as adept in actual 'in-the-air dogfights,' as they have displayed in their Top-Gun exercises, they should have no difficulty with keeping front-line battle positions against hardened Cricket aviators! They understand completely what's at stake. They, too, are willing to take the necessary risks to defend our safety!" With that, the women began to cheer and weep. This applause, however, was not so much to say they agreed women should be fighting the enemy in the skies while patrolling the Jordan River's seashore, as much as the applause made a statement by females, for females! It shouted "Thank you, thank you, over and again, thank you! Your brave commitment is almost more than we can bear. May the Eternal Force ever be by your side! Good hunting!"

As they were speaking, a courier dressed in Navy blues came into the assembly and said that a newscaster had announced that the enemy was spotted just one hour northeast of Jericho Pass and would be attacking our main line of defense near the Port of Samuel. "Plan Zero" was now in effect! Plan Zero was a military directive that compelled all disabled citizens and children to find shelter at the nearest centers: these centers had previously been designated by the civilian authorities to protect the most vulnerable citizens of Frogland. These centers, speedily created, were intended to provide food and water and a temporary place of residence, until more suitable lodging could be constructed.

Seneca, now more rested as a result of not having to speak awhile, assumed complete control of the audience and simply stated:

> Let's keep our heads. You all know what to do. I would ask the Boy and Girl Scouts to provide the necessary leadership in making certain all of our older, respectable citizens find their way safely to the shelters under your control: check with your Scout leaders if you have any questions. The rest of us must be prepared to aid our military personnel by working in the hospitals, assisting in the arms plants, working in the factories, helping with communications, food distri-

bution, water sanitation, transportation, if necessary, and all the fine things we are capable of doing to help our forces defeat the Crickets!

Surprisingly, everyone jumped into action and not a minute was wasted. Who would have thought that thirteen- and fourteen-year-old Boy and Girl Scouts could function with such diligence and ease, but they did! It helped alleviate a big burden: it freed the adults to perform their tasks, as well. Seneca, Ruth, and the other Frog Defense League board members rapidly descended the stairs and made their way to the awaiting vehicles that scurried to Josue II's Summer Castle grounds. The three limousines, with red lights flashing, were escorted by four motorcycles that moved quickly through the throngs of Frogs, citizens going to their respective assignments. Before the Board members knew it, they were going through the Palace gates that opened electronically under the watchful eyes of decorated paramilitary Frog MPs. Normally, palace guards would adorn the entrance to the Summer Palace; however, since they were mostly ceremonial, they would be attending to Palace officials inside the Castle's complex.

Once inside the beautiful Castle, they were quickly ushered into the King's situation room. On arrival, those who had never before been to the Castle could not get over how elegant the interior was! Expressions like, "ooh," "ah," "wow," "gosh," "gee whiz," "holy cow," and "awesome" could be heard from some of the board members, much to the delight and amusement of the palace guards. The ceilings were, it seemed, as high as the sky. They were decorated with scenes of past great Frog Kings and their heroic deeds. One thing for certain was how colorful the various paintings appeared: gold, silver, royal blue, emerald green and a regal purple, with accents of crimson, dominated the saliency of the murals, frescos, and tapestries.

All of a sudden a cheerful but concerned voice came booming through two huge doors, pushed aside by the tall, rotund Frog King: Josue II. He had not waited for the entourage to be presented to him; instead, his concern for his people overwhelmed him and protocol was circumvented. Once again in a booming voice, he beckoned them to come in: "Please, my loyal subjects, come in, come in and make yourself perfectly at home: My castle is your castle." The King's warm disposition made them feel welcome; his subjects were relieved; many had been nervous about meeting their King in a personal setting.

"Do tell me about your meeting with our fellow Frogs; how are they taking the news of an imminent attack? Are the children and the seniors protected? Are they confident, we can defeat the menace before us?" the King inquired. Ruth, who would otherwise allow Seneca to speak first, out of respect for his position and age, could not contain herself and jumped in. "Yes, your Highness, they are strong and better informed because of our board's presentation to them; and yes, the children and the seniors are being taken care of, due to the maturity and responsibility of our Boy and Girl Scouts; and, yes again," she uttered with a smile that rivaled heaven's stars, "the community of

Frogs is behind you 1,000 percent. Many were yelling 'Victory! Victory!' as they left the community center and 'Long live Josue!' then 'Viva Josue!' and finally 'May the Eternal Force save our King!'"

The King nodded thank you, with his pursed lips turned up at the sides and eyes sparkling like effervescing beverages ready to overflow. A little misty-eyed, he inquired lovingly, "Have you had anything to eat? Never mind if you have. I don't enjoy supping alone. I insist you all join me for a little something!" With that, waiters immediately brought food and drink to the King and his community leaders. The waiters seemed to come out of the woodwork and moved about quietly, while performing their separate tasks, or much like the mice who created Cinderella's dress. The waiters knew it was an honor to serve their King! The banquet, the guests found out later, had been ordered by the King hours earlier, in anticipation of his loyal guests.

The King continued, with a slight consternation readily visible on his whitish brow, "We can talk while we dine. I have been briefed by our commanders at Military Headquarters, thanks to the able assistance of our latest two-way audio/visual top security telecommunications conference line: fabulous technology that! Frog Military Head Quarters believes our shoreline defenses can tow the line and hold on, until our combined Frog and Toad flotillas are able to enter the battle zone! I believe we now possess a definite advantage over the Crickets; especially, with the addition of His Toad Majesty's newest ships: *The Eagle* and *The Heroic:* Those are first-class aircraft carriers! Our latest version of the *Mushroom Jet Fighters*, moreover, has vertical-launch capability. It will repel, chase, and defeat the best that the intruders can place in the aerial combat zone against us!."

No sooner had the King completed his remarks, than the King's intelligence attaché knocked on the large doors! The attending palace guard, outside the King's private dining room, spoke to the intelligence officer and demanded the nature of her visit. The officer declared, "I have special and confidential news from the front!" The guard ushered the officer in immediately. The intelligence officer, in an urgent voice, asked the King for permission to speak. The King replied, "By all means, tell us what the latest information is!" The intelligence courier divulged that the second phase of the war was now well underway, with more and much larger shells, from the Cricket flotilla, now bombarding the Frog's shoreline. "The scenes reported from there have just been terrible," the visibly shaken officer exclaimed! She found it difficult to continue, while bravely holding back her tears; nevertheless, she managed to regain her composure and stated, "There are numerous casualties, Your Highness!

At this point, even though the Frogs were entrenched in their fortified positions, it was uncertain whether or not the Frogs would be able to hold the line, until the combined forces of the Toads and Frogs entered the war zone. *The Mushroom Jets*, it appeared, while within flying distance from the aircraft carriers, still needed to be checked out to insure the pilots' safety. These airplanes were very sophisticated: They came completely digitalized, with the latest electronic heat-sensing devices that favored their aircraft over the enemy-fighters. The new devices made their missiles unbelievably accurate, even at a considerable distance. The heat sensors, within the missiles, made it possible for the *Mushroom Jets'* weapons to seek out the exhaust of the enemy's fighter, make contact, and destroy his or her aircraft!

Both camps were conducting high-level meetings to provide their respective armies and navies with the best possible logistical support. The Crickets had a major offensive underway, in their attempt to establish a beachhead on the western slopes of the Jordan, just south of Jericho Pass. The Toads and Frogs, on the other hand, had finally been able, after a great deal of effort, to amass sufficient air power. *The Mushroom Jets* now numbered twenty five—even though more than 300 additional aircraft still remained to be inspected and fitted—and these paltry twenty five would have to suffice as the kingdoms' first-strike force. Time was of the essence! The top commanders, both Frog and Toad, agreed that the ill-trained Frog reserves, entrenched on high ground, could hardly be expected to hold. The city's necessary defense shield appeared very vulnerable against the more experienced, overwhelming, tyrannical enemy.

At sea, the number one admiral in the Frog Navy, Admiral Wisemann, had suddenly and mysteriously taken ill. Admiral J. "Cheetah" Obian, already aboard *His Toad Majesty's Heroic,* was immediately put in charge of the Frog Naval Forces. Cheetah, as his staff referred to him, was also an excellent choice for the newly created post of Supreme Allied Commander: This post would, however, be shared with Toad Admiral Da Vinci; the post involved both administrative and at-sea operation command. While it is true that the Frogs had not been to war in scores, they still had continued to develop the best aircraft in the entire region. In addition, it was Cheetah who was largely responsible for keeping the Frog Air Force ahead of the competition! For example, he offered the navy new high-tech designs that far surpassed what other naval air forces could create.

No one knew for sure, from just what part of Africa Cheetah's ancestry hailed. They only knew that they could use ten other men like him: he was, as they say, "tall, dark, and handsome," with a touch of genius. Stories circulated that he was a Nubian prince and had escaped death when his father, the King, sent his son away, just before being killed, himself. His kingdom, one story continued, was overrun by marauding hordes. With no homeland to return to, at a seaport where refugees came for asylum, Prince Cheetah was adopted by a spiritual family in Frogland,. As to his name, well, Cheetah, as a child, had demonstrated exceptional speed: "Fleet of foot." His grandfather had often called out to him, "Run Cheetah, run," and the nickname stuck. None of the other boys could ever catch him. He was, it seemed, a cheetah in human form!

The *main corpus* of the Cricket Navy, meanwhile, was also moving under the cover of darkness as the command had earlier agreed. It was a good plan that, with the moonless night and only a few stars out, allowed the Cricket Flotilla to hit the shoreline with their heaviest artillery. The Blue and the Red

Vampire leaders were beside themselves with joy—no, with stupendous glee and excitement! All was going exactly as plan. Maybe they were right: The "Blitzkrieg," after all, was the right answer to the invasion of Frogland.

High on the ridge, overlooking the great Jordan River, two Frog observers were speaking rapidly about the Cricket Invasion underway! They thought they had already seen the bulk of the enemy's naval force arrive; incredibly, they were still witnessing even more of the main Cricket Navy advance!

Joel (*speaking to Amos, the other lieutenant*): Amos, I don't know how much longer we can hold our defensive positions. Our army is just not equipped to handle such a heavy bombardment! What more can we do? We've been shooting at the climbing Crickets with everything we have; even our old soldiers have come out to help reinforce our lines with their bows and arrows! Imagine that!

Amos: I guess our binoculars are seeing some of the same action! I quite agree.

Joel: We are NOT a match for them! What is keeping our reinforcements? Where are our troops anyway? And, please tell me what's happened to our navy, to our jets? (*speaking quickly*) Just a minute (*picking up the televideo phone*) Lieutenant Elowitz speaking. Yes sir, no sir, I'm not sure sir, yes sir! Yes sir, right away, sir!

No sooner had Joel pressed the disconnect button than Amos stated:

Amos: What was that all about?

Joel: That was Colonel Jonas. He wants to know: if we are still holding our own or have our positions been overrun; and, how long can we expect to hold out with our current supplies; also, are we in a position to retreat, if the order is given: in order to avert heavy losses? In addition, he wants us to send word to the "Silver Brigade," about what a fantastic job they are doing at reinforcing our most vulnerable position: the right side! Besides a much-needed shield in our defense line, they are providing us with a powerful morale booster!

Amos: I'll send word to the *"Silver Brigade"* right now!

Spartacus: (*answering the televideo-phone*) Major Spartacus, *Silver Brigade*.

Amos: Major Spartacus, pass the word that Colonel Jonas with Central Command wishes to express Command's pleasure at the fantastic job you are all doing at reinforcing our right side! We are checking our lines up and down to see if you are in a position to pull back, when the order is given.

Spartacus: Why should we pull back? We've got them on the run!

Amos: On your side, that's true. We are, nevertheless, responsible for the entire line!

Joel: (*taking the televideo-phone from Amos*) Major Spartacus, we can't tell you anymore, due to security reasons: because, Command is now keeping it to themselves. As Lieutenant Amos has just stated, be prepared to do rear guard duty, if the pullback is ordered!

Spartacus: We'll fight to the last man!.

Joel: Major, we know you are willing to make that sacrifice; however, you are much more valuable to Command, if you work in concert with HQ's orders for *The Brigade*.

Spartacus: I GET your meaning; in that case, we'll follow your directives!

Joel: (*to Amos*) That *Silver Brigade* is quite an independent bunch! Many of these men fought as mercenaries spanning a period of some thirty years. They returned from the Far East about two years ago, to rejoin our peaceful community. They were helping a Nipponese Emperor to retain his position as a defender of the people. No longer able to do more for the Empire, they made their way home to Frogland. The Nipponese Commander Osaka awarded these fearless knights the Emperor's highest honor: "The Order of the Golden Dragon." They were subsequently invited to make Nippon their new homeland. The Silver Brigade graciously declined their invitation stating they wished to be reunited with their families.

Later, a special honor guard accompanied them to their ship, the *Blue Pearl Maiden*. All the ships in the Sapphire Harbor came out to greet the *Pearl* and to escort her out of the Harbor: It was a very sad but festive farewell. The children sang lovely songs, and everyone waved white handkerchiefs! Others threw confetti from the bridge, while the Nipponese Navy fired gunshots from their largest ships: one for each 50 of the 1,500 men, or 30 blasts over the Sea of Nippon. Three months ago, they had received word that the Frogland nation was facing an ominous threat from the Crickets. *The Brigade* promptly enlisted as one of the first groups to defend the motherland!

Amos: Wow, how terrific! What can I say about them after that, except, what courageous men! Why, please tell me, do they choose the bow and arrow over the more conventional weapons?

Joel: When they fight, their "*Holy Code of the Spirit*" allows them to become invisible or at least appear that way before the enemy. They must, however, fight with only the sacred weapons that protected them during their historic past! Only then will this spiritual blessing work! At first, the enemy laughs at these fighting men dressed in Twelfth Century Templar Knights regalia, armed with long bows, crossbows, and slings, too! The laughing, needless to say, soon subsides. What they see, instead, are their own ranks becoming depleted by the sure shots emanating from the weapons of these knights! When the enemy, once again, trains their heavy artillery on the Silver Brigade and believes to have obliterated their position, they are shocked to find that the Knights have reappeared, intact, on the opposite side of the field! Oddly enough, the Brigade's *Blue Pearl Maiden* also seems to share these same mystical powers! Can you see where they are now?

Amos: *(looking through binoculars)* Yes! Wow, I see what you mean. *The Silver Brigade* is now on the other side of the field supporting the weakened left flank. Incredible!

Spartacus: *(yelling to the other Knights)* Men, make a fire roll, 100 feet long and five feet high. Drop it at the point where the climbing Crickets have made their greatest advance up the cliff. Jeremiah, take fifty of your best bowmen and slingers and place them on the right side of the rolling fireball, to prevent any Crickets from making it to the top and over the ridge! The rest of you Knights, form a double crescent, where the ends of each crescent meet at the center; then, recoil the center in our traditional arrowhead fashion and let the magic arrow fly, to attack the enemy at their heart! As the arrow pierces the enemies' strength, both extreme ends can then converge from far left and far right, to squeeze the Crickets and further slow their attack.

This pincer movement was timed perfectly, and the enemy's forward ranks were decimated, while those Crickets close behind retreated and regrouped to attack a weaker Frog position, just to the right of the *Silver Brigade's* stronghold.

Joel: We need to check with Command. In spite of our brave Frogs' efforts and the brilliance of *The Knights of the Silver Brigade,* the overwhelming Cricket forces have finally been able to break through our first line of defenses! Thanks to *The Silver Brigade's* great stance, we have been able to gain valuable time and can now better move into phase two of our defense!

(to Command) Sir, we can no longer hold our positions. We request permission to pull back and initiate phase two. Thank you, sir. I will issue the order to withdraw to Line Two, our second line of defense and in accordance with your strategy.

(to Amos) Issue the Command to withdraw at once! The withdrawal must be orderly, so that our first line of defense, L 1, can join our second line of defense, L 2, without the loss of time, material, and especially personnel.

The *Silver Brigade* had performed admirably; still, the Crickets were too large a force to be reckoned with, at this point in their offensive. HQ issued the command to withdraw to all first-line forward officers in the field, including Joel and Amos. Thus, all of the *avant-garde* was now in full retreat, rushing to join the second-line defenders!

The military genius that first designed the strategy of "Pullback" and later issued the command to do so was none other than the much-acclaimed Frog, Lieutenant General S. Polaski, of Polish heritage. This fiery young leader was under the command of the Toads' General Schwartzwait, the Four-Star Army Field Marshall in charge of all Allied Military Ground Forces. These forces included the renowned 8th Army's 23rd and 59th Frog Battalions and the prestigious 3rd Army's 99th and 111th Toad Battalions. More battalions and regiments were coming in from the First and Third Divisions of the Frogs and Toads' elite Marine forces; still, the 23rd, 59th, 99th, and 111th had been personally selected by General Polaski because of their valor in combat, experience overseas, and mutual heritage. They were homegrown all-star units who had returned from military missions around the world, to lend support to the Frog and Toad's quest to defeat this mighty foe, this malignant threat: the Cricket invaders!

Many additional soldiers came from Central Europe; others came from Scandinavia; while, still others were from the Egyptian deserts. These latter soldiers wore the uniforms of their ancestors, adorned with beautiful bright colors, visible over their white robes that shimmered under the breaking dawn's rays. These fearless leaders rode their white-and-black Arabian stallions, just ahead of their troops, composed of enormous horizontal columns, yet all in meticulous formation! Rumor had it that other troops came from Arabia and as far away as India! What had seemed to be just a war between the Frogs and Toads against the invading Crickets was now a war of international proportion, one consuming the planet!

In retrospect, Prime Minister Plato, it appears, had been allowed to use the Toads' classified computer in order to ask for assistance from the United Nations (UN). It was just about then that a UN official informed General Polaski of the impending war. General Polaski had been representing the Frog presence in the United Nations peacekeeping efforts in various countries around the globe. His principal charge was conducting UN armed maneuvers, at these remote locations. In a special session, the United Nations Central Committee approved the Frogs' request to have General Polaski released from his current assignments and be allowed to, expediently, bring these elite troops to the Middle East.

Prime Minister Plato had stated to the UN Secretary General that the Frogs and Toads were in an all-out effort to counter an enormous threat from the north. "This unknown force, the Crickets," the Prime Minister continued, "originally come from the center of the Earth! They are actually real alien invaders!" Yes, the Frogs, in particular, had hoped for reinforcements, and—at last—these reinforcements would be forthcoming. Oh yes, what magnificent reinforcements these soldiers were, la crème de la crème, indeed, the cream of the crop! It was, thus, that Lieutenant General Stanislaus R. Polaski now found himself, along with his elite troops, facing the dreaded Cricket enemy. The fiery general listened to his heart, as it spoke, "I mustn't fail my people. I must preserve our homeland!"

Chapter Two

The Goh's Risk!

As the war continued, the *Goh* on the Cricket Armada had met and agreed to jump ship, at the earliest possible moment! That moment had arrived! Toru had rendezvoused with Roka and Michio during the night, and Toru had stated at the meeting that a number of gigantic tortoises had been spotted off portside: They were approaching very close to their ship, the prime aircraft carrier, the flagship *Stingray*! The spotter was a close friend of Toru, and Toru asked the observer not to mention anything about the giant tortoises, because it would cause too much commotion aboard ship. The seamen and seawomen had to concentrate on the military matters at hand. His observer friend Keanu was a pleasant young sailor of Hawaiian extraction. He smiled and assured Toru that he would certainly comply by doing his best to assist him, personally! Toro was not the least bit concerned; besides, he was one of the higher-ranking, mid-grade officers. In a situation like this, the observer would simply be obeying the directive issued by a higher-ranking officer or Toro in this case. No one would suspect that anything was amiss; no one would be the wiser!

At 3:33, the *Goh* donned their scuba gear that enabled them to better breathe underwater, than is normally the case for Crickets. They informed Keanu that they were on strict orders to take a closer look at these magnificent tortoises. They wished to see if they had any military use in their campaign against the Forces of the Frogs and Toads. When the coast was clear, they jumped ship and swam out to the tortoises. Oddly enough, from a distance, they appeared quite friendly! The tortoises, they theorized, had made a wrong turn on their normal migratory ocean voyage to their favorite nesting spot on the Galapagos Islands.

The swift and powerful oceanic currents had probably propelled them thousands of miles off-course from their original destination—all the better fortune for the *Goh*! Perhaps an unknown Power was determined to assist them: by using these giant tortoises in the Goh's attempt to return the Frog Princess Sophia, in exchange for a tidy ransom. The capital, in turn, would finance the expenses incurred in the purchase of a ship that would serve to return Fumihiko, their beloved *Shihan*, to Nippon. After so many years, the *Goh* wondered if the Nipponese Emperor was still alive! They certainly hoped so! Together with Fumihiko, they believed they could recruit an army to restore the once-pacific realm to the good Emperor.

As it turned out, although the tortoises were even larger than they first appeared from a respectable distance, they were not tortoises at all—at least none made by Mother Nature. Instead, they were *PT Class 109-9* all-purpose, amphibious sea-, land-, and air-assault machines, equipped with the latest digital electronic gear that made them extremely dangerous to enemy combatants! They could launch torpedoes and missiles, alike; moreover, their machine guns were laser-ready and as accurate as a diamond cutter's eye. The *Tortuga,* as they called their submarine, had a configuration and coloring that made it ideal: an excellent disguise for the *PT Class 109-9* Assaults.

The *Tortuga's* (*PT Class 109-9* submarine's) occupants had been able to intercept and decode Toshiro*'s* messages by using sophisticated encryptology. They were, in addition, waiting for *t*he opportune time to surface, in order to draw the attention of the onshore Cricket spotter. The *Tortuga's* occupants, moreover, had already been provided with additional information from Toshiro, once they were able to communicate and convince the Samurai that they were, indeed, friendly Toad and Frog Seal agents. The *Tortuga's* commander stated they wanted nothing more than to receive assistance in recovering and returning the Princess Sophia to the Kingdom of the Frogs. Toshiro, now more trusting, told the commander that Toro, his Samurai friend, would be at his post, portside: looking for anything moving in the water! From that point on, the operation became much easier! The *Tortuga,* thereafter, easily shadowed the *Stingray.* The onboard *Goh,* the remaining Samurais, had been provided with an exit strategy!

Finally, in Toshiro's last communiqué with Toru, he had advised the latter to be looking for disk-shaped objects approaching the flagship *Stingray*! Toru had kept this information to himself, rather than divulge it at the *Goh's* onboard final meeting. His thinking was: "If I share this information with them and they are captured by senior officers, it could mean their very lives. They will know soon enough!" It was a risk he had to take. Toru trusted Toshiro and knew he must keep the information, the exodus plan, secret. He realized the importance of this clandestinity; furthermore, he knew Roka and Michio would forgive him if and when the subject was discussed.

As they approached the *PT 109-9* Amphibious Assault Units, Roka and Michio were shocked to find that the tortoises were actually miniature submarines. The swimmers became further discouraged, if not angry, to find the Subs' guns duly trained on them. "What?" Toru asked himself, "If these are really friendly agents, why do they appear so menacing towards us?" At that very moment, the upper shells of the tortoises slid back slowly and smoothly to reveal squads of Toad and Frog Navy Seals, all situated in various firing positions! From what the *Goh* members could detect, the respective *PT 109-9* miniature subs were equipped with a variety of the latest laser weapons that could easily repel any enemy, including them.

Once on board, the Toad Seal Commander, a swarthy-complected gentleman, explained: "My name is Lieutenant Colonel Ramirez, commanding officer of combined Toad and Frog Intelligence Seal Task Force or T-Fist for short. We're awfully sorry about having to point our weapons at you, but we have to be very sure you are who you say you are!" Having demanded their true identities be revealed, a series of specific questions that only could be answered by Toru, Roka, and Michio were presented to the three *Goh* members. After they satisfied the questions, the T-Fist Commander proceeded to the acceptance phase of the encounter by offering a toast in honor of their guests: They were now all comrades-in-arms! The toast was a drink made from coconut milk, and they all had a good laugh, since they were expecting, maybe, something else?

A few of the Commander's men helped the *Goh* out of their scuba gear and provided them with an array of Cricket food, that easily surpassed the C-rations onboard the *Stingray*! Just before daybreak, they marched up a hill and through a thick, wooded area with this amazing Seal escort, T-FIST. From there, they reached a halfway house that was dug into a nearby cliff. Lieutenant Colonel Ramirez explained that this secret location, just south of Jericho Pass, had once been a summer retreat for his parents. He recalled, in his discussion, his fond memories growing up here. How could he ever forget those lazy summer days of his childhood? He promised himself to always remember this ideal remote place. "It would become, besides a treasured memory," he elucidated, "a fantastic reserve as the perfect hideaway for some future daring adventure! Yes," Colonel Ramirez smiled and continued, "that introspection had occurred a long time ago. Today, my recollection of that period has not dimmed. Some twenty years have passed, yet it seems more like yesterday!"

No sooner had he finished conveying this sentimental journey, than his speaking was interrupted by a joyful scream! Upon arriving at the summit of the hill, he saw clearly, for the first time, the beautiful Frog Princess Sophia running out to greet him and the others. "I thought you would never, ever get here!" she squealed! The two gazed intently into each other's eyes, she searching for refuge and he searching to understand what strife she had experienced. Just as her beauty was not lost on him, so, too, was his handsomeness not lost on her!

Colonel Ramirez soon released her from a brief embrace, taking into account their different stations in life. Ramirez also reminded himself that she was a Frog and he was a Toad: Both were proud of their distinct cultures and mindful of the civility that needed husbandry, in view of their nations' alliance. The combined Frog and Toad forces would, from all appearances, join these brave Samurai Crickets! In spite of this merry, but somewhat awkward moment, the Frogs, Toads, and *Goh* emotionally joined in congratulating each other on having finally linked-up. Mission accomplished! Or was it? What did their future have in store?

Once the *Goh* and Colonel Ramirez were alone together with the Princess, they inquired about her health and wellbeing. She replied that the Crickets had kept her in isolation; nevertheless, she was, otherwise, treated with the respect and dignity due her station. She dominated the conversation and affirmed that the two brave Crickets, Hiroshi and Toshiro, after arriving here, had returned to rescue a woman named Esther Samson, the Toad Prime Minister's wife.

Esther was a socialite in the Toad community, well respected for the work she was accomplishing for the Toads of lesser means. Samson and Esther had been vacationing on the Aegean Sea, six months earlier, and were delighted that the weather was perfect for sailing. Samson had invited Esther to "go for a spin" on the high seas, but she declined saying she was still tired from all the travel and preferred simply to bask on the seashore. The strong winds, however, carried Samson out farther than he had intended to go. By the time he safely returned, it was very late! She was gone without a trace! Ever since that time, he had inquired everywhere about her whereabouts. Sadly, only a few people had said they thought they saw a woman of her description being led to a helicopter. The helicopter had a foreign emblem that was unrecognizable. It seemed to look like a black scorpion. Other than that, no other clues had been found!

The mystery was solved the day that the Princess Sophia had been brought to the dungeon-like quarters in the Cricket Castle. The Castle, itself, had been won by Cricket conquest. Although the dungeon was heavily guarded most times, there were times when the guards played cards, and it became easier for both Sophia and Esther to communicate, using a special Frog-Toad codification: These two women could emit a telepathic, encrypted code but from no more than a thousand feet. The transmission seemed to work better after nightfall. This telepathic ability would serve them very well in the future!

Late one evening, Hiroshi and Toshiro came to a dungeon in the castle's tower, where the Princess Sophia was being held. They presented false credentials to the guards in order to see the Princess. The guards complied and when they were unaware, the Samurais overpowered them, tied them up, and made good their escape with Sophia. She was taken completely by surprise with no clue as to what was happening! As they passed from hallway to hallway, and corridor to corridor, Hiroshi and Toshiro would alternate displaying their false identity cards; they stated they were transporting the Princess to another location within the complex. Instead, they successfully made their way to the outer perimeter of the castle's walls, where they, once again, used the fake credentials to pass through the gates without any guard the wiser. Once outside the castle's gates, the Princess was told that she was being rescued, and they would have to make haste to reach a rendezvous point. In that precious moment, Sophia asked the Samurais for permission to have a moment to herself, for personal reasons. They reluctantly agreed but urged her to take no more than a minute or two! It was, then, that Sophia immediately went into action to save her newfound friend and to begin "the rescue of Esther!"

Thus, when the Princess Sophia was rescued, during that cold and windy night, she had sent a telepathic message to Esther, telling her not to despair; she, the Princess, would send help! "The rescue operation would be too precarious," Esther had cautioned. She communicated to Sophia not to come, "It is simply too dangerous with the many guards near my cell." Her last words were: "Save yourself!" That event had taken place just a week earlier, before the Frog Princess and the two Samurais, Hiroshi and Toshiro, had departed for the rendezvous point to meet the Toad Lieutenant Colonel, his platoon of Toads and Frogs, and the remaining Samurais. Princess Sophia asked the good Crickets if there was any possibility, at all, of rescuing Samson's wife. To do so, she assured, would result in winning an additional reward: Her government would pay twice the ransom demanded!

It happened, therefore, that under these circumstances, Hiroshi and Toshiro set out on an extremely dangerous mission. It was made all the more risky, since the enemy Crickets would certainly be on the lookout for any further attempts to rescue yet another hostage, Esther! While the extra reward would certainly benefit the Samurais a great deal, it was the *Samurai Code of Honor* that they had taken, calling them to assist honest people in distress, that most motivated them to act. They would, in the end, be upholding the noble and altruistic tradition of the *Samurai.*

Princess Sophia insisted, emphatically, that if Hiroshi and Toshiro—brave and honest Crickets that they were—were to succeed in rescuing Esther, she, the Princess, would have to be part of the rescue equation! The others all seemed to be shocked by what she was saying. "Didn't we just get you out safely, by the skin of our teeth?" Toru demanded, speaking for the *Goh*. The Princess explained, "I was able to communicate with my newfound Toad friend Esther, through telepathic, encrypted code transfer! With me along, I can be of great assistance. Besides, I know the prison complex, the dungeons; furthermore, they would never expect my return! The mean, despicable Crickets are looking for me elsewhere."

Colonel Ramirez had been listening attentively and stepped in to say: "From a military point of view, I quite agree! The element of surprise is in our favor. Also, her ability to communicate by special means is a tremendous advantage that can be invaluable in a harrowing expedition, such as this. I've heard of such a thing in our intelligence briefings. Nonetheless, very few members of our races have this ability, a kind of a sixth or maybe even a seventh, sense. Remarkable! " After some more thought-provoking discussion, the Colonel suggested using the "Ben Franklin" approach of analysis when making difficult decisions: a list of "pros" versus "cons."

As a result, a unanimous vote in favor demonstrated the platoon's solidarity to complete the mission: the rescue of Esther. The Colonel declared that he would lead his 24 men and women, mostly of the Frogs and Toads' Elite Special Forces, to escort them behind enemy lines. Once their destination was reached, north of Jericho Pass, they would find a safe haven to enter the Cricket harbor, known as Scorpion Bay. From there, they would probably proceed on land with their turtle-shaped submarines, their *PT 109-9* Amphibious Assault Units, led by the famous*Tortuga*.

On land, these submarines acted more like tanks, tanks that ride on air. They were also akin to a similar principle utilized by the *air machines of the Everglades*. Amazingly, these *airboats* were capable of attaining speeds of 100 miles per hour over extremely shallow water. Along a similar vein, the *PT 109-9* machines could hover over the sand, without ever becoming congested by the sand itself: an incredible feat. Finally, they could also fly when the need became apparent! For now, these units would function as ground mobility: to avoid giving their position away. It was an added precaution against roving sky detection by enemy radar.

So, the plan was set in motion! After arriving by sea, the platoon of Toads, Frogs, and *Goh* would traverse the mostly-barren desert by land, through the use of the *PT 109-9's* implementation of the *slightly hovering above land by air* principle. The rest of the mission entailed meeting with the remaining two *Goh* members, who had departed earlier following the route from whence they came, but a route too obvious to hide a whole platoon from the enemy. This rendezvous would bring the *Goh's* unit to their original total of five: They would be joining forces and skills, while keeping an eye on improving *esprit de corps*. They were determined to achieve the stated objective: "The Rescue of Esther Samson!" There was no time to waste! After a nourishing meal of Middle East pizza consisting of dried dates, figs, and nuts, sprinkled over moist kosher beef on pita bread, they would leave within the hour. They all looked at each other and realized the moment had arrived! They solemnly knelt, held hands, bowed their heads, gave thanks to the Creator for their food, and prayed for success!

In the meantime, General Polaski's elite United Nations (UN) troops were still pouring in and getting into position, when the Crickets launched yet another major offensive against the Allied second line of defense. This time, however, the Crickets were having a much more difficult time in applying their *Blitzkrieg Stratagem*! Colonel Jonas, overlooking the vast terrain from a position high on a hill, was describing the events as they continued to unfold on the ground. His vista took in both the enemy's forward aggression and the Allied field of defense. All of this action Jonas, and later his associates, discussed with the Frog superior officer, Lieutenant General Polaski:

Polaski: Colonel Jonas, your second line of defense appears to be weakening too soon! I am sending some reinforcements from the UN to shore up the line. The second line must hold sufficiently to slow the enemy's attack; otherwise, they might break through before we have time to fall back. We will move in an organized manner to form our third and final line of defense. Are you getting the message? *(not waiting for a response)* Our two navies are currently fighting the Cricket Armada in a pitch battle somewhere in the Jordan River. Our air forces are participating in this naval engagement with no planes to spare; therefore, for the present, we cannot expect any air support. We won't count on them saving our skins; instead, we will be steadfast in both our determination and use of intellect, set to purposive action!

Jonas: Yes sir and, Sir, I will incorporate the reinforcements to support our center. That's where they will hit us the hardest. Might I say, Sir, those fresh troops are a godsend and will be received by our troops with much jubilation! Sir, a question, if you will?

Polaski: Speak.

Jonas: Am I to understand that the UN officers also speak the Aramaic language?

Aramaic was an ancient language still spoken by a number of the Frogs and the Toads, on both sides of the Jordan River. The language originally came from traders on the Mediterranean who emanated from farther north: some say probably Armenia. The ancient peoples of the Jordan maintained Aramaic as a *lingua franca*: a business language. The language evolved, however, and was now pretty much in the domain of senior officers who studied it in the various military academies. This universal language gave the peoples around the Jordan, a real cohesiveness, a kind of common ground. The culture reflected the language, and vice-versa. Still, it was the officers who mainly used Aramaic in their top military briefings. The language gave those who used it a feeling of continuity; it kept them in touch with who they were and from whence they had come. Besides the cultural imperative, it kept their communication private!

Polaski: Yes. They most certainly do speak Aramaic, along with other languages of the region, for example Hebrew, Sephardic, Arabic, Farsi, Urdu, Turkish, and languages from more distant nations, such as Hindi, Swahili, and Ethiopian. German and Russian are heard as well, just to name a few. Many, of course, speak the English, Spanish, French, and Italian languages that are ubiquitous throughout our Jordan valley. You'll do just fine with them. They're terrific fighters!

Jonas: Thank you, Sir, for apprising me. I will pass the information around to other junior grade officers. It will assist us in our communication with these international troops! I'll get right to work on the second-line of integration, between the UN soldiers and ours. Uh, Sir, one last question.

Polaski: Yesss!

Jonas: Are any of the officers women?

Polaski: Why do you ask?

Jonas: Uh, just curious, Sir.

Polaski: *Captain! (somewhat irritated)* If you must ask, yes there are! Furthermore, they are intelligent and quite attractive; I hope that's not going to be a problem for you! Just salute the stripes. Got it? *(raising his voice)* Salute the *blasted* stripes!

Jonas: *(taken aback and stuttering)* Yes sir, Sir. Salute the stripes. (with vibrato) We will, Sir! Salute the *blasted* stripes, *(recovering his tone* I mean salute the stripes, yes, Sir!

With that brief communiqué, Colonel Jonas set out to initiate and put into practice General Polaski's orders.

Jonas: *(on a classified radio signal with his lieutenants, Joel and Amos, Jonas passing on his frustration to them)* I thought you'd never pick up the *blasted* receiver!

Joel: Sorry, Sir, but we're getting pounded pretty hard right now! Amos is slightly injured but insists on remaining at his post!

Jonas: OK! I've got the picture. Listen carefully! We are getting some new recruits from our UN forces. As you know, they are a mixed force from many nations and include women as well as men. Make certain our men and women officers and regulars, including the Silver Brigade, treat them with utmost respect. Remember: Salute the *darn* stripes and forget the gender. *Comprendo*?

Joel: Sounds like they're really looking good!

Jonas: Did you hear a word I said?

Joel: Why of course, Sir. I was just speculating.

Jonas: *(emphatically)* No time for that! For what it's worth, though, your "speculation" is right on target. Nevertheless, remember what I said!

Joel: *(sincerely)* Absolutely, Sir: over and out!

Jonas: For now, let's show those crazy Crickets what our Allied Troops can do, now that our ranks are replenished! Over and Out!

Joel: *(signing off)* Roger.

The naval engagement, between the two mighty forces of good and of evil, lasted all night and into the next day. There seemed to be little letup in the action. The Vampire commanders, Cornwalter and Reynaldo, were at each other's throats in a tense argument about the stratagem.

Cornwalter (The Blue Vampire): No, Reynaldo, you know I am right! Didn't we catch the enemy off-guard by moving under the cover of darkness?

Reynaldo (The Red Vampire): On paper, I agreed with your idea of moving after dark; nevertheless, you were supposed to be in contact with our flotilla to coordinate ship traffic. We lost a few ships because of faulty or simply no direction from your senior officers! What were they thinking, or better yet, what were they not thinking?

Cornwalter: Why must you always blame me? We share the command, and you are just as responsible for those ships going down as I am. We alternate shifts, and it happened under your watch!

Reynaldo: Yes, that's so right: It did happen during my watch, but it would not have happened if you had given them directives earlier, the way we mapped it out on our electronic charts. Each ship had specific assignments. Now that we have had these accidents, whether by your negligence or not, the formation of our Armada is totally out of whack! What's more, our ships can't turn to defend themselves against the lighter but faster aircraft that the Frogs and Toads are sending against us! They have an ace they call the Emerald Midnight Hornet. He has already shot down seven of our aircraft. Who knows how many more he'll take out. I wished we had someone like him.

Cornwalter: How do you know it's a he? Maybe it's a she?

Reynaldo: You see, this is exactly what I mean: Who in our ancestors' mausoleum cares if it's a male or a female? This flying ace is wreaking havoc on our ships! IT, if you like, has damaged beyond repair one battleship, a cruiser, and one of our best nuclear submarines! How about that? Are you listening to me?

Cornwalter: You're just harping on our losses; what about theirs? Have we or have we not inflicted as much damage to the other side as they have on us?

Reynaldo: We had, until late this afternoon. Now, it seems, their new co-Chief of Allied Naval Forces—or is it co-Supreme Allied Commander? Whatever, Admiral Cheetah! It seems he has outfoxed us! If you notice on our new holographic floor map, they let our ships pursue them and then appear to retreat, only to encircle us! We must move *The Stingray* out of harm's way, or else we're done for!

Cornwalter: Retreat, cut tail, and run? Never! We'll fight to the finish!

Reynaldo: Have you never heard it said: "Sometimes it's better to retreat to fight another day?" I didn't build this glorious navy of ours—with some of your help, of course—to lose it all here!

Cornwalter: With a great deal of my help! Back to the present: If we pull out now, what will happen to our land forces? The last I heard from our Five-Star General Francisco, we were penetrating their second line of defense.

Reynaldo: It appears that their General Polaski is mirroring Admiral Cheetah's stratagem. They are letting us engage them and pulling back: Notice, I said: "pulling back," not "retreating." If our land forces become as exhausted on the land as we are in the sea, we will lose this war! Our days of conquest will come to an end, and we will have no recourse, except, to return to lands we occupy or to return to our home in the center of the Earth.

Cornwalter: Your ideas are filled with hyperbole, and you sound like an old lady spewing sentimentality over her past. I am afraid you've become far too maudlin for my tastes! *(pacing back and forth; then)* After thinking it over, though, I must agree with you. Sometimes I have to disagree to agree! Let's give those green reptiles a taste of their own medicine! We'll reverse the paradigm for a change! We'll pull our ships back and make them think we are in full retreat, only to reemerge stronger than before! We still have our best ships, along with our trusty *Scorpion* that has never let us down and, of course, our own flagship, *The Stingray*. Yes, indeed!

Reynaldo: I couldn't have said it better myself.

Cornwalter: *(now in a better mood, having seen his partner's wisdom)* Oh, but you did!

The two Cricket leaders immediately sent out the command to pull back their ships, in order to deceive the combined armadas of the Frogs and Toads. Along with this feint, they simultaneously continued to press their armies, especially their elite Imperial Guard Units: the 39th, 41st, and 43rd armored battalions. Four-Star General Gerard was the ideal choice to lead these units against the Frogs and Toads and their Allies, consisting mostly of UN ground forces. The Crickets were hoping to break through and go beyond the combined Allied defense line. They agreed that their rationale made sense, The Vampires reasoned, "With all the soldiers we have lost gaining the advantage, why should we stop now, when victory is so close at hand? We have, after all, broken the backs of our enemy's first two lines of defense, haven't we? The two admirals congratulated themselves for having arrived at this momentous decision!

Still, the Crickets knew what the Allied and UN troops were up to: The Allies felt they could stop the Cricket's *Blitzkrieg*. The Vampires joined in saying, "Think again, you sissies; we're coming to get you!" This swift concerted effort, they still believed, would yield just the same results they had achieved in past victories; yet, they conceded, this new enemy strategy of three lines of defense, with each one falling back to create a single impenetrable one, was an intriguing theory. Such a band could be so strong that it might even be capable of repelling their mighty *Blitzkrieg*. Deep inside their bellies, they must have felt some itch of intense concern, but neither Cornwalter nor Reynaldo would admit it had them worried. They had never faced such an idea!

Admiral Cheetah saw through the Cricket feint. He brought in the Frog *Emperor Penguin Spit-fighters*, from the Toad aircraft carrier *Eagle*. The *Penguin* fighters got their name from the amphibious capability of their sleek frames. They could fight in the air and then hide in the water by submerging like submarines. This mechanical marvel required the aircraft to withdraw their outward fins, by pulling back their swept wings, just enough to enter the water. Once again in the water, the wings reappeared as fins for purposes of navigability. Thereafter, they could return to air combat with the thrust of special built-in rocket booster engines. These Frog *Emperor Penguin Spit-fighters* created an incredible sight when they jettisoned out of the water, resembling missiles coming from the ocean's depths! They were submarine-like, yet different from the Turtle-like *PT 109-9* Amphibious Assault Units, whose fighters were saucer-shaped; whereas, the *Penguin* fighters were missile-shaped. The Spit-fighter pilots referred to their fighters simply as *The Pencils*.

Even though the Frog Admiral Wisemann had fallen ill during an early naval engagement, Admiral Da Vinci, of the Toads, was as fit as ever and seemed to be coordinating all his efforts to comply with his Frog counterpart, Admiral Cheetah. There had been rumors that he was very upset when he learned that he had been passed over in favor of Admiral Cheetah to head all Frog and Toad naval operations. Da Vinci reasoned that the Toads possessed a much larger navy than the Frogs; therefore, the assignment rightly should have been bestowed on a *Toad* Admiral! He viewed himself as the logical choice for the new post, if they simply wanted one officer to head it! He recalled being satisfied, maybe even pleased, when he had been named co-Supreme Allied Commander of all sea and land operations of the Jordan and throughout the Middle East! Perhaps he had been misinformed earlier!

Da Vinci continued to ruminate over Toad and Frog capabilities! The idea seemed very plausible, because the real strength of the Toad military arsenal lay in the Toad Navy! While it was true that the Frogs had the superior aircraft, due to their advanced aeronautical research and practice, it was also true that the Toads had the second best aircraft and maybe even the better pilots! This fact was beginning to manifest itself through the acemanship of the Toads' best pilot, the Ghost. The Ghost had amassed an incredible kill ratio. When compared to the Frog's Emerald Midnight Hornet, with three more downed enemy aircraft, the Ghost would be tied with the Frog ace for most Cricket airplanes removed over the Jordanian skies! An enemy aircraft shot out of the sky was considered a "kill;" however, if an enemy pilot successfully bailed out of the plane, he or she was designated "downed." The weight, nevertheless, was equivalent to a "kill," notwithstanding that the downed pilot's life had been spared! Unfortunately, there were pilots on both sides that still preferred the gore!

The Allies were honor-bound not to shoot enemy pilots once they parachuted, according to naval air code. These downed enemy pilots became important in the numerical race for "top ace!" Sea military personnel, in particular, were excited and many sailors took wagers as to who would be the eventual winner; would it be the Frogs' Emerald Midnight Hornet or the Toads' Ghost? Each side believed it would be their ace.

The Ghost had received his name some time ago, while in training at the Toad Top Gun Naval Air School. It was impossible for any of the other naval air cadets to catch him in their sights, much less shoot him down. Throughout his career, a combination of his intelligence and his aerobatics, with his ability to weave in and out and up and down, till it was you the pursuer who was now the pursued, gave enemy pilots much cause to fear him!

Not much, however, was known about the Emerald Midnight Hornet. No one even knew whether this pilot was male or female! A complete mystery seemed to surround the aviator. What was known was that he or she continued to log the most enemy kills, far above any of the other Frog aviators. Other pilots had seen this fighter in the air; however, when they swept by to take a closer look, the most they could see was a dark sheath over Midnight's helmet.

The Frogs and Toads had given as much as they had taken, as their battleships, heavy and light cruisers, destroyers, and submarines engaged the Cricket Armada on the high seas. Also, the superior acemanship of the Frogs' and Toads' navy and air force pilots were now making a major difference in the war at sea! The Frog aircraft had, for the most part, been designed specifically for ground-to-air cover, as opposed to landing at sea on aircraft carriers! Fortunately, through special means that utilized the skills of tool-and-die makers, along with other experts in advanced aviation and aeronautical engineering craftsmanship, the Frog airplanes were, with some effort, retrofitted! With this technical feat accomplished, the Frog airmen and airwomen could now descend onto the Toad landing fields in the sea, their cousins' aircraft carriers!

In the end and through all of this naval activity, Admiral Da Vinci, if he had any emotional misgivings, kept his hurts to himself! Da Vinci, the quintessential admiral, knew that winning the war was more important than his personal pride; after all, he reasoned, without *His Toad's Majesty's Supreme* personal aircraft carrier and *the* King's fleet of first class aircraft carriers, including the Toads' superb pilots, all managed by great officers, like himself, where would their cousins the Frogs be? In a real fix, that's where! Yes, he admitted to himself, when all was said and done, each side needed the other. Together they formed a synergy that was greater than standing apart and alone!

Interestingly, Admiral Cheetah had been aware, from the very beginning that the ultimate leadership ought to have been given to Admiral Da Vinci. He had even offered to step aside, in favor of the Toads' outstanding leader, "The Hawk," as Da Vinci was referred to by most of his colleagues. The name Hawk had as much to do with his outward physical appearance, as it had to do with his military prowess, his sheer tenacity! His nose had been broken, one sailor mentioned to another, when Da Vinci was involved in a fistfight with three marines. He had left the Officers Club late one evening and heard a distress call from a female. In the faint light of the foggy midnight air, he viewed what appeared to be air force blues with white trim, a fellow officer, a female one!

She was being accosted by three marines, who had apparently had more than their share of ale. He rushed to her rescue and took immediate action, only to find out later that they were filming a motion picture! The female officer was just a stunt person involved in stage combat with three male actors dressed like marines! The story was quietly kept out of the papers, but word got out that if you are a woman who needs help, there are still gentleman officers willing to assist you! Whenever women aviators passed Admiral Da Vinci, they smiled broadly and gave him the sweetest salute. He wore His broken hooknose like a badge of courage; it resembled that of a "*hawk*." He had, when you think about it, won the name "Hawk" honorably, performing an altruistic deed: a quixotic one, at least, but never mind the rest!

Prime Minister Samson had discussed the matter with Prime Minister Plato; the two agreed that Admiral Da Vinci had more experience and was the more tactical of the two—a fabulous strategist; yet fighting a war was also a war of hearts and minds; in that capacity, Admiral Cheetah's natural leadership, based on keen intelligence, communication skills, and personal charisma seemed to be what was most needed to pull two ancient friends, the Toads and Frogs, that much closer together. The deed was done and Cheetah, in extreme cases, would have the final word in sea operations; otherwise, Admiral Da Vinci would manage sea strategy. Cheetah had approached Da Vinci, over coffee and tea, one evening in the officers' quarters, after everyone had left the elegant dining room. Under low or soft lighting with only a few waiters around, though not within earshot, he spoke to the Toad leader:

Cheetah: I know how you must feel about not getting sole command over our combined naval forces. Had it been up to me, I would certainly have bestowed that responsibility on you. I believe that your experience certainly exceeds my own. Your skills are without parallel. Please understand that I was sufficiently overjoyed to learn I would be replacing Admiral Wisemann, while, of course, equally concerned about his health.

Da Vinci: *(interrupting)* Before proceeding any further my friend, I do understand! And yes, I must admit that I believed I was the logical choice, taking into account that the Allied Land Commandership, *de facto*, went to your Three-Star Lieutenant General Polaski! Since you have the larger and perhaps better army, Polaski with his overseas experience, I concur, was an excellent appointment! Yes, he can better lead our Allied and UN ground forces! Being younger than our Generals Schwartzwait and Lopez, in time, he will replace them *de jure*. No one likes being passed over for the top spot! Still, we do have the same rank. I am principally responsible for the war at sea and your position is more administrative than tactical. Under these conditions, I am satisfied. I am happiest when I am in the middle of the mix: the fight. That's what I am all about! There's plenty of glory and honor to be won. Finally, if for whatever reason our defense ministries remove you, guess who will take your place: lucky me? I don't want that. Just as I pointed out, I'm happy doing what I do best. So, don't do anything to jeopardize your position. I know you'll do just fine and thanks for your concern. *(Now more relieved, he has spoken his mind as well as his heart.)*

Cheetah: I am honored to be able to work with you and together we will win the war at sea! As soon as we defeat the Crickets out here, we will need to reinforce our fellow soldiers at Cemetery Ridge, where our ground forces are coming together in their third line of defense. We'll repel the Cricket *Blitzkrieg* offensive! I hope they can hold the line till we get there. In the meantime, we both have our jobs to do, right?

Da Vinci: *(extending his arm in friendship and respect)* Right!

That event had happened several weeks ago and now the two were working hand-in-hand to defeat the Cricket Armada.

Cheetah: Da Vinci, I believe the Cricket Flotilla is feinting in their retreat. They seem to have picked up the idea, or something like that, from our ground field commanders' strategy. What do you think?

Da Vinci: Most certainly, Cheetah. Nevertheless, let's continue to press them to the outer limits and away from the few batteries that are protecting our ground forces. If the heavy winds keep up, their Armada will not be able to regroup for another strike at us. In this scenario, we can continue to pursue them until we permanently cripple their larger ships.

Cheetah: A brilliant idea, I quite agree. We can send in some of our lighter ships to harass them, while the terrific storms whip their larger ships about. We'll be able to out-maneuver them and fire at will! Something like what happened when an islander nation defeated a peninsular power. We learned about this strategy when I was a midshipman at our Frog Naval Academy.

At that very moment, somewhere deep within a cave, Lieutenant Colonel Ramirez continued leading a rescue mission consisting of twenty five team members: including himself. The new team members consisted of the Princess Sophia, Toru, Roka, Michio, that is, the three Samurais, and twenty male and female Toad and Frog *PT 109-9* Navy Seals. Five additional *PT 109-9* Convoy Seals, from the *Tortuga*, remained in a cove near the outskirts of Scorpion Bay, the Cricket stronghold. The Seals, there, were positioned to guard their amphibious turtles, until the signal was given to go ashore as tanks. The tanks were not needed for the present, due to the high cliffs and rough terrain. In the meantime, Ramirez's team would make that trek with their mountain-climbing skills. This team could take the field in any Olympics and win!

The team had full confidence in Ramirez's leadership ability: This assurance was based on legend and documentation that listed numerous citations and medals bestowed on the Lieutenant Colonel, for his bravery under enemy fire. He had fought alongside descendants of Cossacks, Watusi warriors, Sikhs, Gurkhas, Chinese warlords, and well- intentioned rebels seeking democracy for their land: all this from the time he was fifteen until the age of thirty three. They didn't come any better or battle-worn than Ramirez! Yet, his hot Latin temper had kept him from achieving the rank of full Colonel. He found it difficult to follow stupid orders! In spite of his emotional outbursts that erupted—when aimed at those he considered insufficiently schooled in the art of war—other superiors saw his innate genius. They knew it was only a matter of time before he would be wearing eagles and then stars on his epaulets.

The military needed more men and women like him, who had fire in their bellies, steel in their eyes, and stood as tall as the redwoods of California—Toads and Frogs who loved their country passionately! For him, the mission was crystal-clear; he was extremely focused. He would find and release Esther from her captors, with minimal or no consequences to his team. If he had to pay the price, so be it! He was determined. He especially loved to beat the odds. This adventure was very risky! It was, his team understood, precisely why their leader had picked up the challenge, the charge! He was born for this assignment; how could he not volunteer?

As they made their way through the cavernous tunnel, he reflected on what had occurred at the halfway house. This house was dug into the upper side of a high cliff, overlooking the Jordan, and it yielded a surprise gift, something that would facilitate the group's effort to save Samson's wife: a faded parchment! Just before leaving the sanctuary, he had sent a young Toad female officer to check the wine cellar for cool water; while Second Lieutenant Jessica Jacobson was doing this, she stumbled in the dark and a tall clay pot fell from the upper shelf onto the brick floor.

Captain Christopher Morris, who was closest to the cellar door, hurriedly ran to see if she was injured. The young Frog officer stared into a bright flashlight, held by Jessica while laughing at her own clumsiness: "Are you all right?" the Frog officer inquired in a kind voice. "Why of course I am," Jessica replied; "Although, I probably could take some lessons on being more careful from you fantastic Frogs, ha!, ha!" Christopher returned, in between their laughter, "I don't know about how careful we Frogs are!" He then proceeded to help her up from the damp floor. Someone above, who had heard the commotion, called, "Is anyone hurt?" The cellar occupants, somewhat dusty, yelled back, "No, we're just fine! Thanks though!"

As the light passed across the room and back to the floor, Christopher insisted:

Christopher: Wait, Jessica, what's that lying next to your feet?

Jessica: Oh, probably just some old papers that fell out of that clay jar that almost hit me on the head!

Christopher: If you don't mind, let's take a closer look.

Jessica: You Frogs sure are inquisitive.

Christopher: Wow! Look at this stuff, would you! It looks like a map of Scorpion Bay!

Jessica: Let me see that *(taking the map away from Christopher)*. My specialty is cartology. I love looking at old maps and this is definitely among them.

The two made their way over to a nearby table. After studying the map for less than half-a-minute, Jessica declared:

Jessica: This map contains underground pathways that lead to various places where the old castle that is holding Esther is located!

Christopher: Holy Cow! Ramirez will want to see this. You know what? I think we've been down here long enough. We'd better get back upstairs: topside. By the way, what were you doing down here anyway?

Jessica: Oh, I nearly forgot in all the excitement. I came down to "fetch a pail of water," ha!, ha!

Christopher: The least I can do is help you with the water. I'll carry the heavier ones. If it hadn't been for your minor mishap, we wouldn't have these valuable maps!

Jessica: Thanks!

The rest was history, as they say. The two young officers brought up more than water, important as that was, especially in the desert. The map was securely tucked into Ramirez's inside breast pocket. The water was also carefully guarded, because they didn't want to chance drinking from a contaminated source; the numerous streams within the cave can vary. Meanwhile, their own supply remained cool as they tromped through the winding hole in the earth. The meandering tunnel seemed to lead nowhere in particular; nevertheless, the path was true to his father's drawing. Ramirez, slightly ahead of the others, began to reflect on his childhood again. At that time in his life, he remembered, his father had had a yearning to go spelunking every now and then. Suddenly, the Colonel had an epiphany and now it all seemed to come together for him! Why of course, these were the maps his father had drawn after he and his friends returned from their caving expedition!

Young Ramirez was not allowed to go, because his father had felt he was still too young, too vulnerable. Perhaps, his father reassured, he would be allowed to accompany him and his friends when he was older: in a few years! Ramirez grew older and that opportunity never presented itself! His father disappeared while he was still an adolescent. Prior to that, his father had instructed him on the dangers of Spelunking. He cautioned: It is a dangerous business; you really need to be an expert in the larger, deeper caves. Most caves are wet, yet some like those that are located in the high mountains of Belize are dry, he informed his son. Ramirez mulled over in his mind these early warnings! His father also mentioned that the ancient Maya had used them to store sacred objects.

Had his father met his fate in one of these dangerous caves, wet or dry? He hoped to learn the answer to that question someday. In his soul there was still such a bond between them. Ever since his disappearance, his father seemed always present and by his side: Ramirez needed only to think about him and there he was, just as he had remembered him! It was impossible to replace him. "True love knows no bounds," a sweetheart had whispered in his ear, some years earlier before she was lost at sea.

The Lieutenant Colonel was jolted from his reminiscences, when the ground began to tremble! The tremors continued until chunks of earth started to peel from the cave's interior walls and ceiling. The jolts became more powerful and the team members seemed powerless, against this horrific act of nature. They found few places to hide: a small alcove here, an inlet there. Others were less fortunate when the soil beneath them began to separate, causing massive rocks to plunge downward barely missing a junior officer, but cornering two others—who now found themselves cut off by an immense boulder! A female master sergeant became trapped under a smaller detached piece of ceiling. Four other team members were altogether missing! Fortunately, Platoon leader Ramirez was only scraped. The tremors seemed endless, until suddenly, they ceased.

Many team members lost their hand-held lights; nevertheless, a few, miraculously, were able to preserve them. As the shafts of lights emitted by these instruments shone all around the cave's interior, Ramirez's voice brought the cacophony of team members to attention.

Ramirez: *(amid coughing by many of the team)* Put on your headgear to protect against any gases that may be coming our way!

Major Mario Giaquinto: Colonel, are you OK?

Ramirez: Yes! Sound off, Major!

Giaquinto: I count *eight* of our team over here: King, Zdunich, Pacheco, Lavot, Sasida, Wetzel, Miya, and me! We hid in the alcove and we're all A-OK!

Boyd English (Senior Master Sergeant): Colonel, there are *six* of us over here. We're fine too! We found cover over there (pointing to an inlet).

Ramirez: *(quickly)* Who've ya got?

English: We've got Nelson, Christie, Propst, Gonzales, Chen, and yours truly *(smiling broadly)*.

Ramirez: That makes fourteen! Who else!

David Cohen (Captain): Two captains over here Sir! Captain Christopher Morris and meself, "Davy Crockett" Cohen! I think I'm all here, just a few nicks and bruises. *(checking himself all round and amused at his predicament, then chuckling as he dusts himself somewhat)* Ya all right Chris? *(speaking with a decided southern drawl, similar to the one the legendary American hero Davy Crockett must have had.)*

Captain Christopher Morris nods and lumbers up and off the damp, cold floor of the cave.

Ramirez: Where are the others? I've got Toru with me. Is that it? Eighteen?

Marvin Chen (Second Lieutenant): *(his voice well ahead of the team, deeper into the cave)* Sir, *(his voice echoing and then slightly reverberating)* I hear someone over here, behind this pile of dirt!

Several of the team members rush over to help. In the darkness, First Sergeant Juliet Miya falls over the side of the open crevice but is caught by Lieutenant Candice Christie's strong right-hand grip!

Christie: I've got ya, Miya!

Miya: Thanks, Candy *(as Miya is being pulled out of the crevice by First Gunnery Sergeant Carlos Gonzales and Second Lieutenant Judy Lavot)*. Hey, I hear some murmuring or moaning beneath my feet. It's coming from deep inside this opening. *(Others begin to run over to discover the source of the sounds)*.

Ramirez: Hold it right there! We don't need *any* more mishaps. Let's check this out in an orderly fashion.

Miya: *(now safely on terra firma)* Thanks, guys!

Ramirez: *(to the four near the crevice opening)* You four: Miya, Christie, Gonzales, and Lavot, be exceedingly careful! Lie prone, face down, and tell me what you see and hear.

About twenty meters to the right and up from the crevice, Chen, with help from King, Zdunich, and Pacheco, are busy shoveling the muck off the body of Second Lieutenant Jessica Jacobson. They complete their task, being extremely cautious not to injure her with their implements.

Jacobson: *(seemingly more dead than alive and very groggy)* Oh, oh, where am I? Is that you, Dad? *(slipping into unconsciousness)*

Major Giaquinto: *(now at her side and checking her vital signs)* Colonel, she appears to be in good shape, aside from a mild concussion!

Mario Giaquinto was one of the best surgeons in the Jordan valley. He had had a successful practice before he entered the military. He knew that the service needed doctors to attend to the sick, disabled, and maybe even the dying. His country needed him and here he was. He was actually half-Frog and half-Toad. His parents were both concert pianists and had fallen in love during a cruise along the Mediterranean. Even though there were raised eyebrows, at the time, most in the Valley now readily accepted the married couple. These were modern times, after all, and more and more people were traveling. The experience of travel seemed to be the best remedy against prejudices. Travelers learned that every race had something significant to contribute to the cause of humanity. For the Giaquintos, it meant the pursuit of life, with a strong dose of liberty, and volumes of happiness. It was this early loving guidance and philosophy that was to shape the idealist Mario was to become. Much like the errant knight, Don Quijote de la Mancha, he hoped to create a perfect world.

Ramirez: That's a relief! You take care of *her (nodding towards Jessica)* and I'll see what can be done over *here (indicating the crevice)*.

Miya, Christie, Gonzales, and Lavot: *(all speaking at once)*
I see one,
I see two more,
There's another one; it's Roka

No, it's Michio
We've found three, no four more!

Ramirez: *(now at the site)* So what have we got, three or four?

Christie: *(the lieutenant speaks with confidence)* Sir, there are four that we have positively identified, and they all appear to be injured or at least mildly so!

Ramirez: We need to begin rappelling now! All free able-bodies over here, on the double!

Giaquinto: Honcho *(another nickname for Ramirez),* Lieutenant Jacobson is coming around!

Ramirez: Great!

Ramirez didn't have time to worry about rescuing Esther, or to think about what had become of the other two absent Cricket Samurais; instead, his full attention was on his fellow team members and the condition of their health! He watched attentively. as Miya, Christie, Lovat, and Gonzales commenced rappelling; in the meantime, some of the other soldiers of the *PT 109-9* Amphibious Assault Team began looking for the two remaining members of their party. By now, they had deduced that the missing were the Princess Sophia and the Samurai Roka. They knew that because Roka had taken it upon himself, as the duty of a Samurai, to guard personages of royal blood, that he would constantly attend to the Princess's need and remain by her side. Captain Christopher Morris, moreover, had stated they were all together when the falling boulders suddenly separated the Princess and Roka from himself.

Christopher Morris: Sir, I think I've found the Princess and Samurai Roka!

Ramirez: Where?

Morris: *(pointing at a huge boulder)* There, Sir!

Ramirez: Wow, *(the wind knocked out of his sails)* that's going to take some doing! Have you heard any noises coming from the other side?

Morris: I heard something, but honestly, I couldn't be exactly sure, Sir, what it was I heard! They've got to be there *(determination in his voice);* the three of us were standing pretty close together when we heard the ceiling start to cave in.

Ramirez: Let's see if we can push a sound locater through that hole, the one up above the boulder. Propst and Sasida over here with the locater and now, please!

The "sound locater" was a device that could be used practically anywhere, whether in the air, in the earth, or in the water. Its purpose, as indicated by its name, was to detect, amplify, and return a clear signal as to any sounds in the area; furthermore, it could be modified, with the moving of digitalized buttons, to separate living voices from ambient, extraneous noise. In fact, a technical analyst could choose to keep certain sounds, while removing others in theory and in practice. A photographic technician is, likewise, able to modify visual images through the practice of technical image crossovers and layovers in the process of editing a frame or frames; hence, the result of image manipulations that results in photographic alterations. Analysts, editors, and technicians combine art and science, in this manner, to create a better mental and physical picture of phenomenon. In this spirit, the audiovisual experts of Ramirez's team went right to work!

Propst threw a grappling hook-type mechanism that was flexible, towards the upper portion of the immense rock. After the second attempt, it caught something and they were now ready to send Sasida up to the top of the rock's surface. Sasida, once he climbed to the upper surface, reached behind his shoulder into his backpack. After a little struggle, he pulled at a black cable that revealed the listening device at the cable's end. One more pull on the cable and the microphone sound-sensing unit was ready for use. Amazingly, the microphone also incorporated a light-emitting camera within the center of its housing. Sasida inserted the cable, with the sound detection unit leading the cable, into the opening of the jagged hole. The cable dropped some distance before it hit bottom. He felt a tug at the cable and heard, for the first time since the earthquake, the Princess Sophia's voice, crystal-clear!

Princess Sophia: Thank Goodness, you've found us! I'm fine, for the most part, but Roka is out like a light! He must have protected me from the falling rocks by shielding me with his body. He is breathing, thank Heaven! Speaking of light, it's awfully dark down here and pretty wet, too!

Ramirez: *(speaking on his televideo wristwatch that ties into Sasida's backpack equipment)* Are you sure you're both all right, apart from Roka's apparent concussion?

Princess Sophia: Quite sure! There it is! I see it now: It's a small bright light on the end of what appears to be a line, or a cable perhaps? It really, really helps in this otherwise forsaken pitch-black hole *(the Princess, usually calm, is expressing her frustration in this dire situation)*.

Ramirez: Yes, I've got you in full view now. Princess, please don't panic when I tell you that I see a massive object swimming in a large underground lake behind you; it appears to be a giant octopus or squid, according to the digital screen on the backpack. (Sasida's backpack is equipped with a video screen on the backside of his gear). It's moving quickly and is now about fifty, no, about forty-five meters behind you!

Princess Sophia: Oh Lord! What now? What to do? *(shouting)* Can someone tell me how on earth a squid gets into an underground lake?

Ramirez: *(quickly)* We'll talk about that later*!* *(very concerned)* Now do as I say. *(firmly and deliberately)* I need you to move into that side dugout, just about 10 meters straight ahead and another five immediately to your left. Check it out first! We're sending in a lot more light on a second cable.

A second cable is produced from Propst's backpack and hoisted up to Sasida. From past experience, he knows a hand-held light will also be needed and he passes that along too.

Princess Sophia: *(picking up the flashlight and moving swiftly to the deep dugout)* It's OK! Perfect! I don't think he'll be able to reach us here, but please hurry it up anyhow! Please, please hurry! Hurry!

Ramirez: Not to worry! Terrific! Now, can you help Roka over there? I see that he seems to be coming around.

Princess Sophia: I'll get him over there, if it kills me!

Ramirez: That's the spirit!

The Princess is tall and strong and she manages to assist him, even though the Cricket is a head taller than she. After much effort they reach the safe haven: the cave, within a cave, within a cave. As she awaits the inevitable, she wonders just how many more caves there must be in this ridiculous mountain.

Captain Morris: Hey, Honcho, we've managed to enlarge a second hole at the base of the boulder using our laser guns. I think we can make it through!

Ramirez: OK! *(referring to the two trapped)* Let's get them out of there!

A few more members of the troop have suddenly arrived to join forces with Ramirez and his party. They explain that the rescue of those who fell in the crevice is going smoothly.

Ramirez: Fabulous! I need you three to help us here! Get your lasers ready for action!

Captain Morris led a squad of five, including himself. Propst removed his backpack and he and the Samurai Toru, Pacheco, and Wetzel followed the Captain into the laser-created hole, where the boulder had previously met the cave's opening.

As they all made it into the cavern, the lights revealed an eerie beauty. The cavern had an extraterrestrial feel about it. The high-powered flashlights, from the various members of the squad, shone on the cavern's inner walls and revealed the most beautiful colors: deep blues, various tones of reds, a bright copper, incandescent yellows, greens, crimsons, azures, magentas, purples, all complemented with deep browns shaded by white crystal that framed them: The whole effect would be a feast for an artist's palette, not to mention enough color to supply any art store for eternity, or so it seemed.

They were in a daze, a stupor, mesmerized, transfixed until they saw the squid's long arms reach out of the dark water, moving to attack the Princess and the Samurai! Just at that precise moment, the squad was shocked out of their hypnotic state; they anxiously went into action to repel the monster from the deep. The squid was like none they had ever seen in the open seas. It was ten times larger than any that had ever been reported at either of the academies, Frog or Toad. As the squad's assault began, in an attempt to put the creature out of commission, the situation was becoming very perilous, to say the least.

The thing now had possession of the Princess and Roka. It apparently had the ability to move outside the water, in the same manner some spiders are able to accomplish that feat. Still, it was not a spider! That was certain! What was it then? Perhaps this specie of squids had been trapped in some underground ocean and was let loose by this last great earthquake. As fantastic as that might appear to someone with reason, theoretically it seemed plausible. It may also have been a carry-over from the last Ice Age. On the other hand, in the not too distant past, people—for more than a 1,000 years in Scotland and in the British Isles—had claimed to have seen a sea monster that patrolled the channels, had they not?

The sea beast was now dragging the two into the deep, murky water. As the long arms of the squid began to encircle them even more, the bodies of the Princess and Roka began to disappear. Their voices and shrieks, too, began to fade! The creature was putting more distance between itself and the troop. Ramirez, now on the scene, took charge. He sized up the situation at once, "What ya doing? Can't you see this creature, whatever it is, has an outer skin that is deflecting our lasers? Our laser beams have no effect on its armor. We need to counterattack by finding its weakness!"

The squid, at this point, had its huge mouth open and was ready to devour Roka. What must have been going on in the minds of the two prisoners is difficult to say. Roka, fortunately, had one arm free and was wielding his saber that sliced deeply into the squid's tentacles. It seemed to wince and loosen its grip on the Samurai. In about the same moment the Princess, still wrapped by two tentacles, came whizzing by, as if on the end of a carnival ride: the Whip! She was, nevertheless, able to scream one last time, before beginning to lose her color; her face appeared drained of all emotion. The squid, completely in command, continued its dive towards its underwater home! Its supper secure, the creature submerged slowly, deeper into the orange-colored water and then shifted its position to expose its underbody.

Ramirez and Morris: *(Ramirez looking at Morris and Morris returning the stare, both declaring at the same time)* That's it! Its underbelly! But it's getting away! We've got to catch it and hit its belly with all we've got!

Captain Morris: Let's get him, or her, or whatever it is!

Ramirez: Like the Captain says, let's go get 'im!

Normally, Ramirez allowed the captains to lead the charge, so to speak; however, the squid's prize was too valuable to lose! He, therefore, prepared himself for the battle of all battles! The three were all excellent swimmers, Frogs, Toads, and trustworthy Crickets. Some adjustments, nevertheless, remained to be made. The selected team proceeded to convert their all-weather suits to wet suits, by simply pulling a ripcord near the collar. It released a special substance that, in turn, flowed throughout the all-purpose suit's outer and inner linings. This seemingly lighter-than-air substance, then metamorphosed by creating linings filled with space-age material. It not only protected the swimmers from the water's elements, but it also provided them with greater maneuverability and propulsion, when in motion.

The swimmer or diver, thus, was enabled to attain incredible speeds! Finally, the converted suit possessed one other terrific advantage! When in the diving mode, the diver pressed a button under his right arm that now made him or her capable of reaching greater depths! After each taking a medicinal pill, that would allow the rescuers to remain underwater for almost an hour, they were ready to pursue the monster! The "humongous" squid continued its downward descent. Within a few minutes, the team found itself deeper into the underground lake that was soon expanding to the shape of an underground sea or even a hidden ocean! No possible way, they said to themselves! There is absolutely no map that conveys this enormous, hidden aquarium that stretches endlessly, for miles without borders!

The chase brought them in contact with other sea creatures, both large and small. Fish of every size and color swam by and then scurried away. A few manta rays were soon replaced by barracudas, and later by sharks. The squid finally arrived at another cave; this one on the side of an underground mountain. Now in its fortress, it would defend the prey it claimed as its own: the Princess and the Samurai!

Using underwater arm signals, Ramirez gave a straight arm up, pumped his elbow in a downward motion twice, and then pointed two fingers at the squid. The cue was a nonverbal command, universally used by the presiding or the ranking officer, indicating to fire at will. It also meant in the language of "salty dog sailors" and "old mariners" alike—certainly in their case—that as soon as the monster exposes its underside "you're all ours, baby!" No sooner had the signal been given than the platoon members opened fire! A number of flashes, laser-power rays, lit up the darkened water! With the squid's ink gone, midnight became daylight!

That was all the ammunition it took, from the six or seven guns that were raining thunderbolts into the squid. The Lieutenant Colonel was correct: once they determined that the underbelly of the monster was its most vulnerable area, the sea beast would be history! The sea monster's tentacles flayed like a windmill struck by Don Quijote's lance, and it vanished, more quickly than it had appeared. It probably escaped to its other kingdom beneath the sea. The Princess Sophia and the Samurai Roka had finally been released from their bondage, once and for all!

The six members of the platoon, joined by the rescued Princess Sophia and the Samurai Roka, were all now safely above the water's edge. After applying corrective, medical procedures to return the injured two back to the living, they resumed their quest to join those left in the cave. Presently, some large decaying trees came floating by and were bound to make a sufficiently large raft. As they paddled, using strong limbs, broken off the tree trunks, the leaders, Lieutenant Colonel Ramirez and Captain Morris, began to plot a course out of these waters. This really was a lost universe! It, probably, had never been correctly identified on any map, by any human being. They drifted awhile. All were exhausted from the ordeal. Toru was resting on the side of the raft when he spotted something very strange. Upon closer inspection, some additional light seemed to emanate from beneath the body of water, as they approached what they thought was a beach. It had been where the huge creature, the squid, first disappeared. Could it be that this light really led to the hidden chamber of the ancient castle?

The castle was among many that had been written about in books, but never found. His father had spoken about a lost city of Atlantis, many years ago. Ramirez pondered the possibility. Why, of course!. He whipped out the map from the inside of his all-weather suit. In his excitement, while the euphoria was still growing within him, he yelled, "we're here!" The crew onboard suddenly began to smile again and their tiredness started to melt away. Yes, they were less tired now. "We're almost where we need to be," someone was heard saying. Another declared, mimicking holding a glass and proposing a toast, "Here's to those brave lads and lasses, the courageous souls at my side!" The others joined in: "Here, here!", "Cheers!", and "*Salud!*"

Ramirez: (*to Morris and Toru*) Thanks for bringing them around! Continue caring for the Princess and Roka. The rest of us will get back to the others. I want to check on the progress of that rescue operation, and I hope our videophones work better above this underground sea, than they did inside the lower caves.

Suddenly, a beep on his televideo wristwatch came to his attention. It was Christie.

Christie: *(interrupting, her voice coming from the main chamber of the cave, at a distance, on the other side of the boulder)* Hey guys, we've got Corporal Susan Smithson up from the crevice, and a net has been sent down so that Miya, Gonzales, and Lovat can hoist up Michio, Murphy, and Minnelli: one at a time, of course!

Ramirez: Ok! We nearly forgot about you all. We've had our hands full with—you won't believe it—a squid that almost ate the Princess and Roka.

Christie: *(laughing out loud)* Hey Colonel, that's one of your better ones! Ha! Ha! That's only too, too cool. It's one for the books? (Pretending to read from a script) Guess who's coming to dinner? Why a squid is coming to dinner, ha, ha, ha, that's too rich!

Ramirez: Remember, Christie, "He who laughs last, laughs best!" *(pleased that both the Princess Sophia and the Samurai Roka were successfully revitalized)* Well, Princess, it's nice to see you are back to your old self! Roka, you look fine, too!

In the days that followed, the platoon rejoined the rest of the troops in the cavernous environment. For a little while, it became their home away from home. While the rescuers Christie, Miya, Gonzales, and Lovat first needed to finish the daunting crevice job, that is, bringing up Murphy, Minnelli and Michio, the rest of the platoon caught up on some much-needed R and R: Rest! Once everyone was safely on the main corridor, of what remained of the earthquaken cave, they set out to rendezvous with the Princess and her entourage: Roka, Morris, and Toru. They found the three under some trees, eating figs, dates, and coconuts.

Captain Morris: *(With a big grin, trying to talk with a mouth full of fruits)* Boy, you guys have had it rough! And, as you can see, we were so worried about you? Ha! Ha! *(everyone joining in the laughter)*

Ramirez: Well, I'm certainly glad to find you healthy and in such good spirits. Now that we're altogether again and rested, let's take one last break before we enter what I believe is the last tunnel *(pointing to the light coming from the water's edge)*. You see that light? *(indicating again with his laser gun)*. When that much light is visible, it tells us that there is an opening on the other side.

Tomorrow, we'll see if it leads to the Cricket stronghold, next to Scorpion Bay: I believe it does! Have a good rest, won't you? You'll need it. And by the way, pleasant dreams, my dears!

It was very likely approaching nightfall. The vivid light coming from beneath the water, where Lieutenant Colonel Ramirez had earlier gestured, was leaving from whence it had first arrived: It began by slowly ebbing away, then measurably dwindling, and finally just vanishing! In each phase of departure, it displayed bright colors that matched those of the cave's interior. The platoon, therefore, hurriedly built a small campfire and posted two sentries. The plan was to alternate sentry shifts every two hours. The team retired believing they had accomplished a great deal! In spite of the earthquake and the ordeal with the enormous squid, the wounded team members were retrieved. After all, had they failed in their attempt to retrieve their lost members from the cave's crevice, the mission might have ended! The Princess and her Samurai guard had also been rescued from the monster's jaws: That called for further jubilation! The wounded, they knew, would soon recover! For now, it was time to catch up on some much-needed and well-deserved rest! The sandy beach, surrounded by a dark blue-vitriol green sea, became the ideal place to experience *pleasant dreams* under exotic palm trees.

Chapter Three

Plato Speaks:
(The Second Town Hall Meeting)

Four weeks passed since war had broken out with the mighty Cricket Empire! Plato had been away when the first town hall meeting had taken place. He had accomplished his mission by bringing the nations of the Frogs and Toads together in a grand alliance. Since that time, the UN troops had arrived and were doing their share to defend against the Cricket *Blitzkrieg*. Thanks to Seneca and to Plato's beautiful, intelligent wife Ruth, things at home were well organized; for example, the Boy Scouts and Girl Scouts had continued helping the senior citizens. Much more, of course, had transpired since the initial Cricket invasion.

Seneca ascended to the microphone to introduce Plato. Television cameras were positioned everywhere there was space to accommodate them. With the UN Forces now in the mix of things, it was also important to carry the message internationally. The televised broadcast would be in the Frog and Toad languages, which were very similar: the main difference was in the accent. The Toads, living just a little farther south along the Jordan, spoke with more of a Hebrew southern dialect; whereas, the Frogs being on the western side of the Jordan spoke with a Hebrew western accent. They both also spoke the international languages that were comprised of Arabic, Aramaic, and Esperanto.

Yes, Esperanto! It served the rest of the nations well: it had become, along with Aramaic, a *lingua franca*, a preferred language of world travelers. It had been invented more than 1100 years earlier, way back in the nineteenth century, by linguistic scholars interested in bringing peace to the world through a common language. Arabic, a natural, regional language, was also gaining international stature as one of the more important languages among traders.

Esperanto aside, these languages, along with Hindi, Greek, Latin, and, of course, Mandarin were among the principal classical languages that would be utilized in the broadcast. Finally, the so-called modern languages, already well established by the twenty first century, were also present in the broadcast, so that those speakers, too, could be apprised of events as they occurred. The All Allied participants, thus, would be informed as to the war's progress. The translators were in their private booths awaiting the speakers, in order to translate the speeches into the specific language, intended for their listening audience!

Seneca spoke: "Ladies and gentlemen, so nice to see you, even if our soldiers have yet to defeat the enemy! Our speaker today, however, has just arrived from the Western Front, and he will speak to you this evening with many words of encouragement!"

Plato rose to speak; his wife Ruth was at his right side. The Assembly then rose to their feet, applauding with tremendous fervor, in the same manner that they had greeted Ruth, almost four weeks earlier. The audience's din was so overwhelming that Plato was unable to silence them. They chanted: "Plato, Plato, Plato, Plato," over and over, again!

Seneca moved to Plato's side, at the podium, and stretched his arms out as far as his old age would permit, to quiet the mass of twenty thousand attendees! The scene was one of *déjà vu* as Seneca began to restate what he had shared with Ruth, four weeks earlier. "Please, please, please be seated. We are all very proud of our illustrious Prime Minister!" Once again, the mass audience erupted into a thunderous, raucous applause!

Plato stepped away from the microphone and moved towards the apron of the stage. He raised his arms to heaven and spoke to the Creator. All suddenly became silent to hear what Plato had to say: "Merciful King of the Universe, The Everlasting Light, be with us this evening that our voices may be as prayers to You, in this trial; that this trail of tears, for those who have lost loved ones, may soon come to an end. We offer to You all our love and deep devotion, Great Spirit." Having concluded the prayer, he now returned to the podium. Microphones had been strategically placed and all in the audience were able to hear without difficulty:

"We are at a great crossroads, as I address you this evening. Oh how I wish I could bring you what you most wish to hear: a word of peace! Nevertheless, that day will soon arrive!" With resolve, he continued: "We will in the end, be victorious!" The audience cheered even more. "We will vanquish this intruder and send him to the lower abyss, back to where he came from! Our Allied Forces have now integrated the famous UN Delta Forces." This was the first time he used the word Delta. For those present, Delta signified honor bestowed on the many who had come to join with the Frogs and Toads, in this, their most desperate hour. The audience chanted, "Delta! Delta! Delta!" and then they became quiet for more of Plato's speech.

"Our dear friends, the Toads and the Deltas, are to be commended for their bravery, that I, personally, have witnessed firsthand. Our combined forces: our alliances with the Toads and now with the Deltas are formidable! These magnificent Delta soldiers of the United Nations are helping us win the war against the Crickets. Even though we are vastly outnumbered, we have been able, these past few weeks, to hold the high ground: the upper hand. Each week the toll on the enemy becomes greater: They are becoming weaker!

"Our Silver Brigade fought admirably during the first weeks of the Cricket assault, and they show no signs of tiring, in spite of their advanced years. The Egyptian soldiers, under the command of Lieutenant General Polaski, have traded in their ceremonial white-and-black stallions for Shermann tanks of the same colors." The audience is amused and laughs uproariously. "Our brothers and sisters, all valiant soldiers from the Eastern countries, have shown the enemy what they are made of: steel! More cheers are heard. "Time does not permit me to mention all who have gained glory on the battlefield. Still, I would like to tell you a little story, about a young lad.

"As you are aware, from bits of news you have received throughout this struggle, our intent has been to slow the enemy's *Blitzkrieg*. We have done so with our first, second, and third lines of defense!" Great applause followed these dramatic words. Up until now the people did not know whether to trust their media or not. These words, from a trusted source such as the Prime Minister, had given them much-needed hope! More cheers and whispers, then, consumed the Frog Stadium. "As to our navies and air forces, we have the enemy almost encircled, and all of this is certainly to the good credit of our terrific admirals! The splendid Admiral Roberto Da Vinci, of the magnificent Toad Nation, (much applause follows) and the fabulous Admiral Cheetah Obian, of our great Frog Nation, (tumultuous applause) are certainly most commendable!

"But, I was about to recount a story of a twelve-year-old boy and his brave exploits. Well, it turns out that the Silver Brigade, after falling back to the second and then the third lines of defense, was cut off from the main Allied Force. The clever Crickets found a way to disrupt the Silver Brigade's radio transmission to the Headquarters (HQ) of General Polaski. Their fate seemed sealed, an imminent and inevitable defeat by overwhelming odds. You can't imagine how alone they must have felt at that moment; knowing they weren't able to get a single message through to HQ. Out of nowhere, it seems, a young boy named David came forth and said to Commander Spartacus: 'I can get through these lines, Sir.' Spartacus laughed at the beardless youth and responded, 'Yeah right, of course you can.' The young lad was not dissuaded and continued in a persistent manner, 'But Sir, please, at least listen to what I know that you don't!'

"All of a sudden, Spartacus's whole demeanor changed. He looked intently into the young boy's eyes and said, 'I do apologize and I do believe you know something that I don't!' In order to make the boy smile he said, 'I'm all ears!' The boy, not to be outdone, retorted 'I see that you are!' Spartacus's close friend, nearby, began to laugh and was politely pushed away by the Silver Brigade's leader. 'To the business at hand!' Spartacus stated, now in a more serious mood. 'Yes,' the boy assured him. 'I live just several kilometers from here.'

"'We kids like to romp through the woods and build our own secret hiding places, so that the adults can't find us! Our parents have never learned the secret as to why we can beat them home, when they are on horseback and we are on foot! The secret is simple. We have carved out a tunnel that reaches from that tree, the one you see there, some fifty meters from here, and continues for a quarter of a kilometer. I can get through the Cricket attack and carry your message to your superiors by following that tunnel.'

"'How about if one of my men accompanies you, for extra security?' Spartacus requested firmly. 'Two reasons to say no,' the boy exclaimed: ' first, the hole is very narrow in some places—In another year I probably won't even be able to get through—secondly, I'd be giving away a big secret I wish to pass on to my younger brothers!' Spartacus exhaled and simply said, 'Well, I don't have much of a choice, now do I, Kiddo? By the way, I don't know your name!' and he smiled at the brave boy. The youth returned his smile and gleaming said, 'My friends call me David, you know, like the boy who beat up the giant in the Holy Book!'

"Yes, by now you know the rest of the drama!" Plato added, "David was successful in delivering Commander Spartacus's military information to General Polaski's headquarters. That most important material, carried by David in his satchel, not only served to save the lives of the Silver Brigade—by bringing much-needed reinforcements to Commander Spartacus' position—but, that intelligence also enabled General Polaski to better define the enemy's position and strategy. Without those maps and the rest, the Cricket artillery would most assuredly have cut into the third line of our defenses. The enemy had hoped that their *Blitzkrieg* would create a highway through our lines. Their strategy was to move their elite Panzer Tank Division, from a flanking position, to a frontal assault.

"Who knows just what might have happened after that! Could we have regrouped or perhaps looked for another miracle? Thankfully, we can put that nightmare to rest! In the end, we were able to reinforce our center: We moved two divisions from our right and three from our left there. The center held! So strong was our reinforced third-line of defense that the *Blitzkrieg* was thrown completely back! It was just like a rock being hurled from a slingshot! No, the enemy would not succeed on that apocalyptic day! David, with the help from above, saved the day and we are now on the offensive for the first time!"

The audience was spellbound by Plato's story, about a twelve-year-old hero, and they came out of their mesmerization with a thunderous applause. Many began shouting, "We are on the offensive. Did you hear that, on the offensive!" Others cried out, "Can you believe it? We are pushing them for a change!" Plato waited a polite minute or two for the crowded stadium attendees to quiet down. Then, with a mist beginning to cloud his eyes and a tear of joy beginning to run down his cheek, he pointed to the young boy on the stage and to his left, saying in an affectionate tone, a kind, soft voice, yet heard by all as he spoke directly into the microphone, "David, would you please, please stand and be recognized!" This time the audience-now-turned-spectators were beside themselves with cheers, applause, and shouts of "Hurray for David!" "Hurray for our valiant youth!" "Hurray for our Boy Scouts and Girl Scouts!" They concluded with a simple prayer: "May the Great One always supply us with heroes"

Later on that evening, Plato and his wife Ruth invited their old friend Seneca out for a late dinner. As usual, Plato was sipping his black coffee, while Ruth and Seneca were each drinking a hot chocolate, with whipped cream, topped off with a large, luscious Maraschino cherry.

Ruth: *(to Plato)* I'm sure you must be tired, dear, going directly from your private airplane to our Frog Stadium. *(smiling)* Oh yes, judging from the many times your speech was interrupted with applause and shouts, your oration was a smashing success. I really appreciate your coming this great distance to speak to our Frog Defense League.

Seneca: Plato, I knew that when the Congress supported you for the position of Prime Minister—after our illustrious King Josue II had appointed you—you would perform fantastically! To be sure, you are *that* right person at *the* right time in our nation's history! You are providing us with the diplomatic leadership our county so desperately needs. We are all so very proud of you and what you are accomplishing!

Plato: What would I do without the two most important people in my life: you!

Ruth: *(to Plato)* Want more coffee?

Plato: That would be fine! I find our coffee more to my liking than that of the Toad's.

All: *(laughter)* Ha, ha, ha, ha!

Seneca: I know that you know much more than you conveyed to our community this evening, concerning the war: Are you at liberty to discuss security matters with a senator, the Chairperson of the Frog Defense League, in addition to your wife?

Plato: As a matter of fact, that was foremost on my mind. I was just waiting for you to beg the question *(big grin)*. Last night at the front, near Cemetery Ridge, I was—as I indicated in my speech—elated to see our troops hold that third-line of defense and then to see our troops quickly repel the invaders. This turnabout of events was facilitated through intelligence brought by David, of whom I spoke earlier. Spartacus, who was also on a reconnaissance mission, had included information in his satchel obtained by some of his best forward observers!

They also spotted the Crickets' Imperial Guard moving to the center of their lance formation, flanked by four battalions: on the left, the 39th and 41st and on the right, the 43rd and the 45th! At first, we had thought their Imperial Guard only consisted of a brigade of three regiments; nevertheless, did we find out differently. As the night progressed, their air support began dropping bombs out of the sky! We never suspected they had that kind of air force capability, that is, of being able to get their military air transports past our antiaircraft defense shields! Worse than that, we didn't even know they had a reserve airborne battalion! For some odd reason, the Crickets have a thing about odd numbers! Our intelligence is checking out this "odd" behavior, pardon the pun *(chuckling all around)*. That's why we've numbered the fourth Cricket battalion as their 45th.

Seneca: Who is their military commander in the field? Any info on that?

Plato: A very good question! Yes! His name is Five-Star General Jose Francisco! He kind of reminds me of our co-Chairman of the Joint Chiefs of Staff and Supreme Allied Commander, Admiral Cheetah Obian, insofar as his background is concerned. He is of Spanish stock, as opposed to the African heritage of our Admiral Cheetah. By the way, we refer to Admiral Obian by his first name: He prefers it that way: hence, Admiral Cheetah! Apparently, General Francisco's family was on vacation when their private airplane crash-landed over Cricket territory! Young Francisco, Intelligence relates, was captured, along with his family members, and brought up as a Cricket.

In their Spartan-like military academy, he excelled in various arts of war; a natural leader from the start, he fast gained the respect of his fellow cadets. Some, however, viewed him in his command position with suspicion because of his ethnicity. Most have long put those ideas to rest, based on his vast field experience with many, many conquests! His closest officers call him "El Matador!" In the Spanish language it literally means "The Killer!" As the Five-Star General, the only persons Francisco reports to are The Cricket Vampires: Admiral Cornwalter, the Blue Vampire and Admiral Reynaldo, the Red Vampire! Interesting no?

Ruth: Those names sound menacing!

Seneca: Yes! So are you saying, Plato, that all it took was having the right intelligence to defeat General Francisco, "El Matador"?

Plato: Yes and No! To begin with, while we are now pressing the attack, it doesn't necessarily mean we have defeated "El Matador" and their other outstanding field marshals. We are, of course, very optimistic about the prospects of an early victory on land. That remains to be seen, as they say. I, personally, feel that our top Frog, Toad, and UN Field Commanders, along with Toad Intelligence, Generals Schwartzwait and Lopez, assisting our intelligence staff—all under the command of Admiral Cheetah—will succeed! Army Chief of Staff, General Stanislaus R. Polaski, our newest Four-Star, is the best man at this critical juncture to lead our wonderful commanders. Yes, we will prevail in the end!

Just after the speech, I received a coded teletext message on my private line *(indicating his interactive televideo wristwatch)*. Admiral Cheetah informed me that the winds were favoring the Toads' smaller ships against the Cricket monster ships. The Cricket larger ships could not turn around fast enough to engage the Toad and Frog navies. The Cricket submarines, moreover, were not equipped with the latest sonar and other electronic devices that, in navy parlance, help subs "run quiet and run deep." Consequently, our ship's depth charges were finding their marks, knocking the Cricket subs clear out of the water. Admiral Cheetah signed off saying, "so far, the hunting is so good!"

Seneca and Ruth: *(together)* Wow! HOLY COW!

Seneca: I have always said that while we have the strongest, best-equipped air force, the Toads have wisely put their muscle into their fabulous fleet! *The Eagle*. Any news on that beauty?

Plato: Yes! I was just getting to that. *(putting on a western drawl)* Sorta savin' the best for the last, partner, at least for now. (now, in a more serious tone) Admiral Roberto Da Vinci, that incredible Toad sea-dog, is piloting *The Eagle*: the world's best carrier! It will match anything out there today. Besides being able to carry a full complement of modern aircraft, it can double as a battleship with its rocket capabilities. Granted, it still needs to be protected on all sides; still, it can be a formidable opponent, just based on its all-range missile launch capabilities. They say the Toad missiles can traverse any large body of water!

Ruth: *(listening to all that has been said)* Besides the favorable winds at our backs, we Frogs have the world's best aviators, don't we, Plato?

Plato: I can't argue with that. From what I have gathered over the last few weeks, there is a contest to see who will end up with the most downed aircraft. The Toads, however, have a terrific aviator known as the *Ghost* with 47 kills! Our *Emerald Midnight Horne*t was ahead for the longest time, until she had to dive into the water and was pulled out of the sea by one of our *PT 109 -9* Amphibious Assault Saucers: specially designed for sea, land, and air operations. I believe, by the way, she has 45 kills to date!

Ruth: This is a little too much to take in all at once! First, are you saying the Emerald Midnight Hornet is one of our women air force officers? Secondly, we have, you say, a machine that can perform in all kinds of environments: sea, land, and air?

Seneca: *(piping in)* Yes to both, if I may answer for the Prime Minister, since I sit on the Armed Forces Security Council. We have had this advanced aviation technology for some time now! While the Prime Minister has been away, shuttling back and forth between our two kingdoms *(referring to that of the Frogs and Toads),* our committee has been kept up-to-date with most of the goings-on, regarding supplying our troops.

We get performance status sheets that tell us what the various armed forces are being supplied. From these balance sheets we can deduce if we are losing ships— every kind imaginable—aircraft, land mobile equipment, such as, tanks, jeeps, and so forth. There are times, however, when we ask to see the armed forces' top brass without much success! I hate to say it, but oftentimes they just put us off! We are told, instead, that certain information is classified, because combat conditions require complete secrecy to prevent a leak that may aid the enemy! So, we have to settle for the next best thing: a mid-grade officer, one who is usually noncommittal in his or her reports to our committee! We understand, but we don't have to like it!

Plato: I am sorry for that, Seneca, but as you succinctly just stated, with the tightness of security being what it is, we have to support our military intelligence community. You are also correct: We can't allow any privileged information getting into enemy hands! There are spies everywhere! Why just the other day, three college students were picked up for hacking onto our mainframe Pentagon computers. It turns out that these same students were selling the info, for extra cash, to an unknown source!

Abruptly, a courier came into the restaurant and went right over to the table where Plato, Ruth, and Seneca were seated. "Sir," he presented his credentials and asked permission to speak. "Excuse me Sir, but I have an urgent message for you from HQ. HQ hasn't been able to reach you through their regular means, due to a power outage created by the enemy. (The courier waits a minute or so). Do you have a reply, sir?" Plato having carefully studied the letter replies, "Yes, yes I do!" (He takes out a piece of paper from his notebook that was tucked in a concealed compartment of his suit. He signs it and then deposits it into the pocket of the military courier's small leather pouch).

Ruth: What was that all about?

Seneca: Do you have to leave?

Plato: No, I don't have to leave just yet, but we'd better call it an evening. I'll have to leave before dawn. I've been asked by King Josue II to have breakfast with him, and then he wants to share some ideas he has, concerning the ground war; moreover, he also wants me there as messages begin to arrive, regarding the war at sea and our effort to regain air supremacy! Lately, our tenacious fighting has resulted with more success!

Plato reads the expression on Ruth's face, and with a sweet smile that only a loving husband can give a wife for reassurance, he says, "Everything is going to be just fine! We've taken on the world's best army and have them running for cover; we have their navy encircled, thanks to heavenly winds! Finally, we've got the most skilled aviators doing a bang-up job in the skies, protecting our shores! We're going to see this thing through with the help of Him Who watches over us all."

With that, they departed the quiet cafe. A white limousine was there, waiting to take them home. The three of them cut quite a figure, having been dressed in evening wear. Ruth was in a long dark skirt with a shimmering royal blue satin blouse; in addition, she wore a diamond necklace that reflected the class she represented; Plato and Seneca were both attired in tuxedos. As the chauffeur held the back door open for them, some passersby waved and greeted them with well wishes.

The telephone rang and Ruth reached over to answer it; she noticed it was 4:09 a.m.! "Who could be calling at this hour of the morning?" she thought to herself: "My husband needs rest." After saying a cautious "Hello," she heard an officer's voice on the other end inquiring, "Is this Ruth"? She answered, "Yes!" The voice revealed his identity, "This is Jonesy...Brigadier General Jones speaking." "Oh, Jonesy, what is it?" "The King has had an accident in the shower and wants Plato over an hour earlier to discuss the most recent battlefield developments. Since his leg is being attended to, he feels it necessary to get an early start in order to make up for any time that might be lost." Ruth replied, "I'll wake him up right now." The General responded, "No, Ruth, let him sleep another half -hour or so. He's been very busy and he'll certainly be busy today. As usual, thanks for your understanding, Ruth."

Ruth brought Plato his favorite dark coffee, almost black. Thus, he awoke to coffee and toast with marmalade. She joined him with tea, a little milk and sugar, and toast with strawberry preserves. After some small talk and breakfast, the Prime Minister was ready to greet the day. The military attaché knocked on the door, indicating he was ready, whenever Plato wished to depart. After a gentle kiss for his wife, Plato was on his way to the King's Summer Palace.

Once inside the King's Palace, the Prime Minister was ushered into one of the Royal Dining Rooms, where Josue II was busy with his breakfast, one of his favorites: a cheese omelet with every vegetable known to man, thrown in for good measure.

Josue II: There he is, Plato. Come have a seat and help yourself!

Just as was the case with King Gideon III, of the Toads, Josue knew he must eat something or risk offending his King!

Plato: Thank you, your Highness, I'll try some of your black coffee with toast and marmalade.

Josue II: *(with his brows wrinkled up)* That's not all you're having, is it?

Plato: I'll also have a few hard-boiled eggs without any salt.

Josue II: No salt!

Plato: No, no salt! I find I'm healthier the less salt I consume.

Josue II: Is that a fact? I'll have to speak to my Royal Physician. Umm, no salt!

Josue: *(to his page)* Call my physician.

Page: Do you mean the one that just attended to your leg?

Josue: Oh, that one, well no! Tell you what… forget it! We'll catch him later. He's been busy with my leg and I appreciate that. Let him get some rest. He's very conscientious. But remind me to ask him about this salt business! Got it?

Page: Yes, your Highness.

Josue II: Well, that's that. Let's eat. We've got a big day ahead of us!

Plato: May we speak about the war, your Highness?

Josue II: I guess you noticed I'm in a good mood, with all the good news!

Plato: I do. *(assuming the King wants to learn more, and becoming exuberant)* If our land, sea, and air forces can continue to out-strategize the Crickets, I believe we can send them back from whence they came, in spite of still being outnumbered!

Josue II: Oh, you mean to Hades! Now wouldn't that be nice. You know, I was thinking along the same lines.

The King and Josue had a pleasurable meal, considering the pressures of state. They were almost done with their breakfast, when the King's Brigadier General Jones was permitted into the dining room.

Brigadier General Jones: Your Highness, Prime Minister Plato, Good morning! *(They acknowledge with a good morning)*. There have been some interesting developments that have occurred late last night and into the early morning. If you wish, we can view the details on our large interactive TV monitors in the communications room.

Josue II: By all means. Page! Where is that page?

The General: That's OK, your Highness. I'll push you along in your wheelchair, if you don't mind?

Josue II: OK, let's get this contraption moving and on to the monitors!

General Jones was careful not to hit any of the potted plants, as he pushed the wheelchair with its special occupant: the King! They passed several corridors, to where armed soldiers were standing at attention. Then, they went towards double doors, just across the great Hall of Frog Heroes, to arrive where two tall MPs also stood at attention; the MPs quickly opened wide the doors. The King, once admitted, along with his escorts, his Prime Minister and his General, began to finally relax. As the three entered they noticed other "top brass," mostly communications officers, already involved with their computers and special communications equipment. Every effort was being made to make certain the transmitting and receiving of signals operated without a hitch! Several TV monitors revealed the battle scenes taking place or about to take place. These pictures were possible because of high-flying reconnaissance aircraft.

The Red Monitor, one of many monitors designated by color, revealed the carrier *HTMS Eagle (*His Toad Majesty's Ship *Eagle*). The Toad carrier was an immense ship, perhaps larger than anything the Cricket Armada had yet created! The *Eagle* moved through the water with ease, powered by advanced nuclear energy that had long since replaced the ancient "gas turbine engines." Yesteryear's engines used gas in their first carrier-class models of the twentieth century for technological and economical concerns. There had been, moreover, a strategic concern about the continued use of gas turbine engines during that period. Ultimately, the use of nuclear power provided a new energy source designed to eliminate oil-dependency (a cost factor). Costs were also significantly reduced, compared to the ever-rising costs incurred because of the ever-fluctuating oil prices: All controlled by the oil cartels!

There had always existed the possibility of "hostile oil-producing nations controlling or frustrating carrier propulsion!" In retrospect, however, the use of oil in the past had been absolutely deemed necessary! The Toads, fortunately, had been at peace with the oil-producing countries for some time now. During this period, the peace reassured them that obtaining future oil would not be a problem. From a safety point of view, however, according to Toad and Frog physicists and engineers, nuclear energy created another great advantage!

It made the new carrier class less vulnerable, than would be the case if attacked while using gas turbine engines. The reasons were: greater carrier speed and distance could be achieved with nuclear energy! Thus, the new energy-enhanced design enabled the *Eagle* to carry seventy-five airplanes; moreover, these aircraft were also modified to use a hybrid of nuclear-powered fuel for their engines! These advances were a far cry from the early carriers that could accommodate no more than fifty-five aircraft. In addition, oftentimes the aircraft they carried were obsolete! Incredibly, the seventy-five nuclear aircraft now aboard the *Eagle* were capable of delivering 100% more strike sorties for only 8% more cost! In brief, the *Eagle* and her aircraft, because of their speed and long distance capabilities, matched or surpassed anything at sea, at a cost savings!

The Green Monitor presented a better view of *The Eagle* launching its nuclear missiles, while at the same time accommodating the comings and goings of airplanes: mostly *Spitfighters* and *Mushroom Jets.* These launches were coordinated, such that none of the airplanes were permitted within the missiles' paths. Simultaneously, **the Blue Monitor** revealed *The Stingray* taking a hit from the *HTMS Heroic*! *The Heroic* also belonged to the new Toad carrier class ships. The Cricket ship was on fire as viewed from aboard the *Heroic,* through the high-powered field glasses of Admiral Da Vinci. While *The Stingray* was not sinking, it was, nevertheless, in trouble! The Cricket carriers, *The Stingray* and *The Scorpion,* could not be lost! As enemy aircraft carriers, they provided the bulk of the Cricket aircraft power.

Several battleships and heavy cruisers moved into a semicircular line of defense to thwart any Frog and Toad ships from entering in for the kill. The Cricket Castilian defense, or horseshoe defense, was working, but for the wrong reason. They had hoped to draw in the Allied Forces and then hit the lighter ships of the Toads and Frogs with all they had. Instead, the Crickets had to move in sooner to protect the *Stingray* from further Allied gunfire. The missiles coming from the HTMS *Heroic* had taken the Cricket Commanders by surprise. They did not think that Aircraft Carriers had the capacity to also launch missiles! The enemy must have been thinking: what was the world coming to with carriers acting more like battleships than as cruisers! Of course, the Frog King was overjoyed at what he was seeing on **the Blue Monitor**! Josue II indicated to Plato and to his generals that the Toad carrier *Heroic* was doing a remarkable job! Another of the King's generals remarked that the Frog Spitfighters, piloted by both Frog and Toad aviators, were carrying the day!

These Emperor Penguin Spitfighters outmatched anything the Crickets could produce, in the way of fighters. Oddly enough, the Frogs had held back their amazing Mushroom jet! The Spitfighters led by the Frog's flying ace, the Emerald Midnight Hornet, who also went by the name "*Midnight*" for short, and the Toad's flying ace, *The Ghost*, were now tied for most kills: seventy each! The battle for air supremacy was beginning to worry Admirals Cornwalter and Reynaldo. If these losses kept up, they declared, we will have to retreat and regroup to fight another day. In the meantime, the Crickets were getting some good news from their submarine commanders.

The Cricket submarines, while not all equipped with the latest nuclear-powered engines and advanced sonar detection devices, were, nonetheless, excellent in every other capacity of running silent and deep. The Frogs, moreover, did not have the class carriers of the Toads; still, they did have an excellent submarine class of ships. The command, Frog submarine captains or higher, however, was of some concern to Admiral Cheetah. He had discussed their deficiencies with Admiral Da Vinci. He had pointed out to Da Vinci, in private talks, that his Frog navy personnel were, for the most part, without battle hard experience on the high seas! Also, the newer nuclear class submarines had sophisticated equipment that required a great deal of expertise to utilize. All of these factors were in sharp contrast to the rest of their fleet, which was old vintage navy from at least fifty years past!

The Frogs had taken out several of their larger battleships and Cruisers from their mothball status. While much slower, these ships could still provide a valuable service as decoys against the Cricket Armada. Their imposing size made them appear more menacing, than they actually were against a modern nuclear fleet. Thus, from these vantage points, the Crickets would have the decided edge over the Frogs, with their more experienced captains and larger navy. The Cricket sea pilots, despite piloting ships that for the most part still maintained older engines, had some that were outfitted with modern nuclear technology; furthermore, they knew naval tactics and strategy that had defeated the best of navies.

The Crickets' two main concerns, having obtained information from spies, were the Toad navy and the Frog nuclear submarines. True, the Toad navy had a modern nuclear fleet including the best class of nuclear carriers in that part of the world. The Toads, however, still retained mostly outdated diesel-type-powered submarines; thus, they would be vulnerable to enemy submarines equipped with any kind of nuclear power! The Alliance reasoned that if they were to succeed against the fierce Crickets' subs—under the sea—they would have to rely on their allies, the Frogs. With their super-class nuclear submarines, the Frogs' undersea flotilla, if commandeered properly, ought to defeat the Crickets. It was a belief that would have to be borne out!

The next question, then, was not entirely one of technology; rather, it had to do with seamanship as well: Who had the best captains? Who had the best strategy? The Crickets believed they had the more experienced captains. They maintained, that even though their submarines still utilized a combination of semi-nuclear-powered turbines coupled with steam turbines, it did not make their navy inadequate or less potent! They understood they possessed an abundance of ships that gave them a two-to-one margin at sea! This numerical advantage could be implemented in their ship-to-ship sea tactics. More players in the field afforded them the opportunity to employ a more sophisticated strategy. Yes, they would win the war at sea, against the Toads and their Frog cousins, based on experience and sheer numbers! Sooner than later, they would claim these lowlands with all their adjacent rivers and seas. These newly acquiesced territories would fit so nicely into their perceived paradigm of world domination. The mighty Cricket Empire had only one axiom: "We know no boundaries except conquest!"

The leadership of the combined Toad and Frog navies understood: They still would be, drastically, outnumbered by the enemy, even with the addition of their allies' ships! The Frog and Toad leaders, thus, devised naval strategies that were ingenious in their simplicity! The Frogs would pursue the injured Cricket Carrier *Stingray* with their own outdated ships! Their friends the Toads, in the meantime, would protect their own *HTMS Heroic and HTMS Eagle* by moving their carriers farther south, thus avoiding close-range action. Their objective was to pin down the Cricket Navy with decoys within the tight confines of the Jordan. The decoys: Frog vintage battleships, heavy and light cruisers, and destroyers would put up the best attack possible and then retreat, before the Crickets could pulverize them out of existence! Frog submarines would be present just below the water's surface to pick up survivors. The Frog and Toad navies wanted to give the Crickets the impression, that while their own *Stingray* had taken a hit, they were, nonetheless, winning the battle at sea.

The second phase of the encounter would cause the Crickets to push farther south to destroy more of the older Frog military vessels. The forces of good, on the other hand, hoped to encounter and then defeat their adversaries in the Dead Sea. The enemy, thus emboldened, glided easily into the trap! The trapdoor appeared closed, or was it? Throughout the battle that seemed to go according to plan, the Frog King was transfixed by what he saw playing itself out on **the Blue Monitor**.

Josue II: What, for crying out loud, is happening? We've hit one of their main carriers and we're sending in our mothball navy to finish the job? I don't think so! Our old fuddy-duddies are no match for their ships!

General Jones: Your Highness *(attempting to assuage his feelings)*, I'm sure they are following orders that will result in losing the battle and winning the war.

Josue II: Oh really! Where are my other admirals? Let's see what they have to say about this foolishness!

Rear Admiral Pointdextras: I'm here, Your Highness. Please let me assure you that we have very able leadership in both our navies. Admiral Cheetah and Admiral Da Vinci are inviting the Cricket Admiralty to pursue them into the Dead Sea.

Josue II: We'll see about that! Put Gideon on the phone.

General: Yes, Highness!

Josue II: *(taking the telephone with an open microphone and demanding to speak with the Toad King)* This here is Josue II; put Gideon III on the phone. *(After a pause)* Now would be a good time!

Toad naval staff officer: Yes, Your Highness, we are attempting to reach him. I believe he is indisposed at the present.

Josue II: Oh, you mean he's in the bathroom. Well, take the phone to him now! I need to speak with him!

Fortunately, Gideon III had returned from using the restroom, and his officer was spared any indignity. The Kings shared their take on what was occurring on the Jordan that both united and separated them. Gideon assured Josue that Da Vinci was one of the best strategists that his country had produced. If he had been a general, as opposed to an admiral, his talents would not have been diminished in ground warfare: He was the best! He knew what he was doing. Josue reflected on Gideon's lauding of Da Vinci and thought that he might have offended Gideon by doubting the other King's leader, who, by the way, was directing the naval engagement with the complete knowledge of his own Admiral Cheetah. They spoke some more and Josue was certain to make clear that in no way did he mean to disparage Admiral Da Vinci; on the contrary, he, too, had great confidence in Gideon's quintessential admiral. He stated that he was surprised that the Toad navy didn't go in for the kill against the *Stingray*. Somewhere along the line, apparently, his own staff officers had neglected to tell him that their retired ships had been brought out of mothball status to act as decoys against the Cricket Navy: Now all was clear and all was forgiven.

Before saying goodbye, Gideon III, not to be outdone, stated that from all the reports he was receiving from the front lines on Frog territory, he was greatly impressed with how the Frog UN commander, Four-Star General Polaski, was repelling and pushing back the Cricket invaders. The Crickets, he was further informed by his intelligence officer General Lopez, were now retreating and being pushed back to the cliffs they had climbed earlier. He wished Josue II the best of victories and once more reminded him that the Toads, with the very able assistance of the Frogs, would defeat the Cricket scoundrels at sea! With that, Josue declared he quite agreed! He thanked Gideon for the excellent support his troops were giving the Frog ground forces. "They have already distinguished themselves in battle, and we will have a ceremony honoring your divisions and the bravery exemplified by your best fighters."

Gideon continued, "Not to have the last word, Josue—thank you! I hope to attend that ceremony and invite you to a similar one on our side of the River, yes! But, I just feel this war has been a great strain on our joint military and the good citizens of Toadland and Frogland, alike." "That is so true" replied Josue. "Nevertheless, our communities are strong, resolute, and determined. They are helping in a thousand-and-one ways." "Yes they are!" Gideon reaffirmed. With that, they each said goodbye to the other quietly and, subsequently, gently returned their respective receivers to their cradles and moved their attention to equally important matters: eating lunch. Gideon called out for an early lunch and shouted, "I'm hungry as a bear—where's my chef?" Josue, too, announced, "Let's break for lunch; I never knew fighting a war could make a body hungrier than a polecat up a tree, who hasn't eaten in three days!"

The fighting at sea went on all afternoon. About twenty ships belonging to the Frogs had been knocked out of the water, more than the Frogs had anticipated in their assault plans. They were sinking and the brave Frogs were seeking help as they floated on the sea's surface. The Frogs and Toads used helicopters, *PT 109-9* Amphibious Assault craft, submarines, and destroyers to pick up as many navy survivors as possible. Time was of the essence! The Crickets were sending their aviators to decimate those sailors still floating in the water: an act unbecoming to naval belligerents, according to the Genevieve Conference and Rules of War. By 17:00 hours, however, the rescuers were able to get out of harm's way and regroup in such a way as to give the impression of a full-scale retreat. Fortunately, more than 95 percent of the troops were rescued.

The *Stingray* was safe, for the time being. The Crickets were working to repair the engine room and to quickly return her to action. The damage was less serious than the fire and smoke suggested. Cornwalter and Reynaldo viewed the day's events with much delight! What had started as a defeat, with the *Stingray* taking a hit, had turned out as a rout against their adversaries: the Frogs. The Blue and the Red Cricket leaders could not believe that the Frogs were so ill prepared to fight an open sea war. They jumped up and down and toasted each other at their officers' dining quarters, with their top brass joining in, exuding smiles and laughter at their strategy's success. Cornwalter rose to speak, and all the senior officers became immediately quiet.

Co-Supreme Commander Admiral Cornwalter: Gentlemen, we are winning this naval engagement and we are going to win this war!

Officers: *(cheering and shouting)* "Here, here, yes, fantastic, we're busting their ships apart!"

Cornwalter: If this keeps up, we'll be able to finish the job in the next few weeks and focus our complete energies at retaking the Frog beaches with our marines. Our aviators have taken heavy losses, especially to their super flying aces: The Emerald Midnight Hornet and the Ghost. Well let me tell you, before this is all over, we're going to make that Ghost into a real ghost, and we're going to eat that "Hornet" at a "Midnight" dinner! Ha, ha, ha, ha! *(all entering into the laughter and raising their glasses to commemorate Cornwalter's words of encouragement and resolve).*

Cornwalter: *(turning to Reynaldo)* What say you, Admiral.

Co-Supreme Commander Admiral Reynaldo: I must say that I am pleasantly surprised and extremely elated! I have felt all along that the Frogs had the weaker of the two navies: Frog and Toad. Still, I can't help but think that we haven't faced their best. They did, after all, manage to take us by surprise and hit one of our principal carriers. Luckily, the *Stingray* should be ready for service by tomorrow. In the meantime we have the alternate *Flagship SS Admiralty*, in which we currently find ourselves, and our old faithful *Scorpion*, to lead us!

Officer Levcoff: If I may be given leave to speak, sir.

Reynaldo: *(politely)* By all means, Commodore Levcoff!

Officer Levcoff: Highest Admirals, our beloved carrier *Stingray, as* you are definitely aware, was hit by their *HTMS Heroic*. Does this mean that we are basically fighting one navy: the Toad Navy?

Reynaldo: Yes and no! To be sure, the Toads have superior nuclear carriers. From what we've seen, these carriers can also launch nuclear missiles. That is something we can remedy, if we can get our submarines to take them out. Our submarine captains are the best in the business of underwater warfare. We don't believe the Toads have nuclear subs; still, their navy managed to rescue many of the Frog sailors from the Jordan today. What puzzles us is that the subs that were spotted today were not Toad subs at all! They were much larger than anything that has been reported in these waters.

They were located by our air reconnaissance from a distance and revealed no Toad markings. The subs in question were moving away from the battle scene. Since we are relatively assured, by Intelligence, that the Frogs have never had submarines, much less the newer class nuclear subs, it seems highly unlikely that they belong to them. We feel, therefore, that they were simply UN observers trying to get out of the line of fire. We must not under any circumstances, however, assume that these subs are not hostile. The UN has been fighting us on land and could do the same at sea.

When all is said and done, we will continue to pursue each and every single one of them until they are all destroyed! With our own nuclear submarines, larger body of ships, and superior seamanship, we will be triumphant! We'll jump on them like jackals do their prey, until their carcasses have nothing left but skeletons!

The officers all stand to give the two co-Supreme Commanders cheers and shouts of support. Suddenly, they start to sing their empire's national hymn that identifies Cricket past victories and conquests: "Crickets, Crickets, Crickets Over All!"

The two co-Supreme Admirals enjoyed the apparent victories the day had brought them, and, after the celebration, discussed whether or not to press the advantage. Cornwalter declared they had no time to waste, and they should advance full steam ahead, until they caught up with the Frog and Toad Fleets. By now, it was dark and Reynaldo had some misgivings. He felt that even with a coordinated attack on the enemy's fleets, Frogs and Toads, respectively, they still could find themselves in a whole lot of trouble! "Three things come to mind," he indicated to his associate: "First, with the number of vessels we have out there, how can we be sure we are not firing on our own ships; do we break radio silence in close quarters? Surely they have broken our code by now. Secondly, what if we run aground? The Jordan is very shallow in some places! Third, what if the ships we demolished today were just a ruse to get us to follow them deeper into unknown waters?" Cornwalter listened attentively to all that his partner was saying. "I see your point. Let me counter your arguments one by one; playing the devil's advocate, as we vampires say, ha! ha! ha!

"To begin with, we can order our slower ships to pull back, thus reducing the number of vessels we have in pursuit of the enemy's armada. We can devise a strategy of containment, wherein we don't fire on them until we have them surrounded. They no doubt are leading us into the Dead Sea: well that's just fine! We'll fight them there. By the time we've got them trapped, the rest of our larger ships can come in for the kill. Since they move more slowly, we will have to coordinate schedules: time! As to their deciphering our encrypted messages? They haven't! If they had, they wouldn't have made such fools of themselves today.

"The Cricket Code given to us by our forefathers has never been broken. There is no language on the earth remotely similar to ours! Our code, you will recall, is taken from the earliest lexical features of the language spoken, that is, when our ancestors lived beneath the earth's surface: In the underworld. No, no one will ever be able to crack our code! Only senior communication officers are allowed to use it: three aboard each ship. But why am I telling you what you already know? To your second point: Yes, the Jordan is shallow in some areas; nevertheless, if they can make it through these waters with their equally large ships, so can we. Furthermore, they have been careless in their retreat, leaving few if any mines. Even so, we have mine sweepers to clear the area, along with tugs that can release us from soil entrapment. Not a problem! Finally, as to your last query, if they are leading us into the Dead Sea to surprise us, it will be their undoing! Once they lead us there, they have no exit! It's doomsday for them."

Reynaldo: I've listened to your rebuttal and have brought many of your same answers to the fore of my mind, considering each possibility: I am not entirely convinced! I understand that war involves taking calculated risks, and "he who hesitates is lost!" Yet, what prevents the Toads and Frogs from bringing in a reserve fleet behind us? As we pursue them downstream, one or more of their fleets could be closing in behind us! We'll be the ones who are pursued, entrapped!

Cornwalter: *(exasperated with the Red Vampire)* There's one way to resolve our impasse. We'll flip a coin!

Reynaldo: What?

Cornwalter: Flip a coin. You got a better idea? Because, I'm determined to go after them by myself, if you are too cautious and prefer to remain behind to fight another day! By then, we will have missed our golden opportunity to annihilate them! If I lose the toss, I will know that the Spirit of our ancestors has willed it otherwise.

With that, they brought in two of their most trusted high-ranking officers. The officers knew from past experiences that the coin-flipping ceremony was a religious act that past Cricket emperors had used to resolve differences between two leaders. A red cloth was draped over the mahogany table that stretched some thirty feet. The coin once flipped had to land on one portion of the tablecloth. Three separate coins would be tossed: two of silver and of one gold. To begin the contest, one silver coin would be held behind the back of Officer One and then with a clenched fist he would present it to Reynaldo. Officer Two would then do the same and with clenched fist present Cornwalter with the second silver coin, one side up. The two silver coins had the images of each of the two leaders on either side. If both sides up of the silver coins were of Reynaldo, then he would have the privilege of flipping the golden coin first; conversely, if Cornwalter won as a result of two coins showing his image, then he would be honored with the first flip of the golden coin.

This first phase of the contest would continue, until a silver winner was declared, in order to begin the actual contest for the gold. Each of the admirals would go to opposite sides of the thirty-foot table to begin the golden coin toss. The best three out of five tosses would result in a winner! The loser would have to support the winner in his choice of battle action: to move now or to wait until daybreak. From Cornwalter's perspective, eight hours would provide the enemy time to escape into deeper waters; whereas, from Reynaldo's perspective those same eight hours of delay might also provide the Crickets with better daylight to reencounter the enemy; only this time, the *Stingray* would be ready for action! Thus, Admiral Cornwalter was for moving now; conversely, Admiral Reynaldo was for waiting until daybreak! Both actions, waiting being one of them, afforded benefits, and both also presented obstacles in revising battle schemes: night fighting! Who would win the toss?

The hour was getting late. Reynaldo had won the beginning phase, thus granting him the right to toss the golden coin first. This right had occurred after the fourth presentation of open palms by both officers showing his image: All the other tosses were mismatched, or showing the image of each leader. The second phase would begin with Reynaldo flipping the golden coin, hoping his image would reappear. If the golden coin reflected the image of Cornwalter, then he would be declared the winner of that toss. Things were beginning to get tense between the two Vampires. As it turned out, Cornwalter won the first two, followed by two wins from Reynaldo. The coin flipping had moved the coin back and forth between the Red and Blue Vampires four times. Now it was up to Reynaldo to flip the golden coin across the 30-foot table to his competitor: Cornwalter. The coin hit the red cloth, but after a high bounce, it spun several times and then slowly went off the table! It was, therefore, ruled a foul!

The turn passed to Cornwalter. He, at last, had the chance to flip the golden coin from his side of the mahogany space. His eyes glistened and his smirky smile betrayed his evil nature. He looked directly at Reynaldo, as his fingers pressed the coin tightly, until it jumped out of his clenched fist, as if it wanted to escape! The coin seemed to pick up all of the light and color in the room, as its golden form moved through time and space, nearly touching the high ceiling, seeming to hang there, until it slowly descended, almost motionless, and came to bounce with a resounding ping, and rest on the bright red cloth. Cornwalter's image on the coin looked back at him. He had won the contest! Reynaldo, in the spirit of his noble ancestors, walked across the lengthy blue runner and, with his right arm extended, congratulated his adversary, who was also his co-Supreme Commander: Admiral Cornwalter, the Blue Vampire!

Cornwalter stated that their ancestors had spoken and had approved of the wisdom in his plan of action! Reynaldo was left wondering why his ancestors had not sided with him. It seemed folly to move at night without their carrier *Stingray*. The night would help the smaller combined fleet of the Toads and Frogs: He just could not understand it! He became depressed for the moment; nevertheless, as a true Cricket, he would commit all of his intelligence, talent, and energies to the cause of conquest! Surely, that's what his ancestors would want, or was it? He would learn the answers to his queries as the war progressed.

The public address system on the *SS Admiralty* carrier was heard stating that their ships were now in combat readiness to deal a fatal blow to the enemy's ships! Cornwalter's voice, over the loudspeaker, mentioned the accomplishments of the day and stated that tonight would bring their greatest victory: the total destruction of the Toad Fleet! Now, with the Frog fleet depleted of their outdated ships, the task would be easier. "Those older, pesky Frog ships were such a nuisance!" he blurted out in what was more of an enraged growl, that later turned into a sardonic grin, than his usual self-congratulatory declarations!

Cornwalter continued, "When we knock out the *Heroic* and the *Eagle*, then the rest of their armada will flee for cover: But they can't hide. We'll scuttle every last one of them!" The Cricket sailors had expected to hear some words from Reynaldo, yet he was conspicuously silent. The men reasoned that he was probably ill. In any case, the co-Supreme Commander Admiral Cornwalter had spoken and, for some, that was final! Cornwalter and Reynaldo may have had their differences; however, they were careful not to show that side of themselves to their subordinates. Theirs was to command and the rest was to follow no matter what, or else swift punishment would follow!

Cricket sailors who disobeyed an order would be summarily brought before a military tribunal, then the appropriate punishment would be assigned and carried out! As a consequence of the military training these sailors had received from early childhood to adulthood—in their respective military schools—few incidents of disobedience occurred. The Vampires ran a tight ship, as they say. Even though the sailors were tired, they knew what was expected of them; they would deliver. Indeed, their whole civilization depended on superb performance! They had arranged marriages with government benefits and these entitlements had to be earned. Only servicemen and servicewomen who had proven himself or herself in battle could participate in the spoils of war: So, here they all were, ready to do Cornwalter's bidding; they would be at their best tonight; yes, they would destroy and board the enemy's ships: take what they pleased as booty!

The pursuit was underway at long last, Cornwalter said to himself! According to their sonar, they were beginning to close the gap between the *Heroic* and themselves. The *Eagle* had not yet been spotted and that caused them some concern. The moon was still hiding under the clouds; however, enough moonlight escaped causing the men onboard to see distant silhouettes of the Toad Armada. Reynaldo advised Cornwalter, who was now serving as the prime commander in charge of the midnight attack, to withhold the ships and bring in their submarine fleet for search-and-destroy operations. The reconnaissance was important: the fear being that one of their own ships may have inadvertently gotten ahead of their own fleet, in the race to see who would be first to strike the Toads.

The Crickets had three outstanding submarines that lead the twelve attack subs in kills: The *Barracuda*, the *Eel Electric*, and the *Piranha*. There was some dispute, however, because the *Sharkfin* claimed it had now overtaken the *Piranha* in kills. In order to certify a kill, an officer of the *SS Admiralty* was selected and placed aboard the sub, in advance, to verify accounts of destroyed enemy ships! For example, the *Sharkfin* had surprised an enemy ship in the Caspian Sea: The enemy ship, it turns out, had been placing mines to keep the Crickets' subs out of their waters. The enemy ship, nevertheless, was passed over; no anticipated kills were recorded—the reason being that the Crickets had not yet determined whether or not they were capable of fighting a two-ocean war! It was then, therefore, they voted for a preference of winning by using the old maxim: "divide-and-conquer!" "Let's gain territories in the south, and then we will turn northward." Needless to say, each of the submarines would contest any downed ships that were not certified kills.

Thus, the carriers, the battleships, the heavy and light cruisers, and lighter craft would remain put until they got word from their attack subs, especially the *Barracuda*. Having achieved the most kills, it earned the right to spearhead the midnight assault! As the Cricket submarine flotilla approached the Frog ships, they noticed that while many of their enemy's ships had sunk, others were still smoldering from Cricket attacks earlier that day. Oddly enough, no survivors were evident! Or, was it possible that most of the survivors had been rescued? Noting the aforementioned, the Cricket submarines approached cautiously, being mindful of the possibility of mines in the area: Danger!

There was no need for them to break radio silence, since they had already been given the directive to fire at will at any of the enemy combatants. The *Barracuda*, first to arrive, sent torpedoes towards several of the Frog ships that were still afloat, until the outdated Frog ships were annihilated beyond recognition! Some of the Frog ships, that met their second fate, were light cruisers, destroyers, and lighter craft. No battleships or heavy cruisers were seen that could be targeted. "Why?" the Cricket submarine commanders asked themselves. The subs came to the surface to take a better look at the devastation they had created. The *Barracuda* noticed, after surfacing, that some 30 or more Frog ships were in the process of sinking and disappearing from the water's upper edge. That indicated to the *Barracuda* Captain Feroz that the *Eel Electric*, the *Piranha*, and the *Sharkfin* must also be nearby! Apparently, these subs had been responsible for this additional destruction, culminating in many, more kills! Captain Feroz, after hesitating, decided to break radio silence and speak directly with Admiral Cornwalter of the *SS Admiralty*.

Admiral Cornwalter: Yes, Captain Feroz.

Captain Feroz: Sir, we have accomplished our mission, as far as clearing the Jordan of all enemy craft at its center. I find it unbelievable, though, that the rest of their armada has slipped away under the cover of darkness: vanished! Most of the ships appear to be the same ships we hit earlier today: old or vintage Frog navy ships!

Cornwalter: I was afraid of that. Don't upset yourself. Thank goodness that we did not delay further. If we press on, we should catch up with them within the next two hours. We will follow your escort down stream. Our destroyers and cruisers will fill in the space between us, with our battleships nearby ready to pounce on the enemy, once we catch up with them! Full steam ahead, Captain, and good hunting!

Captain Feroz : Aye, aye, Sir!

The *Barracuda* Captain felt privileged to be one of only four ships that were nuclear-powered: the other three included the most decorated subs: the *Eel Electric*, the *Piranha*, and the *Sharkfin*. These nuclear subs were well suited for long-range patrols, unlike the conventional subs of early wars. With the nuclear-powered steam turbines, the *Barracuda* and the other three subs increased their endurance and vastly increased their tactical and strategic capabilities, much like the nuclear subs across the Atlantic. Another major advantage was they were not required to surface for long periods of time, to recharge batteries or obtain additional oxygen! The reason was that scrubbers recycled the air in the sub.

The biggest problem that the crews faced on long voyages was their psychological state. In actuality, the subs could stay underwater for an indeterminable length of time, if not for the need to acquire additional food and supplies. The ships' crews, however, were not machines and could only withstand so much time beneath the sea! What the Crickets did not know was that the Frogs' new class of subs was even more sophisticated. Special Frog submarine supply ships were able to dock onto their own attack subs and deliver food and supplies, underwater, without the need of their attack subs ever resurfacing! These submarine men and women were more akin to astronauts of the past; more like superhumans of the future—who might someday live in a different dimension; and yes, more like humans of their own era who could live their lives, for years, under the waters' edge: if it meant protecting their country!

Reynaldo had advised Cornwalter to send out some night reconnaissance aircraft from either of their carriers: the *SS Admiralty* or the *Scorpion*. Cornwalter thought it over and had some reservations, because he did not want to draw attention from enemy aircraft that might fly up to intercept them and later interrogate them, if captured. Reynaldo stated this was ridiculous! Their aircraft could locate the enemy much sooner than their submarines could. Cornwalter laughed and said, "Isn't this a reversal of affairs: first, I am the aggressive one and you are the conservative one; now, you are the one willing to chance giving up our position, in the hopes of gaining the enemy's position." Reynaldo joined in the laughter! After a few deep moments of contemplation, Admiral Cornwalter relented. "If we are to do this, I insist on sending out our two top flight aces: Lightning Striker and Sudden Fury."

Lightning Striker was aboard the *SS Admiralty* and Sudden Fury was aboard *the Scorpion.* It was difficult to say which of the two had the most kills. The Cricket newspapers seemed to alternate between the two heroes. First it was Fury with the latest combat kills and then it was Striker. The two seemed to be held in equally great esteem, for different reasons, by the Cricket community. If one were talking about physical appearance, then the nod would have to go to Sudden Fury! He made a sensation every time he appeared in public. Young girls would ask for his autograph! He would simply smile his broad smile and say sure. Young baby boys were being named in his honor. Girls, too! They would feminize the spelling by adding "lee" to Sudden; thus, one could occasionally hear the name "Suddenlee" here and there. Striker had his following, too. His physical appearance reminded one of a burly bear ready to charge. Cricket men chose to name their boys by Lightning Striker's last name or a variation of that name, for example, "Strike," "Striking," or just "Striker!" To date, no women seemed to want to use his name for their female offspring. The Cricket community knew their ships were off to conquer foreign lands and their good wishes accompanied them. They were pondering who would be the most outstanding aviator; would it be Sudden Fury or Lightning Striker?

The moon was hiding behind the clouds, when Sudden Fury and Lightning Striker left the *Scorpion* and the *SS Admiralty*, respectively, and went into a reconnaissance mode. They both met high above their Armada that looked extremely impressive beneath them in the murky midnight blue waters of the Jordan. From the time they were youngsters in the National Youth Scout Aviation Academy (NYSAA), a pre-aviation school for future Cricket pilots, they were in competition with each other to see who was the best all-around student. While the Cricket society prided itself on being egalitarian, in reality the opposite seemed to prevail. Their society was one led by a *nomenclatura*: an elite class. This aeronautical academy permitted only highly qualified candidates to enroll. The applicant had to be recommended by the leaders of the community; however, if a particular parent had been decorated in battle, then his son or daughter might be given an automatic letter of acceptance, barring any disagreement among the faculty.

Sudden Fury had come from the lower ranks of Cricket society; whereas, Lightning Striker had come from a career military family decorated in aviation combat, mostly in foreign campaigns. They were without a doubt the top students academically and in sports. One could never tell which of the two would come out on top. In school they each had their own following. Sudden Fury had received his nickname based on his ability to come at his opponents with a tempest-like attack: he hit them, it appeared, from all sides at once. Whether he was on the soccer field or whether he was answering a difficult question in physics, chemistry, or biology, he was out front with the goal or the answer.

Lightning Striker, on the other hand, had received his "handle" based on similar qualities, the difference being that they never knew when LIghtning Striker was going to hit them. A cadet might be walking down the hall, minding his or her own business, and Striker would come out of an alcove, grab that cadet from behind, catching that person completely by surprise! Sometimes this action would occur as jest, but at other times, it was done out of sheer meanness, just to show the other cadet who was the boss and in charge! He could not stand to lose!

After the two graduated from the *NYSAA*, attended the main Cricket Academy, and, unlike most, they rose to the top—both tied for honors! While the Goh had been passed over for advancement in the military, Sudden Fury and Lightning Striker had already achieved the rank of Senior Officer because of their incredible intellectual and physical gifts. Pleasing the right people also helped. Politics in the military was no stranger. In time, it was felt, the two would replace the Blue and Red Vampires and carry on the Cricket tradition of conquest by the sword, as it were. Lightning Striker had learned, moreover, that the Cricket leadership had not always been a duo; there had been times in the history of the Crickets, according to his military history professor, when only one Cricket sat at the helm!

As he looked across the open sky, now beginning to show signs of light and color, he thought about the time his team had lost the *NYSAA Basketball Championship* to Sudden Fury's team. His face and jaws would begin to clench and his whole body would undergo a change when those thoughts entered his mind! He promised at the time, that if it took a lifetime, he would get revenge! The game was lost at the very last seconds of the game. Fury had jumped up to dunk a basket and was hit from behind, on the way up, by Striker. A personal foul was called on Striker, and Fury went to the line to take three shots. His team being behind by two points, these shots became critical in winning the game: two to tie and one more to win!

In Cricket basketball three shots are awarded if the foul is considered excessive to the honor of play. In other words, there are accidental hits, but an intentional hit that is aimed at the body, rather than the ball, is something that needs to be assessed with an additional throw awarded to the injured player. Sudden Fury made the first two baskets with some difficulty, due to the injury he had sustained. The last shot, however, was heard throughout the stadium as simply a swish. The game was over and Fury's "Raiders" had defeated Striker's "Commandos"! Crickets are still talking about that stellar game! While most have forgiven Striker for his offense, others have come to understand that this is a man to be feared, and they turn away from him. Fury understood that Striker was a fierce competitor and dismissed Striker's intentional foul as that and nothing more. Over time, Fury became the epitome of what every Cricket youth wants to become: a *conquistador* with honor!

Striker thought that time, place, and circumstance had provided him with the perfect opportunity to eliminate Fury, once and for all. The darkness seemed to whisper in his ear: "Go ahead and do it, you can do it, no one will ever know!" With Fury out of the way, Striker was certain that the sole leadership of the Crickets would pass to him. He decided to act on his plan! He indicated to Fury to take the lead in their surveillance of the Frog and Toad positions, just a few miles ahead and beneath them. After waving his left forearm in a forward manner, with palm extended and then fingers closed, a military signal displayed to avoid breaking radio silence, Fury moved his airplane ahead of Striker; in that instance, Striker closed the gap between them, positioned himself at 6:00 hours, took critical aim and fired a sidewinder heat-seeking missile at Fury's aircraft. With that, Fury's *C111* went into a tailspin, exploding like a supernova. Striker continued with the mission and took photographs of the enemy's locations and sped home.

Everyone was shocked to learn that Sudden Fury had been shot down by enemy fire! They felt a huge vacuum in their hearts! They reasoned that one of the Frog or Toad ships must have gotten lucky with their antiaircraft weapons, owing to Fury's superb maneuverability in space. Striker, after providing the *SS Admiralty Intelligence Committee (SSAIC)* and the Vampires with his aerial photographs and video, was invited to sit next to Cornwalter and Reynaldo, at the officers' breakfast. This compliment was viewed as the vampires' public trust, given to a subordinate soon to be officially recognized as a special senior officer: one to whom utmost respect needed to be shown in all military matters, except when indicated otherwise by the Vampires.

With the new information provided by Striker's material and the dissection of that intelligence, by command, who, in turn, was assisted by the *SSAIC*, the Crickets really felt that victory was just a step away! They strategized that they would now, without a doubt, be able to push the enemy into the Dead Sea and rout them, their being no exit for the enemy. Morale was high among the leadership, the senior officers, and the rank and file men and women. The few Cricket women aboard Cricket ships were mostly of the mid-grade officers level, having been selected primarily for their intellect in naval strategy and their flying abilities. To be sure, there were no female flying aces like that of the Frogs' Emerald Midnight Hornet. Still, the Cricket women who had been allowed to demonstrate their skills and talents, as a result of qualifying tests at the various Cricket Academies, had gone on to prove themselves and to substantiate that they were up to any and all tasks assigned to them.

In the days that followed, the Crickets pursued the Toad and Frog Armadas down the Jordan. At times, there were skirmishes, but the Frogs, who felt themselves more vulnerable than their Toad counterparts, were careful to stay just out of reach. On the other hand, Frog nuclear submarines were patrolling the Cricket areas, midway up the Jordan River, with the intensity of panthers stalking their prey! The Frogs used their aircraft based on their trusted Toads' aircraft carriers, the *HTMS Eagle* and the *HTMS Heroic*, to stave off any serious damage that might be inflicted by invading Cricket fighters.

The time came when the Frogs and Toads were about to enter the Dead Sea! The Crickets became so excited they could hardly contain themselves. As they closed the distance between themselves and the Frog and Toad ships, the Crickets pressed for an all-out attack. To say they were itching for a fight was a gross understatement! They became more emboldened when new information came their way. By the time they began "Operation Devastate," the *Stingray* had been refitted and commissioned, ready for action! The *Stingray*, the Vampires were informed by an approaching liaison Cricket fighter pilot, was moving swiftly down the immense river to join their Fleet. The *Stingray* with four escort destroyers, the pilot relayed, was now less than two hours away!

Unbeknownst to the Crickets, the Frogs and Toads had been conducting their own reconnaissance of the Cricket Armada during dangerous nighttime operations, made all the more dangerous due to heavy winds and rains. Through one of those flights, a Frog pilot spotted a capsule in the water! As she aimed her aircraft in the direction of this speck in the Jordan's turbulent waters, she removed her mask and noticed what appeared to be a downed pilot situated on the capsule. She radioed to a *PT 109-9* Amphibious Assault Unit to pick up the distressed pilot! With that, the *PT 109-9* raced towards the position in the hopes of completing the rescue of a downed Cricket pilot, a Colonel Sudden Fury. Fury smiled up at the attractive Frog pilot as she whizzed by and gave her a thumbs-up for calling in assistance!

She slowly circled his capsule and smiled back, from the cockpit of her mushroom jet! In a few minutes the *PT 109-9* would arrive and pull Fury out of the waters. No sharks had ever been spotted in the Jordan, in the past. Nevertheless, oceanographic scientists had said they could now be found in the Jordan, because of climatic changes brought on by global warming and recent earthquakes in the area! The Frog pilot was cognizant of recent shark attacks and was doing her best to protect the Cricket pilot until help arrived. Of course, this pilot, she mused, might also possess information useful to Headquarters!

The *PT 109-9* crew picked up Sudden Fury and took him to a hospital on board the Frog battleship *Televiva*. It was a ship that had survived the Cricket onslaught, a few nights earlier. The *Televiva* lived up to its name: across life! The admiral of this ship had commandeered other similar ships as a soldier-of-fortune, or Admiral-for-hire, in his case. After a thorough examination of Fury, the doctors determined that aside from having contracted a slight cold from the waters of the Jordan, he was otherwise in excellent shape. Intelligence officers from the *Televiva* and others who had arrived via helicopter from the *Eagle* were anxiously waiting to interrogate Fury. At the same time, Fury's capsule was being inspected: inch-by-inch!

After Fury was served green tea and some delicious food, food becoming a Cricket-with-an-appetite, his Frog doctor, Veronica, stated that he could now get out of his Frog PJs and dress into his more imposing Cricket uniform. His clothes, she divulged, had been freshly laundered and were ready to wear! Fury graciously thanked Veronica, waited for her to leave, and then hurriedly dressed. Fury looked in the mirror and said to himself, "Remember, you, you my friend, are a Cricket senior officer and nothing but name, rank, and serial number need be conveyed to the enemy, based on the Genevieve Conference by-laws." This information he received at the Academy. Just then, two Frog military police entered and escorted him to the debriefing room for interrogation. Once they got past pleasantries, the questioning began:

First Intelligence Officer: Identify yourself, please!

Sudden Fury: My name in your language is Sudden Fury.

Second Intelligence Officer: ...and your rank is?

Fury: Colonel, Third Attachment, 21st Flying Wing Corps, Cricket Air Command.

First Officer: Your serial number?

Fury: 333-99-2006-99-333

Second Officer: If it is not too much trouble, do you mind telling us what brings you to these friendly waters?

Fury: Strange you should ask me such an interesting question, and since you asked, here's my answer: I was night fishing for sharks. Just love that shark meat!

First Officer: Nice to see you also have a great sense of humor, Officer Fury. Now, you must know we have other means of persuasion.

Fury: Well, I suppose if you wish to disregard the Genevieve Conference by-laws regarding the Rules of War and the Rights of Prisoners.

Second Officer: Who says you're a prisoner?

First Officer: Those rules do not apply to spies!

Fury: Since when is accidental, unintentional military surveillance considered spying? As you can see, I am in uniform; therefore, I can't possibly be a spy: Spies don't wear uniforms. You might just take under consideration that I became lost and strayed off-course in tonight's thunderstorm. You see, it was simply an innocent accident: spilled milk. That's the truth of it! If you don't like that story, I've got ten more where that came from.

Second Officer: *(to First Officer, as an aside)* He may have a point there. There were some important changes at the last Genevieve Conference. In addition, tonight's storm was something else!

First Officer: *(reconsidering his previous remarks to Fury)* We're not barbarians here! Torture is unbecoming to the conduct of a civilized nation. We can appreciate nobility in an adversary. Still, we have a job to do and that is protecting our national boundaries and the integrity of our friendly neighbors, as well as, maintaining the peace and tranquility of the entire region. Your Cricket-marauding nation, on the other hand, is more interested in land grabbing, by creating devastation, and by injuring innocent peoples—simply to enrich yourselves!

Fury: Unfortunately, injury and death are byproducts of war! Were that war could be avoided! When the last resort to peace in the diplomatic arena has failed, nations resort to war. Even if I could, I would not speak ill of our leaders! They have made us a superpower in the region and beyond! Our philosophy is to bring a lasting peace to the Earth! We have observed your United Nations and it has been less than successful at administering peace and justice! As the world's principle government, we would have the power to create a "New World Order!" There would be little need to pacify rich, quibbling senior citizens sitting in their comfortable chairs, drinking champagne, smoking Havana cigars while playing guitars, and dining on dominoes in exchange for diamonds!

First Officer: So, my noble Cricket, you take a dismal view of the world's last bastion of hope. How pathetic is your philosophy! Other nation states, empires, and tribes have pursued your narrow-minded philosophy under the guise of peace and well being for all. It simply has not worked and will not work! As a great writer in the West once wrote, "all animals are equal but some animals are more equal than other animals," or something to that effect. Get my drift!

Fury: Yes, but we will prevail; we will succeed! The new generation of Crickets, while respecting the accomplishments of our past and current leaders, will work to include all peoples of the Earth, for the betterment of the whole of the peoples of the planet.

First Officer: Officer Sudden Fury, for the time being, please consider yourself a guest on our battleship *Televiva*! Perhaps, when you observe how we treat each other, you may reconsider your philosophy of creating a New World Order by force, rather than trust! In the meantime, feel free to speak to anyone aboard ship. I am sure to have additional questions for you, after we have completed the search of your capsule.

Second Officer: Welcome aboard, Officer Fury!

With those remarks, First Colonel Sudden Fury was given most of the rights and privileges accorded a Frog or Toad officer of equal rank. Within a few hours, the Alliances' intelligence officers met and analyzed the critical information obtained from the inspection of the capsule. They determined that Fury was, without a doubt, on a reconnaissance mission! A joint search of the area where Fury's *C111* had been shot down, furthermore, resulted in recovering, besides the capsule, additional valuable debris!

The Black Box, along with still-intact computerized maps, memory chips of the specialized guidance instruments and other indicators, gave the Alliance of Frog and Toad agents the kind of intelligence that would make conducting the war much easier. They had suspected, all along, from probes conducted by Frog and Toad aviators that the Cricket Carrier *Stingray* had not yet caught up with the rest of the Cricket Armada. They also noted that the Crickets were closing in on them and hoped to annihilate them, once their own Alliance armada entered the Dead Sea!

Having considered their original plan, to bait the enemy and have him pursue them into the Dead Sea, they came away confident that the Crickets had not yet penetrated their air space further south; otherwise, the enemy would have known what the Frogs and Toads had in store for them! The storm had still not abated, not one iota! The weather, consequently, favored the Frog and Toad Armadas! It became almost impossible to see for any great distance! The storm upset the computer equipment, and it could not be relied upon, with any degree of accuracy. Finally, by 3:00 hours, the complete Alliance Armada of Toads, Frogs, and Allies had entered the Dead Sea! Not surprisingly, however, the carrier *Stingray* was still an hour away, thanks to the same weather patterns. The storm definitely was the primary factor in the few number of knots the resuscitated ship could make per hour.

By 4:00 hours, the carrier *Stingray* rejoined the Cricket Fleet and a tremendous elation, expressed in shouts of hurray and hurrah for the *Stingray*, rang out throughout the entire fleet! The sailors had just learned of its return and awaited its magnificent, triumphant entrance! When the *Stingray* came beneath the misty, dark overarching canopy, this other worldly cloud hastily separated, as if to make room for an incredible undersea monster emerging from its deepest recesses. To the naked eye, it seemed like a harmless speck in the distance, but viewed through field glasses, it surpassed imagination for its potential to make war! The *Stingray* had survived a mortal wound; she was incapable of being destroyed! More than ever, she remained their mistress of the sea! Now fully restored, the Crickets felt themselves invincible!

The result of the *Stingray's* appearance was that the Crickets now had three carriers, each equipped with 55 airplanes: the *SS Admiralty*, the *Scorpion*, and the *Stingray*! The 165 aircraft of the Cricket carriers was greater than the 150 airplanes of the *HTMS Eagle* and the *HTMS Heroic* that boasted 75 each. Granted, the larger sorties of the Toad carriers, as a result of superior nuclear power of its ships and aircraft, more than made up for the difference in the number of Cricket airplanes; notwithstanding this apparent advantage, the Toads could not afford to lose a carrier and expect to defeat the enemy in dogfights! For all intents and purposes, the opposing navies were virtually even; the best strategy would seem to favor the eventual victor! Caesar had defeated Pompeii with half the size of Pompeii's army. Pompeii's effort to encircle Caesar was met with his own encirclement. What exactly did each of the adversaries have in store for the other? Time would tell.

Sudden Fury was taking his usual late evening walk around the deck of the Frog Battleship *Televiva*, thinking of all he had learned, when he heard two women's voices—in the distance. He leaned over the railing and took in some of the salty air that was warm, considering the time of year, November. He had thought about approaching and talking to the two women officers, but decided to meditate, instead, on what had transpired in the sky, just a few nights ago. Fury was watched carefully; still, he had had, as the Frog and Toad Intelligence promised, ample opportunity to visit and interview any of the upper brass. He even had permission to speak with the rank and file of the ship's crew. He couldn't get over how hospitably the Allies were treating him! He thought about what would occur, if the reverse were to happen. For example, what kind of treatment would an allied aviator receive, if he or she were to be rescued by the Crickets? Perish the thought! As to what had happened in the sky, that was another issue; he was not completely sure, nor could he bring himself to believe what his better instincts were telling him.

The Intelligence officers aboard the *Televiva* had assured him that they were not responsible, nor should they receive any credit for his falling out of the clouds. Based on a thorough examination of the debris, aeronautical scientist determined that he had been shot down by friendly fire. A *C111* Cricket reconnaissance aircraft, in their expert opinion, had shot down one of their own airplanes. The Frog's top inspector, Commander Wainwright, was still not 100 percent positive; nevertheless, he concluded that one of the sidewinder missiles had been released from the *C111*, probably accidentally; but how was that possible?

There are all kinds of safeguards against something like that happening! When Frog and Toad aviators fire a missile or any weapon, the safety is removed! When intelligence queried him on that point, Sudden Fury mentioned that his memory was hazy on that episode. All he remembered was being automatically ejected from his aircraft. He could not believe nor support that his comrade-in-arms, Lightning Striker, would intentionally harm him, that is, take his life! It didn't make any sense; none at all; or, did it?

Chapter Four

Rachel and Fury

Colonel Fury's interrogating officers had allowed him to get a breath of fresh air outside, unattended. They felt he did not pose any significant risk. Just about then, the two women officers he had spotted walked up to him and said flirtatiously, "Hello Colonel Sudden Fury" and saluted him with broad smiles: a sign of respect, military courtesy, but mostly fascination at meeting face-to-face this enemy ace! He returned the military formality and courtesy with an even broader smile.

Officer One: Nice to see you. Isn't that harvest moon just the most....

Sudden Fury:....beautiful? Yes it is!

Officer Two: I didn't know that Crickets felt anything for something like a full moon!

Fury: I am quite sure we are just as sensitive to nature's seasonal changes as you are!

Officer One: I have observed that you walk out here about the same time every night.

Fury: Interesting! My captors have arranged that I get a break now and then, and it seems to coincide with your observations. Why, may I ask, has it taken you so long to approach me, if what you say is so! *(Fury is enjoying the verbal interplay, and grins.)*

Officer One: I was placed on duty and it was to keep a sharp eye on you—not to approach you!

Fury: Apparently, everyone is assigned to "keep an eye on me!"

Officer Two: We just want to be sure you don't get lost *(laughing lightly)*.

Fury: Terrific to get so much unearned attention.

Officer One: Oh, but you have earned it, that's for sure!

Fury: How so?

Officer One: I don't think you recognize me, do you?

Taking a closer look, Fury's eyes widen as a flashback in his memory bank instantly produces images of a pilot returning a thumbs-up; it is all coming back to him now! Even in the darkness of the night, he was able to make out the lovely smile of the foreign aviator, he recalls: Wow! She definitely was the one! He realizes she had located him in the dismal Dead Sea. The clouds covered the moon that night. Yet, even with heavy rains, she spotted him! Without that *Mushroom Jet* aviator flying to defend her Armada's exposed flank that turbulent night, he readily affirms to himself, he might never have ever been found! A frightening scenario, Fury concludes!

Fury: You, you're the one! You are the one! *(Now he's excited)*. You are, the, one, who saved my life! *(With that, Sudden Fury dropped military formality and gave her a big hug and swung her around two or three times, planting a big kiss on her cheek!)*

Officer One: Holy Cow, I need to rescue more Crickets*! (all three break into laughter)*.

Officer Two: Well, I best turn in and let you two reminisce.

Officer One: I'll be in shortly.

Officer Two: Yeah, right! *(smiling gently and continuing past the two)*.

Sudden Fury: I just couldn't contain myself. The last time I hugged anyone that hard was when our team won the Cricket National Basketball Tournament. *(recognizing her nameplate and continuing)* Please excuse me over and again! So, you are the famous Emerald Midnight Hornet. At last we meet! And....

Emerald Midnight Hornet: ... and you are the famous Cricket Aviator Sudden Fury! The pleasure is mine....

Fury: Quite the contrary. *(bowing deeply)* the pleasure belongs to me!

Midnight: Pray tell, how did you recognize my true identity, when my name-plate reads Rachel Goldsmith?

Fury: I watched how you commandeered your Mushroom jet. We have studied your airplanes, from some we have been able to capture. We know what they are capable of doing, especially when performing an elliptical orbit. No one in our air force, I don't believe, except perhaps I, could have performed the elliptical swirl you achieved as you passed by my capsule. I knew from your aerobatics, your maneuvers, that you were some kind of special pilot. Now that I see you face to face, I can't tell you how moved I am that this pilot should also be so attractive, if you don't mind my saying so!

Midnight: *(warming to him, but cautious)* Well, Colonel, that's what a girl like me likes to hear. Got any more flattering words?

Fury: None that you haven't already heard a thousand times!

Midnight: You hyperbolize, I am certain. You know what, if the rest of your Crickets were as nice as you seem to be, then this war of ours would be history.

Fury: I quite agree. I guess we are just both serving our respective nations the best we see fit.

Midnight: I don't think we're going to solve all of the world's problems in one night. Speaking of night, it's way past my bedtime! I promised Colonel Sue Edwards that I wouldn't be long! Shame on you Colonel, but *(laughing)* are you keeping a girl from her beauty sleep? I'll tell you what, please join me for dinner tomorrow, that is, if we are given a break: alert status! OK?

Fury: I suppose we have a date; is this dark Cricket Air Force military attire appropriate? I hope you don't mind; I left my dress blues on the *Scorpion*.

Midnight: I know you're fishing for another compliment; well, here goes: Colonel Fury, you would look "smashing" in anything. The rest of the female officers will be beside themselves with envy when they see the two of us together. *C'est la vie!*

The Emerald Midnight Hornet was dead right! Colonel Sudden Fury and she were "showstoppers" the moment they entered the officers' dining room.

In spite of rules and regulations concerning conduct aboard ship, members of the opposite sex were still attracted to each other. And, like the song goes "Standing on the corner watching all the girls go by....ya can't be shot for what you're thinking...." could just as easily be sung "Standing on the corner watching all the boys go by....ya can't be shot for what you're thinking...." There were no regulations against "gasping" or "smiling" when the beauty or handsomeness of the opposite sex caught your eye and took your breath away! Everything, of course, was done in good fun, the kind of flirtation and affection expressed among the well-wishers. Innocent comments by some of the female officers, under their breath, were heard as the couple sat down next to each other: For example, "Isn't she lucky," and "I wonder if he's single," or "Anymore where he comes from?" By the same token, the male officers gazed on Midnight's radiant attractiveness and remarked about her combat skills in the air: She was, after all, the top ace in both the Frog and Toad Air Forces! A guy was also overheard saying, "How do you date a gal who has more medals and better looks than yours?"

Admiral Eisenstein, of the Battleship *Televiva*, addressed all 100 or so military personnel that were present and stated:

Admiral Eisenstein: Colonel Rachel Goldsmith, "aka" our Emerald Midnight Hornet, has requested permission to invite our guest, Colonel Sudden Fury of the Imperial Cricket Armada, to dine with us. We will show him every military civility and courtesy befitting an officer of an opposing nation. Perhaps this war will end soon and the good Colonel will relate to his comrades, family, and friends how we presented our better selves to him and made him at home with us! I, thus, propose a toast to a worthy adversary we can all respect, one who has distinguished himself in battle, albeit against us, yet one who can further the cause for peace!

Colonel Sudden Fury: *(rising, after a polite applause, to receive the toast and to make one of his own)* I thank you, Admiral Eisenstein, and I in turn extend a toast to you, your officers and crew, and to your two great nations of the Frogs and Toads. As a professional soldier, I have been schooled in the art of war and the idea of peace as well. We Crickets have one philosophy and you another. I have learned much about your civilization, during the week I have been aboard your ship; what I have learned is not covered in our textbooks nor covered in the lectures by our instructors. I have come away with a different perspective of your people: You are a proud race, but the kind that emphasizes humility over pride, trust and friendship over distrust and deceit. Would that my fellow officers could experience what I have, since arriving here!

Thank you for understanding that as a Cricket pilot I am, as are your pilots, duty-bound to fight! Those Frog and Toad aviators, who were misfortunate to have died at the expense of my aircraft, died bravely: defending your peace! If our aces and I have defeated some of your best, I can assure you that the legendary "Emerald Midnight Hornet" and the much-dreaded "Ghost " have defeated even more of ours! *(Cheers erupt among those present and then a return to quiet)*. I, too, wish for peace, and may it come sooner than later! *(More cheers and the sound of officers clinking their glasses to "here, here!" ring out)*. Perhaps your other living legend, "The Ghost," in the company of "The Emerald Midnight Hornet" will also join me in this toast? *(Cries of "yes, yes" are heard, then a hush as all look to The Ghost, taking his time coming to his feet and then speaking)*.

The Ghost: *(clearing his throat and looking straight at Sudden Fury)* I am not much for giving speeches, but I have to say that we have met in the sky before, with neither one of us able to gain the advantage over the other; perhaps that's just as well; otherwise, one of us might not be here to enjoy the food that is beginning to get cold! *(All laugh and applaud the four, including the Emerald Midnight Hornet, who, although rising for another toast and to be acknowledged, has yet to speak until now)*

Emerald Midnight Hornet: I quite agree, our food is beginning to cool; therefore, please commence eating whilst I say just a few words. At this moment, we are on schedule. *(Looking at her guest, and smiling)* We have kept few secrets from you. In fact, most who are present probably are not even aware of our "Top Secret" agenda. We will be meeting with Admiral Eisenstein and his staff, immediately following tonight's supper, to discuss "Phase Two" of our naval strategy. Our topic is "The Dead Sea and Beyond!" Thank you for your continued support! Many of you are doing double shifts! Hopefully, after tonight's briefing, we can reduce your hours now that the Toad Armada has arrived. The outer flanking rearguard, that is, our northern exterior defense shield, is secure! *(All cheer!)*

The Frog admiralty had been so impressed with Rachel Goldsmith, that they had put her on their staff. No other woman had occupied such a high post in His Frog Majesty's Navy! Admiral Eisenstein had every confidence in her leadership abilities. You might say she had become his "right-hand man," in spite of being a woman. Rachel believed: In today's navy and marines, it doesn't much matter; what matters is leadership ability! Leaders need to be "cool under fire," and she was one "cool cookie!" Not much "rattled her cage." Other pilots noticed she was "as cool as a cucumber!" Her early training had been at an all-girls school. Her teachers had taught her that she could become whatever she chose to become. She knew how to compete and she loved to win. Sometimes, winning came at a high price. She learned that "practice makes perfect!" If you have natural intellectual and physical talent, you still have to practice; otherwise, a less talented person, one who practices hard, is apt to beat you. There is no shame in losing; the only shame is when you know you haven't put forth your very best effort: She practiced! It was paying off in more ways then one. Her name was on everyone's lips, men and women alike.

Young women looked up to her as a trailblazer, a role model: Colonel Rachel Goldsmith: An Alliance Ace!

As they neared finishing their meal, she was talking, while at the same time wondering how her life had brought her to this officers' dining room. She looked around the officers' mess and observed that those present represented the Frog and Toad elite. A number of Toad officers had arrived earlier, in their *PT 109-9* Amphibious Assault Units, and were dining before attending the "Allied Top Security Meeting." After more than a year of fighting the Crickets, the Allies were gaining more confidence. Much of their high morale was based on the ground forces' military achievements.

The ground war was still a struggle that could be lost to the Crickets, because of the latter's overwhelming numerical superiority. The Allies, with the very able assistance of the United Nations Forces and the Silver Brigade, were, for the most part, working quite well together. It seemed, however, that much like the yesteryear victories of a Gladiator army against Roman Legions, that their own victories over the Crickets were equally short-lived. When they defeated one Cricket army, within a few weeks, another Army, larger than before, was on its way to challenge their various positions. The Frogs, Toads, and their friends, when all was said and done, had thus far defeated every army that the Crickets had thrown against them. They were determined to fight on towards a final Allied victory.

The Emerald Midnight Hornet *r*ealized that she had let her mind wander a little and excused herself to Sudden Fury. He grinned saying, "That's quite all right! I merely thought that you were daydreaming about a boyfriend or someone special." He loved looking into her hazel, blue eyes. His heart stopped as he waited for her response. She replied, "No, there's no one special waiting for me, just 'Mr. Duty': He's a very strict master, but then again, you already have met him once or twice, right?" "Yes, I certainly have met 'Mr. Duty' on more than one occasion; he doesn't take "No" for an answer, ha, ha!"

Midnight continued, "Really, I was just thinking how strange life can be at times." She looked back into his soft, light brown Cricket eyes, and hers seemed to ask, "Why can't we be together, on the same side?" "What are you looking for in my face, Midnight? Do you see something or find anything of interest?" She answered, "I was just studying your features and admiring your swarthy complexion." He replied, "Am I that different to you?" "That's the problem: No, not really, Colonel Fury. Duty calls! See you tomorrow night?" "Tomorrow night it is!" Fury responded. "And, by the way, thanks for the banquet and thanks, especially, for being you! I'll be waiting!"

With that, the two went their separate ways: one to prepare for the next confrontation, for which a battle plan needed to be devised and then presented, thoroughly, to those senior officers present; the other, to stare at the moon and to listen to the music of the waves, as they beat against the sides of the fast-moving battleship, *The Televiva!* He questioned whether or not his growing attraction for a certain female aviator was getting in the way of his better judgment. Perhaps he was moonstruck or just young at heart: He couldn't decide. Had he not said that respect was what was most important? Yes, matters would be much easier if they were on the same side. He took one more look at the moon, before turning in. He sighed and felt a cozy kind of warmth inside his Cricket heart. The breezy, salty air striking his face and the moon glow on the deck combined to make that night very special! He was changing and he knew it. "Get to bed," he urged himself, "you'll see her tomorrow night!" Could he be falling in love? Of course not!

A few nights later at the ship's coffee shop, Rachel apologized for being late and shared with Sudden Fury that their "Allied Top Secret Meeting" had been a huge success. "It's a pity that we are enemies; otherwise, we could be friends," she had declared to him. They both laughed at the strangeness of her comment: It almost sounded like an oxymoron. He had responded, with a gentle smile, that he still believed it was more important that they respect each other. As an example, he offered Field Marshal Erwin Rommel as having gained the respect of another Allied Force, one whom he was fighting. "He did so, by the way he treated his own soldiers and by the way he conducted himself in his military campaigns," Fury explained, "Ya know, there is just something about gaining your opponent's respect. Who knows what will happen after the war is over?" He prognosticated; "perhaps our two distinct races will become friends."

She apologized, again, for not meeting him as they had planned and stated it was just impossible! She then proceeded to, once again, gaze into his deep-set eyes: "Your eyes, those light brown eyes are definitely your best feature. Oh, and as to our statements about becoming friends, once we cease being enemies, well, what more can I say, except ya just never know, now do ya?" Fury responded, "Stranger things have happened, I'm sure. I certainly hope so! You are a special person, very! You've apologized twice and I was so taken in by your beauty that I forgot to accept your apologies; so, I guess I get to apologize last!" Midnight replied, "I think not: sometimes a person can accept an apology simply by being nice and that you are, very!" Fury lightheartedly stated, "OK! I'll accept that. Where do we go from here?"

"Admiral Eisenstein has directed me to inform you that you are being moved to our carrier *Eagle*. The *Eagle*, as I am sure you already know, is one of our newest carrier class ships. The Toads have done a fantastic job with her! General Lopez is on board, and he wants to meet you." Fury replied, "I don't see how I can turn down a general. How many stars?" Midnight answered, "Four!" Fury's eyes widened and he shouted "Four?" "Yes," was the answer coming across the table, "Four." Fury's demeanor seemed to change. "What does a four-star general want with a Cricket colonel?"

Fury, for the first time, seemed puzzled. He became a little nervous, and it showed on his handsome face. Rachel noticed this man she had come to admire had become tense. She, therefore, tried to reassure him that she did not believe it was for additional interrogation. She explained that they, the intelligence team, had felt he would be safer on the Carrier *Eagle* than on the

Battleship *Televiva*. Sudden Fury stopped in his tracks and hurriedly asked, "Will you be coming with me?" She smiled from ear to ear and stated softly, "Yes, they want me to escort you there. They evidently have learned from Admiral Eisenstein that you and I have established an excellent rapport." Now in a playful mood, Rachel declared, "Not to worry, I won't let them hurt you!"

Thus it was the two infatuated warriors left the *Televiva* to arrive at the *HTMS Eagle*. The special *PT 109-9*, that transported them, was designed to land on carriers, in much the same fashion helicopters and mushroom nuclear aircraft do: vertically. Needless to say, Colonel Fury was extremely impressed. He made no effort to hide his exuberance at seeing this multitask, multipurpose light aircraft maneuver on the sea, in the air, and he understood it would eventually descend to the carrier. Speaking to himself, he asked, "What do we have that can perform like this?" The three MPs, who were assigned to escort Colonel Fury, stuck to him as if he was the honey and they were the bees! The Colonel was special cargo and they knew it! They had their orders. He was not going anywhere except where they wanted him to go! The day was just beginning to arrive as the *PT 109-9*, carrying them, moved briskly across the bright Mid-Eastern sky.

They were nearing their destination, at the end of The Dead Sea, when Sudden Fury experienced the surprise of his life: There, stretched out before him, he saw the widest and longest canal he had ever witnessed in his life! It had to be well in excess of 120 miles! From the height the *PT 109-9 Amphibious Assault Unit* was flying, he could make out hundreds of ships passing through the Great Canal. He saw light and heavy cruisers, frigates, destroyers, battleships, what resembled a carrier in the distance, and nearer, even submarines and supply ships: you name it! Finally, what was in the distance began moving beneath them. He noticed the largest of the ships. He recognized the carrier that had been responsible for almost destroying The *Stingray*. He viewed in all its majesty, thanks to the Emerald Midnight Hornet's field glasses, the mighty *HTMS Heroic*!

It hit him all at once: It was like being knocked out of the sky all over again! Only this time, suddenly, all kinds of lights were turning on in his mind's eye! The Crickets were being led from the Dead Sea into the Red Sea! It was here or farther down the waters that his countrymen would meet their demise. The Red Sea led into the Arabian Sea that in turn led into the Indian Ocean! He reasoned, in his convulsing mind, that at any point along the water, the combined armadas of the Toads and Frogs could vanquish them. What chance would the Crickets have? But, how had this canal come about? The Crickets were certain they had played their hand right. The Dead Sea was not supposed to have an exit! But, it did! Was this manmade, or otherwise?

The Crickets, in their pride, had made an unforgivable tactical error: They assumed! They knew the Dead Sea had been disappearing for years; therefore, it satisfied their campaign strategy against the lands of the Frogs and Toads. With a smaller area to navigate in the Dead Sea, they would be able to pin the Alliance against the wall. It was like having the enemy's back against the sea, but in reverse. The Crickets' plan would have worked brilliantly, had that been true. Where had the Crickets gone wrong? They had sent out reconnaissance flights, and all had reported nothing unusual, except that the Dead Sea seemed to be *increasing* in size. That should have alerted the Crickets to the fact that something was going on! When Cricket reconnaissance pilots were queried on that point, they simply responded that day flights would have to be taken, in order to make a better assessment.

Up until now, the Red and Blue Vampires had been reluctant to send out day reconnaissance flights: they rationalized that they had already lost enough aviators, and these pilots were needed for the naval battle of all battles! Ultimately, their scientists surmised that two principles explained the *increase* of water in the Dead Sea: First, the farmers around the Jordan River had previously been siphoning water from it, for many years! In the last decade, however, new means to acquire water had been established; hence, the farmers no longer needed to drain the Jordan that fed the Dead Sea, thereby causing it to rise. Secondly, the unseasonable weather in this arid land resulted in heavy storms, further enlarging the circumference of the Dead Sea. Taking all of this into account, the Vampires were confident that their logistics regarding the geological, topographical, and meteorological changes were indeed accurate: The Dead Sea, they were confident, was now as it always had been, a confined sea with no outlet: a dead end! Had the Vampires taken a giant step back and looked at the larger picture, they might have seen the wisdom in sending out even a single reconnaissance airplane, equipped with infrared cameras, to survey the Dead Sea and beyond; instead, they leaped before they looked! Their apparent lust for land got the better of them. Their vision was by any standard nearsighted: myopic!

The Frog and Toad scientists, on the other hand, had influenced their politicians to pass secret bills in favor of building a canal from the Dead Sea to the Red Sea. Both sides of the Jordan passed similar bills, and their respective governments came together in a joint effort to see the great project through. It seems they received assistance from heaven when an earthquake caused the canal to widen and deepen! The two friendly governments, Frogs and Toads, gave thanks to the Great Spirit with religious ceremonies in their respective places of worship, both in Frogland and Toadland. The "Great Canal," as it was called, was kept "Top Secret!" *Special Emperor Penguin Spitfighters*, *Pencils*, were always on alert to intercept airplanes that flew off course, and these intruders were promptly escorted away from the "Great Canal" zone! When war broke out, it was even more important to keep Cricket airplanes out of the Canal area.

Ironically, the Grand Opening of the Great Canal had had a "blue ribbon ceremony," just weeks before the onset of war. The leading citizens of the two nations had come together to see the first ships pass through its banks. The leaders of both sides cautioned these elite citizens against discussing the canal with anyone, especially foreigners. The reason was: the United Nations had not yet been informed as to the Canal's completion. The leaders stated they wanted to invite all friendly nations to use the canal. They wished not to offend any nation by the misuse of protocol. Those in attendance took the confidential statement very seriously. These citizens, moreover, held "top security identifications" and knew the importance of cooperating with their elected officials. The good of the region, after all, was at stake. The secret became so well guarded that Cricket Intelligence or *SSAIC: Secret Service Admiralty Intelligence Committee* was never able to learn about this mammoth undertaking!

The *PT 109-9,* carrying Sudden Fury and the Emerald Midnight Hornet, along with the Allied Military Police and intelligence officers, swept by the outstretched *HTMS Heroic* and then turned to continue towards the *Eagle*, positioned in the Dead Sea. Fury had inquired as to why they were returning to the Dead Sea, when all of the other ships were headed towards the Red Sea. Midnight replied that the intelligence agents, on board the *PT 109-9* wanted to first survey the ships passing through the Canal, in order to verify ship movement. "We check and recheck and recheck, to make certain no one gets left behind, except those who are supposed to remain," she responded. "The captain is giving me a 'thumbs up', so, from all accounts, everything is going A-OK!" Fury was able to ask just a few more questions, before the *PT 109-9* began its descent to the deck of the massive *Eagle*. It was difficult to say, which of the two Toad carriers was more impressive. These carriers were not mirror images of each other; rather, they had their own unique features.

After deplaning, Rear Admiral Pointdextras, who had just returned from meetings with Josue II, and General Lopez were seen walking towards the *PT 109-9* Amphibious Assault Unit. They stopped short of the machine to receive their Cricket guest-prisoner, accompanied by the Emerald Midnight Hornet, with MPs at either side. In spite of being a prisoner, Colonel Sudden Fury was given all the respect and politeness generally reserved for officers of friendly nations. This treatment continued to befuddle him. No matter, he was going to enjoy the privilege as long as it lasted.

Admiral Pointdextras: Well, at long last we get to meet the best of the Cricket flying aces: Colonel Sudden Fury. Colonel Fury, I am Rear Admiral Pointdextras, the Frog participating pilot of this floating armed city: Admiral Da Vinci is piloting the *HTMS Heroic* and sends his regards. And this here *(indicating to his right)* is General Angel Lopez of Toad Intelligence. But, don't let that perturb you; although he is a pretty good chess player, ha! ha!

General Lopez: *(saluting the Cricket officer)* Such an honor to meet someone of your skill. Wish you were on our side, instead of shooting down some of our best!

Sudden Fury: I must say, Sirs, the pleasure is all mine! Nevertheless, I can't imagine that I am of sufficient importance to you, that you should make all this fuss over me. I have told your senior intelligence officers all that I am able to....

Rear Admiral Pointdextras: We still have plenty of time to discuss some ideas that our intelligence officers didn't get around to, don't we, General? *(Lopez nods, signifying agreement)* In the meantime, would you like to get some chow now, or would you prefer to hear a little bit about *The HTMS Eagle*?

Sudden Fury: My stomach can wait; besides, I had a bite to eat on the way over here (looking over his left shoulder to the *PT 109 - 9*). By the way, that is some kind of multipurpose machine you have there. I'd sure like to have one of those! I've got a birthday coming up? *(They have a good laugh at Fury's expense)*

Emerald Midnight Hornet: *(smiling and beaming)* You do? I guess we'll have to have a party!

Pointdextras: An excellent idea. We'll do that! Got any special kind of dessert you'd like, Colonel Fury?

Fury: Are you serious?

Pointdextras: We Frogs are the serious type. Since you ask: yes!

Fury: In that case how about some of that cheesecake! Midnight bragged you Frogs are famous for it the world over?

Pointdextras: If the Emerald Midnight Hornet said so, it must be so! Cheesecake it is!

Rear Admiral Pointdextras began to move about the deck of the ship, and the entourage followed him, paying close attention to all he had to say. Besides the Admiral, General Lopez, and the three MPs, there were four intelligence officers who stayed close behind. The Admiral pointed out that the Frog Navy and the Frog Air Force had had their differences; thus, the navy came up short in the military budget! Just before the war broke out, however, the Frogs were nearing completion of their own nuclear attack class carrier: *The King David.* Somehow, King Josue II had been able to use his leverage to get moneys passed through the appropriations ways and means committee, to finance the new carrier.

In the meantime, the Toads had schooled him in the latest technology that enhanced navigability and the latest methods of arming nuclear offensive weapons systems. These were a source of pride, since they were contained in *The Eagle,* their most recent carrier. He was super-delighted to command this beauty. King Gideon III felt it very important to include top-ranked Frog naval officers into the ways of the Toad Navy. As they say, "He made it happen!" No other Frog Admiral had ever been accorded such a prestige except Admiral Cheetah. When asked about Admiral Cheetah's whereabouts, Pointdextras responded saying, "Admiral J. Cheetah Obian was needed and remained at an undisclosed strategic military site, along with Four-Star Toad General Schwartzwait. In war," Pointdextras continued, "you need more friends than enemies!" On the whole, the Toads and Frogs were almost indistinguishable, as they worked and participated in each other's military affairs: They were indeed much more than allies; they were friendly, close cousins.

General Lopez: I am certain we would like to hear about some of the ship's characteristics, such as displacement and dimensions, et cetera; that is, if you feel it's OK to discuss that info with Colonel Sudden Fury in tow.

Read Admiral Pointdextras: *(looking at Fury, looking back at Lopez, and then taking the rest of them in)* I don't think you plan to leave the ship right away, do you Colonel? *(they all have a laugh, at Fury's expense; he plays along)*

Fury: Well, Admiral, the thought had crossed my mind, once or twice. *(Now more serious, yet maintains a respectful tone)*. Yes sir, I think you're safe in divulging that information in my presence, considering you have the upper hand. That aside, you can't know how much I would appreciate learning about this beautiful carrier of yours! *(continuing to look at Pointdextras)* Your Toad Navy allies have done a magnificent job, from the looks of things! *(looking at Lopez)* Who knows, maybe I'll be on your side in the next war with your next enemy, if there is one! That is, if we Crickets come up on the short end of the stick. *(Once again, laughter is heard all around.)*

Lopez: *(looking back at Fury)* Sounds like a plan to me. Superb aviators, like you, are a breed-apart.

Fury: Thanks!

Pointdextras: Well, since you've assured us that we can count on you for the next war, I'll tell you a little about some of the features of the *HTMS Eagle.*

The HTMS Eagle was built five years after the *HTMS Heroic!* Even though it has only been five years since our earlier carrier was made, many high-tech improvements have been incorporated, into this latest installment of Toad Carriers. Take into account that *The Heroic* has a displacement of 100,000+ tons, *The Eagle*'s displacement is 10,000 less: with newer technology many of the antennae and other older equipment have been replaced with smaller equipment that is more efficient. We, of course, have found other areas of the ship where this new equipment can be housed, thus creating more space on the flight path of the main deck.

I'm sorry, I can't let you know what the armor is; nevertheless, the armament consists of three REX 30.9-cell Seagull launchers and three 24-cell TRX launchers. Our radar is the latest in radar technology that covers the usual; for example, air search, surface search, target acquisition, air traffic control, and, of course, radar pertinent to landing aid. Our fire control has the newest systems with PDQ 99 radars. We have five new active jamming/deception devices that were just recently installed. Plenty of decoy material is also present. Our aviation facilities consist of seven elevators for rapid movement and safety onboard. Oh yes, we can accommodate a crew of 6,300-6,500.

Intelligence Officer One: Admiral Pointdextras, what about power plant, speed, endurance, and aircraft?

Pointdextras: I was waiting for someone to ask about those. I was leaving some of the best for last. Here goes:

We have three nuclear reactors, six steam turbines, with six screws, I believe. *The Eagle* will do 35+ knots! The endurance, I think is 1.7 million mn @ 20 knots.

Intelligence Officer Two: All right, Admiral, stop keeping us in suspense. HOW MANY?

Pointdextras: How many aircraft? OK! *The HTMS Eagle* with a displacement of 90,000+tons, with extra deck and runway space, will accommodate 90+ aircraft. *(all are amazed and are overjoyed at the news)* She's the best in today's navy! I hope we don't have to use her against you Crickets, but from the look of things...? It appears that your nation is unwilling to broker a peace with us. Time will tell!

Colonel Sudden Fury: *(choosing not to reply to Pointdextras's invitation to a debate)* Admiral Pointdextras, thank you so much for such a thorough analysis of your ship. As I may have mentioned earlier, she's a real beauty *(the rest join in with compliments)*. And, thank you for the invitation to a birthday party!

Pointdextras: Yes! Shall we meet at my quarters, next to the officers' dining room at 17:00 hours? *(All acknowledging yes)* Fine, 17:00 hours. See you then!

That evening Colonel Fury became the delight of the party. "To begin with," he thought to himself, "who ever heard of an enemy officer being invited to a banquet and now to a birthday party, in his honor! This is just too much to imagine, much less to experience! I suppose having a Cricket officer nearby, for these fine folks, is like having a Martian up close for observation, the difference being that this here is a social scene; I'm not in a clinical laboratory, or part of some kind of an experiment. Or am I?" To a certain extent, he was right. Most Frogs and Toads had heard stories of Crickets and how they ate their enemies and drank their blood, but intelligent Frogs and Toads knew better. They understood that oftentimes combatants give their enemies some type of superhuman powers. In reality, however, they could now easily see he was not that different than they. He was accepted simply as a worthy opponent.

Perhaps his presence was for purposes of reassurances. They wanted to match wits with him; they wanted to see if they were smarter than he was; in addition, they also wanted to see if anything they did upset him: They wanted to see themselves in his reflection of them. This point was especially true of the female officers who wondered if he was as nimble, mentally, on the ground, as he appeared to be in the air. The men wondered if the other Crickets were as rugged-looking as Fury. They seemed to want to prove their *mettle*—their strength—against him on the field rather than in the air.

Some went so far as to challenge him to feats of strength in the ship's gymnasium. Questions appeared, such as: "How much can you power-lift; do you play chess and, if so, would you like a game with me; are you a fast runner; and, do the Crickets have Olympics, like we do?" To these questions concerning mental and physical acuity, Fury always seemed to find a tactful way of answering. He would reply, humbly, "You are probably a much better chess player than I," or "I am sure you would beat me in a 100-meter race," or "There is no possible way I could press as many pounds or kilos as you do!" His psychology was better than theirs, for the most part. He knew it took two to argue and he was not going to oblige them, not here, not now. He would have them wait to compete on his terms, not theirs.

His self-deprecating attitude and his unassuming personality were winning qualities that disarmed his would-be opponents. Some of the less belligerent Allied officers would come to his aid, when he was being pressed by the aggressive ones, by saying to their comrades-in-arms, "Give the guy a break, he's our guest;" or "Back off!" In any case, Colonel Fury made it through the evening with flying colors to match his wins in the open air. He was, after all, an ace on the ground every bit as much as if he were in the sky, fighting enemy pilots.

The evening was coming to a close and Rachel Goldsmith, another unassuming ace, came by to escort him to his room. He whispered he needed some fresh air and found the deck more refreshing than the Toads' Officers Club. He mentioned that he had, indeed, enjoyed the evening birthday party, when Midnight had inquired about his feelings. She stated that he was one of the most admirable men there that night. "You have a certain *savoir faire* that most of our officers lack." He responded with a smile and simply quipped, "Your Toads and Frogs are not such a bad bunch. They were just testing my steel. If we are going to fight, I would have to level the playing field; for me, that means meeting them somewhere in the wild blue yonder!"

Rachel smiled and asked if he would like to have a cup of coffee or some kind of beverage to unwind, after so much stimulation at the Officers Club. He replied, "Sounds great!" They continued their walk down the deck. Rachel related that Admiral Pointdextras had mentioned there was a "neat" coffee shop, just a way down from the Club." They stood awhile by the deck facing the ocean's breeze. Rachel inquired, "Doesn't that feel just terrific after being in a stuffy room with stuffy officers?" Fury laughed and replied, "Be nice. Remember, they are on your side. Besides, people are people. Trust me, I would exchange a lot of your officers for some of those on my side!"

When they arrived, most of the Toads and Frogs, who had been at the coffee shop earlier, were just departing. The two received some interesting glances from those leaving. One expression from a passerby seemed to suggest, "What's this world coming to?" Rachel took charge and remarked, "Don't give her a second thought; I can tell when someone is just plain jealous." Fury found the remark quite becoming. It was just what he needed to restore his soul. "She likes me," he smiled within. "She really likes me!" he repeated to himself and it warmed him. "I am, indeed, falling head-over-heels for her," he agreed with himself! He contemplated, seriously, and thought about the future.

He wondered where their relationship was going: wasn't it hopeless? He forced himself to remember that his first responsibility, as an enemy flyer to the Frogs and Toads, was to assist the cause of his nation; but how? He felt pulled in both directions and decided that he didn't have to have the answer right now. He mentioned to Rachel how nice it was of her to bring him to this little shop, where they could be alone for a time and just enjoy each other's company. The waiter dropped by to take their orders and Fury was taken out of his momentary daydream. Rachel inquired as to when the shop closed and the waiter stated they would be open until two in the morning. He then hinted with the wink of an eye, "Don't worry, you've got three more hours!"

As the evening wore on, the two aces of opposite sides talked about many subjects. The most intriguing seemed to be that of politics and religion. Both of these topics are taboo and avoided by polite company, the reason being that most people hold very personal and deep feelings concerning ideas that affect their lives. Politics, they believe, regulates their day-to-day lives on this planet; whereas religion, for most, holds a promise for life after death. Rachel asked Fury if the Crickets' society was democratic or authoritarian, or perhaps pluralistic. He responded that up until now, he was not certain as to what constituted a democratic society: at least up close, never having lived in one.

He explained that what he had learned in the Cricket Academy was that democratic societies exploited those of lesser material means. In other words, the upper classes economically enslave the lower classes by underpaying them for the work they perform. "These poor wretched folk!" Fury exclaimed. He continued by adding that any society that has such a system, where some live in luxury while others can hardly meet their monthly obligations, is doomed to failure! "On more than one occasion, I have flown over your cities and have noticed that some houses are much larger than others," he declared. "Why do some of the Toads and Frogs believe they deserve more of life's material, biological, educational, and medical resources than their fellow citizens?" Fury demanded!

The Emerald Midnight Hornet had never had such an intellectual and emotional challenge to the system she had enjoyed all her life. Rachel was from the upper crust of Frog society and had experienced the best her society had to offer: private schools, the best teachers, one of the most beautiful homes in the valley of the Frogs, and the prestige of belonging to an elite class of Frogs. Of course, the Frogs never referred to themselves as being a class society; it was something most didn't talk about. To begin with, upper social mobility was always a possibility among both the Frogs and the Toads. Rachel took offense that someone, anyone, would categorize her society as an unfair one! Her early education and training caused her to defend her society's position. It seems that the two were having their warfare in the cafe, rather than in the air. The discourse was civil, almost genteel. Still, Rachel felt she must speak for her side! She began by going on the offensive. A strong offense is the best defense, practice had taught her: no matter the venue.

"And your society, Colonel Sudden Fury, is one that does not allow for personal freedom," she began. "From an early age, your youth are forced to enter a track system of education where others determine for them, what they will become in life. Your Crickets are restricted as to where and when they can travel! There is no possibility for free and open elections, with oversight by impartial election observers! Your leaders," she advanced "take more privileges for themselves and their families and friends, or cronies, I might add. In school we learned this elite group of Crickets are called the *nomenclatura*. How then can you imply that your society does not exercise class distinctions? At least in our society, people are rewarded for their talents, special gifts, and abilities, that is, what they in fact contribute to the arts and sciences in our communities."

Fury was taken aback! He, too, had never been involved in a conversation with another person who spoke with such candor and audacious conviction about their life, from a political perspective so foreign to his own. He felt they were in a 15-round boxing match, and he was getting more than what he had bargained for in the contest.

Neither one of the two gladiators wanted to give ground in this match of intellectual titans. After more discussion, that resembled gaining and losing ground on either side, the two came to a moderate consensus for the good of their friendship. They were mutually able to concede that perhaps sometime in the distant future, there might come a period when the peoples of the earth would move towards a more pluralistic form of governance; one that could incorporate the best attributes, the best features, from all the systems of government that had flourished up until that time. They would call that generation the "Generation of Peace," a time when most of the needs and wants by the people were satisfied, as a result of a "kinder and gentler society," a time when true justice would have prevailed!

They acknowledged that while peace was an ideal that seemed elusive, it was still worth every effort made to achieve it. It was and is, they concurred, another word for love! Their distinct beliefs spoke of such a love! It was at this point that the conversation turned to religion. They would link their hearts, minds, and souls towards achieving this spiritual matrix. They would seek not only to better understand each other but to better help each other. Perhaps, they were the beginning of something new, something never imagined, or at least never achieved universally: Peace!

Rachel: We have observed that you worship idols. Is that correct?

Fury: Wherever did you get that idea!

Rachel: Several of our reconnaissance photographs depict large statues around your government buildings, with even larger crowds attending to them, on specific days of the week.

Fury: *(laughing)* That's a good one! I wasn't aware, however, that your reconnaissance had penetrated our air space at the Vampires' Monastery! That's the only place I can think of that fits the description to which you allude. Our nation, as you are aware, is one built on conquest! Each of the 49 statues is 100 feet high and represents Cricket Vampire leaders from our glorious past. The people come to these statues in reverence, that is, as an act of remembrance of the great and noble feats each of the leaders, represented, accomplished during his or her lifetime. Our nation has always been served by two co-leaders; except for a dark period in our history, when only one ruled. With two leaders at the head of our country, we get a balance from both Cricket Houses of State: "The House of the Inside" and "The House of the Outside." Most often we simply refer to them by colors. One we call the "Red House," represented by the Red Vampire; the other is the "Blue House," represented by the Blue Vampire. When one of the leaders passes from this life, he is given a special burial ceremony. Another leader is elected by that House to replace the fallen Vampire, and the new leader dons the new robe, sometimes "Red" and sometimes "Blue," depending on the replacement filled. In any case, those attending these ceremonies take great care to show the utmost respect to our beloved ancestral leaders.

Rachel: Would you mind explaining why your leaders have such scandalous names?

Fury: *(raising his eyebrows curiously)* You are referring, of course, to the use of the name "Vampire." You raise a good point and your question is worth answering. To begin with, no one in our community, including our leaders, is a real vampire; nevertheless, some Crickets have traced their ancestry to gypsies emigrating from Transylvania to the center of the earth! It was said of those early Crickets, that some, indeed, were vampires! How much is true and how much is myth is difficult to say. If there were any credence to those ideas, of which I doubt very much, it would have surfaced by now! Little documentation is available and very sketchy at best: most evidence has long since disappeared! Suffice it to say, the word "vampire" has been kept—since the time of our early leaders—as a way of terrifying the enemy! I dare say, some of our own people believe that when an individual becomes a "Vampire leader," he takes on increased supernatural powers. Sound scary? Trust me; it's all nonsense!

Rachel: *(smiling)* You certainly don't look like a vampire to me! *(opening her eyes wide and making a terrifying face, so they both break up in laughter)* Still, nothing in this world surprises me! We Frogs, like our cousins the Toads, are not at all like the Vikings you resemble. Not that you are fair-skinned—quite the contrary; moreover, your features are very striking, almost exotic. I rather like them, to tell you the truth. But, then again, we were talking about religion. *(speaking in a more serious tone)* Nowhere in your dissertation did I hear of a Supreme Being! I take it that your gods are vampires of power and might? If so, do you Crickets believe that your gods only pass through time and space and, then, cease to exist? That being the case, not having a belief in an Eternal Heavenly Father, do you also not believe in an afterlife, a Heaven, where believers believe the true Eternal Force resides?

From the time we are born, we are consecrated to our Heavenly Father. We believe there is a purpose to life, and that that purpose is to love the Almighty above all others and to love one another, as we would have others love us. Without love, all is naught. Our Holy Book teaches us, through scriptural readings, that to gain all the riches of the world and to lose the Kingdom of Heaven is just an exercise in futility!

Fury: Your Almighty One, we are told, is a myth believed by ancient peoples: an idea with no real validity. If there is a real Eternal Force, as you say, how is it he permits so much evil in the world?

Rachel: Oh! You mean like allowing some to take what rightly belongs to others and then claiming it for themselves: the spoils of war: their land, their peace, their freedom, their loved ones, and even their very lives? The Divine One may allow the Devil to reign on Earth for a period, but the Devil's work will come to a complete end, come Judgment Day! On that wondrous day, the Supreme Being will judge all who have lived and determine their goodness or evil. This Idea, of whom I speak, of a Supreme Being, many of our faithful religious believe! I believe that as the great president of another country once said: until He comes "surely His work on Earth must truly be our own!"

Fury: I am not familiar with that "saying;" however, whether or not there is an "Omnipotent One," as you declare there is, I believe that the president of whom you speak spoke truly! What good is it if there is a "Power" and we behave otherwise: badly. In the case of my people, we believe that our laws govern every facet of our lives. No one is above the law. Our Vampire Leaders, today, must act in accordance with the laws of our forefathers! Yes, it is also true that they have more freedoms; nevertheless, those freedoms only extend to promoting the good of the state!

Rachel: From what we both have stipulated, it seems to me that your nation believes that each individual in your society has an equal share in the wealth and prosperity of the society. Perhaps in abbreviated form: "each according to his or her own needs?"

Fury: And your nations believe that each individual, in your respective societies, is entitled to a disproportionate amount of the wealth or prosperity of that society! Using your abbreviated form: "each according to his own abilities?"

Rachel: That seems to be the case. Religion, economics, and politics come from different directions to create a matrix of any community's norms, however small or large. Our souls, if you believe in a Divine One, our daily physical needs, and our freedoms, that is, our safety needs, all gather like defending angels to protect us!

Fury: *(after a prolonged pause)* You mean, I am sure, our need is to be secure within the confines of any given society? *(Rachel nodding, indicating yes.)* Then you must also consider our identity needs and our need for stimulation, mental and physical...!

Rachel: Now we are getting somewhere. An English writer once wrote "Know thyself" and "To thine own self be true and to no man can thou be false!"

Fury: Once again, I must concur! Are you setting up some kind of trap for me with all these beautiful "sayings"? *(both laughing)* I suppose, the most difficult person to get to know and to understand is yourself! I often question why I said or did such-and-such. I am not always pleased with my conduct or even my own thoughts at times. On the other hand, there is a sense of satisfaction knowing you belong to something larger than yourself. I suppose that identity covers a lot of ground; who we are to ourselves and who we are to others may be exact opposites! As to stimulation, that conjures up another universe with all kinds of images!

Rachel: Stimulation, for me, means allowing our five senses to interact with nature, people, things, or just life itself, in such a way as to continue discovering nature's creation: the Divine Plan....

Fury: *(jumping in)*...through our gifts and talents, we discover the power within, however you may choose to define the source's origins. Our discovery, then, is twofold: that that lies within and that that lies without.

Rachel: Yes! I think the waiter is beckoning us to leave now. I don't know if we have resolved anything; still, I do believe we have been listening to Heaven, if not the stars above!

Fury: Yes!

As the two aviators left the cafe, they seemed a little giddy about the entire evening. The birthday party was a pleasant affair, overall, even if some of the allied aviators were less than polite. Still, the Frog and Toad military had an abiding respect for Fury. They disliked that he had been the cause of many of their deaths in air combat; they wished, vehemently, to challenge him in the skies to avenge their lost comrades, yet they had tried to compare their wits with him and found themselves wanting.

Just who was this strange person from another nation who could bring so much harm to their lands? Face to face and race aside, he didn't seem that different! He might even be affable: Fury had, after all, a very pleasing disposition; he was witty, charming, and easy on the eyes: handsome. The respect they felt for him was based primarily on two facets of his personality: First, he was a modest living legend; second, in spite of any negative comments that came his way, he returned attempted insults and expressed contempt with an inner personal strength, one might call love.

Instead of trying to get even, he demonstrated great patience and poise. In short, he showered them with more respect than they might have deserved, that is, not a respect based on a competitive spirit, but the kind of respect the good Samaritan displayed when he found a desperate man lying prostrate on the ground: The poor soul had been attacked by highwaymen! In the Biblical tale, the Good Samaritan took the injured man, who was badly beaten, to an inn and asked the innkeeper to tend to his wounds. He gave the innkeeper moneys for that assistance and promised to pay any additional moneys to the innkeeper, if the costs exceeded the amount he donated to that cause! Even with the war and its rules of engagement, Colonel Sudden Fury displayed the character of one who would give aid to a wounded fallen enemy.

Rachel found these merits and many others in him most redeeming! She knew their paths had crossed for a reason; their stars, too, had met in the cosmos, maybe predetermined, to join for a reason. Destiny was an idea she had not completely sorted out! She recalled the night she had rescued him, by alerting the *PT 109-9* Amphibious Assault Unit, and all that had transpired since then. She enjoyed being in his company: the military banquet, the flight from the *Battleship Televiva* to the *Carrier HTMS Eagle,* the birthday party, their quite-late night talks, both at cafes and while walking around the various decks. Moreover, there was the whole ordeal of his prisoner status that had perturbed her. Through it all, she was falling in love with him. She wondered if she could resist any demands he might make of her, so that on the way back to their respective dorms, she didn't know quite what to make of his request to see her aircraft. It was, after all, a logical request. He had mentioned that he wished very much to see the airplane she had flown, the one that was responsible for so many losses on his side of the war. She was, after all, as deadly to the Cricket nation as he was to the Frogs and Toads!

When she pondered his question, concerning viewing her aircraft: she affectionately dubbed *The Evening Star,* after Eve, the first woman on earth, she threw caution to the wind and chose, instead, to display the hi-tech attributes of her Mushroom nuclear-powered machine. The after-midnight salt air cut into their respective faces as they climbed into the plane. Fury became exceedingly excited to view the inside front panel, where all of the dials were located. He asked her one question after another. She willingly responded by taking his hand and directing it to this control and then the other. She had him sit in the cockpit, to get a feel for the machine. She said "Eve responds quite favorably to any coded command. She will not leave her position without proper coding of her computerized display board. I, of course, cannot provide you with that information: It is highly classified. I am sure you understand." Fury responded, "That I do!"

Rachel mentioned that it was already approaching 3:00 hours in the morning, and they had better call it a night. Fury nodded yes and stepped out of the aircraft first, to assist her on her descent. After that, Rachel walked Fury to his quarters; she looked meaningfully into his light brown eyes, that appeared black in the shadows of the carrier, and her hazel blue eyes invited him to embrace her. Fury held back his desires, and embraced her with an embrace that betrayed his real affection for her. He kissed her on the cheek, and she returned the kiss on his cheek; they said good night, held hands a little too long, and waved to each other as Rachel walked to her quarters unescorted. She felt like skipping, maybe playing hopscotch. Her feet didn't seem to touch the floor of the deck, even though she was tired.

She awakened to a hard knock on her door. Two MPs asked her to come with them to speak to intelligence officers in the command headquarters. They mentioned one of their Mushroom aircraft was missing. Fury could also not be located. She was horrified at the news! After a lengthy interrogation, the intelligence officers concluded that she had been duped! "That Fury fellow," one intelligence officer stated to the other, "played on Rachel's emotions by gaining her confidence and then deceiving her!" Rachel could not believe it. She had never made an error in judgment in personal relations in her life! Nevertheless, the facts spoke for themselves: Both he and a Mushroom jet were missing. Gone!

That day Rachel was excused from reporting for her regular duties, so she used the time to meditate on all that had transpired. She knew there must be some logical explanation that would clarify the ambiguity that rested in her mind, as well as, in her heart. She recalled one evening when they were alone on the deck looking at the stars, when he whispered tenderly in her ear "If there ever comes a time when we can't be together, look for a notebook under the upper shelf of your tennis locker." They had played tennis just two nights before he left. She had let him have an extra key to her locker. It was located with all the other equipment lockers near the officers' mess. Navy and other military officers would play a set or two of tennis, return their rackets to their lockers, go to their respective showers, and then meet for a not-so-quiet lunch!

Evidently, Sudden Fury felt no one would think to look in her private locker for personal information. He was correct! When Rachel arrived at her locker, she had been careful not to alert anyone by running, even though her heart was pounding a mile a minute! She maintained her composure and put the notebook inside her breast pocket. She smiled at other passersby as she headed for the library aboard ship. It was the perfect place, since the library provided the officers with a great deal of privacy, where they could use all sorts of electronic equipment. It enabled them to work and/or study with interactive material, such as computers, DVDs, even 3-D HDTV, and virtual reality computerized programs with a variety of menus from which to choose. A favorite was *Advanced Tactical War Games a la Holograms*. She took her plastic card and inserted it into the lock, then placed her index finger into another device that cleared her for entry into a private stall. When she was alone, she pulled out the notebook and began to read:

> Rachel, my love, I know how much grief I have caused you! I can't imagine that you will forgive me, after all the kindness and love you have shown me. Please try to understand that we must both do all we can to stop this terrible war that is decimating our nations! By the time you read this letter, I will be interrogated, once again, this time by my side of the contest. I will try to tell them the truth about your nations. I will do my best to convince them that you are a peaceable people who cherish freedom in all its better forms! I now am convinced that I was shot down by friendly fire. The aviator who downed my aircraft is Colonel Lightning Striker. He has always been jealous of my accomplishments and evidently saw a way of eliminating me, the night we were both doing reconnaissance over enemy positions near the end of the Jordan River. I am also convinced that your leaders are leading us into a trap of some sort. The day we were transported from the Battleship Televiva to the Carrier HTMS Eagle, I could see a huge lane of ships making their way through what appeared to be a massive canal.
>
> Don't worry. Since your officers showed me the utmost respect and courtesy during my capture, I will not address the specifics of what I believe you are up to; instead, I will let them, my leaders, figure it out for themselves. If I tell them, they will think I am a traitor and only interested in deceiving them. They can't imagine that your nations are sufficiently industrious and strategically minded to carry out such a brilliant scheme! My hat is off to you! The Red and Blue Vampires must change their militaristic attitude of attempting to conquer all freedom-loving peoples. I have thought the whole matter through, thoroughly, and have come to the conclusion that we have

been the aggressors; aggression serves only to regress the progress of peace.

I didn't join the military; it joined me. As I have mentioned to you, we are a militaristic society in which all participate. Our government, however, has not always been confrontational. Originally, we were a peaceful people when we lived beneath the earth's surface; thereafter, when the giant earthquake interrupted our way of life, we were forced to seek safe haven above the earth. We were attacked by other tribes further north and discovered that we not only could defend ourselves but conquer others as well. We have acquired more than enough space for generations to come. If our leaders do not turn back, then we deserve all we get. Therefore, the time has come to bring a halt to the killing. I will use all my powers of persuasion to bring about a cease-and-desist of hostilities.

Wish me luck and pray for me as I will pray for you. Together, we can make a difference on each of our opposing sides. We will meet again, my love, this much I promise you!

Fury (aka) Colonel Sudden Fury, the Imperial Emperors' Cricket Armada

Rachel having been on the edge of her seat sat back and shut off the light in her stall. She had to compose herself in the dark to see more clearly. She felt her whole world swirling about her. Everything seemed to be like a dream she was in, one from which she couldn't awaken. She recalled when she was just a child and had taken a ride on the merry-go-round for the first time, all alone. It was exhilarating yet quite scary for a six-year-old, even though she was big for her age. She knew the ride would eventually end, and she would get some assistance getting down from the big dragon. Who, she questioned, would come to her aid now? She, of course, was overjoyed to receive such a thoughtful letter, from someone she felt could someday be her life partner in marriage.

Her professional side spoke to her in the darkness and told her she must act! Whom should she speak to, and what should she say? Would she be able to find the right words to convince Toad and Frog Intelligence Officers? They had absolved her of any complicity. Fury's letter might be misinterpreted. Perhaps, they might think it was just another trick of his to have them stand down from their defensive posture. Had they risked too much, in allowing Colonel Fury so much latitude in his comings and goings, in his transport to other ships that presented too much information, for a senior officer of his intellect?

In her heart of hearts, she wanted to believe that everything Fury said in the letter was true. He would speak to his leaders and do his best to have them sue for peace. They need only return from whence they came. But, that was already impossible! At this very moment, the *HFMS King David* was making its way above and behind the Cricket Navy. *The David* had a large flotilla that would block the Cricket escape, should the enemy change their course to return upriver. Her two-way audio video wrist-radio was receiving information alerting all personnel to their battle stations, because, the enemy was spotted entering the upper part of the Dead Sea.

More than likely, from all that she had learned from Sudden Fury about the Vampires, he was probably already in chains. Her best effort at this juncture was to support the defeat of his Crickets. If the two of them were to have any chance at all, it would have to be after an armistice was declared and their respective nations were at peace. In her heart, she forgave Fury; he was, after all, doing what he thought was right. He had been true to her; he had called her "my love." Her lips began to tremble in the dark as she whispered, "and you too, Colonel Fury, I do love thee so." There was no time to waste. She needed to report to her pilots' battle station and become her other self: *The Emerald Midnight Hornet!*

Chapter Five

Vampires and Colonels

In the meantime, Colonel Sudden Fury had lost his case in attempting to persuade the Red and Blue Vampires. While Cornwalter, the Blue Vampire, had listened attentively to all that Fury had said, he could not bring himself to believe that one of their best pilots would go so far as to down another valuable aviator. He was caught between wanting to find out the truth of the matter and the urgency of the moment, which was directing Cricket traffic into the Dead Sea, so he simply said to the Intelligence officers, "I will consult with Reynaldo and give you my decision after supper!" Somehow or other, supper usually calmed his nerves. He asked Reynaldo, seated to his left, what he thought of the whole matter? He inquired as to whether or not he believed Colonel Fury's sworn testimony.

Reynaldo had always favored Fury and had shown a jaundiced eye towards Lightning Striker. He had followed both of their military careers and believed Fury to be the more noble of the two pilots. Reynaldo looked intently into Cornwalter's blue eyes and said, "I know how much you think of Colonel Striker; nevertheless, I must say that I don't think it would be out of character for him to act out his hostilities against Colonel Fury, based on the rivalry those two have had their entire lives!" Cornwalter responded, "That may be so, but how could he imagine he would ever get away with such a foolish, dastardly act like that? Did you observe him throughout the proceedings?"

Colonel Striker had remained calm, cool, and collected throughout the intelligence court inquiry, into the downed pilot incident. At the Academy, Striker had a reputation for being one of the best debaters. When it was his turn to speak, he knew that "silence can be golden" at times like these. Therefore, he chose to speak as little as possible. He tried, instead, to turn the tables on them! He stated that he stood on his academic and military record as one of the foremost pilots the Cricket Nation had ever produced.

In an almost muted voice he spoke softly, as one whose character is being assaulted and said, "If after everything you've heard here this afternoon, you still believe I deliberately fired on Colonel Sudden Fury, then by all means feed me to the sharks; otherwise, release me that I might serve our great empire in its hour of need! I have already explained my missing heat-seeking missile. I gave you the facts! We were under attack from enemy fire below. It was coming, I believe, from their battleship *Televiva* or perhaps from their carrier *Heroic*. I couldn't tell; it was such a stormy night! In any case, I fired at their ship, and it might have hit Colonel Fury's airplane instead."

At that point, one of the inquisitors demanded answers, respectfully, remembering Striker's esteemed position among some of the senior officers, not to mention the Blue Vampire. "How is it you used a 'heat-seeking missile?' Are those not reserved for just enemy aircraft?" Colonel Striker broke into a cold sweat, but corrected himself smoothly, asserting that what he meant to say was that he fired in the direction of the enemy ship to hit one of the Frog aircraft that had come up to intercept him. He mentioned he thought it was probably the Emerald Midnight Hornet's plane! The Vampires had discussed Strikers' rebuttal and found it less than credible, but feasible nonetheless. The Blue Vampire, nodding his head up and down and then looking at his co-leader, declared, "It could very well have happened that way. For the good of the service, the fleet's morale, we need to accept Colonel Lightning Striker's testimony! I think we need to hold Colonel Sudden Fury for additional interrogation. We need to find out if Colonel Fury has concocted this entire story to aid the enemy!"

With that, the Red Vampire jumped up and stated, "You have got to be kidding! If Colonel Sudden Fury is telling the truth, and I believe he is, then we will have locked up the wrong guy! I won't stand for it!" It now appeared that each of the leaders had chosen different colonels to defend. After a few more verbal exchanges, Cornwalter relented and decided that Colonel Fury could return to his squadron: "The Red Demons," named in honor of the Red Vampire. Although sometimes the squadron's aviators, jokingly, called themselves "Reynaldo's Hellcats," not surprisingly, the name quickly took hold! Colonel Striker's muted bravado, on the other hand, was more than sufficient to convince most of the skeptics that he was, indeed, innocent. Lightning Striker, then, was also released and allowed to rejoin his squadron, "The Blue Cobras" named, of course, in honor of the Blue Vampire. Apparently, each of the colonels knew which side their bread was buttered on; specifically, whom they could count on in a pinch: They were right! A display of military pride in their respective leaders went a long way.

After a period of two days and nights, the Dead Sea was in the hands of the mighty Cricket Nation! There could be no mistake about that. They controlled all of the waterways, except for a region to the west that appeared to offer no real threat. It was for that very reason that the *HTMS Eagle's* Fleet

Admiral Roberto Da Vinci had decided to position his carrier there. The element of surprise, always a major factor in any battle, could prove costly to the enemy. Da Vinci hoped to stay hidden until it was opportune to strike the Crickets. Thus, by having extirpated their entire Toad and Frog navies from the Dead Sea, the Allied forces endeavored to provide the enemy with a false sense of security. The Allies knew the Crickets would be disappointed, to say the least, that they had not trapped their adversaries. They further anticipated, correctly, that the Crickets would take heart, knowing that everything above the Dead Sea now belonged to them! The Allies original plan, nevertheless, was still very much in effect; nothing had really changed! They believed the Crickets would not rest until every last Allied ship was eliminated: destroyed!

Thus, both the pursuers and the pursued believed their strategies to be superior over their respective enemies. The Crickets had used their "*blitzkrieg*" to great advantage on land, sea, and air. They hoped to overpower the Frogs and Toads with a rerun of what had become their signature battle plan: winning by conviction, by the power of overwhelming numbers, with lifelong military experience, and sheer tenacity of will! Conversely, the Frog and Toad Nations believed their cause was justified! They knew that they had not started this conflagration, but by golly and with the help from above, they were going to finish it! The Allies believed a larger body of water would be more suitable, more favorable to their combined navies. This notion was based on the designs of the Allied ships: Their ships, on the whole, were considerably faster, and while fewer, their aircraft carriers, individually, carried more aircraft. Of greater significance, however, was the opportunity to utilize a more sophisticated naval battle tactic. In this capacity, Da Vinci was the chess master. The Allies would show these cocky Crickets a thing or two when it came to fighting a real navy!

While the Frogs and Toads had not been to war in decades, still, they remembered the stories their great-grandparents had handed down to their children, and they to their children, until the war stories came down to the current generation. The message the stories repeated, time and again, was "It is better to die fighting for a just cause than to live as slaves to a godless society, one where the *non-believing leaders* assumed the role properly reserved for the true **Eternal Supreme Being**!" Individually, each had been negligent about keeping up with the requirements of a modern military machine: that is, with a large modern army, navy, and air force! In spite of each one's major deficiency, by combining their individual forces, the Frogs and Toads stood to become the most powerful military in the region! We learn by yesterday's mistakes, or we perish!

Notwithstanding the aforementioned, each of the two friendly nations had continued to produce separate increased areas of strength, that together made them a formidable opponent; moreover, with the best of the two nations' military scientists working hand-in-hand, they soon had the capacity to create some of the most unique designs in the fabrication of modern air-, sea-, and land-crafts! As time went by, they began to update ancient Chinese ideas concerning "the art of war." These ideas enhanced their ability to wage war.

The use of modern weaponry became a thing of tremendous concern, especially, when it included weapons of mass destruction! These latter weapons, nevertheless, would only be used as a last resort, when all other methods to establish peace had failed! The idea of using ancient Chinese war strategies, therefore, coupled with modern technologically improved weapons of both design and function, came to produce a first-rate military on land, sea, and air!

Their armed services, over time, became one of such magnificent proportion that in its modern application to make war, it dwarfed all other conventional militaristic strategies that employed arms designed specifically to assail their peaceful way of life. Their enemies, the Crickets, would be in for a rude awakening! The kingdoms of the Frogs and Toads would intend to instruct the Crickets on what real war was all about. How sad so many would have to pay the price for the arrogance and greed of a few!

> Generations after the Chinese, the Spanish had used the same feint, attack-and-retreat, to draw the enemy towards them, only to later pulverize the enemy with their superior long-range Castilian cannons! Once entangled in the web, their defense became an offense, catching the enemy by surprise—in a crossfire that emanated from the outermost ships. It made the Spanish the most powerful nation on earth! It was said of them, "The sun never sets on the Spanish Empire!" Their Empire lasted for some time, before another nation, using lighter ships and keener strategy, was able to defeat them. Fierce winds, also, worked to a tremendous disadvantage against the larger Spanish ships: Spain was ultimately defeated!
>
> England, thus, overtook Spain's dominance on the high seas to become the most powerful navy on earth! Later, the Russians would use a similar technique, this time on land and against what appeared to be an invincible German blitzkrieg! In the meantime, only time itself would tell as to the final outcome! For now, just above the navies of the Frogs and Toads, the winds of war were also pressing against the faces of their nemeses, young Cricket seamen. They stood at attention, wearing blue tops and trousers with white beret type hats, overlooking the bows of their vast armada, all singing with beautiful bravado the National Anthem of the Cricket Nation: "Crickets, Crickets, Crickets Over All!"

It was now mid-afternoon. Clouds were beginning to form in the distance. *The Stingray, who* had rejoined *the Scorpion,* took the ceremonial lead. The two ships were moving slightly ahead of the *SS Admiralty.* The submarines: *Barracuda, Eel Electric, and Sharkfin* were patrolling the carriers by flanking the perimeters of these fine ships. The sleek *Piranha,* though some leagues behind, was fast catching up. The mighty Cricket Armada continued moving deeper and deeper into the Dead Sea to finalize its wresting of these waters from the Frogs and Toads!

Somewhere in the *SS Admiralty's* hospital ward, a dramatic incident had just taken place. The Red Vampire, Admiral Reynaldo, had not been seen anywhere onboard in the last 24 hours! Shocking news, however, would eventually grip the entire Cricket navy. What wasn't known to most of the personnel of the Imperial Cricket Armada was that Admiral Reynaldo had presumably died under mysterious circumstances! On his hospital deathbed, he had asked for Colonel Sudden Fury. At first, some of the navy nurses did not want to comply with his demand, saying they had been given strict direct orders that the Admiral was not to be disturbed!. It was then the crusty Admiral pulled out a lazer-revolver and ordered the nurse present to get on the videophone to Colonel Fury, or else he was going to shoot her on the spot! The nurse, half frightened to death, immediately contacted Colonel Fury. The Colonel received the call when he was about to take off on his seek-and-destroy mission against the Toad and Frog Fleets. As the squadron leader, he normally would be recalled only for an emergency, usually involving a major shift in attack plans. When Fury got the news that Reynaldo was in intensive care, he put his squadron of twenty five superior "Hellcat pilots" on "High Alert Readiness" (HAR) and stated he would return within the hour.

Colonel Fury was beside himself and couldn't quite make out what to think about the whole matter; nevertheless, he had some strong reservations, some ideas that kept swirling inside his head. What if Admiral Reynaldo's being in the hospital was no coincidence, that is, something out of the ordinary? His mind was racing, and he couldn't get to the Admiral's bedside soon enough! He knew that the two Vampire leaders had had their differences. Was he, himself, in some way responsible for Reynaldo's being in his current sad state of affairs! He would soon find out. He pushed past two MPs guarding the Admiral's private ward. The next set of MPs thought twice about detaining him and then stepped aside before he ran them over: They would not take sides in this sordid affair. Fury wondered what they knew that he didn't know? One of the MPs nodded and saluted respectfully to the Colonel; Fury, then, quickly returned the nod with a salute, as he entered the Admiral's room very quietly. He was determined to learn more about the extent of the Admiral's ill health.

The Admiral's face turned from strain to happiness and then sheer delight as he caught a glimpse of his favorite officer, Colonel Fury. Fury, as if speaking to his father, asked tenderly what had happened? The Admiral, for the moment, chose simply to whisper in Fury's ear in a demurred, husky voice. He ordered the Colonel to have the room cleared! Fury stated he would comply; however, he advised the Admiral that it might be better if he were permitted to first caution the nurse. The Admiral understood immediately the wisdom of the Colonel's good advice and readily agreed to Fury's wise request.

The Colonel then proceeded to address the nurse, "If you even so much as mention to anyone that I was here, you *won't* live to regret it, because I personally will deal with you!" She stuttered, "Yes sir, you don't have to worry, sir. I know how to keep my mouth shut. I was just trying to follow orders, sir, but now that I see more clearly, I will go about my regular business. Besides, if I may say, Colonel Fury, sir, I always liked you much better than Colonel Striker!" She smiled and Fury knew when women were telling the truth, no matter their position, rank, or intentions. Men—they were something else—another matter altogether! He had witnessed too much treachery among men, yet in spite of these MPs attempting to pull rank when on guard duty, Fury knew the men were on his side in this messy affair! He smiled at the nurse and half-whispered, "I won't forget this kindness." She let her fingers go through her hair, as if straightening it, then wiggled her hips as she sashayed out the door.

Fury, in amazement, couldn't hide his amusement and shook his head in disbelief. At a time like this, he said to himself! He wiped the expression off his face, turned towards Reynaldo, and asked fervently: "How are you feeling, Admiral?" The Admiral replied, "Don't worry about me. I've had a good life and fought the good fight. It's been fun seeing the officers I most respect come into their own. Now, I want to tell you that things have changed a great deal around here!" He looked intently into Fury's brown eyes, "I believe that I was deliberately pushed off the upper deck with the hope that I would die from the fall. Well, it's going to take a lot more than that to kill an old dog like me!"

The two had a good laugh. "Seriously," clearing his throat, "I know, however, that I am not going to make it this time. Not to worry! I have always believed there was a Greater Power in the universe, but I kept it to myself, knowing that one shouldn't speak about those things in our culture. Still, He will judge me fairly! As for you, my son," there was a warm pause, for he had never before used that term with Fury: "Son, you are in real danger!" Fury, disregarding the Admiral's warning, shot back, "You are going to be just fine, my Admiral!" Fury fought back tears; he knew the Admiral was not about overstating things. He continued, after noticing that the Admiral wished to explain, "What is it you wish to say?"

"They have succeeded, I believe, in taking my life: but you, Colonel Sudden Fury, my favorite son, please, please listen and do as I demand! For some time now, there has been a conspiracy involving a change of command. Cornwalter has always wanted the command for himself. He never liked the two of us, because we stood for principles. He devised a plan whereby I would be nullified, that is, assassinated, so that he could bring Colonel Lightning Striker in as his second-in-command. In that capacity, Colonel Striker would follow his wishes and his alone. I have tried to follow the events that have led us to this sorry state of affairs. In the beginning we were justified in defending ourselves, but now the Cricket Empire has lost track of its initial goals: to capture enough land to meet the needs of our growing population. We have long since been able to surpass that goal! Therefore, this war with the Frogs and Toads makes no sense at all!

"At first I mistakenly felt it would be our last war and then we would quit. We could finally rest! That was a major error of judgment on my part. Admiral Cornwalter will have none of that. He wants total world domination under the banner of the Cricket Empire, where he is the sole Emperor! You have been targeted as well. For the good of our nation, I want you to leave with your Red Squadron intact, all 25 of you, the best! Go to the enemy; go to the only ones who can stop this madness. Together under the foreign flag of the Frogs and Toads, you can defeat our Armada and restore our nation to its original noble quest, one where our citizens can live in peace. I knew that you were different when you returned from your imprisonment with the enemy. They must have treated you with kindness. I also noticed a ring you were wearing. It looks like a promise ring I once found in my mother's trousseau. There evidently is another significant person in your life. Who is she?"

Fury smiled and simply replied, "Her name is Rachel Goldsmith; she is the *Emerald Midnight Hornet.*" Admiral Reynaldo smiled the biggest smile; for a few moments his entire being seemed to revive and then he declared, "She must be as beautiful as she is famous! Go to her then! '*Vaya con Dios*' my son!" Reynaldo fell into that deep sleep that takes all valiant leaders to the Great Beyond: He expired! Fury took Reynaldo, the great Red Vampire Admiral, into his arms and wept. After a few moments that seemed like an eternity, he knew what he must do! He moved into action and quickly joined his comrades-in-arms. He asked them to follow him to a remote island where he would explain their mission.

Once there, Fury described what had occurred and all that Admiral Reynaldo had made known to him. He stated he disliked, very much, the entire notion of fighting against his beloved countrymen! Some, no doubt, would view his actions as treasonous, he mentioned. "Unfortunately," he continued, "to follow the Red Vampire would be great folly!" He was left with no other choice, if he truly wished to benefit the Cricket Nation. His mentor, the Red Vampire, had been assassinated! Colonel Fury declared, "It is the Blue Vampire whom I wish to remove! Ironically, we Crickets have lost our best leader, Admiral Reynaldo, our Red Vampire! Fury had always believed from the start that Reynaldo was responsible for their nation's greatest military victories. He was decidedly the better of the two Vampire strategists. Reynaldo had believed what Fury had stated: "We're being led into a trap!" The Blue Vampire had refused to believe it! He saw, instead, an opportunity to capture the Dead Sea for the Crickets. With Admiral Reynaldo out of the way, this accomplishment would make him the most successful Vampire Cricket in their nation's history, insofar as no other Vampire, or Vampires, had amassed so much territory. Colonel Fury further stated that his very life was in extreme peril.

Admiral Cornwalter had always favored Colonel Lightning Striker and now was making the latter his second-in-command! The repercussion of this act meant that the Blue Squadron would become the premier squadron of the Cricket Navy. The Red Squadron would, in all probability, become decommissioned! If they were not shot, these pilots would probably be relegated to inferior positions, such as flight instructors! In any case, they would not be remaining in their leadership capacity. These heralded fearless pilots had received the most decorated honors! This incredible squadron was known to the whole Cricket Nation and beyond; they were the mighty Red Hellcats—named in honor of one mighty Admiral, Admiral Reynaldo the Red Vampire!

Some of the pilots asked if there was any chance to start a revolt; after all, they were very popular among the rest of the Armada's seamen. Fury responded that the Blue Vampire and his cronies, no doubt, were ready for such a mutiny and mutineers would suffer a terrifying death.

> I am leaving to join the Frog and Toad Air Force Command Center (FTAFCC), if they'll have me—or us! I am quite certain they will! I believe that once Admiral Cornwalter is stopped, our nations can declare a peace and restore dignity to all concerned. Think about it? For the first time, our nations can live side by side and learn from each other; we can help each other! Mostly, we have been a displaced people looking for a home, nomadic hunters moving from place to place. Now, it is apparent, we are conquering just for more land—just for its own sake—without regard to anyone but ourselves!
>
> They, on the other hand, have been cultivators of the earth while at the same time developing a very rich culture: a people enjoying the fine arts and the many facets that make for a good life. The problem has been that in expanding our empire we have forgotten to live as free men and free women. Our libraries are full of military tactics and little else. Admiral Reynaldo, on one occasion, had declared 'Someone needs to stop us before we become robotized animals.' He mentioned to me once, 'There must be something else besides war, don't you think, Colonel Fury?' I answered, 'Yes, Highest Admiral, there is peace!' It was then and there that we became fast friends. We both knew we could trust each other. To speak of such things as peace has remained against all the rules!
>
> We have all served our country with honor, with distinction! Thus, the time has come to help others and in so doing help ourselves! I ask that you help me help us, by stopping our Cricket war machine, one that has become our obsession! Those of you who wish to return may now place your Red Squadron Insignia in the Hellcats' Black Box that is next to this tree. There is no shame in returning. We will always be a band of brothers and sisters, no matter which side you will have chosen. I know it is a very difficult decision for each of you. Those of you who wish to follow me to the Frog and Toad Air Force Command Center need not place your insignia anywhere. We will begin with the most senior officers.

One of the officers, who had been listening attentively with the rest, got up from the soft grass beneath the many gorgeous Royal Palm Trees—where they had all been resting—and asked for leave to address the squadron's pilots. Colonel Fury replied, "By all means, Captain Kahn, be my guest. Speak what it is in your heart and mind; share with us all what you wish to convey."

> For the past ten years we have been, as you say, a band of brothers and sisters. I can't help but think what our countrymen and women will think of us. The label traitor does not sit well with me! Having said that, I must also make mention of what a fantastic leader you have been to our brave Hellcats! *(All cheer these words.)* In the end, I suppose, it's not really about us but about the betterment of our Nation: how best to serve either by the continuation of conquest after conquest and all the death, destruction, and mayhem that ensue; or, to finally take a stand against a dictator who takes the people's choices away: War or Peace. At long last! I can't speak for the rest; they will have to speak for themselves. I, for one, will keep my Red Squadron Hellcats Insignia!

The rest of the Squadron's pilots, who had still been resting in the shade of the Royal Palm trees, listening with complete attention, now stood to cheer the two speakers and started singing their squadron's motto: *Hellcats One for All and All for One!*" Fury went to the Black Box, lifted it and turned it upside down and not a single insignia came floating down; nevertheless, another Hellcat asked to be acknowledged and Colonel Fury also permitted him to speak. He was a lanky officer with curly black hair and a wistful smile.

> Colonel, it is true we've been together for quite awhile, with most of us having served at least three or four tours of duty! I, too, have always felt the Blue Vampire was more concerned about his name in the history books than what was best for Cricketstan and our citizens. I am exceedingly concerned, even though I will follow you to the ends of the earth, Colonel, about what will happen to our families, my family and yours! Will the Blue Vampire seek reprisals on them?

Fury took a long deliberate breath and looked the aviator squarely in the eyes and spoke the following:

> I must tell you that the thought has crossed my mind, numerous times, and it is for that reason that I say once again: there is no shame in returning to your carrier, the Scorpion. Please know this: I am very sympathetic to each of your unique situations. Some of you, like I myself, have families while others do not. Still, it is fair to say, it won't go easy on those left behind. We can only hope that this war comes to an abrupt halt and that we can return to liberate those who may have been imprisoned because of our actions. I hold the Black Box up

to you one last time. Again, you have my utmost respect, whatever your decision!

A warm wind came up from the south, to blow through the fronds of the palm trees, and only the waves in the near distance could be heard to whisper, "Follow your heart, follow your heart, for it alone knows better than your mind." No one spoke, not a single word. Each looked to the other for a change of heart; none was forthcoming! It was, thus, decided by all to keep the Hellcats together, down to each and every member present. The men and women there on that eventful afternoon, this outstanding band of brothers and sisters, truly epitomized their squadron's motto, *"All for One and One for All!"*

Colonel Fury stood tall and handsome, facing his Hellcats with a look of deepest love and concern for each member of the unit. They had made a major sacrifice to stay with the Hellcats and with him, as their leader. His Red Squadron, staring back at him, from a slight distance could see a few tears or more finding their way down Fury's left cheek. He smiled bravely, blinked his eyes, and gave the Cricket salute; they all stood at attention and returned the salute and then threw their hats into the air to confirm their unity! After a quick lunch of sandwiches, they were somewhere in the blue yonder heading towards the amassed Armada of the Frogs and Toads. They must have questioned, now that they had taken this momentous step, what would be their fate? There would be no turning back! Still, how would their enemy, the Frogs and Toads, treat them? It remained to be seen.

Colonel Fury radioed to the Emerald Midnight Hornet for permission to land. Rachel was ecstatic to receive his call. Her prayers had been answered. It was almost too much to be believed! She replied to his coded message, prearranged from one of their late-night conversations over coffee and cake, she began: "Make certain not to enter the Red Sea, or all of you will be shot down as enemy combatants! Follow these strict coordinates and enter in groups of five, with each wave ten kilometers apart, while maintaining your air speed at no more than 200 kilometers per hour; or, send in each wave of five aircraft a minimum of three minutes apart. Our aircraft will ascend to intercept each wave and immediately escort you to our Command base. Be certain to disengage your missiles! It will be so good, so very good to see you, Colonel Fury!" Fury simply responded, "The feeling is mutual, Emerald Midnight Hornet; thanks Rachel; we will follow your directive exactly!"

With that, the Hellcats came in five groups of five, with Colonel Fury arriving last. In this way Fury could lend assistance to the other members of the squadron, should the need arise. Obviously, the Frogs and Toads were taking no chances that Fury and his Hellcats were defecting to their side. They were at war and no one was above suspicion, especially if he or she was a Cricket aviator. Against the now-beautiful blue sky of the desert region, the waves of five aircraft appeared as five falling stars, each descending from the Heavens. Somehow or other the word had gotten out that these Cricket aviators were coming over to their side, and the village people, allies of the Frogs and Toads, came out to view this most beauteous sight.

The Cricket aircraft looked strange, compared to the *Mushroom* and *Emperor Penguin Spitfighters* of the Allies. They appeared larger with black and red markings. Each had four jets, with two on either side of their wings. Like the mushroom jets of the Frogs, they could land vertically. Of course, they could also land in the traditional manner: horizontally. Their missiles, while disarmed, had not been dislodged! Fury, for obvious reasons, had made certain of that. Thus, the friendly Crickets could easily rearm their missiles if given the order.

Fury, though well-intentioned, was cautious! He was concerned about the safety of his squadron. Modern naval Toad technology, he believed, had made it possible, through wave propagation, to detect whether or not an incoming aircraft was armed or disarmed. Omni-directional wave propagation, for example, made it possible to detect sounds and to perceive motion based on the principles of wave behavior within the electromagnetic spectrum: radar. The spectrum, itself, encompassed all waves including, of course, those of the broadcast spectrum. Through the special utilization of wave detection, then, the science of physics became an ally to that nation that understood its potential for communication and its marvel at the manipulation of physical objects in space: Time and distance, seemingly, evaporated in its presence. Fury senses were alert to any danger in the air and on the ground. He knew of the risk and of the vulnerability he had placed his squadron and himself! Once all of the Cricket airplanes had landed, Fury noticed numerous armed vehicles of mechanized Frog units encircling the airfield and positioning themselves in a defensive posture! They were ready to commence firing at the friendly invaders, if the need occurred! They also had risked!

Colonel Sudden Fury was the first to open his protective visor and alight from his airplane, he called *The Meteor*. One could easily see a hundred stars, etched on each side of his fuselage: These two hundred stars represented enemy aircraft he had shot down in past and present Cricket missions! They caused awe and fright among those present to witness this historic event. Almost immediately, Colonel Rachel Goldsmith was there to greet him! Their world, it seems, had come full circle.

Apparently the Command Center was also a Frog Naval Air Base. The airfield overlooked a group of buildings used as an advanced flight college for rookie pilots. Occasionally, a ceremonial parade was conducted to receive important and distinguished guests. Due to the brevity of time, the members of the Flight School were not dressed in their ceremonial garb, as usually was the case when more advanced notice had been given for such high-ranking guests. Still, the full complement of 111 soldiers with a reduced band of fifty were present and began to play sturring field martial music, while the Frog air cadets stood at attention. Ironically, the cadets were only one day away from being commissioned full pilots. The long-awaited honorary pinning of the wings to their blue lapels would be delayed a day or so. That event would require dress blues, but for today khaki dress would have to do. In spite of the underdressed cadets, the ceremony was elaborate in every other respect. History was in the making!

The 25 Hellcats stood at attention with Colonel Sudden Fury proudly in front and the might of the Hellcat air power behind them, on the airfield. Their Squadron's colors of red, black, and white were visible on the flagpole carried by one of the *leftenants*. It was briskly waving in the breeze. The elite of the Frog and Toad officers were also at attention. Admiral Cheetah, who happened to stop by to see if the cadets would be ready for combat, was leading a delegation of other high-ranking officers. Among them were Admirals Da Vinci, Pointdextras, and Wisemann, who had recovered from his illness. Generals Lopez and Schwartzwait had come to the base to report on the land war, while General Stanislaus Polaski remained at the front, with the United Nations and Allied Powers fighting the war on land: They were all there that sunny mid-afternoon to coordinate their defenses against the Cricket land, sea, and air operations! No doubt, information available from their recently arrived guests would be of tremendous assistance and would result in a modification of logistics and strategy.

Admiral Cheetah, as the head of the delegation, stopped to position himself just in front of Colonel Fury. The Admiral waited momentarily, for the rest of the Top Brass to line up squarely behind him, and then saluted the Cricket Commander and his Hellcat Squadron. Once the formal salute was executed, both sides happily broke ranks and began shaking hands all around, freely. The military cadets and band, however, were expected to maintain their positions, until the newly arrived guests were escorted to one of the secured buildings, on the campus of the Frog Aeronautical Military College (FAMC).

Once there, the Cricket pilots were invited to eat from an assortment of foods that had hurriedly been prepared for the occasion. The Emerald Midnight Hornet was given permission to join the Admirals and Generals, because of her contributions to this event and because of her standing as the preeminent Frog ace. The Allies knew the importance of getting on with the questioning of these former enemies; notwithstanding this need, they also knew the significance of adhering to military protocol and treating the Crickets with utmost respect. They would not breach impropriety.

Admiral Cheetah's eyes flashed as he eyed each of the Cricket aviators. He stated to Colonel Sudden Fury, "To say that this is a momentous, fantastic reunion of our two sides is a gross understatement! Therefore, I will simply say, welcome Colonel Sudden Fury, and welcome, also, to you famous Cricket Hellcats!" Fury raised his glass of wine to join Cheetah's and those whose glasses were already raised. He responded to Cheetah's invitation with, "Admiral J. Cheetah Obion, we are gratified that you have provided us with sanctuary! We hope fervently that our presence will hasten the war's end, with the Allied Powers restoring a lasting peace to both sides." All participated in the toast and signified their approval with "Here! Here!" "Cheers!" and "May it be so!"

After some polite conversation and exchanges of pleasantries, Admiral Cheetah asked Colonel Fury if he would please fill them in with what inspired his group to come to the Frogs and Toads' side. "We know of your accomplishments and that of your squadron and find it almost impossible to believe you have come over to us. Why?" Over the next hour-and-a-half, Fury went over much of the same ideas he had shared earlier with his own aviators at the remote island, describing for Cheetah and his most senior officers the details of the Red Vampire's assassination! Cheetah needed to acquire more information from them, but decided that the more these special Crickets were made to feel at home, the more forthcoming they would be about military strategic matters: that could wait until after late evening supper, when Fury and his aviators were more relaxed.

After the mid-afternoon dinner, the Cricket aviators were taken on a tour of the Frog Aeronautical Military College (FAMC). It was an impressive site with an immense number of buildings overlooking a high bluff. The entire complex appeared to be very well fortified, with ground-to-air missile installations. The Hellcats, who had understandably been nervous, asked numerous questions concerning the specifics of the College. They listened attentively as their various guides narrated and described the history of this aeronautical learning center. The FAMC was an idea Admiral Cheetah had pursued to fruition, some fifteen years earlier.

He had run into some opposition from senior Frog Admirals then; at the time he was not yet a full admiral. Nevertheless, his persuasive communication skills and his winning personality gained the confidence of certain high-ranking officials, who in the end made his dream of a college become a dream realized! Cheetah shared with Fury that he realized, early on, a lasting peace exists only when a nation is militarily strong! He further stated that, while war will come when it will come, in the end military men of peace must do what they must do to honor the Almighty and country. There is always the hope that casualties will remain limited, at a minimum, and that politicians will come to their senses to forge a peace! The real difficulty, Fury added, is that each side believes it is in the right and finds ways of justifying their cause to gain a glorious end!

Admiral Cheetah Obian was beginning to size up Colonel Fury and could easily understand why he was so famous and beloved by his Hellcats! Cheetah, himself, was equally popular among his subordinates, and he realized that popularity carries with it great responsibility: Those who are not humbled by the affection of others are doomed! Cheetah believed that "conceit" was a leprosy. Many great military leaders, he introspected, had gotten themselves into trouble, over the ages, by not listening to their better angels. Julius Caesar, Napoleon Bonaparte, Mussolini, Adolf Hitler, and others met their demise sooner than later.

Still, there were some who had a penchant for getting themselves into trouble with their superiors, by overstepping their authority. General George Patton wrote the book on this kind of behavior! His incredible boldness caused his soldiers to claim, "There goes ole 'Blood and Guts': our blood and his guts!" It was not a compliment. In spite of his troubles, Patton's valiant deeds remain in the memory of his countrymen, Cheetah surmised. The memories of dictators, however, have mostly been erased by the removal of their grandiose statues, the ones that glorified their accomplishments while they were in power! Where are the statues of Joseph Stalin, Generalissimo Francisco Franco, and Saddam Hussein, and the like? Gone or reduced! Admiral Cheetah Obian excused himself for his daydreaming and relayed to Fury that he was musing over the kind of men and women that history remembers. He asked of Colonel Fury what he thought others would write about the two of them?

"I have never given it too much thought" was Fury's response. "What I have learned, when reading books concerning you, is that you are much admired by peoples on various continents, because of your generosity to their needs. I believe that charity is the greatest virtue." Cheetah answered, "You flatter me much too much, Colonel Fury. I assure you that if I am well thought of it is not because of my successes; rather, it has more to do with my attempts. The real winners are the people themselves! They continue to remind me that decency still prevails on the planet; what we have to do is nourish it."

The two leaders continued their walk around the beautiful campus and then heard the trumpet sound: It was calling them to mess! The Admiral said he hoped the earlier meal was to the Crickets' liking. If not, tonight's meal would be a whole lot better. Now that the chefs had had sufficient time to research what best suited the taste of the Cricket Aviators, they knew just what to serve. Fury responded with an "I thank you" smile that conveyed his pleasure at Cheetah's hospitality! They were getting on famously, as the Brits say. After a delightful meal, the two sides settled in for some more serious talk, about how best to overcome the advancing Cricket sea- and air-power. For the moment that topic seemed most pressing to the older admirals of the Frogs and Toads! When Fury was queried on his personal views, he reiterated what he had stated earlier:

> My being here is to defeat the Blue Vampire, Admiral Cornwalter! If not for him and the assassination of my mentor and friend, the Red Vampire, Admiral Reynaldo, we might not be in this fix! That's a moot point, now that the Evil One has temporarily triumphed! I know his mind and what he wants. I believe I also know the key to destroying his plans. He desires nothing less than total world domination! His weakness is his unflinching aggressiveness! Your admirals have strategized properly by leading him into a trap. I warned them of your strategy that would ensnare them; nevertheless, I chose not to fully explain that you had built a mammoth canal leading into the Red Sea! Admiral Reynaldo, the better strategist of the two Vampires, suspected that I knew more than I was conveying, but did not pursue the point. He simply accepted what I had implied.
>
> I understand his reasons. He didn't trust Admiral Cornwalter. I suspect he didn't want the Blue Vampire to succeed, if he, Admiral

Reynaldo, were out of the picture. Perhaps he felt it was the last decent thing he could do for his countrymen: keeping quite about a Cricket military success, that in the end spelled the doom of ever having a democratic nation, one where Crickets could live in peace with their neighbors! For me, there was never any doubt about your "Great Canal!" As I have shared with some of you already, I had flown over the Dead Sea area, when one of your *PT 109-9* Amphibious Assault Units transported the Emerald Midnight Hornet, other military personnel, and me from the Televiva to the HTMS Eagle. From a short distance, I could readily see that your ships were disappearing beyond the horizon; therefore, I concluded it could only mean one thing: an exit, that hithertofore did not exist!

What say you of me? Am I here for peace or war? I say to you leaders of the Frogs and Toads, that this Blue Vampire knows no stopping, except he is humiliated on the sea and in the air. While the armies of the Crickets are many and strong, I, nevertheless, agree with those who are for concentrating your greatest efforts on the high seas, where the Cricket Armada expects a sudden and complete victory! If your land militia is to have a real fighting chance for victory in the field, you must first stop the Cricket supply ships that are being protected by the Armada. The solution, then, is to annihilate the mighty Cricket Carriers and the Cricket Submarines that represent the backbone of their naval war machine! In the end, it will come down to the best ships and the best strategists.

The military exchange of information between the Allied officers and Fury resulted in both parties gaining a deeper appreciation of the other! Generals Lopez and Schwartzwait had, unfortunately, left immediately after dinner, earlier in the day. They needed to meet with General Stanislaus Polaski, at the front, to determine if their troops had adequate supplies and equipment to keep them engaged. Just when it appeared that the Frogs and Toads had the Crickets with their backs against the sea, the enemy made an unexpected offensive that saw the Allied Forces lose ground! Admirals Pointdextras and Da Vinci, nevertheless, had remained with Cheetah until after the military convocation that followed supper was finished. The meeting caused them to feel satisfied that they were well positioned to repel the might of the Blue Vampire and his new Second-in-Command, Rear Admiral Lightning Striker!

Special Allied agents, earlier, had gained the startling news of Lightning Striker's promotion. These agents, embedded near Cricketstan, quickly relayed the development to HQ. Admirals Pointdextras and Da Vinci, then, promptly left with the aid of two *Emperor Penguin Spitfighters* that returned them to separate Toad carriers: the *Eagle* and the *Heroic*, respectively. The *HTMS Eagle* still remained undetected behind one of a number of unassuming islets in the density of the Dead Sea. The *HTMS Heroic*, on the other hand, was currently well positioned deep in the Red Sea, with an array of their best and fastest nuclear subs nearby.

The *Javelin* and the *Tomahawker,* the fastest of the *Heroic's* subs, for their part, were moving deeper into the Sea of Arabia. Their mission was to seek and destroy any unforeseen enemy traffic! Admiral Weismann, as it turns out, had asked Admiral Cheetah if Admiral Pointdextras could he shifted, temporarily, to the *HTMS Heroic* now under his command. He reasoned that by reassigning Admiral Pointdextras to the *Heroic*, it would lend much-needed assistance to him in complying with all of Central Command's naval action directives, once things started to erupt....and that hour wouldn't wait long!

As Fury had predicted, the asylum-seeking Crickets under his leadership would be seen as rebels. Their families, as well as his own, would be treated harshly by Cornwalter! The Blue Vampire had given the order to Rear Admiral Lightning Striker to have the families of these, in Cornwalter's words, "absent without leave (AWOL) renegades **punished in *absencia*!**" Thus, the families of the Hellcat Aviators were made to march through the main streets of Cricketstan dressed in black, with the initials of **FTS** (Frog and Toad Sympathizer) painted in large white letters on the backs of their shirts!

They were then sent to the same prison where Esther was being detained. Once they were in prison, Esther made them as comfortable as she could, with the minimum of possessions she had been allowed to acquire. Towels and toiletries were scarce and food was at a premium. Somehow or other, though, Esther had been able to get some of these items with money she periodically gave to the guards! They had not been able to confiscate all of her money at the time of her kidnapping. Fortunately, some of the women Cricket guards had felt sorry for Esther and let her keep most of the sum of money she had with her: They knew the other guards could be bribed and that that money could buy her some comforts, albeit in prison.

Oddly enough, once it became known that the Red Vampire had mysteriously perished, the families of the Hellcat Aviators knew their aviator sons and daughters would have to escape, if they were to save their own lives. They were proud of what their sons and daughters had accomplished for the nation. The families held their heads high, in spite of it all! Still, they knew the country was now in the worst hands possible. Cornwalter was not the compassionate soul that Reynaldo had been. When they had marched down the main street of the largest Cricket city, *Cricketstonia,* many of the Blue Vampire supporters came out to jeer them and throw refuse at them. The families, nevertheless, continued to maintain their dignity and never bowed to any of the hecklers. It was one of the saddest days for the Empire! The other Crickets were afraid to speak out at the injustice of it all, for fear that they, too, might suffer the same fate!

The exterior of the prison was much like a small fortress, dug into the side of a huge cliff. The only entrance to the prison was a large long ramp that pulled cars upward, or lowered them downward, as the case might be, to allow traffic both ways. The distance for the ride up and down was two hundred feet each way. These tram cars, that carried guards and prisoners to and from the prison, could accommodate about twenty people. On the day the families of the prisoners were taken up to the prison, it had been raining very hard! The children huddled together to keep warm. The parents reassured them that someday, soon, good Crickets and their friends would come to liberate them! When they entered the prison, itself, they found a gruff group of guards, who went about their business, checking the papers of each of the new inmates. A few of the guards knew some of the family members and seemed to be more sympathetic. They, lovingly, let these families keep some of their personal belongings, in spite of regulations to the contrary.

The interior of the cells was of a modern design with electronic gates that opened and closed with the push of a button. The children were wide-eyed at the technology that made all these iron-barred walls move so smoothly. Once inside, however, there was no mistaking the feeling of confinement. As nightfall came to Cricketstonia's military prison, the parents would tell the children stories about the past glorious days of Crickets, a time when good leaders prevailed. They would tell them stories about how things were going to be, when nice leaders once again would govern their nation. Until then, a mother could be heard rocking her child to sleep, *"Hush, little baby, don't you cry, the moon is near and almost high; hush, little baby, don't you sigh; your mommy's here—and with thee* (pause) *very soon ...will lie."*

Rachel Goldsmith was eating lunch with Fury and his Hellcats, and she mentioned how impressed everyone was with the way the Crickets had conducted themselves throughout their stay. After lunch, she was told by the commanding officer of the hangars that the Cricket Aircraft would be ready for their inspection. They learned the airplanes had needed to be checked out to make certain of their combat readiness; moreover, a slight modification in the airplanes' exterior color design also had needed to be made; otherwise, there would be no way of differentiating between the friendly Crickets and the enemy Crickets, when the dogfights, that were sure to come, came!

Thus, after eating lunch, Rachel, Fury, and the Crickets walked towards the hangars to inspect their airplanes. Things had quieted down, now that all of the top brass of the Frog and Toad leadership had departed for other military strongholds. Admiral Cheetah had stated he would be joining other senior officers on the battleship *Televiva* that was now entering the Red Sea. He had given Rachel and Fury orders to inflict as much damage as possible on any enemy that might come upon them. When and if necessary, he further stated, you must evacuate this remote military base for duty aboard the *Eagle*.

The newly commissioned Frog and Toad Cadets, now aviators, Cheetah explained, would be providing aerial support for the land forces near Frogville, if a retreat from the base became necessary! In their walk towards the hangars, Rachel and Fury communicated to the rest what scenario would take place, for the preservation of military lives. The strategy, then, was to fight, evacuate the base, and then join forces with stronger military units. If after you've given it your all, and your force is weakened, the Emerald Midnight Hornet promulgated, the noblest thing to do is to retreat so that you can live to fight another day. "Yes!" they all agreed, "first we will fight!" And "No!" they all affirmed, "there will be no *flight* without first a *fight!*"

The remote base, that also housed the military college and served as a rendezvous for senior officers of all the various armed forces, stood in sharp contrast to Cricket bases Fury and the Hellcats had seen. To begin with, in spite of its size, the college and the dozen hangars that could accommodate at least ten planes each, for the Crickets, seemed smaller; moreover, it was adjacent to the seas. Cricket bases, on the other hand, were all inland and protected by mountains. They were much larger to be sure, at least twice as large as this one! What the Crickets could not know was that this base was also very small, compared to other Allied bases scattered along the Jordan and beyond.

The "Canal Base," as it was sometimes referred to, was located some ten miles from the canal that now linked the Dead Sea to the Red Sea. At the base's highest point, where the lookout tower was situated, communication officers, with the aid of field glasses, could clearly see the canal area. Most of the antiaircraft guns pointed towards the seas. A few faced inland. In theory, it was felt that any enemy approaching the canal would most likely invade by sea. The canal, of course, had additional protection from guns positioned on either side of its construction. A great deal of security surrounded the base! Any roads that approached from fifty miles or more were off limits. Most comings and goings were done by air and sea.

As to the Great Canal's security, Admirals Cheetah, Da Vinci, and Pointdextras believed the enemy Crickets would not want to eviscerate the canal with air raids that would make passage impossible. The Great Canal was an engineering marvel! The Crickets, they continued, felt they could still destroy the Allied Fleet and keep the Canal as one of their most prized possessions! Strategically, it also left a door opened, in the event that the Upper Jordan was closed to them. The Crickets, they realized, had ships up and down the upper and lower portions of the Jordan. In their aggressiveness and overconfidence, the Crickets, the Allied senior officers felt, would move all of their ships south for the Armageddon that was to come.

In that scenario, the *HFMS King David*, a carrier not known to the Crickets, could approach from above the waters of the Jordan and make its way south! It would, they hoped, be largely undetected as an Allied ship of war, because the unique design of this Frog carrier was vastly different from that of the Toad carriers *HTMS Eagle* and *HTMS Heroic!* These were all tactical and strategical theories, including calculated risks that warriors create, in an effort to outwit the enemy. In war, deception is the greatest art!

Rachel, Fury, and the Hellcats arrived at the hangars and were very pleased that Fury's airplanes had been given a fresh paint job. The new design would also help distinguish the friendly Cricket Squadron from the enemy Cricket airplanes. These friendly aircraft were now a sleek black, with three red diagonal stripes, resembling chevrons, located on both sides of the aircraft's fuselage: They still resembled the fighters they once were, only this time their new appearance provided them with a new identity! They would be fighting for liberty alongside the Frogs and Toads: In short, they were now the most famous of the new allies!

Their mission was clear: defeat the Blue Vampire, Admiralissimo Cornwalter! The task would not be an easy one. He knew his countrymen. They were disciplined and resourceful. They had never lost a war since coming to live on the crust of the Earth. The Crickets believed it was their destiny to rule all the peoples and tribes of the planet. Defeating the Frogs and Toads would give them possession of the entire Holy Land. Colonel Fury also knew that once Cornwalter was removed, along with his senior officers, there would be a much better opportunity to achieve a lasting peace. Peace was an interesting word that conveyed an ideal not sought by the various Vampire leaders in generations. It was not a word that true warriors welcomed, Cornwalter had once declared, at a graduation ceremony honoring the installation of new Cricket officers, at the Air Force of the Cricket Military Academy: AFCMA. To say the new officers were now eager to test their mettle would be a gross understatement!

As it happened, Rachel had asked Colonel Fury and his Hellcats to bow their heads for a moment of silence, in honor of all those who had died on both sides of the conflict; in addition, for those who were about to die in the cause of freedom. The Hellcats followed Fury's example and bowed their heads in unity as a display of respect. They had all lost beloved friends. Now it was time to finish the task that lay ahead of them. She asked Fury if it would be all right to recite a short prayer that had given the Frogs courage. He smiled and said "of course!"

> Dear Great and Noble Spirit of the Universe, help us as we go forth to defeat an evil force. One nation stands for conquest, while the other is so desirous of an enduring peace. Empower us to win so that all may live together harmoniously, bringing us to a much better tomorrow. Mostly, thank you for the services of these brave, noble, and friendly Crickets who join us in our quest for achieving victory over a powerful adversary. Bless us, too, this day, as we valiantly go forth to lead our comrades in harm's way. Give us, therefore, strength, courage, wisdom, forbearance, and the love for others, as you have loved us. Amen.

Having finished this emotional and heartfelt prayer, the friendly Crickets looked into the eyes of their once adversary, the Emerald Midnight Hornet, and a mist shone from the Crickets' eyes communicating that they were cognizant of an aura that seemed to settle and then imbue the entire group. There was an air in the room that brought about a transformation in each of them: that they were fast becoming kindred spirits was no longer in doubt! In the past, when they had prepared for battles, the Crickets would call upon their ancestors for strength; but Rachel's prayer did not reflect the pompous bellicosity of speeches made by former Cricket senior officers. Instead, those sincere and quiet words, ushered forth from Rachel's lips, were more of a declaration, or better yet, a testimonial of love. It humbly called upon the Creator of all living and nonliving things to mitigate a solution, to the unpredictable situation that lay ahead: the kind that occurs when warriors are pitted against each other!

One of the pilots spoke up and asked if it would be all right to take their freshly painted airplanes for a spin, in the blue yonder. Fury looked for some reassurance from Rachel and they both uttered "yes" at the same time. Much laughter was heard and then they all quickly got into their respective airplanes, that is, the Crickets did. Within a few minutes they were all airborne, except for Fury and Rachel. No sooner had the Hellcats made their circumnavigation of the airfield, when they were seen heading due south, In their famous, traditional Red Raider formation—just out of sight of those still remaining on the airfield.

Soon after, dark clouds began to appear and the winds picked-up with force! At about the same time, coming from the north, another formation was rapidly moving into the Academy's airspace. At first, the shape of the airplanes looked like those that had just abandoned the hangars; however, these wore the familiar colors and insignias that Colonel Sudden Fury had seen for the better part of his adult life: yes, they were blue enemy Cricket Fighters! As they approached closer, Fury could clearly see that they were the elite Blue Squadron, most likely being led by Lightning Striker! But, how could they have possibly known where to find them? Fury was positive he had covered his tracks! Rachel was beside herself. She was in total disbelief. This couldn't' be happening! She looked at Fury with much scorn.

Rachel: *(totally disregarding safety or running for cover)* Well, Colonel Fury, is this what I should have expected from someone I trusted!

Fury: *(grabbing her and dashing for cover to a nearby hangar)* Look, Rachel, I am just as surprised as you are! I have no idea how they managed to find me: *(correcting himself)* us! I promise on my mother's grave that I would never betray the love I have for you and the esteem I hold for your comrades! *(Taking Rachel into his arms he attempts to embrace her, but she fights him off.)* What can I do to convince you?

Rachel: It's a little late for that, don't you think?

Fury: *(After seeing she is relatively safe, and running onto the airfield to direct traffic, as many of the Frog and Toad aircraft attempt to leave the field to encounter the enemy, now directly above)* I hope this counts for something!

Rachel: Please no! You'll be killed! I believe you. I love you!

Incredible as it seems, even though many of the Academy's hangars were being decimated by the Blue Squadron's surprise attack, Fury seemed no worse for his efforts to assist his new friends, the Frogs and Toads. Bombs and bullets were dropping out of the sky, all around! Some bullets had narrowly missed Fury's shoes! Yet, no sooner had the enemy arrived, than Rachel saw the friendly Red Raider Squadron joining forces with the Frog and Toad Air Force, doing aerial battle against the aggressor! The Red chevrons on the black aircraft made the friendly, brave Crickets stand out quite distinctly from the Blue Squadron, whose colors were actually a lighter shade of blue, with a hint of yellow on the aircrafts' noses. The yellow was added to give the impression of a flame fanning out from the nose of the aircraft. These colors, for the most part, acted as a good camouflage in the sky and made the enemy aircraft difficult to see in the daylight!

The black color of the friendly Crickets—except for the crimson chevrons, on the other hand, was almost impossible to see as night approached. In addition, the Frogs and Toads' aircraft was a sky green that also possessed three diagonal crimson strips, but these chevrons—unlike those of the friendly Crickets—were displayed on both wings, instead of on the fuselage; the nose of their aircraft, moreover, was a dramatic forest green. These colors, it turns out, became more difficult to see as the afternoon turned into evening. Thus, the various squadrons: the "lighter Blue" of the enemy Crickets, the "sky Green" of the Frogs and Toads, and the "midnight Black" of the friendly Crickets brought distinct colors into the combat zone! The activity in the sky, oddly enough, seamed to misrepresent itself! If not for the killing, the festive colors gave one the impression of seeing youngsters at a state fair or holiday outing enjoying amusement rides! Here, each of the respective sky riders was trying desperately to catch the other, with—as in a carrousel—no one ever gaining the advantage. This menagerie, however, was neither a fair nor a carnival: It was war!

Rachel had been looking skyward, when she heard an airplane approaching from the right. The sound of the aircraft was not that of her squadron. As she continued turning to her right, she saw another pilot in a black aircraft. When it appeared closer, she saw that it was Fury's airplane leaving the runway. He waved at her as his machine left the ground. Rachel jumped up and down! This time Rachel was furious for a different reason: He had left without saying a word! She wanted very much to be up there, to be a part of the action; instead, she was watching the aerobatics from below. "No," she said to herself, "not at all, this simply will not do! Not in the least!" In no time, she, too, was in her aircraft, zooming down the runway and then pulling up the wheels, as her jet moved swiftly to join Fury and the rest, against the aerial might of Cornwalter's elite Blue Raiders.

Now that the fight among the three combatants was in full swing, the antiaircraft guns had momentarily stopped shooting from below. They, obviously, were concerned that they might, inadvertently, hit one of their own airplanes defending the base. The newly commissioned Frog and Toad pilots were, absolutely, no match for the much more experienced enemy Cricket fighters. The Blue Squadron was having a field day tearing the freshman pilots apart! It almost seemed like a complete rout of the defending "Greenbacks," as the Frog and Toad Air Force referred to themselves, until senior pilot Greenbacks, from across the Canal, came to their rescue!

When these *Mushroom* and *Emperor Penguin Spitfighters* finally arrived, the tide started to turn in favor of the Frogs and Toads. It was, to be sure, the arrival of Colonel Sudden Fury's "Black Hellcats" that ultimately made the difference! The black airplanes, with their crimson-red chevrons, contrasted and shone quite vividly against the backdrop of the other aircraft, since it was still light. It was, as they say, an incredible sight to behold: the two opposing Cricket air forces, now, challenging each other for dominion over the skies! Fury knew these fighters meant business. They were, after all, the Blue Vampire's elite, his favorites! These Cricket fighters, moreover, had an additional incentive besides staying alive; they would be rewarded handsomely for each enemy aircraft they smoked out of existence!

Fury and Rachel each had an advantage of engaging the enemy for different reasons. Colonel Fury had flown with them and knew their unique, flying habits, their individual styles, and their various strategies! The Emerald Midnight Hornet had engaged them as enemies before and lived to tell about it. Cornwalter had offered a huge reward for any of the heads belonging to the friendly Crickets. An even larger reward would be forthcoming, if the Emerald Midnight Hornet were killed, or even incapacitated. The highest reward was saved for Colonel Sudden Fury's scalp! Cornwalter preferred taking him alive, so that he could later torture him. Fury, however, was not about to be taken alive. He sought only one reward for himself and that was bringing the Blue Vampire before an international tribunal, to be tried on numerous crimes against humanity and the good citizens of the world.

As the fighting continued, Fury and Lightning Striker passed each other in the sky. Striker pointed to Fury, indicating that Fury was going down and out! He seemed to be saying, "I've got you, you traitor!" They passed each other again and this time Fury gave Striker an old Cricket salute that meant "You are finished; make your peace with your ancestors!" The salute began with closed fingers and an open palm moving across the throat then eventually a positioning of the fingers across the upper brow of the right eye; ultimately, the hand moved rapidly down the right side of the cheekbone.

Fury didn't care what it took. He was determined to remove the second most decorated Cricket pilot: one who had almost caused the loss of his own life! Fury remembered that stormy night when Striker had shot him out of the sky, and then, he, Colonel Sudden Fury, had spent some horrific hours in the cold, tumultuous sea! "If not for Rachel," he thought, "I would not have survived!" It was payback time! Justice owed Fury and his Hellcats a long overdue installment, at the very least! Once accomplished, it would go a long way in defeating the evil, enemy Crickets.

The Frog and Toad aviators and their friendly Crickets were outnumbered two to one by Lightning Striker's Blue Demons. As Admiral Cornwalter's Second-in-Command, Striker recognized that he had a tremendous opportunity to win greater fame by defeating, of all aviators, Colonel Fury. Striker enjoyed his new position as Admiral Lightning Striker. He felt, however, that he had to defeat Fury or else face a demotion in rank or possibly dismissal! The Blue Vampire had been very clear about that: He was not given to losing. The world would be his at any cost. As the sky battle raged on, the Allies were holding their own! The reason for their success centered on the performance of their *Mushroom* and *Emperor Penguin Spitfighters*; moreover, two new weapons in the sky made their task all the easier. They had just commissioned two new fighters: The Frog *F-77 Silverbird* that could reach speeds of up to 2,500 miles per hour, and the Toad *T-111 Delta Dragon* that was just a trifle slower but carried more weaponry.

After twenty to twenty-five minutes of combat in the upper stratosphere, Striker decided to retreat to fight another day. He had not fully accomplished his mission, since Fury was still shooting down some Blue Demon fighters; nevertheless, Striker considered that he had caused substantial damage on the ground, with his surprise attack that left half the hangars smoldering and still others in flames; in addition, he had reduced some of the Allied Air Force by twenty percent, or fifteen downed aircraft. The Allies, on the other hand, could claim thirty percent enemy shot down, or forty five downed Blue Demons. The aftermath left Fury and the Emerald Midnight Hornet with a total of 60 fighters still intact; whereas Striker returned to his home base with a total of 105. To be sure, the Allies lost more airplanes than the enemy. When the aircraft in the hangars were added to the lost column, another 42 aircraft brought the sum to 57 lost!

The Allies had acquitted themselves remarkably in the air, especially taking into account that their pilots—for the most part—were recently commissioned and with little or no experience in real air engagement. Still, they were caught flatfooted on the ground! Not only did they lose airplanes, they lost lives! Fortunately, most of the Allied pilots were eating at the mess; on the other hand, some mechanics, sadly enough, had been killed while servicing aircraft. An early count, for those on the ground, left the wounded and dead at 20. In all, the final count would list 19 dead and 16 wounded, as sky and ground casualties for the Frogs, Toads, and Hellcats. The enemy Crickets, conversely, would list 42 dead, with an additional three downed aviators—as possibly taken prisoner: Apparently, three enemy parachutes had been sighted near the base floating down to earth, early in the engagement.

In spite of not being able to eliminate Colonel Fury, Admiral Striker was received with much fanfare. The whole mission was viewed as a huge success! As Striker and his Blue Demons landed on the various aircraft carriers, that is, the *Stingray* and the *Scorpion*, they were treated to a fabulous welcome-back-to-ship dinner. The Blue Vampire had hoped that Fury and the Emerald Midnight Hornet might be listed among the dead; still, he was very pleased.

They had surprised the Allies and had taken the advantage for the second time. The submarines: the *Piranha*, the *Eel Electric*, the *Barracuda*, and the *Sharkfin*, he relished in reflection, had been responsible for pushing the Frogs and Toads out of the Jordan and farther south. Cornwalter was so jubilant that he threw a ball for his returning aviator heroes. He wanted to enjoy the moment and to fortify the already high spirits of his aviators, by pinning combat medals on his favorite pilots at the ball.

Admiral Lightning Striker received the highest award for the most kills: four. The devastation his flying armada had caused, to the Frog Academy, however, was viewed with even greater applause by all attending the ball. The enemy Crickets had no way of knowing exactly how many Frogs, Toads, and members of Fury's Hellcats had perished on the ground, while in the hangars. They mistakenly thought there must have been an additional 50 or more. No matter, half the hangars were gone! That, of course, meant half of the airplanes stationed there were now history: *finito*, finished! What great deeds would they accomplish next? They whirled and danced the night away, as their mighty navy made its way through the Great Canal and into the orifice that became the great Red Sea.

All this time the Frogs and Toads and their friendly Crickets took stock of what had transpired. In sum, they had lost fewer aviators; however, they also believed they had lost more aircraft. Fortunately, the airplanes that had been lost in the hangars were of an older vintage! Furthermore, the hangars, for the most part, had contained far fewer aircraft than they were capable of storing. It was ultimately revealed, at the high-level aftermath security meeting, that Admirals Cheetah and Da Vinci had suspected that Cornwalter's agents had given the Blue Vampire the necessary information. This intelligence not only provided the location of the Academy, but also specified the area's military strengths and weaknesses. The report suggested the Academy was indeed vulnerable to attack! It strongly advised Cornwalter to attack suddenly and with force. It further directed that by flying low, the Crickets' Blue Squadron could lead their aerial strike force in a blistering mission against their adversaries.

Admiral Wisemann had flown to the Academy in order to brief the senior officers, including the Emerald Midnight Hornet, Colonel Sudden Fury, and the Ghost, who had also flown in to attend the briefing. Wisemann stated that with the aid of the Frog *F-77s* and the Toad *T-111s* and, of course, Fury and his Hellcats, the Allies were able to masterfully thwart the enemy's surprise attack. "In fact," he elaborated, "the forthcoming attack was not a surprise in the least. We deeply regret the loss of life that occurred both in the air and on the ground; nevertheless, our strategy all along has been to give the invader a false sense of security! Their attack has emboldened them to pursue us deeper into the Red Sea; hopefully, they will continue their aggressive posture so that we can annihilate them in deeper waters: the Sea of Arabia! If need be, we'll finish them off in the great Indian Ocean!"

With those encouraging words, all stood to applaud the Admiral. If he had been ill in the past, he certainly did not look it now: He was the picture of good health. No great harm, he assured them, had paid a visit. The Allies continued to be masters of their destiny. After a sincere and sustained moment of silence to honor the fallen, the officers remained for some pastry and beverages. The main talk centered around wanting to encounter the dastardly Crickets sooner than later!

Cornwalter's entire navy was now deep into the Red Sea, as a result of going through the Great Canal and the Gulf of Aqaba. The Toad Carrier, *HTMS Eagle,* was just beginning to move from behind its place of hiding, on the edge of the Dead Sea; whilst the Frog Carrier, *HFMS King David,* was picking up speed moving south from the upper Jordan River. Had satellite imaging been available and reliable, it would have shown the trap beginning to close on the enemy Crickets; however, the United Nations had long since ruled out the use of satellites for anything but peaceful purposes! Even though the UN supported the Frogs and Toads, it had also sanctioned itself against what it called "taking unfair advantage of the skies!" Their Charter continued, "We must take the noble high ground, if we are to claim a morality that truly passes the test of time, one that supersedes our humble existence. In that spirit and with trust in a Higher Power, goodness will triumph over evil!"

One night had passed, with leaders on both sides of the conflict summoning their senior officers to discuss the next plan of action. The Crickets were extremely pleased with what they had been able to accomplish. While the Princess Sophia had made good her escape, they believed she could not outdistance the long tentacles that the Cricket military extended throughout the entire region: She would be caught in time, no matter the cost, they promised. The land war continued to sway, back and forth; hence, all the more reason why the sea war had to be completed. There was no doubt in The Blue Vampire's mind as to what the final outcome would be: another magnificent Cricket victory! He, Admiral Cornwalter, the sole Vampire leader would receive all the glory, now that Admiral Reynaldo, the Red Vampire, had been eliminated through treachery.

Cornwalter made certain, having elevated himself to Emperor, that no vestiges of Reynaldo remained. All statues and images were discarded; moreover, the Red Vampire's name was never to be spoken in public or private. The consequences for disobeying this law would be very grim, indeed! Cornwalter's reconnaissance, in the meantime, had not been able to find any enemy ships along the lower Jordan, in the Dead Sea, or west of the Sinai Peninsula; therefore, things were going according to the Cricket plan of attack. They would consolidate the captured territories and proceed to liquidate the remnants of the Frog and Toad Navies, once they caught up with them. The enemy, they believed, was trying to escape beyond the Arabian Sea. They had to be taught a lesson. He mused; this will be great fun!

Chapter Six

Dreams, Nightmares, and Nightflights

Rachel Goldsmith awakened to a soft knock on her door. She put on a yellow robe her mother had given to her as a birthday gift and rushed to the door. A glance at the clock indicated it was 3:33 a.m.; Rachel wondered who could be knocking at this hour of the night! It was pitch black outside! She looked through the peephole that revealed only a dark silhouette: Rachel deliberated as to whether or not she should put on the outside light but decided against it. The Emerald Midnight Hornet always possessed a sidearm nearby! It was positioned on a high nightstand, next to the door. She wondered if it could be Fury? After several sustained fast heartbeats, the colonel cautiously opened the door that remained partially jammed as a result of a safety chain, at the upper portion of the doorway.

Fury: Open the door!

Rachel: Just a second, I'll release the safety chain! Please come in. What's the matter?

Fury: *(anticipating her questions)* I fell asleep with no difficulty. I guess we've both been through a lot these past few days. Now that we're here, I'm still getting used to the *HTMS Eagle*. What a fantastic carrier! As I was saying, I fell asleep with little difficulty, but I had a very disturbing nightmare. 'Perhaps,' I reasoned, 'Rachel can help me decipher it.'

Rachel: Please continue. By the way, can I heat up some tea or coffee?

Fury: Tea sounds just fine: one lump of sugar with a splash of milk. Thanks, Rachel.

Rachel: Ok. Well, you were saying...

Fury: Yes, thanks! In my dream a small creature the size of your thumb was devouring another of equal size. The one being devoured was putting up a tremendous fight, but to no avail. The creature that struck first caught the other by the throat with several huge bites, using its massive razor-sharp teeth. The rest was just as gory! What do you make of it?

Rachel: I hope the tea is to your liking. Take a sip.

Fury: Great, thanks again and, by the way, sorry to disturb your peace at such an early hour.

Rachel: *(attempting to calm him)* Quite all right! I am pleased you are enjoying the tea. It's a gift from my father! He purchased it on one of his many trips to the Orient.

Fury: That's nice. *(sipping again, now a bit more relaxed)* My dream?

Rachel: Your dream or nightmare, Wow! It's fascinating! Don't you see? It's quite obvious. The creature being devoured—by the creature doing the attacking and devouring—is the Cricket Navy! They struck us first and destroyed our ships: the ones taken out of mothball. It gave them the impression that their vessels were superior to ours, but it was all a ruse! We knew we would lose the first round. We were giving them just the bait they needed, and they swallowed it hook, line, and sinker! Now, we are ready to attack them as they leave the Red Sea and enter the Arabian Sea. We will hit them with all we've got! We have the mighty *HTMS Heroic* that struck their carrier *Stingray*; in addition, we've got our majestic battleships, along with our many other ships, not to mention our stupendous Tiger Submarine Fleet that is ready to pounce on them. Those razor teeth, you were dreaming about, are the individual submarines that make up our Tiger Fleet's mouth!

Fury: Thanks for the interpretation. You seem to be echoing the Frog and Toad naval strategy against the evil side, of what used to be a mighty nation; albeit, one that had won one-too-many victories!

Rachel: I know how arduous this new alliance must be for you. In your heart you know you've done the right thing by supporting us over the Blue Vampire. *(giving him a loving smile mixed with pathos)* I can't help being a little biased; given your situation, I hope I would have the courage to fight against my own, if I knew that it was their only hope for salvation. No matter, we are in this together to the finish. I have never really doubted you, even when you escaped with our mushroom jet, only to learn of Admiral Reynaldo's fate. Your nation's loss has been our gain. He who knows all and loves best will stand by you, as will I! Your men adore you! The Eternal One loves you, as do I! You truly are a leader among men!

Fury: You are far too kind. I do, however, welcome your words of encouragement. I am not as strong as you think I am. You, my dear, are the best of the best!

Rachel: Is this what they call a mutual admiration society? *(both beginning to laugh in each other's arms and then breaking away)* Something else is bothering you. What is it?

Fury: You read me like an open book. Yes, you have observed correctly. Before the Hellcats and I came over to your two nations, I learned at one of our senior officers' meetings about a new nuclear high-tech carrier that was being built. No mention was made as to the date of its completion. As you might imagine, the construction of this giant, ultramodern carrier was all hush, hush: top secret! One evening when i stepped outside to get some fresh air on the deck of the *SS Admiralty*, I was admiring the midnight sky as I stood in the shadows of our large 16-inch guns. I heard two voices in the distance. The two men felt they were entirely alone and could speak their minds freely. I inched closer to hear, better. It was then that I recognized the voices to be those of the two Vampires: Admirals Cornwalter and Reynaldo.

They seemed to be arguing over where to launch the new carrier. As I have explained on previous occasions, Rachel, the two seldom agreed on anything. I find it incredible that we were able to win so many battles under their joint leadership, but never mind that! What I am taking forever to say is simply this: The two admirals flipped a coin on the deck to see whose opinion would ultimately prevail. Cornwalter won the toss, and it was decided the new ship, they called the *Orca*, would move through the Mediterranean and continue its voyage from Port Said through the channel and then through the mighty Suez Canal. At one point, I was almost discovered when I accidentally kicked a soda can left behind by some careless sailor, no doubt. Fortunately for me, just about that time, a spotted cat ran from under one of the many stairwells on our ship. The cat's presence made the Vampires more at ease, believing it was the cat that had caused the disturbance! Whew!

Rachel: Why have you not discussed this episode with me earlier? This information is crucial to our plans of attack! Why, Fury?

Fury: There are two reasons for my reticence. First, I never believed the ship, if they were ever building it in the first place, could become seaworthy for another year or two; secondly, I didn't want to appear foolish, if my information was incorrect! I have been studying your research on flight information taken over the Mediterranean, the Gulf of Suez, and the waterways in between Port Said and the Suez Canal. Nothing, whatsoever, resembling a buildup of enemy seagoing craft has *ever* been mentioned in your reconnaissance reports! From that perspective, I believe there is no imminent danger posed by the enemy Crickets, that is, a naval amassment on the Western Front. Conversely, as my nightmare may suggest, if the *Orca, instead,* is the creature with the teeth to be launched during nightly maneuvers, then we most certainly could be in for some serious trouble!

Rachel: *(listening, spellbound)* I don't know what to think. I am totally numb all over! Your nightmare has suddenly become my nightmare—I pray that's all it is. I'm afraid, however, that there is something to what you say. I don't doubt for a moment that this carrier, if not completed, is soon to be completed. I get cold chills up and down my spine when I think that it could be moving closer to us, by the minute. I am trying to still my heart so that I can collect my thoughts.

Fury: What do you propose, Rachel? Should we take this matter up with Admiral Da Vinci?

Rachel: That was my first thought. I rather feel we should investigate to see which pilots have been conducting the reconnaissance. We might have a few rotten apples in the barrel. If there is such a ship as the *Orca*, then why hasn't it been reported?

Fury: Let's say you and I go take a look-see!

Rachel: You're on. We haven't any time to waste!

The hour was now 4:00 a.m.; the two colonels were wide-awake! They realized that time was of the essence. Rachel stated that she knew of one *F 77 Silverbird* and one *T 111 Delta Dragon* that had just been armed for combat; furthermore, the two aircraft carried infrared cameras that made it possible to take photographs at night, from an altitude above five miles. The cameras could pinpoint a postage stamp on the ground! Fury responded, "What are we waiting for then? We can be there and back before breakfast!" Rachel replied, "Right on, partner!" With that, the two compatriots got ready to leave, when Fury shot back "Rachel, you've still got on your robe and night wear!" Rachel giggled and murmured, "Well what do you know about that Colonel, I didn't think you even noticed!" Fury smiled and answered, "Um, ah, I better keep my thoughts to myself; you know how much I care for you, so get into something before you catch cold on the deck: The wind was quite brisk when I arrived!" "Yes Colonel, anything you say," Rachel saluted and then giggled some more.

The moment passed and Rachel got serious. "I'll get into my pilot jump-suit. You should be able to find one your size in the hangar lockers." Fury asked, "Which plane should I take?" Rachel, getting dressed in the other room, shouted back, "The *T 111 Delta Dragon*, of course. It more closely resembles your Hellcat aircraft." "We call them the *007 Red Razorbacks*," Fury hollered. "With the new red chevrons I guess we should modify or rename them." Rachel now coming into the receiving room of her small cabin exclaimed "I like the sound of the *007 Red Razorbacks*; I wouldn't change a thing!" Fury replied, "That's what I like about you: You're always taking my feelings into account. Thanks!" Rachel smiled her winning smile and yelled, "I'm ready; are you?" This time Fury saluted her and with a slightly wry smile declared, "That I am, Emerald Midnight Hornet, that I am!"

Within minutes, the two were leaving the flight deck of the *HTMS Eagle* and were on their way to the Mediterranean, via an over-flight of the Suez Canal and then up the waterway past Port Said. The flames from the *F 77* and the *T 111* jets' exhaust made the two aircraft appear like meteors, shooting back into the night's sky. Sudden Fury and the Emerald Midnight Hornet had discussed the flight path alternatives before takeoff. They had agreed that the long way around was the short way home, that is, the longer route was preferable to flying directly to the Mediterranean, because if the *Orca* was already downstream, so to speak, they could provide an early radio alert to the *Eagle*.

Within a few minutes they were leaving the Dead Sea and traversing the Sinai Peninsula. As they traveled through the darkened night, their infrared cameras were recording the landscape below. The land war had spilled into the Sinai and it was difficult to ascertain who had the advantage. Some photos seemed to indicate that the Crickets, with their superior numbers, had retaken a substantial bit of real estate, by capturing the high ground; other photos indicated an almost complete encirclement of the enemy Crickets, by the Allied troops: Frog, Toad, and United Nation flags could be seen at the various positions. A chess player could appreciate the tactics employed by both sides. Napoleon, centuries earlier, had demonstrated that a powerful army, led by competent and imaginative generals, could dominate in matters of war, even without a strong navy.

The Emerald Midnight Hornet felt pangs of discontentment, understanding how crucial her mission, together with Fury's, was: the presence of another carrier could mean that the Allies would be outnumbered on the high seas. If such a sea creature exists she rationalized, perhaps the *Eagle* could intercept it at *Shorm el Sheikh* or just before the *Orca* left the Gulf of Suez. First things first, she said to herself! She wanted to share those thoughts with Sudden Fury but recalled that she and he had also agreed not to break radio silence, unless absolutely necessary. The time now was 4:30 a.m., and night was beginning to give way to day. Rachel looked to her left and caught a glimpse of the Colonel; he was holding his right thumb up, in order to bolster her confidence. He knew instinctively and through experience how much was at stake: they mustn't fail! They continued their mission as the sun began to chase them across the rainbow sky of the desert. Its reds, blues, and magentas, interlaced with pinks and purples reflected off the noses of their respective airplanes.

By now they were coming around the horn of *Shorm el Sheikh* and moving north by northwest up the Gulf of Suez. Thus far they saw nothing unusual. They slowed their *F 77* and *T 111s* down, so as not to miss any of the adjacent areas. They almost passed *Abu Zenima,* when Rachel buzzed Fury and indicated with her left hand, pointing downward, that she was dropping down to take a closer look. Fury nodded he understood and pointed with his right hand that he would proceed to *Ras Sudar*. She returned the nod.

Fury then crossed his wrists, with both hands forming closed fists, except for the index and middle fingers that were outstretched and closed together; with both hands now pointed in opposition, he displayed his "X" signal to Rachel. She recognized and comprehended its significance: It meant, "We are separating for now, however, we will soon meet at the next major junction"—in this case, the mighty Suez Canal! Now that Fury was farther up the Gulf of Suez, he floated down to inspect *Ras Sudar.* Rachel, moving toward her target first, was taken aback, when she saw how much the area had changed since she was a child.

As a child, she and her family had crossed the Sinai to vacation in Egypt, to see its wonders: the Great Pyramids! She always looked forward to those summer vacations. Her parents felt that travel was one of the best ways for her to expand the knowledge she had acquired in school. The Arabic language fascinated Rachel. In school, she had learned that the Arabs had controlled the sea-lanes to India, many years before the Portuguese. They also were responsible for bringing advanced mathematics, silks, perfumes, rotation farming, the Arabic numeral system, cartography, medicine, astronomy, and much more to the four-fifths of Spain they had conquered. She learned that the Moslems had been benevolent rulers during the eight centuries they occupied the Iberian Peninsula; later, the Spanish, under the monarchy of King Ferdinand and Queen Isabella, had retaken the lost territories and pushed the Moors (Moslems) out of Spain. Her teachers taught her that the Arabs had a long, noble, and illustrious history! Way back in the nineteenth and early twentieth centuries, moreover, the Moslems, mostly Arabs, began to reunify their nations. They controlled much of the world's energy by owning vast amounts of crude oil.

As these thoughts passed through Rachel's memory—along with those of her childhood treks up the Gulf of Suez—she observed that her instruments were reading her location as: latitude 29:02 N and longitude 33:07. She wondered, after closely examining all the vessel transit services moving about below her, if she should hurry to the Suez Canal and join Fury. "No, nothing here looks like a Cricket supply vessel, much less a Cricket man-o-war or carrier," she whispered to herself. "Time to climb back up," she continued murmuring.

Her *F 77 Silverbird* had been flying low, so as to avoid detection by radar. Within seconds, her ultra-high-speed jet had her out of the area. She was pleased that the *Orca* had not made it down the Gulf of Suez, not this far, at any rate! "If it does exist," she reflected, "we're going to find her! You can't hide a carrier. Or, can you?"

Fury, in the meantime, had been inspecting *Ras Sudar*. It was a logical place for the *Orca* to stop to pick up supplies. *Ras Sudar*, Fury noted, was a rich port that offered, among other things, vast quantities of oil. The oil fields stretched for a great distance. After making several passes, the Colonel was secure in the idea that the *Orca* was not here. Just like the Emerald Midnight Hornet, Sudden Fury flew below radar to avoid detection. On one of his passes, he saw older children playing soccer. Fury recalled that soccer was a similar game to the Crickets' *Passcore:* the basic skills involved passing and scoring. In the Crickets' game, though, the striker was able to handle the ball once, with his or her hands, as well as kick it, for sure.

How things had changed in his life! For a moment or two, he wished he were a teenager again who could join them. He'd show them a few of his own tricks. Alas, he would have to wait until he had children of his own. For the moment, he just wanted to say hi; so he tipped his wing to the youth on the field, and they waved back as he made his getaway, returning into the upper crystal-blue atmosphere. They had never seen a black airplane with red chevrons and thought about how wonderful it must be to fly that beautiful plane with the flashy chevrons: The paradox of life!

Fury was mildly upset and bothered. While he was very impressed with the *T 111 Delta Dragon* he was piloting, except for a gleeful expression he had conveyed to Rachel, he had not properly thanked her or at least not sufficiently so! He appreciated this new aircraft; he admired how the painters had provided the Hellcats' with the new black color, along with the dramatic insignia that now appeared on the center fuselage. He would most definitely have to take her out to dinner, he mused. For the present, it was on to the Suez Canal! His thoughts were temporarily interrupted with a vision of the youngsters playing on the soccer field. How was it, he wondered, that the youth were playing so early in the morning? Then he realized, as the sun began its full ascension, that in a few hours it would be too hot to play comfortably. "These kids are pretty darn smart," he smiled to himself. "Yes, they keep getting smarter by the minute!" His expression turned more sober, "Hopefully, we can restore peace in the valley, so that they won't have to go to war!"

Fury's attention was brought back to his mission, when he noticed his instrument panel informing him that another aircraft was entering into his air space. The flashing red light on the panel pointed to the speed, altitude, and attitude of the incoming airplane. "It must be Rachel," he thought. "But, why in the world is she approaching so quickly and from the east? She's directly behind me. No! That can't be Rachel: the attitude and swiftness are all wrong!" Fury immediately dropped the nose of his *T 111 Delta Dragon* down, in order to outmaneuver the incoming invader.

Fortunately, his correct reading of the instrument panel and the correct interpretation of the information it conveyed, along with his natural instincts, propelled him out of sudden destruction! No sooner had he moved to position himself behind the other pilot, than he noticed two missiles whizzing by him. He recognized the enemy aircraft as belonging to Admiral Lightning Striker's Blue Demon Squadron. He locked onto the enemy Cricket and released a single missile that found its mark. The Blue Demon airplane was now a thing of the past: It matched the sun's brightness, as it exploded with a tremendous burst!

"I can't believe it! Who would have thought that one of Admiral Striker's aviators would be this far west. What's going on? Oh, I've got it! It must have flown here from a position further north, performing its own reconnaissance, and then headed west where it found me! Wow! That can only mean one thing. It came here from another carrier: not the *Scorpion*, not the *Stingray*, and not even the *SS Admiralty*, they're too far south: but, yes to the *Orca*! It couldn't be anything else!" Rachel at last broke radio silence. "Colonel," she exclaimed almost out of breath, "I saw the whole thing! I didn't arrive soon enough to warn you. Thank goodness you were quick to see it wasn't me sneaking up behind you. You were superb! Fury, we may be in trouble! If there is one out here, there might be others, yes? Do you think we should turn back?"

"You may be right, there could be others," Fury responded, "or this may have just been a stray looking for glory that, instead, became trouble. Well, he or she found it! But no, Rachel, we've come too far to turn back! Our mission is still incomplete, except for the fact that we now know the Blue Demon had to have come from the *Orca*, because there are no enemy airfields on the Sinai. The Allied Forces have destroyed them. We've got to go on, Colonel Goldsmith." Rachel replied, "Thanks for that. I needed it!"

Rachel wasn't afraid for her own life, as much as she didn't want to compromise Fury's. In her estimation, he had already done more than his share by coming over to the Frog and Toad's side of the battlefield; in addition, he had brought twenty five fabulous pilots with their aircraft: the Hellcats! She pondered that for a moment and felt warm all over, that a former enemy could also become, at the very least, a best friend. Besides, she though, to herself, "He's kind-a cute. I think I'll keep him! If we go down in combat, we'll go down together.

"There are times in life," she further reflected, "when a person needs to choose sides and this certainly was one of them!" She also recognized that although she was a female fighter, there were many other women fighting on both sides of the conflict. While she wasn't exactly sure what this necessarily meant or what the consequences represented for women, she hoped it might become a giant step forward for her kind! Indeed, it leveled the playing field between men and women and for their respective races, in the manner in which people treated each other. "What is a person's sex or race anyhow," she thought out loud? "Most people are baffled by it," she determined. "It's simply a cover wrapped around a book and you can't judge a book by its cover!"

Her Holy Book had spoken about such things. Somewhere it mentioned that a good friend can be more valuable than a brother, that is, someone not related by blood, marriage, or adoption. "Now that the world was getting smaller and people were traveling more," she contemplated, "perhaps they would come to the conclusion that we are all pretty much the same. Then what is still keeping the world apart? If it's not race, is it religion? Isn't religion, and government, for that matter, supposed to bring us together! How much more of war can the planet take?" she asked herself. These thoughts occupied her mind during her renewed radio silence, as she and Fury flew towards the looming Suez Canal. At long last, there it was! What a beautiful canal, the two pilots agreed; they each gave the other thumbs up, accompanied by broad smiles! "We're here and all we can do at this point is pray and hope for the best. If there are enemy fighters down there, we'll soon find out."

While the Emerald Midnight Hornet had been meditating on the meaning of life, Colonel Sudden Fury was concerning himself with Rachel's safety. Perhaps he had spoken too soon! It was one thing to risk his life, but should he include her in all of this? He knew her well enough; she would never leave his side. They were most definitely a team, with a capital "T"! Fortunately, for the two attractive aviators, the pilot that Fury had just shot down was a stray. The enemy intruder, in his excitement at seeing an opportunity to make a kill, had forgotten to contact his base; therefore, the Cricket pilot's absence was viewed by the enemy command as simply another of their lost airplanes. For the time being, Rachel and Fury were safe. Both pilots gave each other the signal to descend. This time Colonel Fury was first to swoop down past the terrain. Rachel was covering him as she joined in the search for the *Orca*. Once again, the airplanes slowed their speed, so as to view the various sites more carefully. Their scrutiny revealed a great many vessels, of all types, passing through the mighty work. The United Nations had declared the Suez Canal a neutral basin.

The ships were not required to divulge anything about their intentions or circumstances, except: to identify themselves, to declare the contents of their respective vessels, and to indicate where they were bound. Fury and Rachel could see flags from every nation in the world, or so it seemed: Some were countries from the Middle East, while others were from Europe, Africa, America, and Asia. How beautiful they all looked to the two Colonels! After what seemed enough time, they agreed to call off any further searching of the Suez area and headed toward Gaza! "One more stop," the Emerald Midnight Hornet whispered, "This will be enough to complete the mission."

Colonel Fury was thinking similar thoughts. It would be nice to get back to the *Eagle* and relax with a favorite beverage or two: with Rachel of course! The *F 77 Silverbird* and the *T 111 Delta Dragon* had performed admirably. The colonels both understood they were flying two of the finest machines ever conceived by aerospace engineers! The two airplanes had passed every stress test conceivable. Yes, they felt quite secure that the Frogs and Toads joint military alliance had provided them with the best in modern avionics. Before long, the two were flying well within the coast of the Gaza Strip. They each noticed that their respective aircraft was becoming low on fuel. Rachel motioned with appropriate hand signals that they couldn't make too many passes, if they were to make it safely back to the Dead Sea, where the *Eagle* was already moving down the other canal: the Great Canal that led to the Red Sea. Before either one could indicate a word to the other, they became utterly speechless. There it was: ***The Orca***!

Sometime earlier and aboard the *HTMS Heroic*, Colonel Marvin Rosencrantz, known to most by his famous nickname the *Ghost,* had just finished playing a scorcher of a tennis game with his younger brother Jonathan. It was then his brother asked him, "Do you love Rachel?"

The Ghost: *(breathing heavily)* Fine time to ask me, when I'm out of breath. I beat you! I believe that puts me ahead of you by one set, Jack!

Jonathan: Just answer the question, Marvin!

The Ghost: *(still a little out of breath)* Why do you ask?

Jonathan: Well, before Colonel Sudden Fury came over to our side, you had as much as challenged him to a duel in the sky. You and Rachel had been an item, ever since we joined forces with our cousins, the Frogs. I saw how you saw Rachel admiring Colonel Fury, the night of the banquet. She couldn't seem to take her eyes off of him. Now that they have become so chummy, your demeanor has changed! You don't seem to smile as much anymore. Well, do you?

The Ghost: Jack, I'm five years older than you. I've had other loves in my life and I'll have others in the future. Right now it seems like the best thing for us to do, Rachel and me, is to give each other a little time and space to sort things out. If we are meant to get together again, we will; if not, then I wish her well! *(pausing)* Yes, I wish the very best for her! She is one fantastic person and a formidable leader: The Frogs could use more pilots of her caliber.

Jonathan: *(issuing a cold smile)* You are much too kind! I don't like the way she's treated you. If it were up to me...

The Ghost: *(interrupting)*...but it's not up to you. I appreciate your concern; nevertheless, these matters are best left up to those directly involved. Thanks, just the same.

Jonathan: *(sober)* Sure!

The Ghost: I have a question of grave consequence. *(looking Jack squarely in the eyes)* I must ask you: what has been transpiring with your reconnaissance flights over the Gulf of Suez and up to the Gaza Strip? I know that's classified information; however, I'm the one that recommended you to head that mission. You've made official reports on those sorties, I'm sure! And, I can request to see those reports, if need be.

Jonathan: *(nervous)* Marvin, there's no need to requisition reports; besides, you are on the *Joint Toad and Frog Top Secret Committee*! not to mention your senior officer status! *(now, more in charge)* Finally, the last time I looked we were still brothers! I don't keep secrets from my big brother.

The Ghost: And the answer is...?

Jonathan: The answer is we canvassed the entire area thoroughly and found nothing that came close to looking like a carrier. Oh, yes, there were plenty of huge oil tankers going through the Suez Canal, but that's all! I might add that each time we ventured there, there was a great deal of cloud cover, mist, and fog that is quite unusual for this time of year and in this area of the world.

Jonathan wasn't being forthright with his brother, the *Ghost*. He loved him dearly, and hated the fact that Rachel preferred Sudden Fury! According to the reports, the first and second reconnaissance only went as far as the Suez Canal. The reports stated that on each occasion, bad weather had caused them to return to the *HTMS Eagle* sooner than anticipated. The third one, however, took him all the way to the Gaza Strip. Jonathan had told the other two Toad aircraft to return to base. He stated that it wasn't necessary for the three aviators to place themselves in harm's way, when one pilot could just as easily find the presence of the suspected carrier. So, he made the journey alone. Jonathan, thus, was the first Allied airman to behold the unbelievable *Orca*! His reason for not reporting it was simply to embarrass Colonel Sudden Fury!

In order to achieve this dastardly deed, Major Jonathan Rosencrantz believed he needed to allow the *Orca* a surprise attack on the Toad and Frog Fleet. In this way, Colonel Furry would be held responsible for withholding military intelligence! The Allied Intelligence Committee (AIC) would rationalize that Fury had had this intelligence all along! Thus, the major reasoned, the *Ghost* and the rest of the AIC should be kept in the dark: nothing, whatsoever, regarding the *Orca* must be made known.

When Jonathan returned, he found most of the senior intelligence officers were well pleased to learn that "no news was good news!" Still, a few others, like the *Ghost*, were not so easily persuaded. They found it incredible that the Crickets were only mounting a single frontal attack, with no additional fleets. It just didn't make sense! Colonel Marvin Rosencrantz couldn't help but believe that his kid brother was holding something back. He had been listening attentively to all that Major Jonathan Rosencrantz had divulged, concerning his mission to Suez and Gaza. At long last, the colonel looked at his brother, the major, and spoke: "I sure hope that you've told me all there is to tell! We'll be in a terrible fix, if you've missed something during your last reconnaissance flight!"

Colonel Sudden Fury and Colonel Rachel Goldsmith, that is, the Emerald Midnight Hornet, swept down to take a closer look at this amazing floating fortress. There were at least ninety airplanes on the deck: No, more like a100! No sooner had the two colonels spotted the *Orca* than at least a half-dozen *808 Double-Swept Missile Fighters* came off the carrier's belly to intercept them. Fury and Rachel didn't give the enemy aircraft the opportunity to attack them in an established formation. Rather than cut and run, Rachel signaled to Fury to assist her in creating a wedge, by taking out their two closest *808* inside fighters. She would then turn left and he would turn right to outmaneuver and destroy the other four fighters.

The *808 Fighters* were something never beheld by Rachel! Fury, on the other hand, had viewed a prototype just fresh off the assembly line. He was startled to see that they completed the fabrication of so many aircraft, a full six months ahead of schedule! The double-swept design, with missiles on each of the four wings, gave the *808s* a menacing look. In spite of the airplane's unique characteristics, such as reaching speeds in excess of 2,000 miles per hour, it lacked the ability to make tight turns in a dogfight situation. Still, it had more missile power than anything built by the best of the Frog aircraft contractors. The Toads, with the help of the Frog aerospace engineers, however, were developing a new model that combined the best features of the suspected Cricket *808s* and the recent Frog *77s* and their own Toad *111s*.

The Emerald Midnight Hornet's experience paid off! She had met and defeated numerous Cricket pilots, earlier in the war. She knew that the Cricket aviators fought best when they were in formation. By taking out the lead pilots, they were most likely eliminating two of their best leaders. Having killed two of the enemy, Rachel and Fury turned to position themselves behind the remaining four. It was a strategy taught over and over in the Frog Academy Top Gun Strategic Center (FATGSC).

After a near miss by one of the *808's* missiles that almost hit Fury, his *T 111* rolled over to make yet another pass at an incoming *808*. Rachel, in the meantime, had her hands full with two *Double-Swept-back Missile Fighters* trying to pin her down. She performed several aerial loops with her *F 77* while firing missiles that each hit her intended targets. Colonel Fury had greater difficulty, now that four more *808 Fighters* had entered the killing arena. He, nonetheless, was able to count two more kills and then proceeded, in daredevil fashion, to eliminate two more! The Midnight Hornet, not to be outdone, rejoined the battle and destroyed the remaining two. Both were now practically out of fuel! Fury signaled to Rachel to leave the killing fields in the clouds and head to home base: the *Eagle*. With the superior speed and agility of the Allied pilots' airplanes, the two were able to make good their escape.

Now it was difficult to see who had the better positions! On the one hand, Colonels Fury and Goldsmith had discovered the whereabouts of the *Orca*. Allied Intelligence could say, with confidence, that the *Orca* was no longer rumor but a reality! That, of course, meant the Allies had to contend with one more carrier: a huge one at that! The contention for sea supremacy had tipped the balance of the scales in favor of the Crickets! For one thing, the enemy could proceed immediately down the Gulf of Suez after making its way westward from the Gaza Aquifer to Port Said, and then it could continue southeasterly through the mighty Suez Canal. The Crickets, shortly afterwards, found that the *HTMS Eagle* that seemed to have vanished —as if by magic— had reappeared! It was presently moving through and almost out of the Mighty Canal that majestically linked the Dead Sea to the Red Sea!

The Crickets would, conceivably, prefer to allow the *HTMS Eagle* to continue its voyage from the Red Sea to the Arabian Sea, where it was pursuing their Imperial Cricket Armada: The *SS Admiralty*, the *Scorpion*, and the *Stingray*. This strategy would allow one or two of the Cricket carriers to turn about and face the *Eagle*, as it made its approach. The *Orca*, in this scenario, would come from behind and the *Eagle* would, in a manner of speaking, be squashed in between the ferocious Cricket air and sea power. According to Cricket logic, this plan, if successful, would leave the Allies with only one seaworthy carrier: *The Heroic*! The Crickets would have the *Heroic* for dessert!

On the other hand, the Crickets had no knowledge of the *King David*. They believed, for some unknown reason, that this carrier was the United Nations Carrier, delivering aircraft to nonaligned nations, nations that were neutral in the war between the Crickets and the Frogs, Toads, and their friends, the Allies. The Frogs, it turns out, had built an earlier yet smaller version of the *King David*: This UN Carrier had been built under new UN guidelines that permitted it to ferry authorized airplanes to peace- seeking nations. Thus, it had circumnavigated the seas of the earth during the past five years, assisting nations who wanted to beef up their air force, in order to protect themselves against rogue states.

When the Crickets had last seen the actual carrier, the *King David*, it did not appear to be flying a flag, according to a Cricket reconnaissance aviator. The aviator, in question, also reported that dusk had turned to night, allowing her to make only one pass over the spied carrier's deck! It was then, when she decided to return to her place of origin because of inclement weather, poor visibility, and low fuel. A meager intelligence follow-up, on the part of the enemy Crickets, would have yielded a treasure chest of incalculable, highly valued information! Someone, apparently, had dropped the ball where the mysterious Frog carrier was concerned; no more, however, was spoken or mentioned about this carrier, except to say it was friendly! "Wow!" How totally fortuitous for the virtuous Frogs and their side! To say it was a missed opportunity would be a gross understatement! It would later be exclaimed by Admiral Cornwalter, "Heads are going to roll over this unspeakable, malicious error!"

In the meantime, the Crickets felt they were only going against two of their adversary's carriers: the *HTMS Eagle* and the *HTMS Heroic*. The Cricket's with four carriers, they believed, would easily carry the day. By the time the Cricket's mighty *Orca* made it down to *Shorm el Sheikh,* the horn of the southern tip of the Sinai, however, the *Eagle* had already passed by and was well on its way to catching the Imperial Cricket Armada.

The *Orca* pressed on to reach the *Eagle*. Further north, now through the Dead Sea and entering the Great Canal, the noble and majestic *HFMS King David* moved as swiftly as the Canal would permit. After what seemed like an eternity, the *King Davi*d arrived at the Gulf of Aqaba! From here the *David w*ould continue to make every effort to catch the *Orca* from behind. As the minutes turned into hours, all of these warships continued their journey into the jaws of heaven or hell. Ahead, much rejoicing remained for the victors.

While the United Nations could contribute soldiers to protect citizens, where land engagements were concerned, it forbade itself to become involved in sea militancy. The UN, however, decided it would be within their rights to monitor sea conflicts, if it did not use that information to the advantage of one contestant over the other. The United Nations' ships, moreover, made themselves easy to spot on the high seas. The many light blue flags, embossed with the familiar UN emblem, flew high above the masts they adorned and were strikingly visible to the naked eye! These ships were surveying the naval engagement of the Crickets and their intended assault on the Allied Navies. Almost a week had passed by, before the United Nations' ships observed the unique positions of each of the combatants' carriers and their respective battle groups, that is, battleships, heavy and light cruisers, frigates, destroyers, cargo vessels, and the like. What they saw or didn't see was absolutely astounding! Except for the *HTMS Eagle*, there were no other Allied carriers in sight.

The UN had learned of the *King David's* existence, but had not been able to locate it. The *HTMS Eagle*, majestically sporting the Toad's royal blue and white colors, on the other hand, had been spotted as it attempted to reach the outer perimeter of the Cricket Armada. The United Nations observers also noticed and were amazed at the size of the *Stingray*, the *Scorpion*, and the *SS Admiralty* that had all begun to enter the Arabian Sea! The *Eagle,* seeing itself in danger, was now making a deliberate run for it, to avoid getting trapped between the *Orca* that trailed it and the Cricket carriers it had been pursuing. The *Eagle,* having lost touch with the *Heroic,* felt it had no other choice than to fend for itself: to survive to fight another day!

As the Red Sea embraced the Arabian Sea, the commanders of the *HTMS Eagle* felt it could better defend itself in these open waters. Meanwhile, the *Orca* was gaining on the *Eagle*. Fortunately, for the Allies, the *Orca* had *also* temporarily lost contact with the rest of the Cricket Armada. It appeared, therefore, that there would be a face-off, between the *Eagle* and the fast-closing-in *Orca*.. At this point, as viewed in the aerial photographs taken by the UN observers, there were absolutely no other carriers in sight, except these two titans! The UN photos, thus, did not reveal the *King David* that evidently was still too far north!

At precisely 19:00 hours, the monster *Orca* located the *Eagle* but had orders not to fire until the dense fog lifted; otherwise, it might later be charged with shooting at some of the rear guard of the forward-moving Cricket Armada. In reality, the rear guard had by now moved alongside the rest of the Armada. In the Cricket naval strategy, the rear guard and the avant guard, composed mostly of light cruisers, rotated positions every 36 hours. Thus, it was better prepared to cover the entire sea-lanes that might, otherwise, make the carriers vulnerable to attack by the Allied enemy.

All of the *808 Double-Swept-back Missile Fighters* were itching to leave the *Orca* and descend on the *Eagle!* Their shiny black surfaces, with the yellow *Orca* emblem encrusted into the gray Cricket flag, painted on both sides of their fuselage, made them seem invincible. Not unlike the pilots of the Frogs and Toads, many of the *Orca's* aviators were going into combat for the first time. They had written letters to sweethearts about how they were going to teach the Frogs and Toads whose navy was the best. Admiral Lightning Striker had visited the beautiful carrier, equipped with all of the latest technology, and reassured these greenhorns, that once they got up into the open skies, their jitters would leave them. He bellowed there was only glory awaiting them: promotion in rank for those with the most kills! He further declared it would be his distinct privilege to pin medals of commendation on those most deserving!

Aboard the *HTMS Eagle*, many of the most experienced pilots had gotten sick in the senior officers' mess. It would be up to the freshmen airmen and airwomen to prove their mettle in the fight for air supremacy that would lie just ahead. Admiral Da Vinci, now on board the *Eagle,* called all of his pilots, including those sick but still well enough to attend, to meet on the deck of the *Eagle*. He began his speech saying:

Da Vinci: *(in a sober and noble voice)* My dear pilots, airmen, and airwomen, defenders of our beloved nations, this day we are met with a mighty challenge! We are asked, for the first time, to really take the fight to the enemy. Not like before, when we used our mothball fleet to deceive the enemy, but this time with our superior ship the great *Bald Eagle*, His Toad Majesty's Ship. The *HTMS Eagle*, along with our defense shield, ships of every size and shape, will support you youth of our nations, as you take control of the skies to eliminate those cocky Crickets! (A huge roar of approval is heard from every sector of the carrier!) Make no mistake about it; we will be victorious over the *Orca* and its accomplices!

At this time I would like to honor the Frogs' Emerald Midnight Hornet, Colonel Rachel Goldsmith and our truly heroic friend and comrade-in-arms, the pride of the Hellcats: Colonel Sudden Fury *(enormous applause and shouts of 'yea, yea, yea!')* Would you both please step forward? By order of His Majesty, King Gideon the III, I bestow upon you the ***Order of the Toads*** for alerting our ship to the presence of a new threat: the *Orca*. Your reconnaissance has already saved many lives in our preparedness. We are now more ready for combat with this new intelligence. I salute you, Colonels Goldsmith and Fury, for risking your lives and for downing at least ten of the enemy aircraft; moreover, for proving that our airplanes can outmaneuver theirs. You are the pride of our nations. A grateful Allied force extends a-heartfelt thanks! *(They are pinned and perform the customary salute and handshake.)* Would you offer any additional advice to our pilots, especially the newer ones?

The Emerald Midnight Hornet: *(Fury nudging her to speak first)* Thank you for this most prestigious award, Admiral Da Vinci. We were only doing our duty. I am sure that anyone else here would do as much, given the same set of circumstances. *(Speaking more directly to the pilots)* It's OK to be a little nervous, or even frightened; still, I believe this is a fight we didn't ask for, but a fight we welcome to protect those we love and cherish. You are the best trained, and I have every bit of confidence that you will perform admirably! And now I know many of you have still not met Colonel Sudden Fury; well, here he is! *(Tremendous cheering for the famed aviator and new friend)*

Colonel Sudden Fury: *(pleased, yet somewhat surprised at being put in the spotlight and for all of the unforeseen attention, accompanied by the award; also, a little misty-eyed)*. My friends *(clearing his throat and beginning again)*. My friends and fellow aviators, I am truly and sincerely grateful for this award that I believe belongs to all of you as well. Together, we will win the final victory: Each of us, in his or her own way, giving all that we have, will defeat the Blue Vampire Admiral Cornwalter and his jolly companions! *(Jubilant applause ringing out with some scattered laughter, as well as at the word "jolly")* We must not allow that darker side, of an otherwise noble race, to conquer us and in so doing enslave one of the last vestiges of freedom in this region. Yes, together we will share the final victory that only true brave men and women can expect! Thank you from the innermost recesses of my heart, for all that you have done, to accept me, and my fellow Hellcats! *(Cheering extended all around)*

Admiral Da Vinci: Thank you, Colonels Goldsmith and Fury! This moment is yours! All of you to your quarters and prepare for the battle of all battles! May the Supreme Force of the Universe accompany us as we move to eradicate the enemy!

The call "to your quarters" meant they could get a quick bite to eat, but had to be able to drop everything and get into their respective airplanes within two minutes. Most airmen and airwomen ate their meals hurriedly and then positioned themselves next to their *Mushroom Jets*, *Emperor Penguin Spitfighters*, and *Dragonfly Attack Helicopters* and the few new *F 77 Silverbirds* and *T 111 Delta Dragons.* Senior officers were responsible for making certain their squadrons were ready to go! Maintenance officers, of course, had the awesome responsibility of making sure each aircraft had passed the meticulous inspection necessary for the various sophisticated flying machines.

Obviously, the Advanced Computer Age made many things a lot easier, but other things became much more demanding; for one thing, the calibration systems, used by aviation mechanics, allowed for very little margin of error: either the inspection indicated that all aspects of the airplane's electronic, pneumatic, and weapon systems were within the specification guidelines, or they weren't! This act of inspection never ceased! Aircraft were inspected and re-inspected. The mechanic in charge had to ascertain, with his/her signature, that everything was fit for flight! The idea of human error was always a factor; therefore, nothing could be left to chance! The pilots, once aloft, relied completely on their flying machines! The two were as one and became inseparable!

As the pilots rushed to mess hall, Fury caught Rachel by the hand.

Rachel: Hi! *(a little out of breath from the brisk walk to the cafeteria)* Should you be holding my hand?

Fury: I don't know, should I? Besides, your touch warms me all over, and I want to slow you down to share something. *(smiling and indicating it's pressing)*

Rachel: We haven't much time. Did you want to talk?

Fury: Yes!

Rachel: I'm starved. Perhaps we can pick up a sandwich and go somewhere else.

Fury: Sounds great! I know just the place, if it's not too far!

Rachel: Oh really! Where?

Fury: On one of our late-night coffee outings, you mentioned something about a place where military personnel could go to meditate or pray?

Rachel: *(raising an eyebrow and a little amused)* You want to go there, now?

Fury: Yes, is it nearby?

Rachel: Yes. Let's get some chow and we can be there in a minute's time and still be close to our fighters.

Fury: Our trusty *F 77* and *T 111*. Very well!

Rachel: A cricket at prayer; should be an interesting sight *(she smiles coyly)*.

Fury: You're not making fun of me, are you?

Rachel: *(now very accepting)* Not in the least! Let's hurry!

Within a few minutes, the Emerald Midnight Hornet and Sudden Fury were seated on cushions, at the end of an all-faith and meditation room that served as a chapel, a temple, or room of worship. Fury determined, as his eyes scanned the interior, that it had little furniture. It was almost bare, quite plain: simple: It was, he whispered to Rachel, "pleasing to the heart." On one side of the room, their hung an ornate small Crucifix, on the other side there stood a crafted wooden Cross, and in the middle a bright Menorah placed on an alter with the familiar Star of David; moreover, a symbol "though not in uniform use among Muslims," the appealing Crescent Moon and Star symbol. Just outside there was a bench. Rachel mentioned it would be improper to eat inside and suggested they eat their evening snack outdoors. Once outside, they seated themselves close to each other. From there, they could make out the changing hues of the dark-blue evening sky peeking through the persistent fog. Rachel moved a little closer to Fury and held his hand firmly.

Rachel: Is something really bothering you?

Fury: *(sighing heavily)* Yes and no. I am not really afraid of going into battle as much as I am afraid of losing you. I know you have experienced the sting of aerial combat and are about as calm as any pilot can be, that is, before he or she flies off the carrier's deck to encounter the enemy.

Rachel: More to the point? And, yes, I too am feeling the same way about losing you!

Fury: *(Fury now a little more in charge; Rachel, thus, releasing his hand and looking into his soft, yet lively eyes)* When we took on the Crickets' *808s*, the *Double-Swept Back Missile Fighters*, I felt as though some external force was taking over the *T 111 Delta Dragon*. I have never experienced that phenomenon with the *007 Red Razorbacks* we Hellcats fly! It was such a strange, yet pleasant sensation! I might even call it ethereal. I recall Admiral Reynaldo, the Red Vampire, stating that there exists a Force in the universe that is greater than our own. That experience, of which I speak, has made me believe that he, too, must have had a similar experience sometime in his life! Do you know what I'm talking about; do you?

Rachel: I believe I do. Are you saying that when this Force took over your *T 111,* you were able to perform better than usual? We were outnumbered to be sure!

Fury: Yes, that's exactly what I'm saying. Did you experience anything of that sort?

Rachel: To tell you the truth, I did and I do: each and every time I get into a dogfight! I believe there is a Divine Wind that embraces my airplane, no matter which one I am flying; although now, I prefer the *F 77 Silverbird. (getting up and moving towards the all-faith and meditation room and beckoning him, with a smile, to follow. The two sitting side-by-side towards the middle back of the room)*

Fury: Rachel, thanks! I know we're going to be all right now!

Rachel: Fury, you are one heck of an ace! You never cease to amaze me. I come here from time to time just to settle my thoughts, to meditate, and yes to pray! I've been praying for you.

Fury: I guess I should return the favor. How do you pray? Do you have to belong to a certain faith?

Rachel: There is some debate about that; personally, I believe that the Eternal Force hears anyone who calls on Him.

With that, the two sat for a prolonged silence, hand-in-hand. After these precious minutes, that seemed more like moments, the two aviators picked up their helmets and headed for their respective fighters that were stationed next to each other.

Fury: I want to check with Major Ana Zeitsev, the Hellcats' second most senior pilot. She's next in command. I've got to see if we are in a *GO* position, that is, if we are OK for liftoff!

Rachel: I did that just before Admiral Da Vinci presented us with our awards. I'll, nonetheless, double-check with my Major Stewart Hurst for his confirmation! *(asking him to approach her and giving Fury a loving and penetrating gaze and then tenderly kissing him)*

Fury: *(beside himself, with stardust in his eyes)* Wow! *(smiling broadly)*.

Rachel: I guess it's all right to do that? *(returning his smile)* Think of that as insurance! Ha, ha!

Fury: Oh, that I will, oh most certainly, that I will! *(with a twinkle in his eyes)* Can't wait to see you when we get back*! (walking backwards a few paces, gazing at Rachel while he moves, then turning quickly, with a jaunt to his step that becomes a brisk dutiful walk, as he joins the cooler night air)*

Rachel: *(With a tear or two coming down her cheek, knowing the dangers they soon will be facing against the mighty* Orca, *its menacing* 808s, *along with its battle group, and pondering the outcome of the contest and their fates; waving to Fury and he turning back to return the wave, they both continue walking into the fog and mist that still persist, on the flight deck. In a hushed tone, speaking to the wind, uttering softly)* I love you my Fury; I just love you.

An hour or so earlier and at a great distance away, the *HTMS Heroic* was rendezvousing with another equally impressive ship. A few years back, it turns out, there had been a tremendous lightning storm over the entire island of Diego Garcia. This ship, the one the *Heroic* was meeting, had been built on that very same island, shortly after the unique event. The lightning storm that assailed the island had incredibly lasted three full days and nights! It mysteriously changed the composition of the earth there! The ore, now, was like nothing that had ever been encountered by human beings. Its properties were such that after its careful smelting, it became a new metal: twice as light yet twice as strong as anything that existed until then. Thus was born a prized substance for those who would fashion it to create machines of war: aircraft carriers, for example! The new metal was called **Laserite**!

Until recently, the Frogs had had the most advanced aircraft in the Jordan region; nevertheless, their cousins, the Toads, had steadily maintained their lead in the fabrication of navy ships. After realizing the impending threat from the north, the Frogs moved to rectify past errors or lack of navy readiness: They strove to build a new navy! Thus, they commissioned, along with smaller ships, two new gigantic carriers: the *HFMS King David* and the *HFTMS Eternal Grace*. The Toads, likewise and for similar reasons, decided to vastly improve their aircraft. A new version of the *Pencil,* for instance, demonstrated that they, too, could compete with some of the Frogs' best aeronautical engineering. With these newly improved additions, the cousins felt they both had achieved their goals: military preparedness! It would remain to be seen if their strategic skills matched their manufacturing ones.

The original Allied plan, all along, was to entice the Crickets to pursue them, by making the enemy believe they were in a position to decimate the Allies in the Dead Sea. Once the Great Canal had been built and later discovered by the Crickets, however, the Crickets realized they would have to pursue the Toad and Frog navies into deeper, larger bodies of water to punish them! Everything was going according to plan. Unfortunately, for the Allies, the Frogs and Toads would have to re-strategize as a result of incontrovertible evidence of the *Orca's* existence! Instead of trapping the Crickets between the *Eagle* and its battle group and the *Heroic* and its battle group, the *HTMS Eagle* was now desperately consumed with a fast-trailing *Orca,* nipping at its rear guard.

The question remained, how would the *HTMS Heroic* be capable of taking on three mighty Cricket carriers: the *SS Admiralty*, the *Scorpion,* and the *Stingray* in open waters? The *HFMS King David,* it appeared, might not arrive in time to lend assistance to the smaller *HTMS Eagle*, presently just two hours away from entering the mouth of the Arabian Sea, at the Gulf of Aden.

Admiral Cheetah had received alarming intelligence and was very concerned! If the *Orca* defeated the *Eagle,* the *Orca* —having learned of the *David's* true identity and position— could turn its massive force to face the *King David*! With all of these possibilities for defeat, Cheetah, nevertheless, assured himself and was gratified that the Allies possessed a new stately friend: the *HFTMS Eternal Grace!* A joint venture between the Frogs and Toads. Hope was not lost. On the contrary, the *Eternal Grace* provided the much-needed shot in the arm the Allies desperately needed!

The *HFTMS Eternal Grace* was a ship with an *ethereal* quality. It glowed as it moved swiftly through the rough waters of the Indian Ocean. The more one stared at it, and it was difficult to look away, the more the ship's colors seemed to change. At first it was a glistening bluish silver and then a golden bright yellow that turned to purple. Every color of the rainbow made its appearance as the carrier glided through the waters. Its heavenly and celestial beauty gave it the appearance of another world's grace that was beyond description. To experience its majesty and command of the ocean's waters was indeed spellbinding, if not mesmerizing! As the *HTMS Heroic* approached the newer ship, it was met by seven of the *Eternal Grace's* fighter aircraft. The *Grace* had sent its *T 111 Delta Dragons* to survey the *Heroic*. The meeting of the two carriers had been part of the new strategy. The two ships were extremely fast, for carriers, and they both carried heavy payloads; that is, their separate 100 or more airplanes were loaded to the teeth. Almost immediately, the *Heroic* returned the compliment by sending five of its new amphibious *Toad Pencils* airborne, to meet the *Grace's* seven *Delta Dragons*.

Before losing contact with the *HTMS Eagle*, Admirals Weismann and Pointdextras of the *Heroic* had learned of the *Eagle's F 77 Silverbird* and the *T 111 Delta Dragon's* accomplishments, against the *Orca's 808 Double-Swept-Back Missile Fighters;* however, the seamen and seawomen of the *HFTMS Eternal Grace* had never before seen the newer version of the amphibious *Pencil*. Those on the flight deck of the *Eternal Grace* were impressed with what they saw! The five *Pencil* aircraft seemed to part the clouds as they smoothly harpooned through the air in formation; or, perhaps, more like the fingers of the Olympic champion's hand that releases the Javelin, thus extending the champion's reach with full energy to find the mark! Therefore, in this turbulent Indian Ocean, just before sundown, the astonishment, amazement, and wonder of the new technology and firepower caused the ships' crews to revel heartily at the scene just played out in the skies! The tempestuous, rough waters, oddly enough, began to discontinue their nagging cough and spit that seemingly had been directed at the intruders. As if commanded by a Heavenly Voice, suddenly, all the waters nearby became pacific, and the various aircraft returned to their respective carriers safely.

A strange phenomenon occurred at about the same time the seas quieted. The clouds gave way to a funnel of glorious light that seemed to indicate which way the *HTMS Heroic* and the *HFTMS Eternal Grace* should proceed. It was unmistakably clear! The Supernatural Light pointed west by northwest. While

Diego Garcia, an Island of some 35 miles long, 5 miles wide, and only 22 feet high in elevation, was indeed small, it also benefited from being so remote. At a distance of 1000 miles due south from India, it lay in the middle of the Indian Ocean. An attacker could easily be spotted at a great distance, with radar: as a result, that alerted the defense shield of Diego Garcia to react immediately! The remoteness of the island had afforded the Frogs and Toads sufficient privacy to build the *HFTMS Eternal Grace,* in secret. Small wonder that the enemy Crickets had no knowledge of it!

Once complete, the *Grace's* mission was:

> "*Cover 500 international nautical miles to rendezvous with the HTMS Heroic.*"

That it did, effortlessly. After joining forces with the *Heroic*, the admirals of the *Heroic,* led by Admiral Cheetah, came aboard the *Eternal Grace* to finalize their strategy against the Crickets. At this high-level officers' meeting, they discussed the phenomenon and its significance. They agreed that the light was coming from a Supreme Force. One admiral recalled how Job put his trust in a Higher Wisdom. Another admiral stated he saw the light had now taken on a strobe-like quality. It could only mean the ships were to follow its rays into battle! Thus, the two carriers began moving westward, leaving the Indian coast behind them. Once they had gone the necessary distance, they made a hard right to continue northwest. The battle-ready cousins, the Frogs and Toads, arrived near the edge of the Arabian Sea, where they spotted and encountered their nemesis: the Cricket Armada!

Outnumbered, three to two, the Allied navy moved their ships into the Arabian Sea, just outside and east of the Gulf of Aden. The *HTMS Heroic* was positioned off the coast of Yemen, near the port city of Qishn; whereas, the *HFTMS Eternal Grace* was set near the horn of Somalia. From there, the two carriers could act like Napoleon's cannons of old and make the Crickets run the gauntlet. The *SS Admiralty*, however, seeing what the Allies were attempting to do, made a run for it. Miraculously, it managed to get through with minimal damage to its flight deck. The *Heroic's* airplanes had a better shot at the *Stingray* that was coming in high and fast off the Yemen Coast. Likewise, the *Eternal Grace* had the better hand, as it moved from behind Somalia's horn to surprise the *Scorpion.* The pincer strategy was working very effectively, with *Mushroom Jets* and *Emperor Penguin Spitfighters* from the *Heroic* taking control of the skies. The *Eternal Grace's T 111 Delta Dragons* and *F 77 Silverbirds* were also dominating the skies over Yemen's waters. About then, the *SS Admiralty* made an about-face, inside the Indian Ocean, and returned to assist the embattled Cricket fleet.

The Blue Squadron, led by Admiral Lightning Striker, moved against the *Heroic* that was smaller than the *Eternal Grace*. Obviously, Admiral Striker felt that eliminating the older *Heroic* would be an easier task. The *Heroic,* therefore, was now, itself, caught in a crossfire! The Blue Squadron was the best of the

Cricket Navy's Air force! Between the two Cricket carriers, the *Heroic* appeared doomed! The battleships, cruisers, frigates, destroyers, and submarines from both of the combatants' sides, Crickets and Allies, had taken their private battles deeper into the Indian Ocean. Battleships were attacking battleships and cruisers were attacking cruisers, and so forth. It was as if each of the various classes of navy ships had paired off to outperform their enemy, in the same weight class.

Clearly, this just happened! In some ways, however, it seemed logical; even though war is seldom logical! Lighter ships, especially the nuclear submarine class, could be devastating against a much larger ship. Their torpedoes, once launched, could easily bring down a frigate; moreover, it could seriously impair even larger ships. Depth charges, nevertheless, often kept them away. Each of the warring sides made good use of their battle groups. As always, the side best utilizing their fleet: in the sea and in the air wins the naval engagement. From this vantage point, the *HTMS Heroic* was now taking a pounding from the *SS Admiralty*. It had focused primarily on the *Stingray,* before it noticed the carrier *SS Admiralty* climbing up its backside. The *Stingray* hadn't forgotten the humiliation it suffered at the hands of the *Heroic*, earlier in the war. It was time for revenge, their admirals announced over the ship's speakers!

Just as the naval engagement appeared to be favoring the Crickets, from out of nowhere, the *HTMS Eagle* entered into the fray! Admiral Da Vinci, who had been flown to the Eagle, was now commandeering it. Apparently, the Admiral had decided the better part of valor was to hold the *Orca* at bay. Slyly and skillfully, Admiral Da Vinci managed to elude the enormous Orca! The Eagle, thus, quietly slipped away downstream—using the fog as cover. It could, hence, augment the Allies' firepower in the Arabian Sea. His new strategic orders had boldly initiated a better battle plan:

> "Send out our *Tiger Class Submarines*, accompanied with half our battle group, to face off with the *Orca*, until the *HFMS King David* might arrive: At any cost, do not let the *Orca* through!"

It was a tall order! No matter what, the Tigers, with half a battle group composed mostly of light cruisers, frigates, and destroyers, had to fight the *Orca* and its complement, a full battle group; it would, as charged, hold the line, in hopes of eventual reinforcement. If only the *King David* would arrive sooner than later!

Just like its sibling, the *HFTMS Eternal Grace*, the *HFMS King David* carried 50 *F 77s* and 50 *T 111s*. Its superior speed, too, was now paying off as it moved within striking distance of the *Orca*. The *Orca* found itself unable to move down the waterways, much less able to turn around to face the *David*; it was, seemingly, blocked-in by the *Tiger Subs*! By the time the *David* arrived, more than half the *Tigers* had been sunk! *The Tigers*, nevertheless, had performed brilliantly! The battle group, that had remained to support the *Tiger Subs,* was largely destroyed by the *Orca's 808s*. The brave seamen and seawomen of the *Eagle*, commissioned to hold or slow the *Orc*a, had paid a high price indeed! They would go down in the historical annals of Toad and Frog naval battles as the courageous sailors who gave their lives in order to buy the *HTMS Eagle* precious time! This outstanding action also bought time that permitted the *King David* to attack the *Orca* and, thereby, keep the *Orca* from linking up with the Cricket fleet.

The *King David* went immediately to work by sending out half of its air force to meet the *Orca's 808 Double-Swept-Back Missile Fighters. The 808s* were the best the Crickets had, but they couldn't turn quickly enough to counter the *David's* F 77s and *T 111s.* After the first wave of airplanes returned to refuel, it found the second wave of *F 77s and T 111s* on their way to finish off the *Orca's* aviators. The *King David's* pilots were all very young. What they lacked in experience, they more than made up for with their rigorous Top Gun training. Their enthusiasm to prove themselves was unparalleled. Their superior airmanship became evident as more and more of the *Double-Swept-Back Missile Fighters* fell from the sky. Within a half-hours' time and with the sky now black with the smoke of downed Cricket fighters, it became evident that the Northern Crickets were finished!

The *Orca*, that had promised so much, was now smoldering! Its young aviators had tried to carry the day, but lacked sufficient technical training in supersonic flight. Had more of the older Cricket pilots been available, perhaps they might have fared better. In addition, th*e 808s,* although very advanced in their weapons systems, in the end, were no match for the superior maneuverability of the *Silverbirds and Delta Dragons*! Now that the *Orca,* apparently, was slowly sinking, making sounds all around like those of a dying whale, it, along with the vestiges of its battle group—in total disarray, headed towards its most northern port in the Black Sea. The Northern Cricket Navy, thus, limped back through the Suez Canal. Fewer than half would make it home! It was time for the *HFMS King David* to join forces with its cousin: *The HTMS Eagle*.

"What about the *Grace*?" someone in Allied Command Headquarters yelled into the 3-D videophone, held by Admiral Cheetah, now aboard the *HFTMS Eternal Grace*

Admiral Cheetah: *(with a big grin on his face visible to King Josue II, on his side of the videophone)* Your Highness, I am happy to report that we are fine, yes, very fine indeed! With the arrival of the *HTMS Eagle*, we will now take the advantage away from these feisty Crickets!

King Josue II: That's terrific! You've had us very concerned on this end. *(wiping his brow)* Our reconnaissance, however, shows that the *HTMS Heroic* is really getting hit from both sides. It appears to be their *Stingray* to the west and their *SS Admiralty* to the east.

Cheetah: Yes, Highness, that's very unfortunate! Please let me explain! It was pure luck on the part of the Blue Vampire's ship, the *SS Admiralty*, to get through! Somehow or other, his carrier was faster than we anticipated and was able to make it through our gauntlet, sustaining only minor damage. Well, won't the Blue Vampire be surprised when we happen by? *(firmly)* Yes, we've finally got things back under control on this end.

Josue: *(excited, yet cautiously elated due to the vulnerability of the Heroic's situation; hoping that with Cheetah, things are really improving for the Allies)* Tell me more!

Cheetah: We hid behind Somalia's horn, in order to surprise the *Scorpion*. I directed my Vice Admirals to send out two-thirds of our aircraft. The *Eternal Grace's T 111s* and *F 77s* performed exceptionally well! Those *Delta Dragons* and *Silverbirds* are just fabulous! They really took the fight to the enemy. Our position behind the horn and the aircraft's' speed made all the difference! We were able to hit their carrier's airplanes, before most of them got off the flight deck. The few that did make it out to challenge us were taken out by some of our best pilots. Our younger pilots also performed superbly! Nevertheless, we were not expecting their battleships to put up such a stalwart defense! I've got to give them credit there! Their big guns outmatched our battleships—we lost a few—and then they turned to further defend the *Scorpion*. All of this is to say, we were kept more than busy in our effort to defeat the *Scorpion*. With the aid of their larger ships including heavy cruisers, they also attempted to attack the *Eternal Grace*. His Majesty's *Grace* would have none of that, and its new **laserite** metal was almost completely impenetrable!

In spite of our great victory over the Blue Vampire's *Imperial Scorpion*, the other side of the coin or sad news is: we were unable to assist our beloved *Heroic!* As a consequence, I'm afraid the old workhorse is starting to sink! We're underway now and I've got to go! We've got some unfinished business! We're going after that crafty irascible Admiral Cornwalter. *(With tears in his eyes and with resolve)* Highness, I hope we capture that scumbag alive! He has plenty to answer for, don't you think, my King?

King Josue II: Admiral Cheetah, this is an order: Turn that ship of his into a tugboat, won't you? And while you're at it, save as many lives as you can. I understand those are shark-infested waters! It doesn't look good for the *Heroic's* sailors in the Arabian Sea. I hope the *Eagle* can handle the *Stingray!* You know the *Eagle* is not as large as theirs!

Cheetah: I hear you and understand! We, as you very well know, have a super-intelligent Admiral in Roberto Da Vinci! The lighter *Eagle* he commands will outmaneuver the *Stingray*. Moreover, the *Eagle* has our most up-to-date aircraft! Finally, Admiral Da Vinci has two of our best aviators: the fabulous

Emerald Midnight Hornet and that charismatic, terrific, friendly Cricket aviator, Colonel Sudden Fury! They will do just fine, really fine, your Highness. With your permission, I'll speak with you later.

Despite Admiral Cheetah's bravado, Cheetah knew they could still lose the sea and air war. The *Scorpion* was, at the very least, disabled: probably out of the real game for sure! The *Scorpion,* in spite of all, had achieved an illustrious naval pedigree, by amassing a large win column against some of the best navies of the strongest nations around the globe. Still, it was no match for the *HFTMS Eternal Grace*. The surprise tactics and the pincer movement, originally designed by Admiral Cheetah at command center, worked very effectively against the *Scorpion*. With the *Scorpion* barely hanging on, there was no need to scuttle it: too many of its crew would perish! This war was not about killing unnecessarily; instead, it was about winning through the depletion of the enemy's resources to make war on the high seas. As to the land war, no one could say for certain how it was proceeding. The two wars seemed worlds apart. At best, the information obtained was dated and too sketchy; time would tell. Right now there was the *SS Admiralty* and the *Stingray* with which to be concerned!

The fate of the *Heroic* seemed sealed: At a distance, it could be seen sinking! Its navy personnel, composed of as many women as men, could clearly be seen jumping from the deck of the *Heroic*, into the frigid, whirlpool waters of the sea. With special observation field glasses, the officers of the *HFTMS Eternal Grace* witnessed and could almost hear the screams and yells of these noble creatures: Their situation was now desperate! Unlike Admiral Cheetah, the Blue Vampire would not let up on the *Heroic*. Cornwalter wanted his battleships to send it to the bottom of the Arabian Sea, along with all of its crew. Cheetah, through the use of his long lenses, appeared transfixed at the scene being played out before him; suddenly, over and to the extreme right of the sea, he spotted Cornwalter, now sporting a long gray beard, on the upper deck of his *SS Admiralty*. The Blue Vampire's laughter seemed to skip along the waves of the Arabian, crossing the sea to where Cheetah could make out its ugly sounds.

The rescue operation had begun! Cheetah and his senior officers were making every effort to quickly cut through the bellicose waters. The order of the day was to defeat the mighty Crickets and send them to the lower abyss. Both the *SS Admiralty* and the *Stingray* had to be permanently removed; otherwise, the *Heroic's* crew might succumb in the murky waters, where lurking sharks were waiting to feed. The cry went out on the *Eternal Grace*, as well as the *Eagle*: "Save the *Heroic's* brave sailors and aviators!" The sharks, nearby, began to make their way to the bodies in the waters of the Arabian. From his ship, the *Eagle,* which had commenced its firing at the *Stingray*, Admiral Da Vinci spoke through his intercom and declared, "The reason for immediate haste is upon us; we will not allow the Vampire and his sharks to devour our comrades-in-arms!"

Da Vinci's blood boiled as he saw the *Heroic* begin to sink! It sickened him, but more than that, it reinforced the enormous resolve in his gut, heart, and soul. He would avenge his brother and sister officers of the *Heroic!* He continued to fire his guns at the gigantic *Stingray.* The courageous admiral, unexpectedly and at great risk, positioned his carrier, battleships, and heavy and light cruisers between the sinking *Heroic* and the *Stingray* and its largest ships. Two advantages accrued from that daring strategic exploit: First, he was shielding the *Heroic* from any further bombardment, issued by the great guns of the *Stingray* and its complement; secondly, by approaching at a closer range, his smaller but more dexterous and faster force could inflict serious damage to the *Stingray* and its escort of magnificent battleships, large and light cruisers, including several first rate frigates.

Moving from left to right, so as not to get hemmed in off the Yemenite coast, the *HTMS Eagle* and its rapidly moving ships came upon the *Stingray* suddenly and with great ferocity! Admiral Da Vinci ordered his fleet to fire-at-will! In some ways, it was like a turkey shoot! All of the enemy's ducks were in a row and amazed, if not shocked, at the Toad Admiral's audacity! By the time the larger ships of the enemy caught on to what was occurring and started to reposition themselves, to better strike the Toads' fleet, it was almost doomsday!

The Crickets' airplanes, nevertheless, were still swarming around the *HTMS Heroic,* that is, until a fresh group of aviators from the *HTMS Eagle* moved in to chase them away; moreover, by now the *HFTMS Eternal Grace* had made its way up and across the stretch. The *Grace,* however, had its hands full trying to pry the *SS Admiralty* off the eastern backside of the slowly sinking, but still afloat, *Heroic*. Thus, the *Stingray* was now the most westerly positioned carrier of all the fleets: enemy and allies. The *Eagle's* intrusion had come as a result of approaching from its northwesterly position in the Red Sea and moving southeasterly into the Arabian Sea, then swinging around the *Stingray* to come to rest between the centrally located *Heroic* and the *Stingray*. The *HTMS Heroic* had, until then, endured the full firepower of the enemy, including the enemy's airpower.

The positions of the respective carriers and their battle groups could, therefore, be witnessed and determined, from an aviator's perspective flying high above the Indian Ocean to the Yemenite coast, as follows: from left to right, *(west to east)*, the *Imperial Stingray*, the *HTMS Eagle*, the *HTMS Heroic*, the *SS Admiralty*, and coming quickly—from a slightly southwesterly direction—the *HFTMS Eternal Grace!* Finally, the Crickets' *Imperial Scorpion* was out of commission, but the *HFMS King David* was still an hour away. The two sides, then, were effectively even, considering that the *HTMS Heroic*—at the very least—was seriously damaged! The *SS Admiralty* and the *HFTMS Eternal Grace* were evenly paired, except for the ethereal strength of the *Grace's* outer **laserite** skin. In addition, the *Grace's* aircraft, that is, its *F 77 Silverbirds* and *T 111 Delta Dragons*, had already proven they were significantly superior to the highly armed *808 Double-Swept-Back Missile Fighters* of the enemy Crickets.

To a statistical, scientific entomologist, safely perusing the scene from above, the stage below was reminiscent and characteristic of various genres of wasps and bees, fighting for territorial dominance. The airplanes' bee-like dives of the Allies—when attacking the wasp-like aircraft of the Crickets—was an amazing sight to behold! The wasps had had their way with the *Heroic*, but the tide had changed and now the wasps could no longer attack in formation; instead, it became, for them, a matter of every aviator for him- or herself! The better discipline of the Allies—or was it their dogged determination and sheer tenacity— was now beginning to prove itself. The result: a few of the enemies' *808s* were leaving the sky's fiery theatre and escaping to safer skies, over the inland Yemenite territory. The absence of these few did not amount to much, since the Crickets had numerical superiority over the Allies.

Still, the Blue Vampire had to be very concerned about the way in which the naval battle was currently being waged! The *Eagle's* appearance was demoralizing, yet the *Stingray,* he carefully noted, was more than holding its own, but after a mere thirty minutes had passed, the impenetrability of the *Eternal Grace's* hull and outer shell became an evident cause for despair! These facts overwhelmingly manifested themselves, when several of his submarines' Captains reported they had attempted to scuttle the *Grace* with the latest Cricket *606 Torpedoes*, with no positive results: at first the *Barracuda* and a while later the *Eel Electric*. Both subs were noted around the world for their devastating accuracy! Other reports were coming in from the Piranha and Sharkfin that read: "*606s* dead on arrival with absolutely no good effect!" It became more than Admiral Cornwalter could stand.

The Blue Vampire went into an uncontrollable tirade, kicking chairs and throwing objects at senior officers, unfortunate enough to be in his presence. He just couldn't quite comprehend why his airplanes' bombs, too, were exploding above, near, and on the flight deck with little or no damage to the *Eternal Grace*! His officers, cold with fear of him, dared not even mention "that the better part of valor was to retreat to fight another day!"

Chapter Seven

Two Admirals—Two Lovers—Two Brothers

After observing The Blue Vampire's emotional upheaval and after listening to Admiral Cornwalter's most senior advisors, Admiral Lightning Striker, who had been summoned from his distant post, started to speak with fire in his eyes:

Lightning Striker: Listen, my fellow patriots! There has never been an army, navy, or air force without vulnerability! Moreover, since our forefathers emerged from their native home in the center of the Earth, we have never lost a war. Our brave brothers and sisters are waging the land war with welcomed news of a new victory on the Sinai. I expect, that if they are true to form, as in past conflagrations, in the end they will be victorious! We have already shown our dominance over all of the ancient lands known as Chanaan; although our secret service agents inform me that there are numerous rebels fighting in the enemy's underground army. Make no mistake about it, the land war is far from over. Once again, the latest reports are very favorable. We have very capable commanders in the field. No, let me correct myself: We have a brilliant new field marshal in General Boris Ovcharenko, leading very capable commanders. Together, they will lead our land forces to achieve the ultimate objective: Victory!

Cornwalter and the senior officers were now moved to listen to more of what Admiral Lightning Striker had to say.

Lightning Striker: As most of you know, we have devastated the *HTMS Heroic*. We said we would get even with that no-account ship, after it was fortuitous enough to damage our *Stingray*. Fortunes change and this time it's our mighty *Stingray* that is also getting the better of their other no-account ship, the *HTMS Eagle*. I suppose the much-heralded Toads just plain forgot how to build ships, don't ya think? *(The sea personnel starting to laugh and yell with bravado)* I know that some of you are distressed at the loss of our *Orca*. Yes, some reports indicate it might now be at the bottom of the sea; still other reports declare that our valiant *Orca*, while damaged, made it safely back to its Black Sea Harbor. In any case, I strongly believe that it is being rapidly repaired to reenter the fray! I predict the *Stingray* will defeat the *Eagle,* and it is up to us, of the *SS Admiralty,* to defeat the *Eternal Grace!* Our military scientists have designed a new mid-sonic underwater torpedo: the *6060*. It will penetrate any metal around. It is classified information and it will remain that way: You understand; I am sure! All intelligence stays here, onboard! The Allies must not and cannot learn of this development!

Our revised strategy will be to entice the *Eternal Grace* to follow us into the Indian Ocean, where we will also be accompanied by our immense task force, our ***Black Widows Submarine Fleet***: that, of course, includes our *Barracuda, Eel Electric, Piranha, Sharkfin,* and our latest addition, the *Devilfish*. Once our submarines and aircraft can be loaded with the *6060* series, we will reengage the *Grace*, only this time with weapons that will bring it to the bottom of the Indian Ocean. (More cheers by all. Presently, there appears a new revitalization of the ship's officers). One final detail: If the *Eagle* and its group are still afloat, after the pounding it is receiving from our *Stingray* and its fleet, and if the *HTMS King David* arrives to rescue it, then the *Stingray* will disengage. It will proceed to follow us into the Indian, where it too can be retrofitted with the new *6060s*! Does anyone here doubt that we are going to win this air and naval war?

Officers: *(answering in unison)* No sir! *(The officers of the SS Admiralty are primed for action; whereas before, there was a pall of uncertainty that permeated the very air they breathed)*.

Lightning Striker: Admiral Cornwalter *(deferring to his superior)* I believe that's all I have to relate.

Cornwalter: *(bringing his two large thick hands together, more like paws than appendages, and beginning to clap them: The rest of the officers following suit)* Your speech, it was an excellent speech Admiral Lightning Striker. Yes, simply an excellent speech! *(addressing his senior officers and advisors)* Well?

Officers: *(after being cued, beginning to applaud long and loud)* Hip, hip, hooray, hip, hip, hooray; Striker's our man! You're the best!

Vice Admiral: *(after glancing at Admiral Striker for permission)* Attention!

Cornwalter: *(in a much-improved mood, receiving the officers' salutes and returning a slow resolute salute)* One last thing: we will reconvene at 5:00 hours to discuss the latest developments. We will be leaving, then, the Arabian Sea to rendezvous with our supply ships in the Indian Ocean, off the Kenyan coast, within the hour. *(giving another quick salute from the Blue Vampire to his officers)* Dismissed!

As Admiral Lightning Striker had asserted, the *HTMS Eagle,* despite its bold initiatives, was, in his words, "taking a pounding!" Notwithstanding this assault, the *Eagle* was doing better than expected. Cheetah was right, when he declared to King Josue II, that Admiral Da Vinci was intelligent, brave, and determined. Besides, he had two superior pilots who were also capable squad leaders, the Emerald Midnight Hornet and the Hellcats' leader, Colonel Sudden Fury. These two aviators might easily be considered among the world's very best: rated in the top, of the top ten fighter pilots! Therefore, it came as no great surprise to learn, by evening's end, that recently the two colonels had shot down thirty more enemy fighters! Rachel logged 14, while Fury logged in 16. Infuriated, Lightning Striker had returned to the *Stingray*, via his night jet-helicopter. He had been informed that while the *HTMS Eagle* was really getting hit, along with some of its battle group, it was faring much better in the air! Better strategy was needed to put the *Eagle* out of commission! Striker, thus, was taking over! Major issues would require his final approval. He called an emergency meeting of his high-command officers.

"What is going on with this ship?" he started in on his officers. "Are we or are we not the military envy of the world? The Blue Vampire has given us everything we need to make the *Imperial Stingray* the pride of the Cricket Fleet. Yet, your command doesn't seem to get the job done! Well, I'm here to tell you that things are about to change. To start with, we are going to take out the *Eagle's* defensive shield, its battleships and carriers and the rest, just like we did with its twin, the *HTMS Heroic*! We are going to fight through the night, without sleep if necessary, until not a single one of their ships is left standing! *(in a booming voice)* Do you hear me?"

Command Officers: Yes sir!

Officer Number One: *(frightened, however, still willing enough to make his case heard)* But sir, our pilots are not as experienced as theirs; besides, in spite of our outnumbering the enemy with bigger guns, they keep shifting their ships' positions; and, they continue to remain elusive; and, they just won't sit still; and...

Admiral Lightning Striker *(having endured the diatribe)* Enough with the 'ands' and the excuses! Anymore of that and I'll have you shot! Besides, that's what a good Admiral does. He keeps his enemy off-balance. That's what Admiral Da Vinci is doing to us. He's keeping our larger fleet almost completely off-balance. I won't have it! No sirree! He's the best Toad Admiral the Allies have. But I've got news for the Allied leaders: Our Admirals are even better! Does anyone else have something to add? I didn't think so! I personally am going to direct the air attack. I will be leading the magnificent Blue Demons—the only squadron on this ship that seems to have a respectable kill ratio against those mongrel Frogs and Toads. I will be leading them to victory! After we dispense with the *HTMS Eagle* and its stubborn escort, we will take on a bigger prize: their noble *HFMS King David*. We will restore honor to this mission and bring greater glory to our imperial cause, so help me and in the name of all our illustrious ancestors! *(in an even louder voice)* DO YOU HEAR ME!

Command Officers: *(with renewed vigor)* Yes Sir!

Admiral Striker: What? *(once again, more boisterous than before)* I CAN'T HEAR YOU!

Command Officers: *(practically screaming)* YES SIR!

Striker: That's the spirit! Everyone back to your posts. We've got work to do! We're going to clean house! *(The officers are saluting, while Striker returns the salute with great gusto!)*

Striker was a complex person. As a child, he always needed to bully somebody. The rest of the kids respected him, not because they liked him, but due to the fear he instilled in them! Striker had learned at a very early age that "might very often means right!" As he grew in age, he would frequently go off by himself and wonder why he had such a rough childhood. Looking for answers and finding few, he would put his hands to his face to cover the tears. Once or twice he found himself sobbing almost uncontrollably! He, of course, could never bring himself to divulge these incidents, to school counselors. When trouble broke out, he cleverly found ways to avoid detention, pinning the blame on a weaker child.

The weaker child would rather spend time in detention, than have to face the wrath of Striker! Although he could beat the best and biggest of the other kids his age, he still felt inadequate. Something was missing in his life, and it had been missing for a very long time! He was an only child. His mother always seemed depressed. Even though he tried, he could do little to console her. Sometimes for no apparent reason she would yell at him. He recalled she had once taken out a strap to punish him for stealing. She later found that it was she who had lost the bracelet! She felt terribly guilty for having threatened her only son. The damage, unfortunately, had already been done! Lightning Striker would not accept her apology. He wondered if perhaps she had been the reason his father had left.

When he became an adult, he and his mother would eat supper in silence, for the most part. She would try tenderness, as a way of finding a way to his heart. Often, his mother would ask about his professional duties as an admiral, of which she was very proud. He would simply say "Someday it's all going to be mine. No one will dare ridicule me or laugh behind my back. You'll see!" She would promptly refute him, "No one, absolutely no one is doing that my son. Everyone loves what you are accomplishing for our land and us Crickets: Our Cricketstan enjoys all the fruits of your conquests. Why, the *Cricketstan Military Gazette*, just the other day, ran an article declaring that you are the first in succession to become Emperor, when our valiant Blue Vampire steps down or passes away! What more could you want?" Lightning Striker would not be appeased. Once again he would retort, while grinding his teeth, "I want it all, Mother. How many times must I tell you, Old Woman, I want it all and I'm determined to have it!" His mother, on this last occasion, frightened at his outburst, weeping and speaking through tears accompanied by heavy breathing, cautioned him. "My son, don't be foolish. Be careful of what you wish for; you just might get it!"

To say that Lightning Striker had fits of paranoia would be an understatement, according to one of the Cricket psychologists. Nevertheless, the military needed strong men who could issue commands to subordinates and get results: This, at great cost to his childhood, Admiral Lightning Striker did exceedingly well!

The night wore on, and many decisions were being made that would adversely affect the outcome—on both sides—of the air and sea war, if they were not corrected! The ground campaign, of course, was another matter. The latest Allied report was not good! It indicated that the Crickets had been able to disembark thousands of soldiers from their troop transport ships, when the *Orca* and its battle group were making their way down the Gulf of Suez. Consequently, these fresh Cricket recruits reenergized the Cricket campaign against the Frogs, Toads, and friendly nations who had joined the Allies. The Allies had not arrived at the point of desperation—fighting the land war; nevertheless, the tide did seem to be favoring the awesome, relentless Crickets! For these reasons and others, such as the safety and well -being of the region's citizenry, the Allies absolutely had to win the war at sea!

The rescue of Esther, in a manner of speaking, also depended on a naval victory. Unfortunately for Esther and her rescuers, no other naval support would be forthcoming at this time, other than the *PT 109-9* Amphibious Assault Units. The units, according to army intelligence, had left a year earlier, with the dashing Colonel Ramirez as their commander. The Colonel and his platoon of 25, a multiethnic task force, would be required to perform the rescue completely on their own!

At home, in his castle, King Josue II, in the meantime, was growing weary of the war and heartsick at the absence of his only daughter, the beautiful Princess Sophia. The whole situation was becoming clouded with adversity! Notwithstanding the aforementioned, occasionally, rays of sunshine made their appearances. For example, In various regions of Frogland and Toadland, where Cricket occupational forces were in place, the people kept vigilant with many joining the resistance: It came to be known as M-50! They struck terror into the hearts of the enemy Crickets. On this cold November night, decisions were being made at home, as well as, on all the war's fronts!

Aboard the *SS Admiralty*, the Blue Vampire and his senior advisors knew they had made the correct strategic decision to reach the Kenyan coast. Here on an undisclosed island, Cricket chemical, biological, mechanical, electrical, structural, and even civil engineers, as well as physicists and biophysicists, were working hand-in-hand with comparable renegade scientists and contractors. Their aim was to create and fabricate weapons of mass destruction, including super-powered torpedoes and missiles. In addition, by leaving the Arabian Sea, the *SS Admiralty* would cause the *HFTMS Eternal Grace* to pursue them. By this stratagem, they would also be rescuing the *Imperial Stingray*; otherwise, it would stand little chance against the impenetrability of the *Eternal Grace!*

Meanwhile, Admiral Cheetah and his senior staff officers had to decide whether or not to pursue the *Admiralty*. They were torn between helping the *HTMS Eagle*, that was also laboring to pick water logged seamen and seawomen out of the Arabian, and the worrisome idea that the *SS Admiralty* was escaping to fight another day! They, after much heated discussion, decided that the Cricket **flagship** must not be allowed to make good its flight from the present conflagration! Cheetah reasoned, with his officers, that the *Eagle* could hold on a few hours longer, when the *David* would arrive to enter into the fray. After all, the *Eagle,* although not as large as the *Stingray,* had proven itself time and again throughout the night; moreover, did the *King David* not defeat the invincible *Orca*?

Reconnaissance flights, conducted by the *HFTMS Eternal Grace,* at last spotted the glorious *HFMS King David,* with all of its battle flags swaying and then fluttering against the breezes of the chilly Red Sea. *His Frog Majesty's Ship* was just on the verge of entering the Arabian Sea, when they were informed of new developments! Several top senior officers, apparently, disagreed with the handsome, dark-complexioned Admiral, stating It was still risky business! Many Allied lives might be lost at sea, if the *HTMS Eagle* were abandoned! Whereas If the *Grace* remained, they logically argued—and certainly with the *SS Admiralty* gone—their *Eternal Grace* would send the *Imperial Stingray* to the lower depths! The Allies, in effect, would have decisively won, by having destroyed three of the four Cricket carriers, including their escorts!

"On the other hand," Cheetah, with stern conviction evident in his baritone voice, shot back, "the destruction of the *SS Admiralty* will end sea war hostilities once and for all! Having cut off the monster's head, most definitely," he continued, "the war will be abruptly halted. The Crickets, hat in hand, will sue for peace! They will have no other choice; this much I promise you!" *The King David,* he also argued, would save the *HTMS Eagle* along with the *HTMS Heroic's* men and women sailors, both afloat in the Indian Ocean. With that, the issue was settled and, once again, Admiral Cheetah demonstrated why he was head of the Allied Naval Operation Command: Cheetah wanted nothing less than the Blue Vampire's head!

Aboard the *Stingray,* Admiral Lightning Striker had issued the directive to move all remaining squadrons out against the enemy. He had the killer instinct and understood that he who strikes first and hardest will "win the day": In his case "win the night!" While morale was high aboard the *Stingray,* the Admiral was pushing his men and women almost beyond their limits to endure: they were at the point of exhaustion. Many of the Cricket male and female aviators had not slept in 24 hours. He would not tolerate slackers! Anyone not ready for combat would be severely punished. In some cases they would literally be fed to the sharks!

Striker believed that the *HFTMS Eternal Grace* was closing in—within the hour. He must do his level best, at the very least, to incapacitate the *Eagle* while evading the *David*. The *HFMS King David* and the *HFTMS Eternal Grace* were the largest of the enemy's carriers; of equal importance, they also possessed the largest complement, including fabulous battleships, with long-range missiles, and vicious submarines to match their own. The Tiger Subs had added to their reputation when successfully confronting the *Imperial Orca.* If the *Orca* was no match for the *David* and its battle group, what chance did his *Stingray*, with an exhausted crew, have?

Aboard the *HTMS Eagle* morale was even higher than on the *Stingray!* For one thing, Fleet Admiral Roberto Da Vincii: Supreme Allied co-Commander of Naval Forces insisted that each pilot have at least four hours of sleep! A pilot, he proposed, needed to feel razor-sharp in the air. A four-minute dog-fight is an eternity in the sky. Incredibly, a millennium earlier, a pilot by the name of Colonel Epstein had endured eight minutes of dogfighting over the Sinai. He withstood the assault of eleven of the enemy, completely by himself! He downed four of the enemy airplanes and the others, one by one, left the field of combat. Apparently, they were facing a force they couldn't defeat. They were outnumbered by this lone pilot's stupendous airmanship! Perhaps there was a mysterious copilot riding with Epstein that day? No one can say for certain. His efforts, indeed, helped to save a nation! Likewise, the Allies intended to save theirs!

Rachel's alarm awakened her and she got up like a shot! A few cabins down, in the male quarters, **Fury's** alarm also went off. He was "up and at 'em" before you could say "Jack Robinson!" They had agreed to meet in the officers' dining hall. The breakfast was to both of their liking: French toast, a side of meat, and hash browns. Fury began the conversation by asking Rachel to pass the marmalade. She smiled her usual bright smile and politely whispered "Sure." Fury asked, "Why are you whispering? The enemy Crickets can't hear you. They're making too much noise sending stray missiles this way." **Rachel** responded, "The answer to your first question is that I'm still asleep! The answer to your second statement is that the enemy is simply trying to serenade us, with the whizzing and screaming rockets." **Fury** couldn't help contain his laughter and stated, "You just know how to brighten up a feller's day, don't ya?"

After some more bantering, Rachel confessed to Fury that for the first time she was very apprehensive, very concerned! "You know," she began, "We have got to hold out until the *King David* arrives, and as far as I'm concerned, *His Frog Majesty's Ship* can't come soon enough!" "All I can tell you is to keep the faith," Fury assured her. "You've taught me that! Besides, I am here to protect you, ha, ha, ha!" Rachel smiled an even bigger smile now, more like a cheshire cat. "Oh really? Who, pray tell, pulled whom out of the stormy sea last year? Ha, ha, back to you." "Well, you certainly got the best of me there," he responded.

Fury more serious now began to open up his heart. "To tell you the truth, Colonel Goldsmith, I don't want to live in a world without you!" His exotic brown eyes zeroed in on hers and his betrayed much more. Rachel coolly replied, "Listen Mr. Smoothy, Sir Knight-in-shining-armor, I can very well take care of myself. I've been a big girl for some time now. Furthermore, if something should happen to me, there would be an army of women who would love to take care of you!" "Rachel, Rachel, don't ya *see*, there's only one gal in this whole wide world for *me;* Rachel, Rachel, to be *sure*, for you, there's nothin' in the world I'd not *endure*!" Rachel finds Fury amusing and begins to sing, "So, now you're the poet, too!" Rachel's coquettish demeanor soon changes to her musing about family. "Seriously, Fury, if I was overly concerned before, you've brought me back to reality. And, by the way, your poetry isn't half-bad! It's all about enduring, isn't it? We Frogs and Toads, over the eons, have endured. I am confident that your good people will endure as well!"

A call over the loudspeaker in the mess caught their attention. "All able pilots to your aircraft!" Fury, once more, was looking at Rachel as they both left their seats, with unfinished food on the table, "Here we go," he calmly stated. "All able pilots to your aircraft!" The voice over the loudspeaker seemed foreboding. A few minutes later, the two pilots got within a short distance of their respective airplanes, stationed side by side: Rachel's *F 77 Silverbird* and Fury's *T 111 Delta Dragon*. They were, instantly, drawn to each other by the Holy Spirit! Without saying a word, they looked quickly and deeply into each other's eyes. This time, it was Fury who reached to embrace Rachel. Neither one of them wanted the strong, yet tender, embrace to end. Then, Fury broke the silence saying, "I hope I don't get fired for what I'm about to do." With that, he gave her a most passionate kiss, the kind that actors of the silent screen gave to their sweethearts, before danger separated them!

An hour had passed and still there was still no sign of the *HFTMS Eternal Grace!* Rachel and Fury, high above the waves of the Indian Ocean, each from their own canopy, could see for a considerable distance all around. They had hoped to observe something that resembled the *David*, but their efforts to locate it were in vain! In a few moments, they would be locked in mortal combat against Admiral Lightning Striker and his Blue Demons, among other

Cricket squadrons. It had been pitch-black out, when the Hellcats had followed Admiral Fury's lead off the *Eagle's* flight deck.

As more pilots left the ship and looked over their shoulders, they could see Toad Navy firemen putting out various fires, caused by Cricket battleships hurling payloads from their huge cannons. The Hellcats were itching to take on Striker! They were obsessed with the idea of retaliating against the Blue Vampire and Striker for having imprisoned their families! An elite Toad squadron known as Gideon's Raiders also took to the air. These young aviators hailed from the prestigious Majestic Toad Flight Academy that, although small, produced the best of the nation's pilots. Thus, the Emerald Midnight Hornet, Colonel Fury and his Hellcats, along with Gideon's Raiders all joined in formation, high in the still chilly Indian sky, as they prepared to descend on the *Stingray*!

One individual who was missing in the lineup was *The Ghost*. The Toad ace had fought brilliantly the night before; unfortunately, his time in the air became excessive, during the prolonged dogfight, and it caused him to run out of fuel. Before ditching into the wintry waters of the Arabian Sea, however, he was able to take three of the enemy with him! After plunging into the Arabian, he encountered a new enemy: sharks! The sea could be less forgiving than the sky! Twenty terrifying minutes would elapse, fighting off hungry sharks, when much to his surprise, his younger brother, Jonathan Rosencrantz, arrived to rescue him in an *Allied PT 109 -9 Amphibious Assault Unit*.

The younger Rosencrantz, it turns out, had been allowed to remain in the Toad Air Force, after an incredible Toad Court Martial Hearing that lasted two days. The Military Tribunal found him temporarily insane, due to combat fatigue, as a result of too many reconnaissance flights! Jonathan, nevertheless, was summarily demoted from the rank of Major to that of Captain. An additional, special condition was placed on him that required he be remanded to the protective custody of the Ghost. The slightest infraction would land him in a Toad Military Prison! There was no doubt in anyone's mind that The Ghost's reputation had kept his younger brother from sitting out the war in the stockade. Thus, when Jonathan successfully pulled his older brother from the Arabian's jaws, it served as evidentiary proof that the Toad's Military Tribunal had not been remiss in permitting Jonathan to continue in the King's service.

There was anger enough to go around! Admiral Lightning Striker was angry for his lost childhood; the pilots of the Blue Squadron carried an intense anger directed at Colonel Sudden Fury, whom they viewed as a turncoat; Colonel Fury was angry for the attempted murder resulting in the death of his mentor, the Red Vampire; the Hellcats were angry, as was Fury, at the imprisonment of their families and the humiliation they had had to suffer while being paraded through Cricketstonia; Colonel Rachel Goldsmith was angry at the hardships the Frogs were going through, just to survive day to day; and, finally, Gideon's Raiders were angry at the devastation the Cricket invasion had caused Toadland, with so many of their cities now ablaze. The night sky went from black to gray when the firing of the various guns of the two competing sky armies went into action. Initially, Striker's Blue Squadron seemed to have gotten the jump on Fury's Hellcats: Both air force squadrons had trained at the same Cricket Top Gun Academy and, therefore, knew each others' every move.

Still, beyond the normal Cricket strategy of flying in formation, over the years, the Hellcats had developed their own style of aerial combat. It now differed ostensibly from that of the Blue Squadron of the enemy Crickets. The Hellcats, rather than making a full bend to the left or right, when caught from behind, would flatten or tilt their wing upward to catch the air so that it would slow down their machine. This lifting of the wing, thus, would facilitate their airplane's ability to come out of the arch sooner. The result of using this technique saved many of the Hellcats' lives; whereas, the old technique exposed their aircraft to other enemy fighters. The enemy could then pick them off while they were still in the bend.

Another technique they used was to fly straight up into the sky, knowing they could outlast the pursuer. When the chaser gave up, finally breaking to return downward, the Hellcat pilot would immediately break after him giving pursuit, until the pilot had a clear shot. At that point, the Hellcat pilot would release a heat-seeking missile that caused the enemy's aircraft to explode, lighting up the sky! If the Hellcat had expended all of his or her missiles, then he or she would get close enough to drill the enemy's airplane with his machine gun. Still another technique utilized by the Hellcats, when caught from behind, was to loop perpendicularly to the earth. This act permitted the chased to become the chaser!

Any initial advantage, the Blue Squadron may have had, soon evaporated. Except for a few of Gideon's Raiders being shot down, the Allies performed admirably! The Hellcats made mincemeat out of the Blue Squadron, downing three times as many of the enemy. Many of Gideon's Raiders, despite having less real combat experience, also performed meritoriously! As the fight raged on, over the ships below, airplanes could be seen dropping out of the sky and crashing into the choppy, churning sea! A thin light was beginning to appear from the east. The awesome warring gave the whole scene a macabre atmosphere. A visitor from outer space might believe he or she was witnessing the end of the earth: Armageddon!

Somewhere in the middle of everything that was occurring, high above the Indian Ocean, Rachel Goldsmith found herself holding her breath, desperately attempting to reach the water's upper surface. Apparently, one of the Gideon Raiders had mistaken her for an enemy aircraft, in the still-darkened arena of death in the sky. The young Raider pilot shot Rachel out of the night sky by mistake! While Rachel's new *F 77 Silverbird* did somewhat resemble that of the Blue Demons' *808s,* because of large, triple blue stripes located on both sides of the center fuselage, still, it was sufficiently different, such that it should not have drawn fire from a friendly pilot!

No doubt, the novice aviator panicked after making a straight barrel roll and then arching down and left to avoid being killed. When re-ascending, up and to the right, she was temporarily blinded by all the gunfire and shot at a silhouette. The Gideon Raider must have imagined it was an enemy *808 Double-Swept-Back Missile Fighter*! Not realizing what she had done, the young Raider continued to fight on, thinking all the while she had downed one of the enemy!

Sudden Fury, from a distance, a moment or two after downing two *808s,* saw instantly what had happened! He immediately radioed in for assistance. Within five minutes another *PT 109-9* rushed to rescue Colonel Goldsmith. Incredible as it may seem, the captain piloting the *Amphibious Assault Unit* was none other than Jonathan Rosencrantz! Already dressed in a wetsuit, he jumped into the shark-infested waters, without regard for his own life, and managed to pull the Emerald Midnight Hornet to safety. Once she was aboard the *PT 109-9,* Jonathan winked his left eye at the Colonel, saluted respectfully, and then cheerfully identified himself as Captain Jonathan Rosencrantz of His Toad Majesty's Royal Air force. "At your service, Emerald Midnight Hornet" he exclaimed!

Then, in a more serious tone, he stated: "I apologize for any inconvenience I may have caused you!" Rachel, still the colonel, returned the courtesy by saluting and saying "I guess we're even now; the past is passed. I'm gratified that you are really on our side! Now for more important matters, I'm dying for some Frog coffee or just any coffee!" Jonathan, more at ease, "It so happens we do have some of your famous Frog coffee: coming right up, Colonel!" "Thank you, Captain," Rachel, all smiles, replied. "By the way," she continued, "thanks, too, for the blanket; it sure beats getting kissed by a shark!" They both laughed at the picture of her perfunctory remark! The Frog Prime Minister Plato had once stated: "The better part of valor is genuine friendship!"

What seemed like an eternity—falling more than floating in the sky—became a thing of the past: Rachel was safe! Admiral Striker and his violent band of killers, on the other hand, seeing the attrition of their airplanes, headed home for the *Stingray*. Their mission was not a total failure; although unable to defeat the Emerald Midnight Hornet and Sudden Fury, the Crickets successfully destroyed a number of the Allies' airplanes, including a couple of Hellcats! Striker, however, had lost numerous Blue Demons; moreover, the best of the *Black Widows Submarine Fleet*, including *the Barracuda, the Eel Electric, the Piranha, the Sharkfin,* and *the Devilfish* had left to accompany the *SS Admiralty*. The safety of the *Admiralty* held a higher priority than the *Stingray*! The Crickets, Prudently, had left their *Southern Underwater Fleet (SUF)* to protect the *Stingray*: among those were the *SUF 6, SUF 16, SUF 26, and SUF 46* but not the *SUF 36*. It had met its demise at the hands of the Frogs' *The Tigerfisher*! Conversely, the Frogs' *Tigerfisher* and the *Spearfisher* were now assigned to protect the *HTMS Eagle* and what was left of the *HTMS*

Heroic, while the Frog *Harpooner* and *Tomahawker* were charged to escort the *HFTMS Eternal Grace*.

The private war being waged by the *Eagle* and the *Stingray* seemed to present such a huge and relentless barrage of firepower that it lit up the almost-night sky, as if it were day. The bombs exploding in air, ironically, gave the entire environment an atmosphere of jubilation! Yet, there was nothing to celebrate except death and destruction! The fleets, those of the Allies and those of the enemy Crickets, were at loggerheads or more like two rams, butting heads! Neither could get the advantage of the other! The giant battleships of both navies, in addition, fearing being hit by the torpedoes from enemy subs, couldn't get close enough to their respective enemies' carriers to inflict serious damage.

Therefore, at about the same time, the two sides switched tactics and began to employ the use of their much lighter, faster ships. The Frog Battleship*Televiva* issued six destroyers to lead the fight; while the Cricket Battleship *Cricketstonia* also enlisted the same number. Perhaps, the reason their private war was at a standstill was due to the complete balance in both sides' naval vessels. The war's Arabian Sea outcome would rely more on strategy and cunningness, than on even numbers: until one side obtained the advantage. The destroyers would make the difference!

As daybreak arrived, with the aircraft of both groups regrouping and refueling aboard their respective carriers: the *Eagle* and the *Stingray,* a final effort was underway to finish what had been so energetically and so valiantly started. There was absolutely no question that the destroyers had the awesome responsibility to win the battle for their respective nations! The destroyers, as in days of yore, still found it necessary to group themselves in numbers of six. Six destroyers, then, like six Musketeers guarding the Queen, provided the escort for her majesty, the grand carrier. Other naval vessels, of course, also accompanied the fleet; especially noteworthy were the heavy and light cruisers, the dukes and earls. However, much like heirs to the king's throne, battleships were in a class of their own: a special breed apart! Being the largest of the offensive attack naval vessels, these majestic ships moved in the ocean's realm, more like giant sharks than whales.

To be sure, the other battleships were having their own private war. Some speculated these ships were now deep in the Indian Ocean, perhaps in the vicinity of Diego Garcia! No one knew exactly. As to what the projected outcome might be, that was a complete mystery. In any case, it would be a horrendous battle! Incredibly, here again, both sides seemed evenly matched. "Stop to think about it," one sailor said to another, "at this very moment, they are positioned toe-to-toe, punching each other out with all the guts they've got in them! I can see the scene now, with flashes of light coming from their great guns! Wow, what a battle that must be!" Officers aboard the *Eagle* were also discussing similar scenes of battleships at war. The unforgettable images, the officers vividly recalled, were from historical filmic archives they had viewed, while still in training as cadets at the various Allied Naval Academies. These films depicted major naval battles fought in the Pacific Ocean, that is, in the vicinity of the Philippines, many centuries past, a millennium or more, almost though not entirely forgotten! History had recorded it as *The Battle of the Philippines*!"

"In the next few days," Admiral Da Vinci on the *Eagle* was overheard saying, "We will either win or lose our fight for freedom! The bulk of our battleships are dueling near Garcia; the *HFTMS Eternal Grace* is pursuing the *SS Admiralty*; moreover, we are in a death-grip, hoping against all hope that our destroyers will win the day against those of the mighty Crickets! The *David* seems to have lost its way, or, worse yet, it may have hit a mine field! For now, however, the fate of our carrier is at stake! The difference in the Arabian Theatre, incredibly, will be determined not by our largest vessels; rather, it will be the result of our smallest yet fastest ships. These little warriors, these mighty little guys, yes our destroyers, it is they who will make all the difference!"

That night, the night Admiral Da Vinci was to send his mighty destroyers into harm's way, he murmured a silent prayer. He was asking the Supreme Power in the universe to work a miracle for his most courageous, little ships. "Help them defeat the awesome Crickets, their larger destroyers, yes, the same way David defeated Goliath in the plains!" He thought about his family and the families of all the navy personnel aboard the various destroyers. He couldn't sleep! His head was filled with too many thoughts, so he went over to the officers' mess and poured himself some black coffee and grabbed a doughnut. They looked so tempting! He decided that the last jellyroll just might need a new home, and he could think of no better place than his tummy!

After he had his fill, he meandered up the observation tower and spoke to the officers present. They came to attention and he told them to stand at ease. They informed him that all had been quiet for the last two hours. "We were going to awaken you;" one of his senior officers mentioned, "however, we felt it more important that you rest. All the same, things are just too quiet. We feel the enemy is up to something!" Da Vinci replied, "Well, for what it's worth, I am glad you let me grab two hours' sleep. I wouldn't have been much good without the rest anyhow!"

He continued, "Just before I retired, I spoke with all of the commanders aboard our seven destroyers, and they assured me they are itching to outmaneuver and pound the enemy!" One of the officers spoke up and asked, "How is it we now have seven destroyers, instead of the customary six, admiral?" "The seventh ship has been sent to us by the Admiral of the *King David,*" Da Vinci answered. All of the officers shouted in unison "the *King David*, sir?" "Yes," Da Vinci exclaimed, "the *King Dav*id! We now know our *King* struck a mine; consequently, she has been delayed. Keep the faith! She is due to arrive tomorrow, around 16:00 hours or just past mid-day." Another officer, somewhat confused, asked, "How is it, if I might be so bold as to inquire, Admiral, that you waited until now to inform us?" "That's a fair question, Commodore. The answer is we needed to be absolutely certain the information we were receiving was true! We received confirmation just as I was walking this way. A courier gave me a decoded message concerning the whereabouts of the *David;* it was sent from one of our submarines, the *Tigerfisher*. The *Tigerfisher's* captain stated he had spotted a destroyer approaching one of our heavy cruisers, undetected! It appeared to be in a belligerent attitude. Let me read this passage to you:

> We were just ready to take down the destroyer, when we recognized it was one of ours—that is, one belonging to the *King David's* avant-garde! We noticed a flag with a bluish star, with six points to it, flying high above its guns. We proceeded to surface and board the *Heavenly Angel*—that's the destroyer's name. She's a real beauty to behold, especially in the moonlight! Of course, we made contact with her *beforehand*; otherwise, she might have knocked us out of the water instead!
>
> She's sporting her new and improved laser-tech torpedoes and depth charges, not to mention her latest incredible guns! These new guns surpass anything a comparable ship of her size can accommodate: They are lighter in weight yet pack twice the punch! Yes, help is definitely on the way, Admiral Da Vinci. Wish we could get there sooner!

"That's all the info we have been able to receive on our printout. The air is full of static and all the audible messages are garbled! I trust, no, I hope it isn't a deception by the Crickets. That ole Blue Vampire—a certain Mister Admiral Cornwalter, that monster—may be up to some of his old nasty tricks!

"The incredible thing is: the *Tigerfisher* is supposed to be off the Kenyan Coast, with the *Eternal Grace*! And, if I may add, what is the *Angel* doing this far from the rest of the *King David's* avant-garde? I wish it were true. Then I wouldn't have to send out our destroyers in desperation to beat those rascals! Our carrier is still busy putting out fires, and some of our firefighters have slept less than I have! I just love those swabbies, those brave firemen and firewomen are terrific, too! I can't believe we are still afloat! If we are in trouble, I can only imagine what is going on, this very minute, aboard the *Stingray*! We have to have hit it pretty darn hard! What has saved us is the magnificent job our pilots have done. Sadly, at last count, we've lost more than half our planes; we just can't afford to lose too many more!

"To the point, I still think our best bet is to take them off guard with our destroyers. If they can get in close and drop a few Easter eggs in the enemy's belly, then we will all, finally, get some much-needed R and R! For now, I want you all to hit the sack for the next hour, and that's an order! I've made arrangements for replacements on the bridge."

They all saluted and shouted "Yes Sir!" With that, Admiral Da Vinci stood on the bridge, quite alone, thinking of his family and of all his sailors aboard the *Eagle*. In a brief extended moment his thoughts returned to the commanders and their men and women aboard the destroyers. Once again, he found himself in prayer, only this time he asked for guidance. Looking skyward, toward the full moon, he petitioned, "Shall I send in the destroyers and catch the enemy off-guard, Sir, at the risk of losing all or most of these fine officers and the brave men and women they command, or shall I wait for His Majesty's Ship, the *King David,* to arrive? Give me, please, You Most Holy One on High, a sign! I pray thee on bended knee."

The officers hadn't been asleep more than twenty minutes, when they were awakened by a tremendous blast! It appears that Admiral Leopoldski—now commanding the *Stingray*—had the exact same idea as did Admiral Da Vinci: a renewed surprise attack! None of the intelligence officers aboard the *Eagle* could ever have imagined that the Crickets would attack with a full moon in plain sight! Still, they did! They did so with all the venom their twelve destroyers could launch! The Allies had not realized that an additional six destroyers had been commissioned by the *SS Admiralty's* command, to assist the *Stingray's* destroyer-initiative! It was both a daring and brilliant move issued on the part of the Blue Vampire. If the Toad carrier was in trouble before, the ole gal's spirits were now sinking, or so it appeared!

The Allied destroyers—all seven including the newly arrived *Heavenly Angel* from the *HFMS King David*—were caught flatfooted, as they say; nevertheless, the seven made an enormous attempt to contain further enemy damage to their carrier, by establishing a defensive guard. These Allied destroyers, now placed on the defensive, were able, nonetheless, to create a most effect shield. The Frog and Toad destroyers tightened their perimeter, just like Roman Legions of old. They brought their shields, their small destroyers, together to form a giant tortoise! It worked!

The Allied destroyers in their new positions, between the incoming Cricket destroyers and the *HTMS Eagle*, held off the enemy invaders! At that pivotal moment, the outnumbered Frog and Toad destroyers went on the offensive! They took forward positions and commenced action against the aggressors! Amazingly, in spite of fewer ships, the Allied attack was showing positive results, due to the Allies' superior tactics. This smaller fleet outperformed the larger fleet of Cricket destroyers. As a result, many of the Cricket destroyers began to meet their doom on that moonlit night.

While the destroyers, along with larger ships, were battling in the Arabian Sea and a complete conflagration of both navies was taking place, Colonels Goldsmith and Fury, in the company of a few Hellcats, joined the upper night stratosphere. Within minutes, from a great height, they, too, began to engage the Crickets by swooping down on the incoming destroyers and other larger belligerents in the proximity. Many of the *Eagle's* aircraft, however, were less fortunate. They were caught by the enemy's ferocious bombs, delivered by the *Stingray's* best dive-bombers.

It was, thus, that the Frogs and Toads became outnumbered in the night's sky. With all of the enemy's fire raining down on the Allied fleet, incredibly, only one torpedo had hit the *Eagle*, and it had landed just below **Catapult**

#4. Fortunately, there, where the hull is rounded, just under the water line and where it begins to narrow, the *Eagle* was protected due to its unique feature of a triple bottom. The two additional layers of the hull, each over the first layer, consisted of steel plating with a gap between each of them. The triple bottom, therefore, provided the much-needed protection from the *Stingray's* torpedo and insured the *Eagle's* safety! These extra layers had performed superbly by preventing a massive leak! The *Eagle* continued to fulfill its design mission: to transport its fighter aircraft, to launch its airplanes, to serve as a mobile command center, and to house its military personnel.

An hour earlier, apparently, Admiral Lightning Striker, now aboard the Cricket battleship *The Emperor's Tempest*, also known simply as *The Tempest*, had received a secret communiqué from The Blue Vampire, still aboard his flagship, the *SS Admiralty*. In that midnight missive, Admiral Cornwalter had directed Admiral Striker to re-attack the *Eagle*, immediately, along with all available destroyers. The missive continued: "Bring deliberate destroyer-hostility to the enemy, regardless of any casualties the destroyers, themselves, might receive!" Admiral Lightning Striker, therefore, ordered the *Stingray's* Admiral Leopoldski to place the plan into effect, immediately! While that action was taking place, the *Stingray* was to slip away and rejoin the *SS Admiralty*, off the Kenyan Coast. The missive concluded with:

> It is vital! You must make haste! Together we can defeat the *Eternal Grace!* Once accomplished, we can also defeat the *King David!* Our giant *Orca* has speedily been restored at a naval yard, at an undisclosed site, off the Black Sea Coast. Praise our forefathers: it has been saved! As I transmit this coded message, the *Orca*, once again, is making its way down the Gulf of Suez. If we act quickly, we will definitely hold the superior hand: moreover, in spite of the damages you have sustained, according to information passed on to Vice Admiral Baryshnikov by Chief Warrant Officer Five Maliknecov, we believe the Stingray can now make the necessary repairs as it rendezvous to meet us, in the Indian Ocean off the Kenyan Coast. In the name of our ancestors, good hunting! Get moving! Hurry!

The poet looks at war and calls it madness unloosed on Earth! Yet, at a distance, from a place of safety, war can appear to be quite beautiful with all of the bombs creating huge, massive fireworks. Even the roaring of the ships' giant cannons, causing a deafening exhilaration, stirring the hearts of some, while still frightening others, can continue to excite those who have made the military their career. Other patriots come away with a different sense of war: they understand that sometimes destruction is a necessary part of life, like tearing down a building that, otherwise, might collapse on the innocent.

Yes, Fury thought, maybe I have been concluding falsely. It was, thus, that the friendly Cricket, Sudden Fury, contemplated the effects of the torpedoes he had just dropped on the battleship, *The Emperor's Invincible!* He must have made a direct hit, judging from the way the battleship began to list to one side. Fury wondered if his nemesis Lightning Striker was on that ship. If so, maybe everything had been squared: maybe he had gotten revenge without meaning to do so. As the friendly Cricket zoomed back into the safety net of the still-darkened sky, he also asked himself if Striker had a family. In the span of less than a minute, he began to feel, more than ask, with an uneasiness arising from the pit of his stomach!

He questioned anew: had he, Colonel Sudden Fury, formerly of his Emperor's Air Force, made the right decision by going over to the Allied command, over to the Armada of the Frogs and Toads? He couldn't entirely convince himself that he had. Oh yes! The Red Vampire, that fabulous old man, his mentor Reynaldo, had insisted he follow his heart. Reynaldo, Reynaldo, Reynaldo, where are you now? Are you up here somewhere in the Arabian night sky? Are you still counseling me even after your demise? The minute had disappeared just as quickly as it had appeared. The Colonel turned his magnificent machine to the right and returned to his base on the *Eagle*. The flight deck had been cleared and it was now safe to land. As he descended from his airplane he noticed that Rachel had just landed before him. They greeted each other with exuberant grins that suggested: let's have coffee!

When Fury quickly crossed over to meet Rachel, he noticed that her arm was bleeding. "What's that!" he exclaimed. She smiled and then collapsed in his arms. He called for a medic, and within a few minutes the doctors began examining her to determine the extent of her wounds. Apparently, her suit had been penetrated by a steel object flying in her direction, after cutting through the canopy of her airplane's visor. Her right arm had been slashed, and she had rapidly been losing blood. In no time whatsoever, the doctors were able to stop the bleeding of the wound that had occurred just below the upper right shoulder. They immediately started a transfusion to replace the lost blood. Throughout the procedure, Colonel Sudden Fury remained at her side.

After what seemed like an endless night and when the sun began to make its appearance, Rachel, too, began to awaken and mumbled she was hungry. The doctor said that was a good sign; however, he noted she would be placed on a special diet, and they would need to make certain that no infection manifested itself. "She'll be good as new in a week or so!" the head surgeon had assured. The doctor's name was Roberts, and he had volunteered to serve with the *Eagle* since hostilities had broken out against the Crickets. He was a rather tall man with kindly eyes. His full head of hair made him appear younger than his years.

He spoke with Colonel Fury and, once again, reassured him that she would be just fine; nevertheless, "she should not return to duty until she has made a full recovery," he cautioned! Fury inquired, "And how long might that take?" Dr. Roberts replied, "Well, it shouldn't take more than a month." "A month?" Fury countered. "She'll never stand for it!" "That's the reason we're having this talk," Roberts stated, looking squarely into Fury's eyes. "She'll listen to you; we all know she is sweet on you; moreover, you must promise me, for her good, to do everything in your power to keep her out of any cockpit: She mustn't fly, at least not for a month!"

Colonel Fury, who had been returning the good doctor's gaze, grit his teeth and then replied, "That's a tall order! But, you've got it: affirmative. I'll keep her out of the air if I have to...If I have to do whatever it takes! She means more to me than I can put into words." The two men shook hands after Fury, once again, thanked him for his attentive skills applied to the woman he loved. The doctor said she was resting now, and there was nothing else to do but for everyone to get some shuteye. Fury nodded in agreement. Fury looked as if he needed a hug and the doctor obliged. He patted the Colonel on his back and in so doing felt some of Fury's tears glancing off his own cheek as they parted.

The doctor began, "We owe you and your Hellcats such a debt of gratitude that I doubt we can ever repay you." Fury replied, "No, sir, it is we who owe you for allowing us to join you in the cause of freedom. You are helping us regain our nation by ridding us of the evil that has dominated for far too long!" Their eyes met, one last time, and as the two stood, a special moment passed between them, these two men of resolve, these titans of principle.

Less than a week had passed since Rachel's brush with death, and much had transpired! Fury, after attending an officers' meeting, dropped by the *Eagle's* hospital quarters to check on Rachel. He had not missed a day visiting her since she had been admitted. He was, therefore, surprised to see her out of bed and fully dressed in her flight suit. As he greeted her, in her private room, he presented her with flowers. "Hey, how ya doin', pardner," he said with his best western-movie drawl. "These thangs are fur the dag-dern most beautiful coyote this side of the Pekoes!"

She came over to greet him, slowly, and beamed saying, "Wow! Where and how did you ever get these gorgeous flowers?" "That's a top secret, but—suffice it to say—a certain admiral gave them to me to give to you, provided I didn't divulge his name." "I see," replied Rachel. "Well, you both certainly know the way to a Colonel's heart," she stated and then began to giggle as she fussed over the multicolored flowers that made up the bouquet. "I think I'll put them right over here by the window, where they can get some sunshine!"

Colonel Fury was pleasantly surprised, himself, when Rachel turned from the window to plant a huge kiss, finding its mark, right on his lips. He, shyly, returned to his western drawl and said, "Why mama, how'd ya learnt ta kiss like that?" With that, they both laughed and it felt good! There had not been much to laugh about in a long time. Rachel started again, slightly changing the tone and the mood of their encounter by saying, "Fury, I wish we had more to laugh about and smile about." This time Fury, in a more serious demeanor answered, "We do, we do. Let's sneak out and get that coffee I almost promised you, and I'll tell you all about it!" A few minutes later, he hoped, they might be found sipping coffee and enjoying a doughnut at the ship's cafe.

Even though Dr. Roberts had still not released her, he had mentioned she was recovering more rapidly than even he had expected; nevertheless, he had felt it was just too early for dismissal. "It's necessary for her to remain under close observation, until the sutures are ready for removal," were his orders to Fury, beforehand. Colonel Fury, however, felt the Emerald Midnight Hornet, she, herself, needed some sunshine; moreover, the flight deck was a lot more peaceful than it had been for a long time! Thus, there was no real danger outside. With little difficulty, extirpating Rachel from her hospital ward, Fury took Rachel's arm and placed it in the crook of his arm. The two, then, commenced to walk arm-in-arm to their favorite onboard coffeehouse. Life was beautiful. They would at long last share a cup of Joe!

Rachel: Well, now that we're here, with few people around, please, please tell me everything that I've missed!

Fury: As you can see for yourself, the Cricket offensive has almost subsided, except for a few submarines that are still lurking—in deeper water—still trying to sink us! The *Stingray*, evidently, was not as damaged as we had hoped. She made good her get- away and is presently en route to join the *SS Admiralty* in the Indian Ocean, off the Kenyan Coast! More exciting news! I've been almost bursting at the seams by keeping this information to myself. Try and guess!

Rachel: The *King David* has arrived!

Fury: Yes! And that's not fair; you stole my thunder! Under the circumstances, nonetheless, I forgive you and you win the prize!

Rachel: And what might that be?

Fury: A trip for two aboard the *HFMS King David*!

Rachel: You and I are going? Just the two of us!

Fury: Yes again and again. We have both been reassigned to that beautiful lady! If a ship is a she, I guess I can refer to he as a she, you know, using seaman's vernacular?

Rachel: *(chiding)* As long as you remember she is really a he (both chuckling) As to our new orders, I don't know if that makes me happy or not. I've got so many questions. To begin with: What's going to happen with the *Eagle*. And, how did I get reassigned to join the *King David* in my broken condition?

Fury: Those are two questions I am more than happy to answer. I'll take the last one first. You are, judging from your x-rays, going to be just hunky-dory.

Rachel: What about the sutures?

Fury: Doc says that's the easy part. He just wants you to lie low for a spell. The Allies can't afford to have their best aviator on the ground for too long!

Rachel: But you're not! I can tell you've been up there… in the blue horizon!

Fury: Hey, Silly, my reference was not to me, but to you! You're the best!

Rachel: No, we're the best! *(changing the mood with caution)* What haven't you told me?

Fury: I was getting to that. Not a biggie, not one to be overly concerned about.

Rachel: And ... the answer is...?

Fury: *(a bit more serious) The Orca* has been restored. She has, however, bypassed us and is steaming to join the rest of the Cricket fleet off the Kenyan Coast.

Rachel: Wow, wow, wow! That means the *Eternal Grace* is at a tremendous disadvantage, being out there all by herself!

Fury: All the more reason we are going to close the door behind them. They may have the advantage for the moment, but we are going to turn the tables on them real soon.

Rachel: Tell me more!

Fury: As I mentioned earlier. The *King David* has now joined us here in the Sea of Arabia, and our Arabian fleet is intact, for the most part. On the other hand, the word is, we have definitely lost that magnificent Toad carrier, the *HTMS Heroic*. You recall it being hit?

Rachel: *(hanging onto every word)* Yes! Yes, I do! *(with a mixture of sadness and anger in her eyes and in her voice)* She took three torpedoes! The *Heroic* will go down in our history books as one of our greatest carriers!

Fury: You can depend on it! When I was on the other side, Rachel, the Vampire Crickets often talked about her military feats! Admiral Reynaldo had declared that if and when we engaged your navy, she, the *Heroic*, would have to be removed; otherwise, we would scarcely have a chance of defeating you. The sides are, you will agree, even again! The reason why is because the Crickets, too, have lost a carrier! *The Scorpion*. You, of course, already suspected that, since you and your squadron helped destroy it!

Rachel: Yes! I remember that afternoon, after an all-night battle between our opposing navies. I left you to go on a special mission to assist the *Heroic*. You, in the meantime, were still occupied fighting the pilots of the *Stingray*. Before she started to list, the *Heroic* had already lost so many airplanes in the surrounding aerial combat-zone. I led my *Midnight Hornets* against the might of the *Blue Cricket Naval Air Force*. Admiral Da Vinci, at first, had objected to my taking my entire *Midnight Hornet Squadron*. He had stated, "We can't spare the entire group!"

What happened later was that Da Vinci received a call for immediate assistance from the admiral of the *Heroic*. You remember meeting him, Admiral Weismann? (Fury nods yes). Well, almost simultaneously, a second communiqué was received from the battleship *Televiva*. It stated that a squadron-strength group was needed to take out the aggressors, specifically the *Stingray's Vipers*. By the time my squadron arrived, the Crickets' aerial bandits had done their draconian job of destroying our beloved *Heroic*. We took them on, just the same! One by one, my *Midnight Hornets* and I began to take control of the skies! The problem, earlier, in all this mess, was that most of the *Heroic's* naval air force were young graduates from the Frog Air Force Academy. They, literally, had no real dogfight experience beyond top-gun training. They were not only outmatched by experience, but they were outnumbered by surface-to-air missiles, emanating from the Crickets' heavy cruisers in the zone.

Fury: Incredible! I bring you out for fresh air and coffee, and you seem to have more information to share with me than I with you. *(both laughing, in spite of their serious summary of recent events)* You never shared that info with me before. Why?

Rachel: *(sighing and looking at Fury with tender loving eyes)* Perhaps it's because you men are worse than we women are, when it comes to worrying. Besides, you had enough on your plate!

Fury: I suppose you're right. Still, please, next time—let me know.

Rachel: Agreed, on the condition you return the compliment. Let me know if you are leaving the area!

Fury: You've got it: I promise, on the grave of my ancestors!

Rachel: You don't have to get that melodramatic. This war is simply beginning to get on my nerves. I've lost count of how many reconnaissance flights, missions, air raids, dogfights, and the like I've been on. I am sure the same goes for you, Colonel Fury.

Fury: May I ask you a silly question?

Rachel: Sure. What is it?

Fury: How is it you first started calling me by my last name, instead of my first?

Rachel: Because you told me to.

Fury: I did? Are you sure?

Rachel: Why of course you did! It was that night we first met on the deck. I was walking with one of my female officers and, after recognizing me, you picked me up from my waist and swung me around, more than once, in circles!

Fury: Indeed! I do recall it with no effort at all, but...

Rachel: *(interrupting)* Are you saying now that I should address you as *Sudden*?

Fury: No, no, not at all! I was just curious as to how you arrived at my name. Please understand, I like that you call me by my last name*! (jokingly)* It kind of goes with Air Force General Fury, of Their Majesties' Joint Frog and Toad Command!

Rachel: But neither one of us is an air force general, Colonel Fury. *(returning the banter)* How about, *maybe in your wildest dreams, General Fury!*

Fury: You win! I surrender!

Rachel: Seriously, do you want to be a general—someday?

Fury: We're both professionals. I think it's kind of expected of us: to climb. I must confess, though, as long as I can be with you, it really doesn't mean a sack of beans to me.

Rachel: That's interesting. Very interesting! The other day, Admiral Da Vinci, the Big Enchilada himself, came to visit me. He said I had to get well soon, because they were planning a surprise for both of us! Just what do you think he was talking about?

Fury: Well, let me guess. Maybe we're being asked to test-fly that new *Saber Tooth Tiger 222*! You think?

Rachel: Perhaps. Anyway, I like the Admiral! He even gave me a tender kiss on my cheek.

Fury: He did! Why that ole rascal, trying to take away my gal, ha, ha, ha!

Rachel: *(blushing a little and, suddenly, seeming to have completely come to her senses)* Through all this talk, back and forth, I've not asked you about the *Eagle*. What about the *HTMS Eagle*?

Fury: *(trying to imitate W. C. Fields)* Not to worry, my little chickadee, the *HTMS Eagle* is an *Eagle*. Nothing can destroy her! *(now serious)* She has survived, in spite of being hit near the breadbasket. We are for the present on course towards a friendly port, just off the Yemeni Coast. It shouldn't take long to patch her up and make her look "as good as gold"—all the necessary repairs and stuff like that.

Rachel: I'm going to miss her. She's a *Grande Dame*. When do we leave for the *King David*?

Fury: Tonight, if Dr. Roberts gives us the highball!

Rachel: The highball, what's that?

Fury: In Cricket language it means the green light, the A-OK, the walk in the park, the...

Rachel: *(Laughing and excited)* Enough already. I get the idea!

The couple didn't have to wait long, because Dr. Roberts came into the coffee shop and asked politely, if he could join them. Needless to say, Fury and Rachel were surprised to find they had been discovered. When they inquired as to how he had found them, he responded that their secret was probably the best-known secret on board. "I suspected you two lovebirds would make good your escape and come to your favorite place for a cup of joe" the good doctor stated. He continued by saying it was necessary for Rachel to return to the medical center for a complete checkup, since High Command wanted her to leave that very evening, if possible, to join the *Golden Raiders* stationed on the *King David*. Fury, of course, would be going too! With that, the three went to the hospital, and Rachel was more than pleased to learn she was fit to travel. The wound that had caused the bleeding was now sufficiently healed; consequently, Dr. Roberts gave her a release.

That evening, Fury and Rachel flew their *T 111* and *F 77* to the *HFMS King David*. High above the *David,* the two aviators could make out its contour. Its silhouette was made all the more dramatic with the sun setting to the west of it. The sun's rays complimented the ship's size from stem to stern, illuminating its beauty. The carrier was, as they had previously learned, bedecked with flags of every color that signified the ship, itself, representing the entire Frog Nation: These individual flags, furthermore, identified the twelve regions of Frogland that had, in one way or another, contributed to the ship's fabrication. Thus, the *King David* was both—in a manner of speaking—Frogland at sea and Frogland at war! It had already won its first battle flags, based on its confrontation with the *Orca*. The *David's* objective would be to chase the *Orca*: to finish the job it had begun! By destroying the *Orca*, the *Eternal Grace* would stand a better chance against two enemy carriers rather than three.

Once their airplanes landed safely aboard the *David*, the two pilots met with the *King's* top brass. Up until this point, neither Rachel nor Fury had any idea as to who these officers might be: Everything surrounding the *HFMS King David's* upper brass had been so hush-hush. With top security documents, Rachel and Fury would, at long last, learn the identity of these individuals. Surprisingly, they were immediately met by the carrier's two newest and highest-ranking officers: Admiral Leviton and Vice Admiral Amsterdam: The Admiral was a short, slender man with gray-white, wavy hair that complimented the tan he was sporting. His clear blue eyes moved like penetrating lasers, found in the faces of some action heroes, of science-fiction animation or computer games! He moved more like a dancer than an athlete. The Vice-Admiral, on the other hand, was a large, robust man, with a ruddy complexion, and probably at least six-feet three-inches tall! He seemed as though he could hold the earth on his shoulder, much like the mythological Atlas! It was comically evident he had outgrown his uniform from, too, many exquisite meals! That aside, he projected confidence: authority! Yet, a pleasant fellow resided inside him. Years of acquired knowledge and experience were unmistakably visible on the dark brow of his oval, plump face.

The *David's* upper brass extended a late-supper invitation to the new arrivals. Rachel and Fury quickly accepted on two accounts: first, the supper would give them an opportunity to learn what their next mission would be; secondly, they were both tired and famished! The Admiral's quarters were more elegant than anything they had ever seen aboard any ship. The interior of the room was oval with round windows facing in every direction. The paintings on the walls complemented the royal blue of the interior walls and the carpeting, which was of a golden wheat appearance.

As they walked over to a table, already set for dinner, they felt an airy bounce beneath their feet, probably due to the plush carpeting. Two waiters promptly appeared and asked them what they would like to drink. Fury said that he would be pleased with simply a cold soda: a root beer, if possible. The waiter nodded; then, he asked Rachel what her preference might be. She said she would prefer some hot tea. Once again, the waiter nodded respectfully and departed.

The supper had been sumptuous, in every respect! Admiral Leviton communicated to the two famous aces that they were hand picked for a top secret— and very dangerous—mission. They could, of course, refuse the mission, he stated. The admiral proceeded by saying they needed the very best pilots to undertake this difficult task. Since the two of them had already obtained combat experience against the *Orca*, it was felt they would be the ideal pilots to lead a squadron of the *HFMS King David's* best airmen and airwomen, in a strike against the *Orca*. Rachel asked when this mission was to take place.

Admiral Leviton, at this point in the briefing, stated he would defer that question to The Vice Admiral Amsterdam. The Vice Admiral was excited to discuss and explain the more salient aspects of the mission. "To begin with," he declared, "you will be leading thirty of our finest airmen and airwomen: *The Golden Raiders.* They have been preparing for this mission for the last two weeks. These sailors have personally asked for the two of you. They feel that the *Orca* will have a different strategy in place for the next encounter with the *David*. So, a different approach, as you might expect, is necessary: something tactically creative! They have studied the way you both have performed raids in the past. They want and need the two of you"

Fury and Rachel were pleased that their reputations had preceded them. Rachel spoke first, "Well then, what are we waiting for." Fury nodded in agreement. "Not so fast," the Vice Admiral responded. "I'll have one of our captains show you to your sleeping quarters, and we'll talk some more at breakfast. You can't go on a mission without a full belly, ha, ha, ha!" "I suppose you are right," responded Fury. With that and some small talk, they were led to their separate sleeping quarters. Fury declared, "I don't know about you, Emerald Midnight Hornet, but this cowpoke is dead-tired! I hope you have a pleasant sleep. Sleep tight!" Rachel answered, "Colonel Fury, don't let the bedbugs bite!" With tired eyes, together, they stared at the waning moon that was fast becoming just a slip. They hugged—an exhausted hug—leaned on each other for support—kissed softly then drifted their separate ways, unescorted, for some over-due but well deserved rest.

Chapter Eight

Briefings, Strategies, and Rachel's Nightmare

The next morning Vice Admiral Amsterdam met with Fury and Rachel, along with some of the *Golden Raiders'* captains and commanders. The menu consisted of eggs, meat, pancakes, sweet rolls, and an assortment of other breakfast staples, such as various fruits and juices, along with cereals, and beverages: coffee, tea, milk, or just plain water. The officers were asked to listen and watch the presentation, while they enjoyed their breakfast: a kind of oxymoron. Still, time was of the essence! The Vice Admiral introduced Captain La Fontaine, a blond good-looking fellow about age 35. His expertise was reconnaissance. He began his presentation by stating the mission info would go down better with a hearty breakfast and a cup of coffee. To this, much laughter erupted. Someone shouted, "Sorry sir, but we've heard that excuse before!" to which more laughter swept the officers' dining hall!

Captain La Fontaine, pointing to a *smartboard*, began: "If I may direct your eyes, for a moment, to this video, taken by Colonels Goldsmith and Fury, you will note immediately that on their mission against the Crickets, they met heavy resistance from the *Orca's 808 Double-Swept-back Missile Fighters*! You can also see that our aircraft is superior in many ways to theirs; nevertheless, they still possess more airplanes than we do. Notice how they fight. They come in pairs and seem to remain so for the duration of the dogfight. Their strategy is to double-team our aviators. Of course, it must be stated that Colonels Goldsmith and Fury were acting alone on this surprise mission: I might add it was a surprise to us as well." Much laughter is heard. Most realize this mission was not authorized by Allied command.

"The thing is, we experienced the same tactics from the Crickets, when the *David* last engaged them at sea and in the air. This idea of double-teaming, two against one, has an advantage when one side has superior numbers over the other side. We have to find a way to reduce their numerical superiority! We strongly believe that a raid on the *Orca,* where we catch them by surprise, will do the trick! This raid, of which I speak, should be performed at a time when they least suspect an attack from our Allied Forces. It is for this reason that we are sending in a destroyer fleet, led by our *Heavenly Angel*, along with the battleship *Televiva* and its convoy.

"The plan is to make them think our attack is principally coming from the sea, as opposed to from the air: sea craft rather than aircraft! Again, our principal aim is to engage their air force, before they have the time to scramble off the *Orca's* flight deck. Undoubtedly, many of their airplanes will make it safely off the *Orca,* as they rise to meet us; however, we will be able to hit the rest, those that have been caught on deck. I will entertain questions after you finish your meal? So, please finish your breakfast, before it gets too cold. I will resume in ten minutes. Hopefully I can satisfy any queries you may have."

Later, one of the *King David's* premier fighter pilots asked, "Why don't we just go in and finish them off?" Captain La Fontaine responded, saying, "I appreciate your enthusiasm, so let me say this about that. At present we have only two carriers against three of theirs. As you are aware, the *Eagle* is presently being repaired off the Yemeni Coast; therefore, we can't afford to risk the *David* against a ship that would like nothing more than to engage us in full battle. We aren't a hundred percent sure that the *Stingray* isn't lurking nearby. Our strategy, then, is to feint a full attack and then to move at full throttle to catch the *SS Admiralty*. By doing that, we can accomplish a great deal more. For one thing, if we, on the other hand, can beat them at their own game, we can trap their flagship between our two ships.

"With the *SS Admiralty* out of the way, we will have, effectively, cut off the serpent's head! If the other two Cricket ships wish to continue the fight, that's fine with us. We will be even-steven with two carriers apiece! By that time, our *Eagle* should be ready with her repairs and closing in on our enemy, from behind. They, I am certain, believe the *Eagle* is totally out of commission. Does that give you a better idea of the way things stand?" The *David's* star pilot seemed pleased with Captain La Fontaine's answer and replied, "Yes sir, it does make perfect sense. Thanks for the thorough explanation."

The *King David's* fighter pilots, by now, had finished their breakfast. They had less than fifteen minutes free time before getting to their airplanes and then it was takeoff against the immense *Orca*. Rachel and Fury were surprised, when one of Vice-Admiral Amsterdam's senior officers presented each of them with an official letter stating: They would be flying the new *Saber-tooth Tiger 222s!* The letter continued, "We are honored to have you in our company and wish you good hunting!" It was signed "Vice-Admiral J. R. Amsterdam."

Once on the flight deck, about 7:00 hours, Rachel spoke to Fury and whispered, "I guess this is it, honey!" Fury, mustering all his strength, softly replied, "I believe you're right—light and love of my life!" Not much more was communicated. What was less sober, yet ardently expressed, became readily visible in the wetness of their eyes. They remained intently gazing into each other's souls, studying the expression they each would take with them, that would stay with them as they headed into the jaws of the enemy in harm's way. A last hug and a kiss sealed their mutual expressions.

They were now both aloft and their target, the mighty *Orca*, was within sight! Before they arrived, they could see the enemy's airplanes leaving their newest aircraft carrier to engage them in a fight to the finish. The *Orca's* guns, below, were beginning to fire at the *David's* fighters. Evidently, someone aboard the *King David* had, by committing treachery, informed the *Orca's* command of the impending surprise attack! Just who this spy or informant was, no one yet knew. The Frog and Toad fighters, however, always had alternate plans if something of this sort were to occur. It was then that the Emerald Midnight Hornet radioed to the attack squadron to exercise Plan "X." This change indicated that the *David's* fighter pilots would engage the enemy's fighters, eliminate them, whilst the dive-bombers would attack the deck, and finally, the torpedo aircraft would go in low to drop their payload! A full battle was now evident; it had been forced upon them!

The fight had begun in the early part of the morning, and it was now a full hour later. During the first wave of the *David's* attack, the enemy Crickets were putting up one heck of a fight! The spy's advanced notice had afforded the *Orca's* pilots enough time to devise a plan of their own! For one thing, they had radioed ahead and asked the *Stingray* for support. The *Stingray* had then made an about-face before rendezvousing with the *SS Admiralty,* off the Kenyan Coast. The flagship *SS Admiralty* had given the final "affirmative," allowing the *Stingray* to assist the *Orca*.

It turns out that the *HFTMS Eternal Grace* had all but disappeared. There was, however, a sighting of the *Grace* in the vicinity of South Africa, then later moving between Mozambique and Madagascar. The *SS Admiralty's* pilot, performing aerial reconnaissance in southern Africa, had radioed an incomplete report and had not yet returned to the mother ship; therefore, the sighting could not be completely confirmed or denied by Cricket intelligence. In the meantime, it was the *Orca* that appeared to need assistance! The *Orca* could definitely defend herself, but the Blue Vampire believed that caught between two Cricket carriers, the magnificent *HFMS King David*'s demise would certainly benefit their cause. The Allied navy's aircraft capacity to wage war, hence, would drastically have been reduced—in the short term—by half!

Thus it was that the *King David* became surprised to learn of another Cricket war vessel in the area: the *Stingray*! Fortunately, the *David's* aviators, courageously led by the Emerald Midnight Hornet and Colonel Fury, had been able to sizably reduce the *Orca's* aircraft by one-third. Still, the dive-bombers and the torpedo airplanes, for the most part, were kept at bay by the superior guns of the *Orca*. Before noon, Fury radioed to Rachel that the better part of valor, now, was to return to their base aboard the *King David*. She agreed and the *David's* fighter squadron made a beeline towards their new carrier.

Once all of the *David's* aircraft were accounted for, they were told to stand by, as the *HFMS King David* had received new orders, from the command center, to meet the *HFTMS Eternal Grace* en route to the island of Diego Garcia. Evidently, the *Eternal Grace* was attempting to leave the enemy with the impression that it was fleeing from the *SS Admiralty* and the *Stingray* around the Cape of Good Hope. What the *Eternal Grace* was actually attempting was to buy time, so that the *Eagle* could get repaired and fitted for combat. In the meantime, the *SS Admiralty's* Cornwalter seemed to be buying the ruse. The two Allied carriers, the *Grace* and the *David*, on the other hand, were well underway towards the island of Diego Garcia. At exactly 14:00 hours, on New Year's Eve, The *HFTMS Eternal Grace* commenced its sharp turn towards the east and around Madagascar, all the while moving swiftly toward the islands where it was first conceived.

One full day had passed when the great news arrived. The *HTMS Eagle* was not only repaired and ready for action, but she was also en route to meet the Allied Fleet near Diego Garcia. The problem, of course, was that the *Eagle* would have to maneuver its carrier, in such a way, so as not to be detected by the three Cricket carriers: the *SS Admiralty,* the *Stingray,* and the *Orca.* Yes, the *SS Admiralty* had also decided to join her two warships! The entire Cricket Fleet, therefore, was also rendezvousing just off the Kenyan Coast. It was a strong position for them, since the Cricket Armada now controlled all the waterways: from the Mediterranean down through the Gulf of Suez; from the Jordan to the Dead Sea; and, finally, down through the new Great Canal, connecting it to the Red Sea and, ultimately, spilling into the waters that joined it to the stormy Arabian Sea!

Most important and of equal consequence, the Blue Vampire had reason to believe he, in addition, controlled the entire Eastern Coast of Africa. Admiral Cornwalter was now beating his chest and flexing his muscles, at every meeting with his superior officers, including Lightning Striker, declaring, "I alone rule the largest territory of any living creature on Earth; I have surpassed the wildest dreams of our forefathers by capturing the greatest wealth; moreover, by amassing the largest military power ever witnessed, we will continue to fulfill our ancestors' ambitions to rule supreme!"

The Blue Vampire thought he had, at least for now, scared off the Frog and Toad combined fleets. Also, of great importance, the United Nations had reaffirmed, sometime ago, that they would continue not to interfere in the sea or in the air lanes of combatants. They, however—according to their charter, approved by all of the member nations of the world—could continue to send troops to areas where hostilities had broken out. Thus, the UN troops were helping the joint Frog and Toad efforts at dislodging the Crickets from positions they held that, incredibly, spanned the entire kingdoms of the Frogs and Toads. The biggest fighting, however, continued taking place on the Sinai Peninsula. The land war was very bitter and neither side seemed to be able to dominate the other: It was at a stalemate neither side preferred.

In the meantime, Emperor Cornwalter declared to his senior officers, that with the Frog and Toad's Naval Warships out of the picture—with the UN ships participating primarily as observers—his Cricket War Vessels could now better support the Cricket Land War Machine that was mired in the Sinai! If the Sinai were taken, it meant the loss of tens of thousands of Frog, Toad, and Allied soldiers. A complete rout of the Cricket enemies could be achieved, he divulged, by utilizing the airplanes from the Cricket Flotilla that were now available! Cornwalter further stated the likelihood, now, of the *Stingray* moving into the Red Sea. The *SS Admiralty* and the *Orca* would be following closely. In this scenario, he elaborated, the rest of the Cricket Armada could be free to move through the Great Canal and continue upwards towards the mighty Jordan to attack enemy positions. Other warships would remain to guard the African Coast.

Several days and nights had passed and the Blue Vampire, through all his revelry, was still celebrating. He seemed extremely confident that he could finish off the Allies in a single assault, when he so chose. For now, he saw no reason to rush toward the Sinai, at the expense of ending his party. Yes, he would take more time to fully enjoy the fruits of his ocean and sea conquests. He saw himself as Neptune, incarnate! Yes, he mused with great delight: "I have won!" He controlled all the waterways and in a few days he would also control the Sinai, the gateway to the interior of strategic Africa! The rest, he believed, would come even more easily. Cornwalter had only to act!

While the Blue Vampire was lavishly entertaining his officers, Da Vinci and his *HTMS Eagle* had managed to bypass the Crickets undetected. They were able to follow an easterly route off the coast of India. From there they pushed rapidly toward the Allied stronghold of Diego Garcia. The only concern seemed to be the Indian Ocean's turbulent waters. In another two hours, the *HTMS Eagle's* commander and crew would be arriving at their destination. Aboard, ship Admiral Da Vinci was having a cup of coffee as he spied the Indian's waters. He asked his senior officer what he thought about the unexpected change in the ocean, as evidenced by the increased height of the waves. Captain Antonius Goad responded that he had read and seen videos concerning sudden changes in the Indian Ocean's waves.

"Sometimes," Captain Goad explained, "it simply meant a storm was approaching; at other times," he continued, "it could be a white squall; however, in very rare cases it could also mean a *tsunami*!" The Admiral became very perturbed. A *tsunami,* he recalled, had been responsible for turning over huge ships, including military ones. Even battleships and carriers, if not handled properly, could find themselves vulnerable, or worse yet, capsized! Admiral Roberto Da Vinci inquired of his Captain, "How much more time until we arrive at Diego?" The Captain responded, "The time now Admiral is 3:00 hours. I expect, taking into account the ocean's environment, we ought to put into Diego Garcia at 3:33 hours." "That suits me fine," the brilliant commander returned. "Once we are in port, I will feel more at ease."

After what seemed to be an eternity, the *HTMS Eagle,* finally, was able to weather the storm and make its way safely to the Island. Upon arriving, Admiral Da Vinci was met by none other than his peer, Admiral Cheetah. Even so, Cheetah remained Allied Commander and Chief of Naval

Operations. They both saluted as Admiral Da Vinci walked toward the swarthy, handsome Admiral Cheetah. "Looks like you've put on a little weight," Da Vinci chided his counterpart. Cheetah laughed through his smile of gleaming white teeth and replied, "We just got a new cook! I found him adrift off the Madagascar Coast: His fishing yacht had been pulled out to sea!

"I asked him if he possessed any other talents, besides his boating and fishing hobbies. He replied, he used to be a French chef at a five-star restaurant in Manhattan!" "That's almost, too, incredible to be believe; notwithstanding, coming from you it has to be the truth," answered Da Vinci. "I appreciate that, and you can make book on it, Admiral," Cheetah affirmed. The *Eagle's* Admiral, then, accepted Admiral Cheetah's invitation to join him in his private dining room. Cheetah continued, "He's the best chef around these parts for thousands of miles!" Da Vinci, quite exuberantly, half-shouting, while patting his friend on the back, "Well, boss, what are we waiting for? *Permettez- moi, s'il vous plait*; *je suis un connaisseur international de le boire et le manger*! (Permit me, if you please, I am an international connoisseur of food and drink, literally: drink and food). I'll sample your renowned chef's entrees! If his food and drink passes my palate's test, then we'll both be mighty rich: You for discovering him and I for certifying him, ha! ha! ha!

It was now 4:00 hours and the two Admirals were much too excited to sleep. They were more interested in talking than resting, and they settled down to some serious quality conversation, over what promised to be some fine cuisine. Just as Cheetah had promised, the master chef had a knack for preparing succulent foods of various types. There were choices literally from around the globe. Everything from ethnic, to exotic, to traditional. When asked by Cheetah what his preference was from the menu, Da Vinci replied that he just wanted a good ol' American double cheeseburger. Cheetah, beside himself, yelled, "What?" Da Vinci responded, "Just kidding, Cheetah. I think I'll try some of your chef's world-class *pollo con fettuccine alfredo*." Cheetah, with raised eyebrows, retorted, "Say what?"

Da Vinci explained, "I was just requesting baked chicken with a special creamy Alfredo Sauce, accompanied by Parmesan cheese, over fettuccine noodles." Cheetah, after a moment's pause then smiling, "Oh that, why of course, he can do that; sure thing, coming right up! By the way, here comes our chef now. Monsieur Jean Le Beau, please allow me to introduce you to my very, very good friend and comrade-in-arms, Admiral Da Vinci of the *HTMS Eagle*: in charge of all Allied Naval Front-line Strategic Engagements!" Monsieur Le Beau extended his hand in friendship, and spoke with a charming French accent, "A pleasure to meet you, monsieur Admiral Da Vinci!" Da Vinci, in deference to Cheetah's famous chef, stood up to be introduced and warmly returned the greeting, "The pleasure is entirely mine, Monsieur Le Beau."

As promised, Monsieur Le Beau was able to serve the dish requested by Admiral Da Vinci and an African delight that consisted of lamb and vegetables with a special sauce, for Admiral Cheetah. Even though by now it was close to 4:30 hours, the two distinguished admirals dismissed what might be considered early breakfast or a very, very late supper. During war, oftentimes, conventional time just doesn't quite work, so friends need to create time to meet their own spiritual, emotional, and logistical needs. Thus, the admirals began to strategize their next move against the mighty Cricket Armada, while enjoying their unique meal. Cheetah began by inquiring of Da Vinci what he felt, from his military perspective, ought to be done. "You, my best comrade-in-arms, Admiral Da Vinci, have been on the forefront of the storm, and I believe you may have some information that I am not aware of: correct?"

Da Vinci, nodding his head, while swallowing some of his delicious food and drinking some tasty wine to wash it down, replied, "Indeed I do! The Crickets are positioned exactly where we want them to be. They, no doubt, believe they have won the war; that we have fled to save our skins! Well, thanks to you, Admiral Cheetah, and to your Central Intelligence Officers, we can take them by surprise! We can attack them just as they start up towards the Arabian Sea! With one of our carriers blocking their entry into the Red Sea, with another behind them—moving between Madagascar and their exposed rear—and with still another making a frontal attack, we can take the three ducks out of the water with minimal loss to our own fleet."

Cheetah replied, "You know, I was thinking along those same lines, myself! I believe you are wondering why I brought the *Eagle*, the *King David*, and the *Eternal Grace* to Diego Garcia." Da Vinci, now having finished eating, answered, "Yes, you might say that was an understatement, or underquestion, if there is such a thing?" Cheetah smiled and chuckled and then became dead serious, his penetrating dark eyes, completely concentrated on his friend's eyes. "I've brought you and our other trustworthy officers to Diego, precisely because there have been some incredible findings on this land; here, on our stronghold and base of operations, there are extremely amazing things that have happened that defy complete understanding, to say the least!"

Da Vinci's eyes widen; he quietly put down his eating implements, returned his intent focus on Cheetah and replied, "And that, Sir, is...?" "Well," Cheetah began, "we have known for sometime now, that our famous Silver Brigade has been in the possession of some mystical powers that permit them to, for all intent and purposes, uh, to disappear: to vanish before the enemy's eyes!

"We inquired of their leader to share with us what the specific source of their power was and where it could be found." Da Vinci, all ears, gave Cheetah an urgent expression that communicated his wanting to know the rest of the story. "Yes," he insisted, "Go on with your story, by all means!" Cheetah, more relaxed, continued, "Well, as you might expect, the Silver Brigade revealed the source of their power and where it could be found. And yes, the source comes from the Heavenly Host. An Angel made it known to the Silver Brigade's leaders, many years ago, when they were sailing along these tumultuous waters!" "Wow," Da Vinci exclaimed! "I had heard of their famous exploits, both on the River Jordan and in the Far East, but never quite knew how much was myth or how much was fact."

"Trust me," Cheetah went on, "it's not myth; it's real! The Angel from above directed them to the Isle—Diego Garcia. Discovered many years ago by a Spanish explorer, the Island contains Holy Water that when sprinkled on an object renders that object invisible!" Da Vinci, not waiting for Cheetah to finish his statement jumped in with, "Don't tell me; it's found right here, on Diego?" "Right you are, Sir, right you are!" all smiles, Cheetah quietly responded. Da Vinci eagerly inquired, "Where do we go from here?" Cheetah replied, "We have three members from the Silver Brigade, who have been brought here from the front lines of the Sinai. They will lead us to the Holy Spring. Their leader is consecrated and only he can activate the Spring's Heavenly Power, by reciting a sacred prayer the Angel instructed him to pray. Fascinating, don't you think, Roberto?" Da Vinci echoed, "Yes, fascinating, amazing, and yet almost preposterous, that is, too incredible to be believed; I am completely in awe, in total wonderment!"

Later that afternoon, after Cheetah and Da Vinci, at last, had been able to get some shut-eye, though not much sleep, the top commanders met at the new Allied Central Command Headquarters. Among those present were Colonel Jonas and Major Spartacus, the latter of the famous Silver Brigade. Admiral Cheetah welcomed all present and stated that this would be the final naval offensive against the mighty Cricket Armada: "We will never have another opportunity like this one!" He declared, futhermore, "Our countrymen and women are praying for our success; we mustn't fail them!" The original plan of destroying the Armada in the open sea, he explained, had not been scrapped: rather, it had just been postponed, until today! Cheetah then proceeded to lay out the strategy, "We will move this evening toward the African coast, just as twilight begins to settle. This time, we will have a Heavenly advantage: one that will enable us to creep up on our adversary, before we pounce on him! How this action can be accomplished is really quite simple, and it amazes me that it has taken us so long to think about it, let alone act on it!

"We have heard and learned about Major Spartacus' incredible military feats on the battlefield, while facing superior numbers. The ability of his brigade to remain invisible for a period of time and then reappear has struck terror into the hearts of his enemies. One evening, it hit me like a thunderbolt—from Heaven—while I was peering into a starry night, overlooking the great Indian Ocean from our Citadel, here, on Diego Garcia! I don't know, for certain, if it was speaking to me as an emissary from above; I simply know that it was a presence, and It spoke in a way I presume angels speak. The voice directed me to welcome Major Spartacus to our headquarters, in order that he might divulge the source of his mystical power. Thus, it was so, that Spartacus and select members of his brigade came to us last week.

"Since arriving, he and two of his men have performed some exciting experiments that indicate we can use the Holy Water on our ships, too! We have determined that our vessels can remain invisible for a period of three hours! After that, the power begins to wane. If I may call your attention to the large panorama of windows behind you and the harbor beyond, you will immediately notice that, while there are three carriers stationed there, only two are readily visible: *The HFMS King David* and *The HTMS Eagle*. In three minutes, according to my watch, the third one will reappear!" Those words caused an audible gasp, from the newly arrived senior officers present, and then a hush, as they leaned forward in their seats to learn more from Cheetah. "We sprinkled that carrier, *The HFTMS Eternal Grace,* fifteen minutes later than the other two," Cheetah resumed. "If you wish, you may go outside on the verandah, or closer to the balustrade. In either case you shall see what you shall see!"

At that moment, everyone rushed through the open doors to the verandah, all the time looking at their watches. Sure enough, in exactly three minutes flat, *The Eternal Grace* made her reappearance! From the spectators, a spontaneous chant arose of "Hurrah! Hurrah! Hurrah!" "Long live Spartacus and his Heavenly potion!" one officer exclaimed, while another more humble whispered, "Long live the Eternal One's Holy Spring, His Divine Water."

Just before sunset, the enormous Frog, Toad, and Allied Navy went out in unison to do battle with the Blue Vampire's Cricket Armada. The *HTMS Eagle* was positioned between the *HFTMS Eternal Grace* on the left and the *HFMS King David* on the right. Between the carriers there stood a vast array of escort ships: These mainly included destroyers and submarines. The great battleships, such as the *Televiva* and others, were moving just ahead in the Allied formation towards the African Coast. Their respective battle groups consisted of heavy and light cruisers, frigates with some destroyers, and submarines, as well. By nightfall each of the battle groups had taken positions assigned to them. *The Televiva* moved swiftly towards the Arabian Sea and then turned left, due west, towards the Gulf of Aden, thus, effectively cutting off the Crickets' escape through the Red Sea! The battleship *Judea* that had been stationed west of the Cape of Good Hope was now making its way up the African Eastern Coast. It reported its position to Central Command as having passed South Africa, Mozambique, Malawi, and nearing Tanzania! The battleship *Jordan* was moving from east of Madagascar towards Seychelles and then towards the Kenyan Coast.

Meanwhile, the Heavy Cruiser *Exodus* and its battle group were fast approaching Somalia. The Frog Submarine Fleet, consisting of *the Tigerfisher, the Spearfisher*, *the Harpooner*, and *the Tomahawker*, was about to engage the Cricket's Submarine Fleet, including *the Barracuda, the Eel Electric, the Piranha, and the Sharkfin,* about 50 nautical miles above the equatorial divide and between the Maldives and Somalia's Mogadishu. The Frog Submarine Fleet was awaiting a reply from Allied Command Center to begin its attack. Within a few minutes, Command responded stating the Fleet should remain *silent running,* until the waters quieted. But, there seemed to be no abatement in the Indian Ocean's enormous waves and its hidden undercurrents!

Command Center was fast approaching a great deal of consternation! At 4:00 hours, the decision to sprinkle all ships with Holy Water had gone out.

Now it was 5::00 hours, and the stubbornness of the weather seemed to be favoring the Crickets! In another two hours, any advantage the Allied Forces might have had, by using the protective shield of the Heavenly Water, would have come to an abrupt end. The question, as is always the case in a crisis, was what do we do next? Cheetah, who had remained at Diego Garcia, to personally direct the Command Center's Communications, could easily see the positions of all his battle groups and the entirety of the Allied Fleet, spread across his computer screen, in color! Thanks to Spartacus and his blessing of the screen, Cheetah was able to view not only the whereabouts of his naval forces but also those of his enemy! The Admiral was looking at the Command clock, and he began to reflect on a major battle he had studied, long ago, while he was still in Officers Candidate School. His instructor had referred to it as D-Day! Cheetah turned to face his team and soberly proclaimed to his tactical officers, "I believe this is our D-Day!

"Sometimes fate and circumstances, beyond our control, make us act sooner than later. As you can see on our panoramic screen, the Crickets are now beginning their move towards the Arabian Sea! If we do not move within the next twenty minutes, our battle group, led by *The Televiva,* will be unable to forestall the enemy, in spite of her temporary invisibility: They will be overwhelmed by the superiority of the enemy's numerous battle groups, in convoy. Whatever our informants have told us, concerning enemy movement, you can see that the Cricket battleships are running an *avant-garde,* in order to protect the *Stingray* and the *SS Admiralty*. It appears that the *Orca* is remaining off the Kenya's Coast, just due east of Kilimanjaro. Evidently, they believe she will be able to protect their African interests. They have provided the *Orca* with only two battle groups. That certainly favors us, if we can strike them first! Therefore, let's turn our battleships *Judea* and *Jordan* loose on them! What say ye, mates?" The officers yelled in unison, "Let's get'em, Chief!"

Some viewed the battle as a prelude to the Battle of Armageddon and one of Biblical proportions! Not only was the fate of the Kingdoms of the Frogs and Toads at stake, but the fate of the entire world lay in the balance! At this point in time, the United Nations had almost become obsolete! There had been many times in its early history that it had performed as originally envisioned, way back in the 20th Century. In those exceptional periods it had settled major disputes, or it had been a good arbitrator. Now, times had changed. The world, since then and during the past millennium, had been accustomed to peace. There really was little or no need, at the present, for the kind of services the UN had provided.

With war a thing of the past, famine had been eliminated; precious water restored; clothing and shelter made available; health care and pharmaceuticals improved: these were all offered in abundance at no charge to the recipient. Since vacations and holidays were also viewed as a benefit to good health, they, too, were a right given freely to the Earth's people. Costly wars had demonstrated once and for all the folly of war, or had it? No one could have predicted a time in the future when creatures from the earth's center would come out to wage war against those on the Earth's surface! Yet, here it was staring them in the face! Yes, the green light and all systems go had been issued by Cheetah! The moment of truth had arrived! The fight to the finish was on! *Gloria! Gloria! Gloria* became the battle cry!

In the early evening and just before nightfall, Sudden Fury was in his cabin, alone. He opened a chest of drawers and pulled out a small blue box. Except for a dim red light and another shaft of light emanating from the vent to his front door, the room was rather dark. He preferred less light in times of major decisions. Somehow or other he could think more clearly with less distractions from outer sense stimuli interrupting his thoughts. He spoke softly in almost a whisper and said, "This evening I will propose to the Emerald Midnight Hornet, to Colonel Rachel Goldsmith, my Rachel, my true and only love!" As he opened the box, the available light in the area hit the diamond's delicately cut shape that made each facet glisten like the crystals of new-fallen snow on unperturbed ski slopes. He smiled and said to himself in even a softer voice, with a lump in his throat, "Well, this is it! I hope she accepts my offer of marriage; I just don't see how I can live without her."

A short time later, just after supper, Fury invited Rachel for a walk out on the deck. Once again, a gorgeous moon appeared over the horizon and soft winds caressed the two soldiers. The two seemed to have arrived at full circle. He remembered the night when he had first met Rachel, on the deck of another ship, along with Rachel's friend, another female officer. He had picked Rachel up with his arms—wrapped tightly around her waist—and he had swung her around several times in a spontaneous moment of exuberance, to demonstrate his appreciation for her having saved his life! Now he wanted to share it with her forever!

When Fury asked Rachel if she would be his wife, she gasped and then let out a pleasant scream that said all he wanted to know. "Yes, yes, and yes a thousand-and-one times, I will be your bride, Colonel Sudden Fury!" With that, he picked her up and swung her just as passionately as he had on their first meeting two years earlier. "I love you so very much that," and then he suddenly stopped speaking for he was too caught up with emotion to continue; finally, he regained his composure and declared, "I just can't find any other words to say what I am feeling at this very moment and what I have felt from the first time I laid eyes on you: I love you, Rachel!" "And I love you, Fury," Rachel responded, "I love you from the innermost recesses of my soul." The two embraced and tenderly kissed, a prolonged kiss that echoed their love. Fury and Rachel immediately sought the ship's captain, to ask that he perform a ceremony of marriage.

Just as the two were walking hand-in-hand, looking for the ship's captain to marry them, a heavy rain approached that caused them to find shelter off the deck. The waves were getting heavier now! An announcement came over their wristwatches. With the press of a button, on each of their watches, they could see and hear Admiral Leviton of the *King David*. He greeted the ship's crew and stated this was an update on the *David's* strategic plans. "You are advised that due to circumstances beyond our control, you are, immediately, to meet with your senior officers. Best of luck, as we move toward our objective: D - 777!"

Fury started to speak, but Rachel pressed her fingers to hush his lips. "I feel the same way, and it really doesn't matter just now, because I've got this golden-diamond-ring that says we are engaged to be married! It will do until the Celestial Power decides the time and the place; till then, you're mine; if not here then somewhere in His Kingdom!" She withdrew her fingers and Fury spoke. "Yes, my most precious Rachel, you have spoken my thoughts, as well! We will never part. I pray that He will keep us in the palm of His hand, until the day we can wed." With that, they sought each other's eyes—for a fleeting moment the earth and time skipped a beat: then stopped. Their eyes greeted each other, akin to a love-light mist rising from the sea when it seeks to reach its coast. Once again, they looked deeply into each other's eyes, sighed, smiled with tears welling up, and not being able to hold them back, the tears flowed down their cheeks! They so wanted to say they were husband and wife, but that, apparently, would not happen just yet. After a passionate hug and a tender kiss, they parted to their separate stations.

They had already been briefed on D-777. They knew this code meant a fight to the finish! They would move closer to the enemy's position and strike with all the thunder they could muster! Before the next day's end, they would either win or lose. The Allies had four advantages that could not be wasted: (1) The bad weather favored them with their ships further out to sea; whereas, the tremendous waves were now hitting the African Coast where the Cricket Navy was positioned; (2) the enemy had finally dropped into the Allied trap: they were surrounded and enclosed by the powerful Allied Navy to the east and the African Coast to the west and at their backs; (3) the Frog and Toad ships would virtually be invisible for the next hour-and-a-half; finally, (4) the Frogs and Toads knew, in the inner recesses of their souls, that His Strength emanating from above would be with them throughout this Heavenly undertaking: They would do the Almighty's work, here on earth! They would remove this insidious, hideous vermin from the planet. Peace would once again reign supreme.

Just as the Frog and Toad fighter-planes were about to leave the *King David*, an incredible event occurred aboard ship. A group of some 100 middle school military junior cadets, in raincoats, began to play music: first the Frog National Anthem, then the Toad National Anthem; finally, these anthems were followed by martial music. Their music and their presence was enough to bring tears to the pilots' and the crews' eyes. No one seemed to question how the precious youngsters made it aboard ship. The airmen and airwomen simply accepted it as another of the Divine's blessings. In the past it had been customary to invite the youngest of the military students to tour the carrier: Perhaps, in the excitement of an impending attack against the Crickets, each of those responsible—for shuttling these beautiful children to their academy—had somehow or other thought the children's departure had already taken place, that someone else had fulfilled that duty! No matter, it was inconsequential; the courageous, attractive young boys and girls were right here, in plain view, for all to see and hear!

The youngest cadets played with bravado and a dreamlike quality that was not hampered by the downpour that gave signs of ebbing, on the flight deck. Yes, it was a spectacle to behold! There, on the soaked deck, they proudly wore their white uniforms covered with sky blue capes, easily visible through the transparency of their plastic raincoats. Ten white flags, each bearing a six-pointed star—commemorating the young David who slew Goliath, flew gallantly! The flags were positioned in front of the band. The heavy wind, ripping across the deck, seemed to almost blow the flags away, but the flag bearers held fast to their poles. The spirits of all aboard the *King David* were lifted to heights that even their airplanes could not reach. The music was being broadcast live to the entire Allied Fleet. The Crickets, too, were able to intercept the music that flowed beautifully and brilliantly across the Indian Ocean! Admiral Leviton, when questioned by Vice Admiral Amsterdam, as to whether or not the music should be transmitted to the rest of the fleet—for fear of alerting the enemy—responded soberly by saying, "By the time they hear the music, they will also be feeling our bombs: some emanating from below the water's surface with still others… from the sky!"

Thus, each of the men and women as Frog, Toad, and Allied airmen and airwomen went forward, toward their respective targets to claim a much-needed and much-deserved victory! The ships that had been moving from their positions off the southern African Coast, with still others speeding from just east of Madagascar, were now engaging the Crickets: *The Judea* was first to let the enemy feel the sting from her enormous guns by pouncing on *The Orca*! *The Televiva* in the north, not to be outdone by her sister ship *Judea* in the south, was performing admirably in its will to decimate *The Stingray*! This punishment was long overdue. *The Jordan*, likewise, moved into her position from the east to strike *The Orca* with great ferocity—lying in the west; then, she quickly turned just due north, to blast the *SS Admiralty* with equal determination; whereas, the heavy cruiser *Exodus* could be felt from a distance—caused by the vibrations of her superior weapons, stomping on the *SS Admiralty*, yet no sooner had she arrived than she quickly departed, moving in a northerly direction to assist the battleship *Televiva* that was, indefatigably, doing her level best to stop the *Stingray's* northerly escape!

While the battleships and the cruisers were softening up the enemy, they reported that enemy submarines were in the area and moving toward them at breakneck speed! In the meantime, the Frogs' *Tigerfisher, Spearfisher, Harpooner, and Tomahawker* submarines had been busy eliminating the armed periphery that was to protect the Cricket Carriers. This immense Cricket defense shield consisted of several battle groups, each group acting as escorts for *The Orca, The SS Admiralty, and The Stingray.* With their huge battleships and heavy cruisers, now caught by surprise by fast-moving Frog torpedoes, the Cricket Carriers became even more vulnerable to the Allied assault! While, yes, it is true that the Frog and Toad Navies were invisible for a time, now no more than a half-hour, it was also known to Frog submarine captains that sonar could detect their presence in these infested waters! Evidently, the mood on the Cricket ships was such that the Cricket radar engineers were too busy celebrating, rather than manning their radar posts! Otherwise, there seems to be no *technical* explanation as to why the Crickets reacted only after the first wave of torpedoes exploded and sank many of their largest ships. To all effect, the backbone of the various battle groups had now been broken!

In spite of these catastrophic setbacks, there were still the Cricket submarines. They had always proven themselves to be one of the most formidable components in the Cricket arsenal. *The Barracuda*, *The Eel Electric*, *The Piranha*, and *The Sharkfin* were the scourge of the oceans and the seven seas! They had been responsible for midnight- and surprise-attacks on foreign vessels that had been attempting to supply the Allies! They had assisted the Cricket Armada whenever it was felt necessary to search and destroy enemy ships, of all sorts, including potential enemies. In brief, this special, unique submarine fleet presented an awesome threat to all seagoing vessels that had opposed the Crickets or those that had repudiated—in the media—the Cricket-forced amassment of territory acquired by the sword: conquest!

The captain of the *Eel Electric* was a very distinguished, older-looking gentleman. His eyes, like Admiral Leviton's, were steel blue and his white wavy hair, along with a suntanned face, made him look years younger. Probably, it was the many times he had put-to- port that gave him that salty, windblown look. No one knew exactly from where he had come. Some had inquired about his ancestry; he didn't look at all like the swarthy Crickets; nevertheless, he was someone with whom to be reckoned! Besides his rugged, handsome face and tall frame, that carried the captain's epaulets with four bars and a single star, he was more easily spotted because of the gold necklace he wore: His sweetheart had given it to him years earlier, for good luck: A golden locket suspended from the chain, and it opened to reveal an image of her on the left with another image of the two of them on the right. The pictures had been taken the night they had become engaged. Their love had been written in the stars and they proclaimed it to all the celestial bodies that were listening. This had all happened on a blissful summer night, amid soft ocean breezes, and beneath the shelter of tropical palm trees.

Before parting to join his *Eel Electric,* the pride of the Cricket submarine fleet, he had promised his sweetheart his undying love! She, in turn, had declared her pledge to him: "My precious gift of enduring love and commitment, to thee I do plight!" She had, that evening, asked her one and only beloved captain, never to forgo wearing the golden necklace: "May it never leave this manly neck where rests thy beauteous face!" Incredibly, she had vanished during a winter storm. A new breed of Barbary Pirates had attacked her passenger ship! The brave captain had, these past five years, vowed to search the world over until he found her! It was not customary for Cricket captains to adorn themselves with jewelry; however, this captain had achieved such fame on the high seas that his leader, Admiral Reynaldo, as a token of his esteem, had given him that extra dress privilege.

Similar to the Red Vampire, Admiral Reynaldo, the handsome captain had had his differences with the Blue Vampire, Admiral Cornwalter! Of equally great significance, it so happens, that at one time in the recent past, just before Reynaldo's death, Reynaldo, Colonel Fury, and the good captain had had coffee together on a remote island— where they were vacationing. There, they felt safe from spying ears and wagging tongues! There, they could speak their minds! Colonel Fury, now more at ease, amazingly discovered that the *Eel Electric's* Captain was none other than the legendary Captain Vladimir Vestinova!

Like Fury, himself, Captain Vestinova had listened attentively to and admired Admiral Reynaldo: who had become his mentor. Even with all of his experience, Vestinova was incredibly amazed at how very little he, the most senior officer of a major Cricket submarine, understood about the inner workings of Cricket politics! After teaching Colonel Fury and Captain Vestinova the political ropes, the Red Vampire, ever the sage, commenced advising his two protégés to guard the language they used with senior officers: These officers were most assuredly under the Blue Vampire's spell; it intoxicated most in the Cricket military who lusted for power: No, these officers were not to be trusted!

As Vestinova, while looking through his periscope, contemplated his past association with Admiral Reynaldo and Colonel Fury, he wondered to himself why he was still fighting on the side of the Blue Vampire. Why, for instance, had he not left Admiral Cornwalter to join Colonel Fury and the Frog, Toad, and Allied Forces? These people had not sought war. These worthy enemies were peace-loving, and they were only attempting to protect their homeland through self-defense initiatives! Reynaldo and Fury had been right, during the last time they were to meet, when they declared the Blue Vampire must be stopped, but what was he, Captain Vestinova, to do? After replacing the periscope, he deliberated with himself? Yes, Cornwalter was bent on world domination: first in the Middle East, then the vast continent of Africa, and, soon afterwards, the remaining democracies that lay just across the Atlantic Ocean. After those conquests, Cornwalter would be ready to attack Asia! The Blue Vampire was a malignant megalomaniac the world could well do without!

It was then that Captain Vestinova decided that although it was the eleventh hour, he could still cross over to the side of his worthy adversaries. He would join forces with Colonel Fury and the Emerald Midnight Hornet, Colonel Goldsmith, of whom he had heard so much: she was a legendary ace, a noble fighter whom he respected. What could he say of Colonel Fury except that he was unique! His ancestors broke the mold when they made one Sudden Fury. He displayed enormous, natural leadership skills, always a majority-of-one, yet, as the Red Squadron's leader, their welfare ever came before his own. His airmen and airwomen respected him, and these pilots would follow him in any just cause!

Thus, Vestinova, having scrutinized his ruminating thoughts, concluded that the Red Squadron had been right to follow Colonel Fury to the other side. Yes, even in the act of fighting against their own kind, in an effort to restore peace to the planet, they would gain redemption! The question remained: As the captain of the *Eel Electric,* would his seamen and seawomen follow his orders? Would they, indeed, change sides in this conflagration? It would be a bold move in an effort to defeat the menacing dictator, Admiral Cornwalter...Vampire extraordinaire: the embodiment of sheer evil!

What if there were traitors? Some may be too intimidated by punishment at the hands of the Blue Vampire, if things went awry. Still, had his navy personnel not been loyal to him, through thick and thin, in all the days of his command? Nevertheless, there were a few who just might want to challenge his authority. How should he proceed? Ought not he contact Colonel Fury immediately about his intentions? He knew exactly how to do that, based on a previous sign he and Fury had agreed upon, or should he first inform his Cricket submarine sailors? He contemplated the two possibilities and concluded the former was far more advisable and expedient to the latter.

Captain Vestinova, thus, immediately contacted Fury, via a high-speed computer, using an encrypted message sent to a site only known to the two of them. Colonel Fury, on the other hand, had a computerized watch that would light up and vibrate, alerting him to enter a sequence of numbers, in order to retrieve the Captain's message. Fury was alone when he felt his wrist tingle with the incoming message. He sensed it was very important to read it, so he dashed away to the men's room and entered a stall where he had complete privacy. There, he quickly entered the numbers that would reveal the information from Vestinova. The message was concise and stated all the parameters of Vestinova's *Eel Electric* submarine, including, of most importance, his position and speed in knots. The message began and ended with:

"We are coming over to your side. Need protection from hostiles!"

The Colonel knew exactly what that meant! Fury, immediately, pushed a button that replied to Vestinova's message by stating, in a preconceived message of his own:

"What took you so long? Help is on the way! You've made the right choice!"

Fury, of course, knew it was imperative to inform Rachel! He always took her into his innermost confidence, because of his deep and abiding love for her. He held the utmost respect for the intelligence and the trustworthiness she shared with him. She often advised him on delicate matters. The situation, of having the top submarine commander and his submarine come over to the side of the Frogs, Toads, and their allies, seemed like an open-and-closed affair; nevertheless, Colonel Fury and Rachel—always on his side of any issue—

would have to consider that the admirals, especially Admiral Amsterdam, might consider Captain Vestinova's move a tactical action intended to undermine, or at least slow, the allied offense now well underway! These were some of the critical misgivings Rachel had shared with Fury, before they met privately with the Admiral.

Fury: Excuse me, Admiral Amsterdam. I know that you must be absolutely certain that Captain Vestinova does not intend to strike or divert us, if we accept his request. I wish I could provide you with more assurance. The only thing I can tell you Sir is that when I asked to come over to your side, your government trusted the Emerald Midnight Hornet. Now I am asking that you, Admiral, also trust the two of us.

Rachel: If I may speak freely, Admiral Amsterdam.

Admiral Amsterdam: Please do, Colonel Goldsmith!

Rachel: When Colonel Sudden Fury came over to us, with his brilliant and courageous Red Squadron, we were very careful to position our most advanced aircraft—in the air—in order to return fire, if fired upon first! In taking this calculated risk, as a defensive initiative, I knew that Colonel Fury and his fighting airmen and airwomen would be a valuable asset to freedom's cause. Sir, you must agree that the friendly Crickets have fought splendidly, thus advancing our campaign against the evil Crickets! To cut to the chase! We can better accomplish our immediate objective, of defeating the enemy, by sending out our superb submarine fleet, *The Victorious*—-or *The Invincible* as you refer to her! By assisting Admiral Vestinova, we are helping him to help us! Likewise, he will prove a great asset to our illustrious navy! Furthermore, Captain Vestinova knows just how the formidable *Black Widows* fight!

Admiral Amsterdam: You both present rational and logical arguments! On the surface, it makes sense; nevertheless, just because Colonel Fury has turned out so right for us does not necessarily mean Captain Vestinova will. *(smiling)* Your years of experience, however, are on your side Colonel Goldsmith. Your sound judgment, based on the former, may tip the balance in your favor. Colonels, I will consult with Admiral Leviton. You will have your answer in ten minutes! In the meantime, make yourselves, perfectly, comfortable in my office, until I return! By the way, did you both study drama or elocution in college? I can't recall when I last heard such passionate speeches! *(They have a hearty laugh!)*

Colonels Sudden Fury and Rachel Goldsmith: *(both smiling to each other and a little embarrassed as they returned Admiral Amsterdam's glance. Speaking in unison)* Yes indeed Sir; we did Sir! Thank you, Admiral Amsterdam, Sir! *(They both salute the Admiral, and he returns same with a twinkle in his eyes.)*

The meeting between Admirals Leviton and Amsterdam went very well! Almost Immediately—in five minutes flat, Leviton ordered that the *Victorious* move into harm's way, in order to protect Vestinova and the sailors of the *Eel Electric*! By now, Admiral Vestinova had spoken with his crew and explained why he was taking their submarine and crew over to the other side. His argument went along four or five veins.

> First, the Blue Vampire had been responsible for the death of the great Red Vampire, Reynaldo! Reynaldo had communicated to him, just before his death, that there was no time to lose! They must stop Cornwalter at all costs! The reason he had not acted before now, Vestinova articulated, was that he refused to believe The Blue Vampire was as evil as Reynaldo had indicated. Past events, however, particularly the drunken party that Cornwalter had thrown, had convinced even the Blue Vampire's lap dogs: closest associates that Cornwalter would not rest until he conquered the entire planet! Our forefathers are no doubt turning over in their mausoleums! They never wanted this!
>
> Secondly, not only do the Frogs, Toads, and their Allies have the moral high ground, they also, strategically, are better situated to bring this naval war to an abrupt halt. Most of our battleships have been decimated; furthermore, our ships' escape route has been all but cut off! Our carriers' backs, unbelievably, are hemmed in against the rugged African Coast. With the entire might of the enemy to our west, facing our Black Widows submarine fleet, we as a naval force stand very little chance to maneuver our ships! We, in fact, are blocked in! Consider, especially, that the enemy has proven their superiority in the skies. If their submarines don't do us in, once we surface, their air armada will! Our leadership, as you already know, has shown itself to be not only corrupt but, also, inept! That last statement, my comrades, is a gross understatement. Like Nero, they fiddled when they should have fought!
>
> Thirdly, we also know that Admiral Lightning Striker committed a treacherous act of sabotage by downing one of our aces: Colonel Sudden Fury!
>
> Fourthly, by entering on the side of our noble enemy, this late in the ball game, we can still reclaim the dignity of our ancestors! Most important, we can, thereby, reduce the amount of devastation on the high seas that will result in saving thousands of lives: on both sides! With a weakened submarine fleet—our glorious Black Widows—the Blue Vampire must sue for peace! In addition, we can encourage our Cricket comrades to rebel!

Finally, in the end, we will be free of a our evil dictator who has steadily and most assuredly been leading us down to the lower depths of Dante's Inferno, an abyss reserved for the lowest of the low! Do we noble Crickets, even if we were to win, want this holocaust on our shoulders? I think not! What say you, my brave comrades-in-arms?

(All sailors in unison): "We are with you! We are with you to the end! Long may you live!"

Most of the *Black Widows* were still some distance away. They had been surveying Diego Garcia Island, investigating information they had obtained about the Frog and Toad stronghold. It was getting dark, and they were hurrying toward the African Coast, to lend support to their countrymen and countrywomen. It would take some time before they made contact with the enemy fleet. It stood in the way of their ability to link up with their fellow Crickets. Radio silence was at a premium. The order went out, not to alert the enemy Frog and Toad ships that continued to menace their mission; consequently, Captain Vestinova had to make a critical decision: whether to wait until he was closer to the Frog, Toad, and Allied Forces—to radio for assistance---or whether to simply make a dramatic dash toward the haven, of former foes!

The *Eel Electric* had been having some troubles with their nuclear reactor that propelled their submarine. In one of their last engagements with the Allied Navy, they had taken a hit. The damage was insufficient to bring them to the lower depths of the Indian Ocean; still, it was sufficient to cause their submarine to act peculiarly, that is, to respond accurately to various commands regarding speed and depth control. In short, he felt he could not risk making a run for it! There was also the concern of several members of the crew who could not be trusted. These were mid-grade officers loyal to the Blue Vampire. Fortunately, Vestinova knew who they were and had some of his most trusted officers keep a watchful eye on them.

After drinking a cup of coffee with two of these trusted officers and discussing their options, he put a plan into play. The procedure would be a compromise between his two options. While he felt he was still, too, far from making contact with the Frog and Toad Fleet, Vestinova knew full well that Colonel Fury, by now, had alerted his new friends. These Frog and Toad ships, Vestinova believed, were already well underway to rescue his submarine. Therefore, the Captain opted to move toward his new security blanket: the friendly Allied Armada; this he must do at the earliest possible time, he assured himself. According to his latest coded information from Colonel Sudden Fury, the rendezvous meeting would be at approaching 20:00 hours or an hour away.

At about fifteen minutes before 20:00 hours, Vestinova gave orders to have the *Eel Electric* surface, realizing that he could make better speed above, that is, on the ocean. Ironically, just about the time that his submarine was surfacing, the two untrustworthy officers made their move! They attempted to scuttle the *Eel Electric* by placing several sticks of dynamite near the reactor.

These two officers wanted no part of the ship's mutiny against their nation. They viewed Captain Vestinova as a treacherous traitor: a disloyal patriot of the worst kind, only to be surpassed by Colonel Sudden Fury and his happy band of traitors. *The Red Vampire's Squadron*, now *Colonel Fury's Red Raiders*, was often referred to as *"Fury's Scummy Red Traitors."* Most Crickets simply referred to them as *Sudden Fury and his scum!* The attempt by these deceitful officers was short-lived! In no time at all, the Captain's faithful officers overpowered them! They were put in irons and confined to an onboard detention cell.

At around the same time, Rachel suddenly awakened from a nightmare! Perspiration covered her tanned face. The upper portion of her nightshirt's collar was completely wet! She had eaten something that, evidently, was disagreeable, and she had returned to her cabin to rest but had fallen asleep. In her dream, she was reliving the recent battle she and Fury had fought with the enemy's battleships, cruisers, and destroyers that had been trying to create an escape route for the larger Cricket carriers. She saw herself diving from a great height toward a dark enemy destroyer that was sending rays of fire toward her airplane!

These rays appeared as giant lasers that crisscrossed her path. As she attempted to swerve to the right, to evade the rays, she saw herself getting closer and closer to the destroyer's belly; she found she needed to pull up in order not to crash into the destroyer's armed side. At the last minute, she dropped her payload of torpedoes, while at the same time maneuvering her airplane skyward. Her *1205 WIN torpedo-fighter's* nose barely missed hitting the destroyer's observation tower, as she attempted to evade more firepower emanating from the destroyer's great guns! A few moments later, the concussion of the explosion, caused by the two torpedoes hitting the destroyer, sent her *1205 WIN aircraft* into a tailspin; moreover, enemy aircraft, approaching from the *SS Admiralty*, were speedily zooming toward her for the sole purpose of expunging her from the sky!

While Rachel was still deeply beside herself, recovering from her nightmare, Captain Vestinova, less than an hour away from the main Frog and Toad Armada— positioned slightly to the west—was making a desperate run for it, with his gallant crew of the *Eel Electric*! Vestinova, soon afterwards, received another coded message from Sudden Fury that stated the *Victorious* submarine fleet was within a quarter-of-an-hour away and would be in range to support his escape! He could no longer wait; the *Black Widows* were quickly converging on the *Eel Electric's* position! Obviously, one of the saboteurs, now in irons, had earlier alerted the *Piranha* that in turn alerted the remaining *Black Widows*. In the excitement that followed, the *Piranha's* captain immediately fired two torpedoes at Vestinova's submarine. Fortunately, for Vestinova and the crew, the other Cricket sub was out of range; the torpedoes, however, barely missed their intended target: *The Eel!*

The *Piranha's* captain, therefore, gave the order to surface at once, in order to pick up speed. The *Barracuda*, on the other hand, had seemingly, all along, been quite close to the renegade submarine. It had been shadowing the *Eel Electric*, without even realizing its sister submarine was going over to the enemy! Once it had garnered this knowledge, that Captain Vestinova was leaving the Blue Vampire's protection, the *Barracuda's* commander made a formidable effort at extirpating the turncoat sub from the ocean's waters. Now within range, the *Barracuda's* commander fired his newest laser missile, to accomplish the obliteration of the *Eel* and its crew. *The Barracuda's* amazing missile, while not making direct contact with its target, nevertheless, came sufficiently close to destabilize *The Eel Electric's* computers; moreover, it also caused significant harm to the *Eel's* propeller shaft! When the *Eel Electric's* engineer conveyed the severity of the damage to Captain Vestinova, the latter quickly took evasive action by giving the re-submerge signal and the command to go deep into **silent-running**!

Rachel peered at a shaft of light coming from beneath the foot of her cabin's door. She was beginning to get a handle on her nightmare. Yes, it had all been true! She, thanks to fellow Frog and Toad aviators, had been able to fend off the Cricket aces. The aerial dogfight had seemed more like a dream within a dream. The fighters of both enemy and foe, she recalled, had swirled at each other like so much large confetti being blown by a giant wind machine. At times these airplanes seemed to collide, only to be separated by stronger winds. The air spewed and was replete with colorful smoke: the result of gunfire being shot from the various ships just below.

Abruptly, the scene changed to that of a movie shot in slow motion, where the fighters' maneuvers seemed to approach a standstill: more like frames being shown one-at-a-time. All of a sudden, the fighters resumed their whizzing about, very similar to a strafe of bullets pouring from the muzzle of a machine gun. Ultimately, the Frog and Toad fighter pilots, once again, proved their superiority in the skies. This victory was the result of possessing slightly better aircraft, not to mention a combined Frog and Toad squadron that, continually, manifested: courage, expertise, and tenacity... in the face of death!

Captain Vestinova had no other choice but to hurriedly drop his *Eel Electric* to the Indian Ocean's bottom! By performing this dive, he was able to elude his former navy, now determined enemy, and find safe haven in the immense darkened waters of the Indian. Most certainly, as he already knew, the *Barracuda's* commander, Captain Malencovsky, would be dropping depth charges. Vestinova and Malencovsky had been close friends at the Cricket Naval Academy, near Cricketstonia. They had both come from the lower classes of Cricket society, and, as such, had needed to compete with some of the sons and daughters of Cricketstan's most privileged families, if they were to earn a place in the prestigious Officers Training School (OTS).

Captain Malencovsky was torn between his duty to his country and his long friendship with a fellow OTS classmate! Sure, he had fired a missile that almost took out Vestinova's sub; nevertheless, if he had really applied himself, diligently, Malencovsky was certain he would not have missed his target! He had Vestinova right where he wanted him, or al least he thought so.

Malencovsky also knew the deadly Frog and Toad submarine fleet would be approaching from the west within minutes! If he tarried, he would be breaking out of the *Black Widow's* submarine attack formation that was absolutely necessary in defeating the enemy's *Victorious Fleet*.

Chapter Nine

Submarines, Former Enemies, and Rescues

Rachel had wanted to find Fury and tell him about her nightmare. He was always so attentive. The fact that he was such a good listener made him an even better conversationalist. She decided to take a quick shower and then meet him at their favorite on-board coffee shop. In about fifteen minutes, she was ready to meet the love of her life. She checked herself and realized she had not yet placed a call to him. Once on the telephone, Rachel asked Fury if they could meet for coffee. The hour was getting late and the shop might close soon was what she had mentioned to him. He quipped, "Not a chance they'll be closing early tonight, honey, not with a battle in full swing." His reply was witty and not at all sarcastic. The two lovers would rather tease each other than fight. So, within a few minutes, they met at their favorite little coffee shop—just around the corner!

Fury: Well, fancy meeting you in place like this!

Rachel: *(taking in his smile with the smooth voice)* Well, the same to you, sweetheart! *(Fury takes her in his arms and gives her a long hug and a brief kiss on the cheek.)* That's what I like most about you, Fury. You always show me affection and you fill my emotional bank.

Fury: It gives me great pleasure to be able to assuage your anxieties.

Rachel: Honestly, Fury, don't you ever get frightened? During the many missions you have flown, have you ever once been afraid? I mean really afraid!

Fury: I would be an out-and-out liar if I said no! I used to be a little bit of a fatalist. I believe that, as you say, He has a plan for us. And, when that plan doesn't work, The Immortal One has another plan for us! Before I met you, I didn't believe there was a rhyme or reason to life. Sure, our leaders talked about our ancestors, but it makes more sense to me now to comprehend that there is a Divine Force in the universe. If we are doing what we know to be right and just, everything else will take care of itself. I now enter the field of battle with much more conviction and a lot less fear. The Heavenly Spirit is on our side. We will prevail. Truth and goodness will put evil to shame! Now, please tell me about your nightmare. Are you scared?

Rachel related to Fury all of her dream. After some time, she began to breathe more easily. She, once again, declared her love for Fury and prayed they would make it through this night!

Fury: I have a confession to make. I, too, had a nightmare.

Rachel: Are you kidding me? If so, I don't think it's funny!

Fury: I wouldn't kid you about something like that, after what you have shared with me, just now!

Rachel: Then, I am truly sorry. Please tell me about your dream, that is, your nightmare?

Fury: Not a problem. In my dream I was fast approaching one of my former country's battleships, the *Cobra.* You may recall, they hadn't yet left the African Coast, and they were sitting ducks. What actually happened though, as soon as our Allied airplanes hit them, they very quickly returned fire! To make matters worse, after a brief time, our airplanes began losing their magical and invisible shield! One of the Blue Vampire's elite squadrons, then, started to find their range. We, of course, began to lose more of our airplanes to them!

Well, as I was saying, I came upon the Cricket *Cobra* when I felt the reverberation of my new *Sabertooth 222*, like the one you've also been flying. Suddenly I felt scared, quite alone! I mean, I began to perspire—no, sweat! The sweat was getting into my tired eyes; I could feel my eyes burn all the way inside my head! I promptly wiped away the cold sweat from my eyes; when I once again turned to look, I was about to hit the *Cobra*, not with my missiles, nor even with my rapid-fire laser guns, but with my *ST 222*! It was then that I sat up in bed—still attempting to save my airplane and myself—then, suddenly awakening, I saw your image coming to me through the darkened room!

Rachel: Wow! My poor Fury! *(leaning over and embracing him, putting his head on her lap)* You were probably also target-fixated! You have nothing to worry about now! It's over! What you just described really happened. As you may not clearly recall, you did fire your missiles. They made a direct hit! The reverberation, in part, was the internal explosion of the *Cobra*. The battleship started to break apart. It broke in two! The prior enemy's guns may have come too close for comfort; nonetheless, they caused no harm to you or your *Sabertooth. (Fury is now sitting upright)* You are as you always have been: the epitome of courage lodged into one hunk of a man! *(Fury and Rachel embrace tightly)*

Fury: I guess my biggest fear was beginning to realize that I am mortal—more than that, realizing that I may never have seen you again!

Rachel: *(softly and tenderly)* Nothing can ever separate us! *(Now, both begin to smile between their combined tears; they gaze at each other, momentarily studying each other's features, before Rachel continues to speak)* We really put it to their best battleships, didn't we?

Fury: Yes, that we really did! You, Rachel my sweet, hit their other great battleship, The *Cottonmouth*! The two battleships were, for some odd reason, within sight of each other, poorly placed to defend or attack. I guess they were enjoying a victory over us, prematurely! Your *222* certainly found its mark. What type of missile did you use?

Rachel: The missile, I believe, was our new XY Zoom Splitter**.** I was so excited when I saw that I could take out the *Cottonmouth* that I just pushed the computer screen icon, without even realizing which of the missiles I was firing! It felt so exhilarating to know, that within a few seconds, we would have one less of their great battleships with which to contend!

Fury: What can I say; you're the best, Rachel!

Rachel: No, you are the very bestest, Fury!

Fury: No, you are the veriest bestest ever! *(both laugh then, later, in her apartment, they begin to kiss when they hear a knock on the door)*

An ensign appeared stating that they were both needed at the Admiral's quarters immediately! With that, Fury and Rachel quickly composed themselves to leave on the double. When they arrived, the admiral was drinking a midnight cup of green tea. He smiled as he greeted his two aces and then returned their salutes. He begged them to sit down and began to briefly compliment them on their extraordinary feats in the sky, against a very determined enemy. He mentioned, that while it was true that, for now, it appeared they were eliminating the Blue Vampire's mighty forces, they still, nevertheless, had major work to perform. For one thing, he explained, the enemy's carriers were still menacing! Yes, he continued, the Cricket defensive shield, their destroyers and battleships, had taken a beating at the hands of the superb Frog and Toad aviators and battleships; however, incredibly their own carriers had hardly been touched. Apparently though, Admiral Amsterdam emphasized, Admiral Lightning Striker's Blue Demon Squadron had performed remarkably, in spite of being surprised by the invisible Allied Forces!

The *King David's* admiral declared that it would be up to Colonels Rachel Goldsmith and Sudden Fury to continue to lead and inspire their squadrons' fighters to, once and for all, remove the Blue Demon scourge! "If we can accomplish this deed, and I know we can," Admiral Amsterdam reasoned, "then we will have defeated their navy! Without the benefit of their best aviators defending their main carrier, the *SS Admiralty*, we will have effectively cut off the ugly dragon's head! The remaining carriers, that is *the Stingray* and *the Orca,* will either fight on to an end with no purpose, other than bringing complete devastation upon themselves, or they will ultimately see the light of truth: that a noble surrender will best serve both sides, by saving many lives!

It was now up to the two colonels to finish what had been started more than three years ago: The defeat of an invading navy! Throughout history, there had been great leaders who, through superb leadership, were able to gain the upper hand over their mighty nemeses. Examples of this, in antiquity, were stunning victories by Greece over Persia, England over Spain, Japan over Russia at the turn of the twentieth century, and the United States of America over Japan at mid-twentieth century. Of course, these had all happened more than a thousand years ago! Nevertheless, if they could do it, so could the Frogs and Toads and their friends defeat the seemingly invincible, terrible Crickets! During the mid-twentieth century, it was the American aviators who carried the day against an invading Japanese Imperial Navy, thus proving the remarkable advantage of aircraft fighter-power, itself, in naval combat. Now, it would be up to the Emerald Midnight Hornet and a certain Sudden Fury who could make all the difference in **the war at sea.**

It was thus, that within the hour, Rachel and Fury, once again, found themselves high above the Indian Ocean, flying toward the three huge Cricket aircraft carriers. The Cricket Armada was attempting to break out of its confined space, where it was still pinned with its back against the African Coast. Yes, it was true, updated information indicated the *SS Admiralty*, the *Stingray*, and the *Orca* had just recently taken some serious hits; remarkably, however, the ships were able to extinguish the fires and sufficiently do onsite repairs, enabling them to be at a 97-percent fighting capacity!

At last, the moment of truth had arrived for both sides in this final battle of *Winner-take all*! It would be a fierce engagement between the two major powers, to say the least. For now, all that could be heard, high above the Allied ships that appeared as toys *strategically* placed below, was the hum and purr of the jet-like engines that propelled the two aces ever closer to their enemy. As they came within sight of each other, Rachel and Fury, once again, acknowledged each other with a thumbs-up! Then, suddenly, they both lowered the noses of their fighters to attack the *SS Admiralty*!

The Victorious *Allied Submarine Fleet,* led by the nuclear Frog *Tomahawker* submarine, was fast approaching and within striking distance against the more vulnerable ***Black Widows*** Crickets' *Submarine Fleet* positions. Captain Vestinova and his valiant crew were very concerned about some of the near-hits to their sub, in the silent-running mode. Captain Malencovsky, in the meantime, was beginning to have second thoughts! He had to determine, within a few minutes, what his life had brought him to; that is, what was most important. He asked himself whether his duty to his country was more important than his friendship with Vestinova? He also realized that too many lives had already been lost, as a result of the Blue Vampire's obvious obsession to conquer the world!

Captain Malencovsky recalled a strange conversation he had had with Vestinova, way back in those golden days, when they were still naval cadets at the prestigious Cricket Naval Academy and later at the elite OTS (Officers' Training School). Their tenure had often been filled with fun-loving nights, at the various nightspots in and around Cricketstan. Yes, those were definitely fun-loving times! He had over the past few years missed not being able to see more of Vestinova. He also remembered when he was in a fight with two other naval cadets, in the Academy's soccer locker room, and Vestinova had come to his defense to even up the sides: They cleaned house!

Those two cadets, whom they fought, were eventually removed from the Academy for cheating on tests. It was something else, however, that had happened. It was what Vestinova had said to him afterwards, when the two were just about ready to graduate. Malencovsky pondered that moment in time. What was the exact question? He suddenly had an epiphany. Yes, he remembered! Vestinova had asked him, at first in jest but then seriously, "What, Malencovsky, would you do if for some strange reason we should find ourselves on opposite sides of the fence, as commanders of our own subs; you know, on opposite sides facing each other; what would you do? Would you blow me out of the water, or would you ask yourself, first, 'why am I facing my friend Vestinova? What has changed that we should find ourselves opposing each other! Has Vestinova gone mad,' you well might ask?"

"Let me help you, dear Malencovsky. I should never oppose you, no matter the circumstances or the time of day or night! What say you, my dear best friend? Would you then come to my aid and change sides, too?" Malencovsky noticed he was beginning to perspire. He wasn't sure whether it was the drink he held firmly in his left hand, or whether it was the question his best friend had just asked him! "Well, Cadet Vestinova, I know you to be the most outstanding student at our Academy, and I know you would never desert the Motherland, unless you had very good reason to do so. I should search my heart rather than my mind for an answer, and my love for our friendship would come first! We are as brothers and brothers should never have to oppose each other; is that not right, my Vestinova?" The two cadets sought each other's eyes, held hands as men can, and the gleam amidst their wet eyes conveyed the true feeling of friendship they shared. They, in effect, had performed a pact between themselves! Thus, the two men, long ago, had vowed to always support each other, through thick and thin.

Far beneath the Indian Ocean's upper surface, Vestinova had already launched a pod—by shooting it out of a communications special compartment. When the pod surfaced, Vestinova had informed his naval cadet friend, from years ago, that he would chance bringing his submarine up from its hiding place. "My life and those of our glorious *Eel Electric's* sailors, our precious brothers and sisters, are presently in your hands, Malencovsky! I trust in our lifelong friendship and what we pledged to each other—on that fateful day, oh so many years ago—at our beloved Academy. Together, right now, we can save our country by joining forces! The Kingdoms of the Frogs and Toads, I am sure you agree, never sought to harm us. They are, as the Red Vampire informed Colonel Sudden Fury and as the Colonel, himself, has learned, an honorable and just people! Let us, I implore you, bring an end to the Blue Vampire's tyrannical rule!"

It was then that Malencovsky came to his friend's aid. Knowing he would be giving up his commission in the *Black Widows Fleet* to aid Vestinova, Malencovsky, nonetheless, radioed Vestinova declaring he was going over to his side! His message stated: "Surface Vestinova, before it is too late; my best friend, I am with you!" Vestinova was not entirely sure that Malencovsky was still the same person he had grown to love at the Academy; nevertheless, he was in a very tight spot and decided to risk surfacing. When he arrived at the top of the water's edge, he found the *Barracuda* almost directly above his *Eel Electric*! "Wow," was all he could say. "We wouldn't have had a chance!"

The two, then, decided on an immediate strategy of flight to later fight the *Piranha* and the *Sharkfin*. The reason: The rest of the Cricket subs were also closing in fast. Yes! In a few minutes, the two faithful friends, Vestinova and Malencovsky, would be vastly outnumbered and in peril! Just then, they spotted ***The Victorious Fleet*** coming to engage the ***Black Widows!*** The captains of the *Eel Electric* and the *Barracuda* both radioed the Frog *Tomahawker* saying they were coming over to their side! "Terrific," was the only reply given by the *Tomahawker's* crusty Rear Admiral, no doubt an eloquent man of few words.

Exactly at that specific moment, the captain of the Frog *Harpooner*, in a very excited voice, arrogantly remarked to the *Tomahawker's* flag-officer, "This is our chance to take out the *Eel* and the *Barracuda*: let's take them both out while we can! We can sink them, now!" The *Tomahawker's* admiral sternly replied, "You fire one shot at them and I will personally take you out, completely out of the water! Do you understand me, do you read me Captain Miller, Sir?" Captain Miller sheepishly replied, "Yes, Admiral Posten, yes Sir, I read you loud and clear!"

Somewhere else, Fury's *Sabertooth 222* was zooming toward the *SS Admiralty*, when quite unexpectedly, his mind, for a suspended moment, took a vacation. This had happened to him before and in the recent past. He had explained this phenomenon to Rachel. "At moments of intense combat," he relayed, "I feel the presence of my grandfather and grandmother! It is a very comforting sensation. My grandpa and I are together in his garden performing some gardening chores, such as trimming hedges and shrubs, whilst my grandma is preparing lunch for us and reminding us to get out of the sun's midsummer heat rays, that seem to pound the two of us like a hammer driving spikes into railroad ties!

"I see their faces clearly, just for a fleeting moment, mind you, and then I instantaneously return to my mission: the fight at hand. I can't explain it; I don't seem to have any control over it; it just happens." Rachel, as in the past, always seemed to have an answer to his query. "I believe that during those times, as you have just explained, your grandparents are actually with you! They are reassuring you, giving you that additional confidence—we could all use—in order to help you complete your mission! How fortuitous and how beautiful is that!"

Fury's mind returned from his momentary sojourn: a flashback that had placed him, as an adolescent, once again with his grandparents. A good thing, too! He was just within seconds of crashing his *Sabertooth* into the *SS Admiralty's* starboard side. Such a result would be described as "pilot's target fixation!" Fortunately, he immediately released his two torpedoes and sped his exit towards the left of the *Admiralty*, in the direction of the *King David*. Tracer shells accompanied him on his way out, with some of them barely missing his aircraft.

As his *Sabertooth 222* made an about-face, to observe more-closely, damage done to the enemy ship, he witnessed immense billows of smoke escaping from the carrier's air traffic control center (ATCC)! Without it, Colonel Fury knew the carrier's aircraft could not easily depart or land! He wondered, too, and asked himself, "Had the Blue Vampire been situated there?" He also answered his query, to himself, "If so, with the demise of this evil man, Admiral Cornwalter, perhaps the war might be hastening to an end!" It was almost too much to expect. The Colonel, surprised, noticed that another Frog *Sabertooth 222* had just inflicted heavy damage to the *SS Admiralty's* missile-magazine storage and supply depot (MMSSD).

Fury surveying the scene whispered to himself, "There doesn't appear to be any hope for that dreaded carrier that has, for so long, been the scourge of good navies the world over!" A moment or so later, Fury realized that it was Rachel who had made that tremendous hit! Her *Sabertooth* quickly picked up speed and swerved nearer to Fury's. Once again, as he looked to his left, he saw her fast approaching him. This time, however, it was his turn to present her with the thumbs-up signal, for a job well done! She beamed with delight, knowing they had accomplished their principal mission. He could see it all in her smiling expression—through the canopy of her aircraft—as she turned to face him. Remarkably, as if for the first time, he also noticed her helmet.

Her headgear displayed two light-blue lightning bolts on both sides of her helmet, embossed on a field of white; in addition, there was the three goldstar insignia placed in the front, outlined in a midnight-blue border, that for the Frog Air Force symbolized ***endeavor, courage***, and ***belief***. He wondered if it was a new design. Suddenly, a second or two later, Rachel spotted three enemy aircraft coming at them from about two-o'clock high, just beneath a low-hanging cloud. She motioned to Fury who instantly went into a downward barrel roll, so as to create a 180-degree arch, in order to attack the Blue Squadron from their rear. Rachel followed suit. The enemy airplanes, no doubt, had been deployed earlier from the *SS Admiralty* and were seeking revenge for the destruction of their mothership!

The captains of the *Eel Electric* and the *Barracuda*, meanwhile, having devised a defensive-offensive plan, moved rapidly above the Indian's waves to join ***The Victorious-Invincible Fleet.*** Vestinova's *Eel Electric,* though damaged, was slightly ahead of Malencovsky's *Barracuda* when Vestinova and his senior officers saw the *Barracuda* break up, as the result of a huge explosion! At that precise moment, Vestinova gave the order to turn his submarine around in order to confront the new enemy, ***The Black Widows Fleet***. It would be an impossible task for one sub to engage an entire fleet and a great one at that! He was honor-bound; his friend, after all, had spared his life and that of his crew! Vestinova was once again faced with a difficult decision, whether to pick up survivors or to attack the closest attacking Cricket sub. He opted for the latter, reasoning that other Allied subs could pick up the Cricket sailors who might have survived the explosion. The captain, then, gave the submerge order and the *Eel Electric* responded. Within minutes, the *Eel* was almost back underwater! Vestinova, in the Indian's murky water, spotted the *Piranha*! It was still at a distance, though coming around quickly to better position itself. It couldn't wait to fire yet another volley of its newest torpedoes. This time, the *Piranha's* commander promised he would not miss the wretched turncoats! Well, this turncoat would have none of that!

Captain Vestinova knew the captain of the *Piranha*. Oddly enough, like Colonel Sudden Fury and Lightning Striker, the two had also met years ago at the Cricket Naval Academy. They had been rivals in the Cricketstonia Submarine Special Forces Division and there had been no love lost between them! Captain Smirnov, captain of the *Piranha*, had always been a cold and calculating individual. He never showed mercy or apologized, even in polite company. He came from a privileged class of Cricket elite military families: *The nomenclatura*. His motto was, "The end justifies the means."

In combat he was never one to take prisoners. Yes, Captain Vestinova knew whom he was facing; he had his work cut out for him. Just then he noticed, on his new advanced echolocation-radar screen, that the *Piranha* had closed the gap between them and was approaching swiftly from the east. Fortunately, Vestinova had already acted quickly by immediately giving the command to submerge the *Eel Electric*; otherwise, the *Eel* would be history now! His submarine had not long descended, into deeper water, when two enemy torpedoes whizzed by his propeller shaft.

The *Piranha* belonged to the newer *Typhoon Super-Class Boomer Submarines,* the Crickets had created less than five years earlier. Even so, Captain Vestinova's *Eel Electric,* at close range, would have a slight advantage, since this smaller-sized *Cricket Fast-Attack Submarine* made it possible to outmaneuver the largest of the Cricket subs. The Blue Vampire had ordered these boomer submarines built to overtake the new and comparable *Toad Boomers,* also known as *The Toad Ballistic Missile Submarines Fleet*: The ballistic nuclear missiles, typically, could fly in excess of 3000 nm and were equipped with multiple warheads. Notwithstanding, the Cricket Typhoon subs—also called *Typhoon X Class*—were the largest in the world!

Vestinova knew that despite his fast-attack sub's advantage of maneuverability—over that of Smirnov's boomer—he also faced major disadvantages. To begin with, the *Eel Electric* had sustained some slight damage to its propeller shaft; In addition, the much larger *Piranha* not only contained greater firepower, but it could also submerge to much greater depths, due to its outer metallic skin construction. From these lower depths, the Toad Boomers and the Cricket *Typhoon X'ers* could easily continue to launch their missiles and torpedoes, it being understood that the missiles, themselves, would still have to be launched from a specifically designed vertical launching tube. While military nautical science had made vast improvements over the centuries, the various forms of missile launches, whether from land or sea, remained virtually unchanged during this period of conflict.

The Eel Electric went on the offensive. In some ways it was like David dueling with Goliath. The problem, however, was that Captain Smirnov knew his adversary quite well. They had both argued submarine strategy at the Cricket Naval Academy. Both had received high marks for their separate styles of underwater tactical warfare. As in a game of chess, oftentimes, a player needs to wait for his opponent to show his hand. Thinking ahead several moves may not always help, if the opponent is unable to predict the other's offense: example, improvisation cuts across the grain using deception! Captain Vestinova surmised, correctly, that Captain Smirnov would use the greater distance between them to his advantage!

Therefore, he needed to make himself invisible! Perhaps, he could bring the *Eel Electric* behind one of the many reefs that populated that area of the ocean. The oceans and seas of the world contain some of the tallest mountains in the world. There are many places where a sub can hide. Also, by lying on the ocean's bed, a sub can appear to be any number of foreign or inanimate objects: for example, a sunken ship of days gone by. By scrambling the enemy's radar for a short duration, a vessel could relocate its position vis-à-vis the attacker. Rather than fire the first shot and betray his position, Captain Vestinova would wait for his opportunity to come-a-knockin'.

The *Eel Electric's* captain had disappeared! The *Piranha's* captain was beside himself! Where was Captain Vestinova? Was he behind a reef? Was he one of the many objects that lie motionless on the ocean's floor? Was he responsible for the scrambled screen that had lasted for over a minute? Or was he perhaps, at this very moment, directly beneath the *Piranha*? Captain Smirnov became quite agitated, maybe even frightened. His mind began to race. His hands began to perspire when he exclaimed, "I must find him before he finds me, before it is too late!"

At that moment, one of Captain Smirnov's senior communications officers screamed that two torpedoes were headed their way. The *Typhoon X* was too large to dodge both missiles! While the first missed, the second squarely found its mark, and the mighty *Typhoon* super-class boomer submarine exploded sufficiently to cause it to sink! Unfortunately, now the *Eel Electric* had given up its position. This time, however, it was the *Sharkfin* that would attempt to eliminate her. As the *Sharkfin* made its approach, along with other *Black Widows,* the *Eel* made a desperate attempt to run for it! Vestinova was hoping that the *Invincible Fleet* might soon come to his rescue: His situation was dire: untenable! Tears, however, washed his face when he heard his communications officer yell, "It's here! It's here!" The crew jumped for joy, hugged each other or just slapped the other's hand in jubilation, as the news spread! The captain made it official proclaiming over the address system: *The Invincible* has arrived!

For the next hour the two fleets played a cat-and-mouse game. Each attempted to gain the better of the other through naval tactics they had studied at their respective academies and from what they had learned through actual experience in real naval combat. The ships, on both sides, were being hit with various degrees of intense fire-power. *The Black Widows Fleet* was, decidedly, experiencing far more losses than *The Invincible of the Allied Fleet Subs. The Tomahawker*, *The Spearfisher*, *The Tigerfisher*, and even *The Harpooner* all contributed substantially during this epic battle. Captain Miller, of *The Harpooner,* finally got his chance to take out not one but two *Black Widows*! Likewise, other of *The Invincible* commanders—admirals and captains—also played an enormous role in subduing the enemy! It was Admiral Posten, however, who had been the principal architect of the overall Allied combined fleet attack. His submarines moved through the waters of the Indian Ocean as if they had been born and raised there: They owned the ocean and they proved it by winning the day!

The remaining Cricket subs slithered away towards the safety from whence they had come: distant ports with military installations, in colonies still in their possession. Admiral Lightning Striker, seemingly everywhere, apparently had been in command and responsible for *The Black Widows* naval assault strategy. Having witnessed, first hand, the horrific conflagration that devastated his *Black Widows*, he determined all was lost! It went beyond his means of salvaging his fleet. Instantly, he became the first to depart the battle-riddled theatre of the Indian Ocean! Striker issued new orders for the *Sharkfin: Typhoon class X,* he was commanding, to hastily exit for more secure, warmer, and pleasant waters. It appeared very doubtful if this wily rascal would be heard from any time soon, or ever. Sages tell us that cowardly types tend to shun the light of day! Shakespeare says they die many times before their actual death;

whereas, the brave but taste of death once: when they die. Many also believe these heroes gain their eternal reward, their peaceful bliss, in heaven with their Creator.

Colonels Fury and Goldsmith were, during this point in time, positioned to inflict heavy damage on the enemy Cricket pilots: those who nearly extricated the colonels from the Indian sky! First Sudden Fury and then the Emerald Midnight Hornet moved speedily to eliminate four of the new Z-66s: These new Cricket fighters were capable of attaining speeds of 2250 miles per hour. While it was true that the Frogs' new edition of *Sabertooth 222s* were now at least 250 mph faster, it was also pertinent, if rumors that had been circulating were to be believed, that the new Cricket fighters had greater maneuverability, including upper stratospheric range! Therefore, it became imperative that the colonels not miss their targets; otherwise, they could once again become the pursued—rather than the pursuer. With this thought in mind, the Frog and friendly Cricket went to work!

When Rachel found the dark *Blue Demon* enemy fighter on her radar screen, she locked on the fire component and then released the missile. For a brief instant her radar screen also displayed an image of the fighter within the enemy airplane. His uniform was black; while his helmet was also black; it contained four jagged bluish-green stripes running the length, from forehead to the tip of the base of the skull. She silently prayed for the pilot whose life she was about to take. Next, Fury came upon two of the remaining three and in similar fashion vaporized them from the sky. In the meantime, Rachel noticed that the remaining enemy fighter was attempting to escape into the upper level of the stratosphere. She hurriedly chased the dark *Blue Demon*.

The chase was beginning to take its toll on Rachel's aircraft. She was now certain that the rumors were true: "Their aircraft could climb higher than ours," she whispered to herself. "I must release this missile now," she spoke out loud, "Otherwise, at this high altitude, I run the risk of running into my own ammunition!" Once again, she fired her missile that caught the *Blue Demon* pilot just as he or she was maneuvering to the left. Rachel knew the enemy pilot had made a critical mistake. Had he or she simply continued to climb straight ahead, Rachel doubted her missile could have reached its target.

Once again, she was delighted at her own success; in addition, as was her custom, she quietly prayed the heavens would accept the fallen enemy angel. As the Midnight Hornet began her descent, sixteen more enemy aircraft had entered into death's arena! Sudden Fury was immersed with all the skills he possessed to eliminate as many of his former Cricket airmen and airwomen as possible! Common sense, nevertheless, dictated he should take flight from these aviators who were now his avowed enemy. Yet, Fury faced logic and fear straight in the face—single-handedly for the moment—and continued to fight on!

Did he know something she didn't? Sure enough, a new fighter squadron, that had just been created, appeared high above the horizon where the golden sun was making its ascent. These young men and women pilots constituted

The Freedom Eagles: they hailed from the carrier *HTMS Eagle*. They wanted to demonstrate their ferocity, tenacity, and effectiveness as Toad pilots. Within a minute or two, *The Freedom Eagles* were fully engaging the enemy with much admiration from Rachel and, especially, one Colonel Fury. He blurted out, "At long last, we have some relief!"

Fury and Rachel, incredibly, had been solely dueling the best of the Cricket flying aces from the *Blue Squadron!* They both had hoped to see *Fury's Red Raiders Squadron*—formerly enemy Crickets; alas, they were nowhere in sight! In the ensuing trauma of the battle against the *SS Admiralty,* after the carrier's disintegration, Fury had apparently forgotten that he had given specific instructions to his second-in-command, his trusted and most senior officer, Major Ana Zeitsev. She was ordered to continue to prosecute the war against the escaping *Stingray*, no matter the consequences already perpetrated against the *SS Admiralty*. The *Stingray,* Colonel Fury had stated, must not, under any circumstances, be allowed to leave the theatre intact!

Perhaps it was the mild concussion that Fury had suffered, when he felt his airplane experience heavy turbulence, as a result of the *SS Admiralty* breaking apart. Fury shook his head several times to reassure himself that he was A-OK, 100 percent. Good thing, too, because two more enemy aviators were pressing down on him from ten o'clock high! Once again, Colonel Fury went into one of his famous triple-barrel rolls. As he pulled out of the last roll, he instantly saw three additional Cricket fighters from the Crickets' newly formed *Black Ravens Squadron*. Fury was concerned, and deeply so! All the while, he and the Emerald Midnight Hornet had believed they were up against only one squadron; instead, they were now up against two, no, three enemy squadrons! For in the near distance, quickly entering into the foreground of the open-theatre-of-combat, he could clearly distinguish the diamond-backed design of the Cricket's *Hissing Vipers Squadron*.

In the early morning sky, the *Hissing Vipers* resembled flying rattlesnakes slithering on low-flying clouds! They, no doubt, were approaching at a minimum of double-mach speed or higher. The *Black Ravens*, Fury surmised, had hailed from the huge carrier *Orca*; whilst the *Hissing Vipers*, most likely, he believed, based on past confrontations, belonged to the carrier *Stingray*. But, holy cow! Holy Toledo! How could this be so? How could this be possible? Shouldn't these enemy squadrons be nearer their own carriers, protecting them? All of these thoughts ignited in Fury's tormented brain, with the lightning speed very akin to that of a monster-mainframe computer! No matter, he needed to really, really concentrate—his life and that of his colleagues, his fellow fighters, depended on him! He would sort out and piece together the geography and the rest later: after he took care of the business at hand!

Colonel Fury, having lined up his sights, took careful aim and blasted the first of the three enemy fighters, with a perfect hit. The pursued enemy was performing its own aerial acrobatics, with numerous rolls, twists, swerves, and various other maneuvers attempting, in vain, to elude the brave colonel, his former comrade-in-arms, and the *Freedom Eagles*. Before Fury could strike the remaining two Cricket fighters directly in his sights, he witnessed one after the other disappear like starbursts from where else, but Rachel's missile-firing *Sabertooth 222*! She whizzed by him, once again, with a thumbs-up and her ever-winning smile; while it rivaled the rising sun's warmth, he thought, it also flirtatiously teased him, since she was now ahead in numbers shot down. She enjoyed beating him to the punch.

Fury, however, remained resolved in his effort to win their match. Instead of brooding, he, therefore, simply bobbed his head up and down indicating yes, yes, and mouthing, "I saw; yes, you are winning!" He returned a thumbs-up, displaying his own charismatic grin with enough white teeth that seemed to fill a Steinway piano keyboard. His eyes gleamed and his lips smiled. Rachel knew that expression very well. He had conveyed it many times over, when they were in combat together: it meant that though we are in harm's way, we are fighting side-by-side, together! She also reminded herself of their purpose: performing a heavenly deed to procure and establish a lasting peace for their respective nations, not just for the living but for children yet unborn! "Yes, I will marry this man," she thought, "this tall, dark, and handsome brave Cricket." As they pulled away to continue the fight, she blew him a sweet kiss!

Rachel was somewhat beside herself. She was beginning to experience the effects of flight fatigue. All of the aerial maneuvers she was employing in the chase— and being chased by top enemy aces—were starting to wear on her! The Crickets' individual *Blue Demons Squadron*, the *Hissing Vipers Squadron,* and the *Black Ravens Squadron* were each considerably larger than those of the Frog, Toad, and Allied squadrons; whereas, the Frog and Toad squadrons each consisted of 30 aircraft, the Crickets' squadron each numbered 45. In doing the math in her head, based on information she had obtained during the latest briefing aboard *The King David*, Rachel concluded that the enemy initially had 3 X 45 for a total of 135 aircraft. That left a paltry 2 X 30 for a total of 60 aircraft her side could muster, and that is, if Fury's *Red Raiders* would quickly return from their mission against *The Stingray*.

"For now," she uttered aloud, "we've just got 32: the *Freedom Eagles*, Fury, and me!" Unbeknownst to herself, a tear was finding its way down the left side of her cheek. She removed three more enemy fighters from the sky, before she began to pray for more assistance. "Please send more squadrons, You, Who are all good, Who made us, You, Who are before all and after all time, You Who are all that is love and Whom I love; I entreat You to aid us in this our gravest hour! Fortify us that we may better serve Thee!"

No sooner had Rachel Goldsmith, (aka) The Emerald Midnight Hornet: the pride and joy of all Frogland, finished her prayer than the sky began to darken, like so many ominous dark clouds gathering in position to rain down a tremendous amount of thunder and lightning, on those below! This heavenly storm, however, would be very selective with its fire aimed solely at the Cricket arsenal! The enormous entry of the five additional squadrons: the *Heavenly Angels Squadron* and the *T/F-111 Delta Dragons Squadron*, both hailing from the carrier *Eternal Grace*; the *F-77 Silverbird Squadron* from the carrier *HTMS Eagle*; and, from the carrier *HFMS King David,* Colonel Rachel Goldsmith's newly-commissioned *Starry Sky Squadron*; finally, last, though certainly not least, Colonel Sudden Fury's *Red Raiders Squadron,* also stationed on *The King David*. Rachel and Fury, in separate locations, in the midst of dire struggles, gleefully and momentarily looked up with the innocence of children waiting all night for Santa's gifts! Just as the child screams, "Him came, Him came," all of the previously outnumbered good pilots also began, so the angels say, singing in unison: "Him came! Him came! Thanks and triple thanks! You wonderful, marvelous You!"

Once the enemy recognized there were now 180 or more Frog, Toad, and Allied aviators, representing at least six opposing squadrons facing them, they readily began to have second thoughts about remaining at death's door! Their leaders realized the tables had turned. With only three squadrons, and those already suffering significant losses with many of their airplanes disintegrating left and right, it was time to "fish or cut bait"! They knew it would only be a matter of time before they were totally annihilated; still, they chose to fight on. It was of no use! Their finality was at hand. *The Blue Demon Squadron's* leader, thus, gave the command to head for the African continent's interior; the leaders of the other two Cricket squadrons, likewise, gave similar commands. *The Hissing Vipers* and the *Black Ravens* headed for asylum in Persian territory, far beyond the Arabian Sea.

Future historians would name this theatre as *The Battle of the Indian Ocean*! Here the menacing *SS Admiralty* met its terrible demise when torpedoes from every direction found their mark. *The SS Admiralty* was no more; moreover, no one was exactly sure if the Blue Vampire had been abroad his flagship! In any case, Admiral Cornwalter could not expect to find safe haven anywhere on the high seas! As to the Cricket Air Armada, it was reduced to less than half its original fighting force! Celebrations would long commemorate the heroics of the Frog and Toad Fleets, the six squadrons and their courageous pilots, and the invaluable support of their allies.

Yes, too many lives had been lost! During the final hour of aerial combat, several airmen and airwomen later commented that the sky had been ripped apart, from all the firepower thrown by both opposing air forces! What were once the heavens now appeared more like scenes from Mephistopheles' temptation of *Faust,* that is, an underworld had come from below to take over the upper world, a place where the Devil and his six demon servants had hoped to destroy anything resembling nature and all its goodness. For now, that despicable force was turned back. The forces of Good prevailed over those of Evil! It was time to do a reconnaissance of the ocean to pick up survivors.

In separate flight schools, Colonels Goldsmith and Fury had learned about the causality of downed aircraft. During dogfights, their flight instructors had meticulously explained that some pilots are killed outright as a result of direct hits by missiles. Fortunately for the pilots, oftentimes the hits are only partial, yet sufficient enough to cause the airplane to crash into the sea. Other problems that can occur and do occur consist of engine, electrical, and/or mechanical problems: These are due to the tremendous stresses the machine is exposed to in aerial combat. Faulty production, even after many tests at the manufacturing firm's test-sites, may also go undetected. This kind of serious problem can happen during time of war, when manufacturers are pressed for the rapid production of aircraft and when politics and exigencies get in the way of strict policies that require sound and safe aircraft production.

The list of possibilities—as to why aircraft fall out of the skies—appears endless; nevertheless, two additional reasons their instructors cited were of particular concern: The first, pilot error, often occurs in a crowded sky when the pilot swerves to avoid collision on the one side, only to collide with a pilot from the other side; secondly, a pilot may experience the emergence of interior or exterior trauma, due to gunfire he or she has received or because of a preexisting physiological condition. What then were the causes of why both Colonels Rachel Goldsmith and Sudden Fury, ultimately, found themselves floating on the Indian separately: he in an inflatable life-raft and she in a capsule?

In the Emerald Midnight Hornet's case, just prior to the departure of the enemy to which she ostensibly contributed—considering the number of enemy pilots she removed —her *Sabertooth 222* was mistakenly shot down! One of the Toad aviators, from the soon-to-become-renowned *Freedom Eagles Squadron,* became overzealous! Rachel's *222* was being pursued by two of the enemy's *Z-66s.* As she made her descent, with the two enemy planes in hot pursuit, the three came into the *Eagle* pilot's view. He let loose of a sidewinder, heat-seeking missile. Instinctively, Rachel sensed the friendly pilot was target-fixated or miscalculating that his missile would hit one of the enemy's *Z66s*, instead of her *222*. Unfortunately for Rachel, the pursuing enemy pilots withdrew in the nick of time to save their skins: one escaping to the left while the other sped to the right. The stray missile, seeking a new target, struck the tail end of her *222* instead! The cause: once again, friendly fire! She, fortunately, was saved due to the newly installed automatic ejection system! Her capsule, however, made a hard but safe landing in the Indian.

In Sudden Fury's case, every enemy Cricket fighter was gunning for him! He was considered an outcast and an embarrassment to the Cricket Nation's cause: world domination! If no Frog, Toad, or Allied fighter was killed, on that momentous battle of all battles, one Colonel Sudden Fury must pay the ultimate price: death! Small wonder, then, that this brave, friendly pilot, now considered by the alliance of Frogs, Toads, and the Allied forces as one of the bravest and noblest benefactors to defend freedom's cause, was still alive! Yes, small wonder indeed! Fury had already compiled a significant number of kills before this battle. In spite of being shot at, by three converging enemy pilots, Colonel Fury adroitly found the same enemy in his sights. He, shooting below par, was able to return the fire resulting in the downing of two of the three *Z-66s*!

His airplane, then, no longer able to continue, turned downward and immediately went into a severe tailspin, completely out of commission! The descending force of the *Sabertooth 222* was such, that he found it extremely difficult to reach the eject button. He knew it would be impossible to safely land in his aircraft's present condition. He had only a few precious minutes to evacuate the *Sabertooth*. These would become desperate minutes consuming all his effort, both mental and physical. It was, he was certain, an angel who must have pushed the button that released him; since, he certainly could never have reached it! With that accomplished, his capsule's multicolored parachute expanded beautifully into the air of the bluest sky. The Indian Ocean's semi-turbulent waters opened its arms to receive him. It became his temporary sanctuary. Unlike the Emerald Midnight Hornet's landing, his was considerably harder, much harder! It would take awhile before he regained consciousness!

When enemy warships moved to eliminate the downed Allied fighters, including Frog and Toad pilots, the *Tomahawker's* flag-officer, Admiral Posten, made an urgent call; he commanded all submarines to destroy enemy ships bound towards the downed-pilot combat zone! The Allied submarines were free to participate in the search-and -rescue operation, because the enemy threat from the remaining carriers had passed. When Fury awoke in the belly of the *Tomahawker*, after fully regaining consciousness, Admiral Posten wanted to speak with him, at once! He had heard of Fury's flying escapades: near escapes in the deadly skies; furthermore, he knew, full well, that this noble individual was someone very special! Fury looked into the admiral's steel blue eyes as the top flag officer approached him in the hospital's sick bay. Admiral Posten proceeded to introduce himself, and Colonel Fury attempted to lift his head and then his arm to salute the *Tomahawker's* most senior officer.

Admiral Posten: *(to Fury)* That won't be necessary, son. You've already done enough and we can't begin to thank you!

Colonel Sudden Fury: *(now seated with the aid of the ship's nurse)* Thank you, Sir, for giving me a ride on your *(searching for words)* most incredible sub! I didn't expect anything like this. Quite frankly, I would have been happy with just a little *PT 109-9*; like the first time your navy picked me up! Ha, ha, ha!

Admiral Posten: *(joining in)* Ha, ha, ha, ha! I heard about that. That event, I believe, took place a few years back, no?

Sudden Fury: I suppose you're right, sir. *(feeling his dizziness returning)* This war has caused me to lose track of time. *(feeling not completely himself yet, but becoming more serious)* Have you, Sir, heard anything about Colonel Rachel Goldsmith ... *(his eyes pleading)* ... Sir?

Admiral Posten: *(just getting over Fury's levity and then, likewise, turning serious)* We picked up all the downed pilots on this end of the open sea. *The Tigerfisher* is picking up those just west of here. I am quite certain she is just fine! By the way, how did you know her airplane was hit?

Sudden Fury*: (more uneasy, in spite of the admiral's reassurance)* Well, Sir, I didn't until now! May I ask how the admiral came by that information, Sir?

Admiral Posten: *(raising an eyebrow and then smiling through his steel blue eyes)* Aren't you the clever one? I understand and sympathize with your concern. Well, it's classified information; nevertheless, knowing your rank and who you are, I suppose I can waive protocol and state that her name appears on the list of all downed Allied pilots, as did yours!

Sudden Fury: Thank you, sir. When will you know more?

Admiral Posten: Very soon.

The Tigerfisher, in the meantime, reported it had just *fished* (in seaman's language) the Emerald Midnight Hornet from the troubled waters. Rachel appeared quite chipper as the *Tigerfisher's* navy seals assisted her out of the bobbing capsule.

Navy Seal: How ya doin', Colonel Goldsmith, or should I say Emerald Midnight Hornet?

Colonel Rachel Goldsmith: Right now, my swabbie friends, you can call me anything you wish. Just get me outta here *pronto, amigos!* And, one last *thing (smiling at the two)*, thank you very much!

Navy Seals: *(together saluting and receiving Rachel's salute)* You've got it, Colonel!

Second Navy Seal: Let's take it nice-n-easy. Are you hurting anywhere, Colonel!

Colonel Goldsmith: *(touching her left leg)* I seem to have lost some mobility in my left leg.

First Navy Seal: Why doesn't that surprise me! *(calling for more assistance then pointing above)* Let's place you in this contraption *(indicating she is to sit in the Comanche CH A-77 Attack Helicopter's bed, in a prone position; then, the rescue bed is lowered down from the Comanche Helicopter)* OK, nice and easy. We are going to strap you in now, Colonel. They will be flying you to our hospital aboard the *Tigerfisher*. You are going to be A-OK and 100 percent!

Colonel Goldsmith: *(still smiling, though decidedly in pain)* Thanks, men! You're fantastic! This aging beauty isn't getting any younger! Ha, ha, ha!

All: Ha, ha, ha, ha!

First Navy Seal: Have a safe journey! I am told they have some of that special apple pie *The Military Times* says you enjoy eating so much!

Colonel Goldsmith: Really, apple pie, yum and yum again! Thanks! It's just what a girl needs at a time like this! Bye-bye, boys!

Seals: Bye-bye, Midnight! *(saluting with much respect as she is lifted into the air)*

A few tears of joy crept down the Emerald Midnight Hornet's cheek. She said to herself, as the helicopter's aerial gurney was transporting her to the *Tigerfisher*, "I've certainly done my share of crying in this blasted war! I guess no one is going to hold it against me. Only this time, I don't know if I am happy or sad! I can't help but wonder what's happened to my Fury? Please, You King of Kings, let him be safe!"

The helicopter's trip to the *Tigerfisher* took no time at all! Several of the submarine's top brass were there to receive her. All the while, Admiral Posten had made the scene available to Colonel Fury as a result of closed circuit TV. The good admiral had received a message from his principal communications officer, that an important rescue of a senior officer was taking place off the *Tigerfisher's* area of operation. Admiral Posten then turned on the in-room TV set. As the camera zoomed in, Fury was clearly able to see Rachel's face! The hologram transmission of the on- going spectacle, where Rachel was the main attraction, made Fury feel as though he could reach through the screen to touch her!

He was so moved that tears, once again, began streaming down his cheeks. In a whisper Fury reverently said, through a half-choking voice, "Heaven be praised, she's alive!" The admiral responded, "I wouldn't have it any other way, just like I mentioned!" The admiral asked the colonel if he would like a more realistic view of Colonel Goldsmith. Fury inquired as to how that could be accomplished. The admiral asked the nurse if he could, with a little assistance, make topside. The nurse asked for clarification, "Do you mean outside, on the *Tomahawker's* shoulder, that is, the outer enclosed rim, Sir?" "Exactly," the admiral replied. "I suppose so," the careful nurse responded. Fury then spoke up, "I'm as strong as an ox and good as gold; let's go!" With that, the three were topside!

Through the high-powered field glasses, Colonel Fury could once again see Colonel Goldsmith. This time Fury was smiling from ear-to-ear. "Wow, wow, is she gorgeous, or what?" he uttered. *The Tigerfisher's* medics had just finished examining the extent of Rachel's injuries, when they received a message from the *Tomahawker's* senior communications officer. Admiral Posten's communications officer, after speaking with the *Tigerfisher's* medics, asked to speak with Captain Miguel Gonzales, the head physician onboard. He inquired if Colonel Goldsmith was sufficiently well enough to speak with Colonel Fury, before being lowered into the *Tigerfisher's* belly. "This request, please understand, comes from Admiral Posten," the communications officer stated.

Dr. Gonzales understood the situation quite clearly; the two colonels were engaged! Everyone seemed to know that! Sailors love to gossip; it helps to pass the time! The doctor, after carefully perusing his clipboard, to see if he had missed anything in his own impromptu examination, and after assuring himself that a more thorough examination of Rachel would follow immediately, answered with confidence, "I think we can accommodate Admiral Posten. Sure thing!" The two colonels, then, began to speak and see each other through the use of longer-distance audio-sensitive binoculars. These functioned much like videophones. A major difference being that the binoculars allowed the viewer to actually see and hear the other person, as long as, the direct-line-of-sight-field was available and clear. Fury began very animatedly:

Colonel Sudden Fury: Rachel, are you OK?

Colonel Rachel Goldsmith: *(elated)* Just like a walk in the park! Yes, I'm OK; how's about you, my dearest Colonel, my Fury?

Fury: *(excited)* Likewise, I'm sure! I can't wait until we get together!

Rachel: Neither can I. We have so much to talk about!

Fury: Sounds great. How about right now?

Rachel: What do you mean, right now?

Fury: I mean, let's get married, before another war is started!

Rachel: I've already accepted your proposal of marriage!

Fury: I'm glad you haven't changed your mind. Tell you what, I'll supply the *Tomahawker's* chaplain and meet you between the *Fisher* and the *Hawke*r.

Rachel: You are completely and utterly insane; I love the idea! Let's do it!

Chapter Ten

A Celebration amidst a Parade of Ships

With that, all the arrangements were made. Rachel and Fury, two of the most famous aviators, wearing the full colonel insignias on their epaulets, would meet as planned. In a quickly improvised manner, with a few minor changes, several of the female officers found some material and adornments that would suffice as a veil, a wedding cape, and a train. They each boarded separate *PT 109-9* amphibious assault units, just before dusk, that moved them into the center and in-between two mighty submarines: the *Tamahawker* and the *Tigerfisher*. A number of seagulls, off the African Coast, instinctively knew they also had a part to play in the ceremony. Sailors, airmen, and airwomen were amazed to see these wondrous birds approaching with assorted flowers in their beaks! Word spread, like wildfire, and all of the navy and military personnel wanted to get in on the act: They wanted in on the wedding ceremony!

The vast array of military might manifested itself in ships and aircraft of every ilk! It had been some time since these armed vessels, both immense and diminutive, had come together. The combined armadas of the Frogs, Toads, and Allies stretched beyond the horizon line and further than the eye could see! There were *PT 109-9 Amphibious Assault Units* moving in every direction, alongside other small-armed craft and gunboats. The destroyers and frigates were there, too! Their decks displayed meritorious flags, won in battle, waving from the rigging of their lower masts and topmasts to their respective bows, from fore to aft. A few of the light and heavy cruisers passed near the great battleship *Televiva*. The contrast of these fighting machines especially delighted the civilian spectators aboard ship: journalists, politicians, contractors, and special guests who were politically connected, people with influence.

Most impressive in this parade of navy power came the carriers and the submarines. The submarines, though smaller in size, always seemed, especially, to capture the imagination of the newly arrived navy cadets! Perhaps, it was because of the submarines' ability to fight battles considerably below the water's surface or in the depths of the splendid seas and oceans of the earth. Last and at a considerable distance, not easily seen, came many of the greatest carriers! Whereas the submarines' sailors could boast about *The Tomahawker, The Tigerfisher, The Harpooner,* and *The Spearfisher*, among others, such as *The Javelin* that had served meritoriously, the carriers' sailors had won their own bragging rights! They always stood very tall on the decks of these floating islands as their ships entered the harbor. They bore the biggest responsibility to wage war against the enemy, and they served with distinction! They exemplified duty, honor, and country! As reverent sailors, pride was tempered by humility. With the carriers now visible to the naked eye, one could more easily see the sailors saluting their nation's flag!

Ultimately, it was the carrier *HTMS Eagle* that destroyed, with the courageous assistance of its *Freedom Eagles*, one of the Crickets' best and most dreaded carriers: the *Stingray!* Very similar to previous battles, it had been a horrifically fought battle! *The Stingray* had lost, too, many of their finest aviators, not to mention just, too, many planes! It no longer being able to contend, determined that escaping was the better part of valor! Thus, it chose to go up the Gulf of Suez or perhaps through the Red Sea! From the latter, not necessarily the best course of action, it hoped to arrive at the newly created Great Canal. The Canal, of course, opened to the murky Dead Sea! Eventually, by continuing this escape route, it sought to find safe haven up the Jordan. At long last, it imagined arriving, with its escort, at one of their ports—on the banks of the Upper Jordan River. Sadly for them, it was all for naught: it was futile! She would not survive to see another sunrise where she could freely pillage and wreak havoc!

As one cadet relayed to another: At the end of the enormous battle, the *Stingray*, having sent its pilots out too soon, was left with little protection! They were rushed in the process of loading missiles on the wings of newly returned airplanes, when they were—according to astonished Allied pilots—"caught with their pants down!" The firepower poured from the *Freedom Eagle's* missiles, like a hurricane hurling gigantic red hail from the heavens! *The Tomahawker* and the *Harpooner*, more like prehistoric sharks moving swiftly toward their prey, issued fire from their enormous jaws! On that ferocious day, few were spared! Of the enemy who were pulled from the water, most were grateful just to have survived. Those who did were promptly attended to and given humane treatment.

The carrier *HFTMS Eternal Grace,* a co-produced Frog and Toad carrier, was a different story altogether! Although, according to sketchy intelligence, the infamous *Orca* was of comparable size, it apparently was not as fit for battle as was previously thought by Cricket shipyard inspectors. It had been substantially injured in its earlier engagement with the Allied Navy! As a result, reported statements conjectured, its aircraft launching deck was not completely reliable. The Admiral of the *Orca,* in an earlier desperate call from the *SS*

Admiralty's Blue Vampire, Cornwalter, likewise, had hurriedly dispatched his *Orca* aviators to aid the distressed *SS Admiralty.* Too soon the aerial protection left the *Orca*; too soon without proper protection for itself, it would disastrously meet with its own swift demise. *The Tigerfisher* and the *Spearfisher*, moreover, having completed their mission against the enemy's premier submarines, the *Piranha* and the *Sharkfin*, were now free to continue the hunt for larger game.

According to shaky, military journalistic accounts, the hunt for the *Orca* was on! With the help of aerial reconnaissance—the story goes—they surprised the giant *Orca* and sped towards her at breakneck speed. Each, to outdo the other, took careful aim to sink the giant fish! It would be virtually impossible to see which of their torpedoes hit first: Was it the *Tigerfisher's* or the *Spearfisher's*? They appeared to find their mark simultaneously, based on the enormous groan that emanated and lurched out of the *Orca's* belly! The *Orca* was further put out of its misery, during the night, by waves of swarming aviators with their hourly-long dogged attacks from above. The enormous cry of the *Orca* was heard for many nautical miles around!

The *Eternal Grace's* pilots, especially the squadrons of the *Heavenly Angels* and the T/*F-111 Delta Dragons* performed perfectly, marvelously! The *Heavenly Angels Squadron* was composed solely of woman! These newly-commissioned graduates had finished four years of a rigorous discipline, such as aeronautical engineering and advanced fighter tactics: modern air combat. The foremost Frog and Toad's air military academy, where the concept of the *Heavenly Angels Squadron* was formulated, was named The Chanaan Naval Air Force Academy, in honor of the *Old Testament's* "land of milk and honey." These female pilots, moreover, wanted to prove they were worthy of their officer status! *The Angels*, therefore, entered into the fray against the *Orca*, with stupendous ardor, discipline, agility, effectiveness, and ferocity!

The T/*F-111 Delta Dragons Squadron,* conversely, was composed solely of male aviators. Unlike the *Heavenly Angels*, they were seasoned veterans! The captain of the *Delta Dragons'* aviators, nicknamed Deep Freeze because of his icy-cold glare, had just before takeoff issued a challenge to his squadron: "Let's show the girls how it's done!" "Not a politically correct thing to say," one pilot present shared with another; nevertheless, it was meant more as a positive rather than a negative; that is, more to motivate the male aviators in a mutual effort against the enemy. It was, after all, a tremendous time of stress!

With the apparent sinking of the giant *Orca* and the much-feared *Stingray*, all squadrons could now join Fury and Rachel, who, along with the freshman aviators of the *Freedom Squadron*, had been competing amongst themselves to defeat the three elite Cricket squadrons. These Cricket aviators were at first insidiously protecting and then later avenging the *SS Admiralty's* destruction. The menace of the Cricket might, it was believed, had finally passed and come to an end. They had been vanquished! It was time—was it not—for gaiety, celebration, laughter, and, yes, tears of joy! The sailors and the aviators would be going home, at long last, to see their loved ones, family, and friends. It was about time! What better way to celebrate than a wedding?

The King David, however, had not been heard of or even seen in aerial reconnaissance flights. These were being conducted throughout the Indian Theatre of Battle—around the clock! *The David's* last communiqué had come from Diego Garcia Island, where Admiral Leviton's coded message, originally, had indicated *The David* was resupplied and now fit to fight! *The David*, most had believed, would soon return to defeat the *SS Admiralty*, in this, the last major conflict: a do-or-die proposition! The Allied Navy could wage effective battles, but as to winning the war against the mighty Cricket Armada, without the participation of *The HFMS King David,* this was possible but not probable. The *David* was expected to arrive off the East African Coast. After that, it was to have engaged and annihilated its mortal enemy, its nemesis: the *SS Admiralty*! What could have happened to the Allied Forces' majestic carrier, the remarkable fabulous *HFMS King David?* Would it ever arrive? Had it mysteriously been destroyed by marauding mercenaries, loyal to the Blue Vampire, who paid them well? These were real fears and discussions, by the various rank-and-file of the airmen, airwomen, sailors, and soldiers that had been circulated almost everywhere.

In the interior—just off the African Coast, where a top-secret Toad Radar Installation was located, two Toad intelligence officers were also discussing recent events, more specifically, the mysterious disappearance of *The David*. "But wait," a recently- promoted intelligence officer declared to another. "That simply can not be. No, no, no! *The Starry Sky* and the *Red Raider Squadrons* came from the *David*, right?" The higher-ranking security officer replied, "That's very true, most true indeed, but according to my *Top Level-15 Briefings*, these squadrons were sent inland, to one of our undisclosed African bases, for fast reaction response against enemy positions. *The King David*, moreover, was sent to Diego Garcia for repairs and a resupply of munitions!" The level-12 security officer then responded, "That sounds *mucho* fishy to me!"

The Level-15 security officer remarked, "I know, I know! A few of us, however, now believe, based on new evidence, that they were actually assigned to a search-and-destroy mission: ultra top-secret, code name *Maharba*: Abraham spelled backwards! Except for the departure of the *Starry Sky* and *Red Raider Squadrons*, they have a full complement of squadrons, not to mention a full escort of Allied destroyers, battleships, and submarines: enough firepower to choke a horse! Yep, enough firepower to take on a second Cricket Navy!" The other replied, "Wow, you don't say!" The Level-15 intelligence officer, whispering in Intelligence Officer 12's ear, "Yep, I do say!"

The Level-15 officer was partially correct. Where he got it wrong, based on misinformation or disinformation withheld at the level-15 briefings, was that the message from Admiral Leviton from Diego Garcia was a ruse! For quite some time, Allied Intelligence had found that a second Cricket Navy was being built at a shipyard on the Ivory Coast. The West African country had been taken over by the Crickets in order to promote their own selfish world-domination interests. Allied Intelligence determined that the entire party off the East African Coast, by the Crickets, was staged to deceive the Allies! The enemy knew the Frogs and Toads and their friends would be back. Their enemy, the Blue Vampire had once stated, had too much at stake to simply flee. Cornwalter both loathed yet respected the fighting machines of the Allies. He, therefore—at the time—had devised a final-solution strategy, to once and for all defeat his enemy. These Frogs and Toads, especially, would be taught a lesson, he had boasted!

The Toads and Frogs had special agents throughout the African Continent. The Toad agents, those working within the tiny Northwestern African nations, from Senegal down the coast to Benin, had learned of tremendous work projects being conducted in that region. With the assistance of expatriates from these nations, who sought to remove the Cricket presence, the West Africans and the Toads set out to gain as much information as they possibly could. They concluded that the Cricket's second navy would consist of two carriers, with a full complement of aircraft and escort ships, besides battleships, heavy and light cruisers!

This critical intelligence was instantly delivered to Allied Intelligence at their command headquarters in Diego Garcia. The Allies decided to let the Crickets continue to build their mighty force, unperturbed. This noninterference would give the enemy a false sense of security. Thus, the enemy's plan of sandwiching the Allies between their two navies would backfire. Yes, the Frogs and Toads would attack the Cricket's main navy, off the East African Coast, just to make them think the Allies were not aware of the Crickets' ploy. However, for the Crickets, and this was a big "however," things would play out just a little differently than the Blue Vampire had anticipated, or envisioned!

First, it was felt that keeping the *HFTMS Eternal Grac*e on hand, with its heavenly powers, would be a sufficient force to overpower the enemy, provided that the *Eagle,* with its enormous capacity to search and destroy, could pin the Northern Cricket Armada's back against the rugged African Coast. Secondly, this arrangement would permit *The HFMS King David* to make a run up the West African Coast and, likewise, pin down the enemy before he had a chance to leave his port. Once this mission was accomplished, *The David* would return to assist the *Eternal Grace* who now—correctly reported by the *Military Times*—was taking on the massive *Orca.*

The ever-resilient *Orca* seemed to have nine lives! It was first reported that it had been hit by torpedoes from the Allied *Invincible* Fleet, follow by air bombardments! Later reports indicated it had, remarkably, weathered the fiery storm! *The Orca*, updated intelligence reports mentioned, had received a retrofitting in its last overhaul at the Cricket's secret navy yard located in northern waters. Most likely these were not in the Jordan—probably somewhere in the upper Mediterranean. The retrofitting included a new layer of strong, yet lightweight metal that made it almost unsinkable! Final intelligence stated that what had cried out with the onslaught of torpedo and air fire was a Libyan oil tanker: After receiving numerous hits, the tanker slowly found its way to the lower depths of the Indian Ocean, cascading at times, as the undertow pulled the look-alike monster to the deep, to eternally sleep.

In the end, the Allied modus operandi—utilizing fresh Toad intelligence—worked superbly! The coded message sent from Diego Garcia was not that of Admiral Leviton at all; instead, it was Admiral Cheetah's message to Admiral Da Vinci; moreover, it was purposely sent so that it could be intercepted and decoded by Admiral Cornwalter's intelligence operatives! The Crickets, the Allies believed, would be elated at solving the Allied communiqué. With *The David,* seemingly in the Eastern waters off the Indian Ocean, the Crickets knew they could complete their military project: the fabrication and deployment of their second navy off the upper South Atlantic Ocean! It would, they were certain, arrive ahead of schedule to attack the rear of the Allied lines. In this scenario, catching their enemy flatfooted! The Frogs and Toads, between two mighty Cricket offensives, would be obliterated!

What happened, instead, and unbeknownst to the Crickets—according to the latest and complete military report—was that on that moonless, stormy night *The HFMS King David*, after prayer meeting, went on its perilous journey to find and destroy the Blue Vampire's second navy. During *The David's* voyage, accompanied by its escort of Allied destroyers, battleships, and submarines, up the West African coast, *The David* encountered the enemy! The enemy was already moving southward. They had just passed Cameroon! Both navies' top brass were surprised by the sudden encounter! The enemy's admirals, mistakenly, believed *The King David* was en route from Diego Garcia, to rejoin the *HFTMS Eternal Grace* and the *HTMS Eagle*; conversely, Admirals Leviton and Amsterdam believed the enemy's carriers were still in port! The result: Armageddon (though not the one prophesied).

The *David's* superior submarine fleet went immediately into action. The captain of *The David's* lead submarine—who later would be promoted due to his quick thinking— radioed *The David's* command that they were going behind the first carrier to take out the second one! This tactic, on the part of *The David's* submarine captain, provided great benefit. By eliminating the second carrier first, the enemy's second aircraft wave was abruptly prevented from entering the fight: It was in shambles! The first aircraft carrier was also struck horrifically! Torpedoes from *The David's* other submarines seemed to throw caution to the wind as they mounted frontal attacks on their enemy! Next followed bombs from *The David's* incredible dive-bombers! The enemy's second aircraft carrier's destroyer escort, of course, had already been annihilated as a result of first fire! The first carriers' destroyer escort, likewise, was removed but at a heavy cost and some loss of life. The fight was hard fought! The battleships of both friend and foe squared off and traded punches far into the night, until *The David's* battleships struck knockouts against the enemy!

Thus, and in retrospect, with the first tremendous explosion of the second enemy carrier up and off the Nigerian Coast, *The King David* was now less encumbered. It had already successfully launched its second wave of aircraft against the first carrier, when it contacted the captain of the first wave to lend assistance.

With both waves of *David* aviators converging on the enemy's remaining carrier, the lone Cricket carrier was doomed! All of *The David's* might rained on the enemy, and it quickly found the Atlantic's bottom, never to rise again!

The Battle of Nigeria-Cameroon, as historians would later refer to it, was over! Yet, what of the East African Theatre? *The HFMS King David* and her entire fleet made an about-face and sprinted around the Cape of Good Hope to assist the *HFTMS Eternal Grace* and the *HTMS Eagle*. By the time *The David* returned and spotted the *Eternal Grace*, the *Grace* was, after a four-hour struggle—where both sides punished each other over and again—putting on the finishing touches to end, once and for all, the evil *Orca's* life! The *Eagle*, having on numerous occasions fought bitterly against the *Stingray*, would come away with the victor's crown! Its rival was finished and would never again enter the ring!

The enemy's carriers, battleships, heavy- and light-cruisers, destroyers, frigates, freighters, other transports, small-armed vessels and gunboats, in short, all of their seagoing vessels were either destroyed or incapacitated: The enemy's ships were no more to be seen! Its *808 Double Sweptback Missile Fighters*—mainly from the *Orca*— and the Crickets' other fierce fighter squadrons had also been fervently fought and forever dismissed from the heavens! The Crickets had sought to eliminate all resistance in their efforts to achieve a Fourth World Order on planet Earth: They had envisioned themselves as the supreme master race! They lost.

The mightier Frogs and Toads, and their valiant Allies would not have it so! The evil was confronted and removed! The friends of the oceans and seas of Mother Earth would disallow the enemy's perverse contagion to take hold! Still, there was the war on land that must be won! It had been raging, side-by-side the war at sea. Other evil powers, past and present, mainly in Asia and in Europe, had fought on despite their lost navies. Would the Crickets do the same? Most decidedly yes!

The Cricket generals had, after all, massive armies with newly arrived reinforcements! They were now in control of vast areas they had taken back. The areas consisted of more than half of the Frog, Toad, and Allies' real estate: These were important positions, previously held on the Sinai and other key locations. With the War at Sea at an end, the Frogs, Toads, and their Allies could now expect to reinforce their side! The war, half-won, would continue. For the time being, a wedding would be conducted, war or no war! Much had been accomplished; much progress had taken place! Alas! Absent from the wedding scene were the Princess Sophia and her newly found friend, Esther!

Also absent was a certain courageous young Toad senior officer. This colonel was leading a combined platoon of special-forces made up of Toads and Frogs, men and women. His mission: to rescue the beautiful princess that now included the equally very attractive Esther, Samson's wife? The Toad Colonel last reported that, although the mission had early on confronted nearly catastrophic impediments, such as sea serpents, the mission's light was now back to go-green! The lost platoon (aka T-FIST) would forge full-speed ahead! "May the Heavens prevail," Colonel Ramirez augustly declared!

The horns of the various military ships, including those of an Allied Portuguese Man-of-War began to sound. They seemed to say: we want a wedding! Suddenly there appeared in the distance the silhouette of a great ship. Was it? Could it be? The figure enlarged with the sunset becoming glorious! The sun's rays came in every color of the rainbow: reds, oranges, yellows, greens, indigos, blues, and violets. More ships came into view: several destroyers, followed by huge battleships, and finally an enormous ship. Yes, it was *The HFMS King David*! Now all the ships in the harbor began their clamor by shooting off guns and continuing blasting their horns and then their sirens! The wedding, to say the least, was delayed but not postponed! Rachel shouted to Fury with the two *PT 109-9* Amphibious Assault Units sitting side by side; "We can wait a bit; our wedding gift is still arriving, and I couldn't ask for a better gift than *The King David* home, safe and sound!" Fury responded, "And I couldn't agree more!"

Once *The David* finally entered the main harbor, the chaplain stated in a sufficiently loud voice, "I guess we can get started!" As the chaplain began to speak, a very fast-moving military gunboat appeared to be closing in on them! It captured the attention and startled the *PT-109-9* officers commanding the boat. The officers, with guns locked and loaded, surveyed the developing situation. Was it friend or foe? Through the longer-distant binoculars, they saw the Admiral's white insignia with four gold stars embossed on a banner of cadet blue, fluttering in the sea breeze! The faces of Admirals Leviton and Amsterdam came into view as the binoculars moved lower. Incredible as it seems, it was the famous Duo, the much-heralded pair of admirals. "What could they possibly want from us?" Fury and Rachel inquired, aloud and in unison.

The *Toad 200 XX* Amphibious Assault Unit pulled alongside the other two Assault Units. Admiral Amsterdam began, "We heard on the way up here that a wedding was about to take place!" Then, deferring to the most senior admiral, "Admiral Leviton, I believe, has something he would like to say." The Admiral wearing his dress uniform, as was Admiral Amsterdam, began to speak. "Isn't it customary to have someone give the bride away?" Rachel and Fury are both saluting with Rachel responding first, "It sure is, Admiral Leviton!" "If you will permit me then, I would like to have the honor," the good Admiral responded. Rachel and Fury reached across the edges of their Assault Units to embrace at receiving such a privilege!

The whole affair was taking on a magical, delightful quality. Admiral Amsterdam, wanting to accommodate as well, asked, "And, I suppose it is also customary to have a best man!" Fury needing no more information, "Admiral Amsterdam, Sir, I would be privileged to have you as my best man, if you, Sir, will do me the honor?" "I will indeed, Colonel Fury!" Fury and the *Tomahawker's* chaplain made their way into Rachel's Assault Unit. Next entered Admiral Leviton with the assistance of his two senior officers. Finally, Admiral Amsterdam, a rotund man, with a little struggle and the aid of the same senior officers, made his crossing into the *PT 109-9*. Altogether at last, the marriage began with an air of reverence and dignity. The entire harbor was silent except for an occasional ship passing by. The chaplain, initiating the marriage ceremony, started:

Chaplain: Dearly beloved, we are gathered here today to celebrate the union and marriage of two people, Colonel Sudden Fury and Colonel Rachel Goldsmith ... Do you, Colonel Sudden Fury, take this woman to be your lawfully wedded wife, to love and honor her, from this day forward, in sickness and in health?

Fury: I do!

Chaplain: Do you, Colonel Rachel Goldsmith, take this man to be your lawfully wedded husband to love and honor, from this day forward, in sickness and in health?

Rachel: I do!

Chaplain: With the power vested in me, I, therefore, now pronounce you husband and wife! You may kiss the bride*! (Rachel and Fury kiss and then deeply embrace!)*

Instantaneously, horns, whistles, sirens, guns from the large battleships, destroyers, and other armed vessels began to ring out to salute and celebrate the two newlyweds! Within a few minutes, Fury's *Red Raiders Squadron ("Hellcats"* for short) and Rachel's *Starry Sky Squadron* flew overhead, at separate intervals. Seldom has the earth witnessed such a tumult in homage—to two so much in love—in such an ancient, sacred rite as marriage!

As dusk gave way to night the bright flare of guns from the magnificent ships continued and could easily be seen from a great distance. The effect now was much like that of a centennial Independence Day celebration, however, with substantially more emphasis on the cannons' punch! It was absolutely exhilarating to the nth degree! Everyone present, military and civilian, could feel a surge of blood in their veins. The Frogs, Toads, and Allies, together, had defeated the military might of the most powerful navy in the world! There was so much to celebrate: a victory and a marriage.

Early the next morning, Rachel and Fury awoke in a special cabin aboard the *King David* that had been transformed, by order of Admiral Amsterdam, into a bridal suite for the newlyweds.

Rachel: *(looking sleepy-eyed at Fury)* Do you think we can venture out on deck to see the full moon.

Fury: *(attempting to wake up)* Anything you say, dear; women rule, right? *(They both laugh)*.

Rachel: *(a cup of coffee in-hand and looking over the David's exterior protective fence)* Do you recall, Fury dear, when first we met face-to-face onboard ship?

Fury: *(also sipping his coffee)* I most certainly do; how could I ever forget!

Rachel: Yes, you walked up to me and...

Fury: *(interrupting)* Wait just a minute; you and your girlfriend officer walked up to me and...

With that they began to laugh realizing they had just had their first disagreement. Still holding their drinks, they began to share a kiss and then an embrace. "I'm sorry, Honey, I believe I just spilled some coffee on your sleeve!" Fury mentioned to Rachel. "Don't worry, Fury. If it will make you feel better I will spill some on your sleeve!!" Fury broke away and attempted to run away, but it was too late! She soaked his sleeve. "OK, if you're going to be like that I'll have to throw you overboard!" Next, the friendly Cricket Colonel picked her up in his arms as he had done on their first meeting. Once again he swung her around and around, only this time he held her as if to carry her across the threshold. He politely kissed her and then let her resume her standing position next to the guardrail.

Fury: Rachel, I have never been happier in my life! I love you so, so very much!

Rachel: You are so special to me, Fury! I love you more than any words can express, dearest! You are my love!

Fury: You are my love and my life, Rachel! I promise to cherish you forever!

As the dawn began to break over the Indian Ocean, both Rachel and Fury wondered if after the war a new sunlight of peace might also break into the world. They knew, full well, that they were being reassigned and redeployed to an airfield base near the Sinai. "Who cares, for now we have each other and that can wait," Rachel declared! "Fury, my love, no matter the future, nothing can ever, ever separate us! We are so fortunate that Admiral Amsterdam gave us a week!" "Yes," Fury responded with a smile! Yes, they would have a week to honeymoon! Nothing would interfere, not even the war. Hand-in-hand, the newlyweds walked to their favorite coffee shop aboard the *David*. Here the Emerald Midnight Hornet and Sudden Fury, two colonels very much in love, began to relax and assume their new roles as husband and wife: to love and be loved!

GLOSSARY

Cast of Characters

TOADS

CRICKETS

FROG		TOADS		CRICKETS	

Units

ARMY

FROG		TOADS		CRICKETS	
The Silver Brigade	22	Fighting 333 Scarlet Berets	10	Panther Mechanized Tank Division	10

Armament

ARMY

FROG		TOADS		CRICKETS	
		M-245 Shermann tanks	10		

NAVY

Aircraft Carriers

FROG		TOADS		CRICKETS	
HFTMS Eternal Grace	152	*HTMS Eagle*	63	*SS Admiralty*	69
HFMS King David	106	*HFTMS Eternal Grace*	152	*The Orca*	135
		HTMS Heroic	64	*The Scorpion*	64
		HTMS Supreme (King Gideon's personal carrier)	16	*The Stingray*	11

Battleships

FROG		TOADS		CRICKETS	
The Jordan	198			*The Cobra*	209
The Judea	198			*The Cottonmouth*	210
The Televiva	79			*The Cricketstonia*	215
The Emperor's Invincible	176			*The Emperor's Tempest*	176

Heavy Cruiser

Light Cruiser

Destroyer

Submarines

Amphibious Assault Units

AIR FORCE

Modified Fighters

Super Fighters

Squadrons

Helicopters

Torpedoes

Locations

About the Author

A. Anthony Oseguera, a graduate from Bingham High School (Utah), left early in his life to pursue an acting career in Hollywood. He graduated from the Pasadena Playhouse College of Theatre Arts and then moved to New York where he studied opera. After receiving his Ph.D. in International Broadcasting from the University of Missouri—Columbia, he pursued an educational career by teaching at Chaminade College Preparatory (Saint Louis), Valdosta State University (Georgia), and Eastern Illinois University. As a professor emeritus, he enjoys writing and traveling in the company of his wife Maggie (his editor), family, and friends. Most recently, he has enjoyed returning to teaching at TriCounty Technical College and Westside High School (both Anderson, South Carolina) where he has taught English and Spanish, respectively. His family brings him his greatest joy!

Anderson, South Carolina
March 13, 2010